Wolfblight

Book One of The Wolfblight Saga

Simon Steele

WOLFBLIGHT

Copyright © 2022 Simon Steele

All rights reserved.

ISBN: 9798836444228

To

Lexi + Ariane

Enjoy the book

[signature]

I dedicate this book to all my friends and family of whom I love dearly and whose support made this novel possible.

CHAPTER I:
OUR STORY BEGINS…

Deep within the frozen land of Norway lay the ancient village of Gormstad, a great huddle of colourful timber buildings encircled by a mighty wall of stone sitting amidst vast frosted grasslands peppered by craggy hills and monoliths. During the day, the town's labyrinthine maze of roads, streets, alleyways, marketplaces and many houses would be bustling and brimming with exuberance and life as its citizens went about their lives with carefree abandon and peaceful bliss. But as the cold night had drawn in, the streets were deserted for a snowstorm had blown in and everyone had departed to their warm homes for the night.

Inside one such house, it was tranquil as the Skarlagen family had departed to their beds after enjoying a simple supper of oats and hot creamy milk followed by warming mugs of cocoa. To the sound of howling wind, a couple named Astrid and Wulfric slept soundly as they were tucked up beneath thick blankets covered by fur throws and cotton sheets, blissful and content as they curled up against one another. Astrid was a middle-aged woman of incredible beauty; her long crimson hair was woven into a long braid and she was dressed in a long night gown that was decorated with knotted patterns. Her husband Wulfric was a large man with thick dark hair and a beard. Unlike his wife, he slept in the nude, his bare skin covered in an assortment of intricate tattoos and markings.

As the air was filled with the gentle creaking of timber, there suddenly came a startled scream before a tiny and distressed voice could be heard,

"Mommy!", cried the voice,

Astrid murmured as she stirred from her sleep, opening her weary blue eyes as she glanced around the darkness that had enveloped her room,

"What the…", she uttered,
"Mommy!", came the voice again, this time louder and more urgent in tone,
Astrid sighed before she got out of bed,
"Coming Ulva", she said,
As quietly as she could, Astrid made her way out of the bedroom and walked down a dark corridor whilst passing by several doors, being careful as to not wake her other children, her sons Erik, Falbjorn and Kjalmar and her daughter Thyra. Soon she came to Ulva's room and gently pushed the door open before walking inside.
Astrid blinked as her eyes adjusted to the dark, glancing towards the bed that sat at the back of the room, its form gently illuminated by a small crystal nightlight,
"Ulva, what's wrong sweetie?", said Astrid,
It was then that the blankets on the bed rustled and shifted before a small form appeared from beneath the sheets, a girl dressed in a white night gown, her long, auburn hair flowing down to her waist, her blue eyes shining with tears,
"Mommy", whimpered Ulva as she held out her arms and ran towards Astrid,
Astrid felt her heart sink as she fell to one knee and embraced her daughter before the poor child began to weep,
"I had a bad dream", sobbed Ulva,
"A nightmare?", asked Astrid,
Ulva nodded and held her mother tightly as Astrid walked over to the bed and sat herself down, rocking gently whilst stroking the back of Ulva's head as she cried. As Ulva mewled and clung to her mother, Astrid softly sung to her a special lullaby. It was a song that had been passed down through the Skarlagen family since time immemorial and like magic, whenever a child of the family heard it, it would soothe their troubled soul and ease their upset.

It went as such,
"White wolf Lupa, maiden of night,
Treading neath moon shining bright,
With fangs and fur glistening white,
Taking off in frantic flight,
White wolf Lupa with heart aglow,
Tiny paws strident in the snow,
Cloaked in gleaming moonlight,
Dwelling in shadowed and dark twilight,
White wolf Lupa, your love misses you,
And you know that you miss him too,
He wanders far searching for you,
Cross the land with flaming lamp in hand,
White wolf Lupa, lost and cold,
Running through gloomy groves of old,
Summon your courage and have no fear,
Harken yourself back home my dear,
Return to your loved one of your own,
So you're no longer alone...no longer alone",
Astrid smiled warmly as she could feel Ulva was no longer shaking and she was beginning to quieten down,
"Feel better?", asked Astrid,
Ulva gently nodded before she glanced up at her mother with big, soft eyes,
"I dreamt that a monster was chasing me, it was big and had horrible eyes and teeth. It was shaped like a man, but it had the head of a wolf", she squeaked,
"Hmmm, it sounds like you encountered a werewolf", said Astrid,
Ulva gasped in terror before she buried her face in Astrid's chest, whimpering as she began to shake with fright,
"There, there my little lamb, it's okay, I've got you", said Astrid,
Lifting her head up so that her teary eyes met her mother's, Ulva sniffed and said,
"It bit me mommy, it hurt me",

Smiling gently, Astrid said in a soft, tender voice,
"No monster is going to hurt you, not while I'm here",
Wiping her eyes with tiny pale hands, Ulva said,
"Promise?",
"I promise", said Astrid before she pecked Ulva on the forehead and gently tucked her into bed, making sure she was snuggled in warm and cosy,
Rubbing her daughter's belly gently in a clockwise motion, Astrid said,
"Dry your eyes sweetie, everything is going to be okay",
Ulva wiped her eyes as Astrid adjusted the nightlight, illuminating the room in a cold white glow,
"Are you comfortable Ulva?", said Astrid,
"Yes mommy", said Ulva,
"Good, do you have Valka with you?", said Astrid,
Ulva reached under her blankets and pulled out a fluffy grey and white malamute doll with beady eyes and a pink mouth. Snuggling the adorable doll close, Ulva said,
"Yes",
"Good, call me or your father in the night if you need anything", said Astrid,
"I will", said Ulva,
"Good, sweet dreams Ulva", said Astrid before she sweetly kissed her daughter on the forehead, causing Ulva to smile as her cheeks flared red,
As Ulva curled herself up in her bed, Astrid was about to leave when Ulva said,
"Mommy?",
Turning to face her daughter, Astrid said,
"Yes sweetie?",
"What's a werewolf?", asked Ulva,
"They are monsters like the one you saw in your dream, half – wolf, half – man monsters who like to eat people", said Astrid,
"Where did they come from?", said Ulva,

Astrid sighed before she walked over to the bed and sat herself next to Ulva,
"Well they come from our stories and are nothing more than figments of our own dark and vivid imaginations", she said,
Sitting herself up, Ulva said,
"Really?",
"Yes sweetie, when I was your age I was told a story by my mother about werewolves. She told me that they were born from the trickery of Loki, the god of mischief and chaos", said Astrid,
"Will you tell me the story?", asked Ulva,
"It's quite dark Ulva, you've had one nightmare tonight, I don't want you to have another", said Astrid,
"Please?", squeaked Ulva,
Astrid sighed before she said,
"Alright, but I'll have to tell you the short version, I don't want to keep you up all night",
Ulva smiled before she clambered out of bed and huddled close to her mother, holding Valka tightly as Astrid cleared her throat and began to weave a dark saga of terrible monsters and gods, a fable of blood, frost, darkness and hope, the Saga of the Seven Heroes,
"Once upon a time there was peace amongst Norway and its people were happy and prosperous. Though the gods delighted in such a sight, one god did not. His name was Loki and he was a wicked and malicious trickster who took delight in spreading discord and chaos by interfering in the lives and affairs of both mortals and gods alike. He saw the prosperity amongst the humans and found it to be incredibly boring and mundane, in such peace he saw an opportunity to conduct some mayhem. To achieve this, Loki used dark and forbidden magic to create an affliction known as the wolfblight, which he would use to turn the people of Norway into werewolves. To spread the wolfblight, Loki knew that he needed help, so he summoned the most dreaded of his five children, the Dark Wolf Fenrir.

After tainting Fenrir's claws and fangs with the wolfblight, Loki ordered him to go to the realm of man and wreak havoc and destruction in his name. With his wicked venom, Fenrir attacked the people of Norway and it was from his bite that the first werewolves came to be.

They would be human by day, but at night they would transform into monsters and attack their fellow kinfolk. Seeing such horror would have brought immense pleasure to Loki, delighted at how such transformations would have torn the land apart. Parents would have slaughtered their children, lords and ladies would have killed the very people they had sworn to protect and families and friends would have destroyed one another",

Ulva gasped in shock as her mind filled with terrible images invoked by her mother's words,

"Those poor people", she said,

"Indeed little one, it was truly a dark and terrible time", said Astrid,

"Did Fenrir act alone? Surely just one wolf wouldn't have been enough to threaten everyone", said Ulva,

"You are right sweetie, Fenrir didn't act alone, he had help from his own children, three monstrous wolves named Skoll, Hati and Garm. Skoll was the eldest child and was a mighty beast known for possessing an insatiable bloodlust and an incredibly bad temper. Fenrir's second child was Garm, a wicked and vicious creature who possessed incredible cunning and intellect, his intelligence matched only by his cruelty. Hati was Fenrir's youngest child and only daughter, a monster whose grotesque appetite for flesh and blood was legendary. Hati would not only turn many humans into werewolves, but she would eat them by the thousands, greedily gorging and consuming with unsurpassed gluttony. So it was that Fenrir and his children ravaged the land together and though they tried, the people of Norway could not get rid of them, even when vast armies were raised under the command of kings and queens", said Astrid,

"So they weren't stopped?", asked Ulva,

"They were, but not by the forces of man. Such carnage was witnessed by the gods and they were outraged by such a blasphemous desecration of the humans they had sworn to guide and protect", said Astrid,
"Who stopped them then?", said Ulva,
"Odin, King of the Gods and Lord of Valhalla sent his two sons Viddar and Tyr down to Midgard to rescue mankind from Fenrir. They were accompanied in their quest by four of Odin's most loyal companions, the wise ravens Hugin and Munin and the noble hunting wolves Geri and Freki. Together, they all set out to find Fenrir and his children. For many days and nights they searched and eventually found them within the depths of a dark lair", said Astrid,
"Then what happened?", said Ulva,
"With help from their allies, Viddar and Tyr fought the horrible wolves and after a long and terrible battle they triumphed and slew Skoll, Hati and Garm. Fenrir however could not be destroyed for he was too powerful to overcome. After escaping Fenrir's lair, Munin told Viddar that the only way to stop the Dark Wolf was to bind and imprison him deep within the bitter wastes of Niflheim, the land of frost, mist and darkness. She declared that they needed something strong enough to chain up Fenrir and that only a master of the forge would be able to create such a powerful artefact. Using her magic, Munin summoned a dwarf, a metalsmith named Thrunnir. With enchanted iron, divine fire and spell – songs, Thrunnir forged a mighty chain known as Gleipnir and used it to bind Fenrir and banish him forever, thus restoring peace to the land", said Astrid,
"Yay!", cheered Ulva,
"As for the werewolves left behind in the wake of Fenrir's defeat, it is said that they continue to roam the land, lurking in the shadows and terrorizing those unfortunate to cross their path", said Astrid,
"They sound horrible, I wouldn't want to meet one in real life", said Ulva,
"You won't Ulva", said Astrid as she stood up,

"Promise?", asked Ulva,
"I promise, now off to bed with you", said Astrid,
After Ulva had got into bed and made herself snug, Astrid kissed her on the forehead,
"Sleep tight", she said,
"Good night mommy, I love you", said Ulva,
Astrid smiled and said,
"Love you too sweetie",
With Ulva now tucked in, Astrid dimmed the nightlight before she made her way to the door.
It was then that the door creaked open and a child appeared standing outside the room, a boy slightly older than Ulva garbed in robes, his round and freckled face framed by locks of red hair, his small blue eyes glistening in the dark,
"Falbjorn, what are you doing up?", said Astrid,
Rubbing his eyes and yawning deeply, Falbjorn said,
"I heard crying, everything okay?",
"Ulva just had a nightmare that's all. Go back to bed, it's late", said Astrid,
"What did she dream about?", asked Falbjorn,
"Nothing to worry about, now off you go", said Astrid,
"I was chased by a werewolf", said Ulva,
Falbjorn's eyes suddenly widened before he said,
"Really? Did you dream about the wolf stone too?",
"What's that?", asked Ulva,
"It's an old stone that lies in the Gormwood just outside of town, it records the Saga of the Seven Heroes. Dad said there are lots of them scattered across the land commemorating the story. I hear they have werewolves etched upon them", replied Falbjorn,
"Wow really?", said Ulva,
"I'll take you to see it one day", smiled Falbjorn,
"Sorry you two, but no one is going to see the wolf stone, the Gormwood is far too dangerous to be running around in, it's dark and full of wicked things. The forest ensnares the curious and drags them away, never to be seen again", said Astrid as she folded her arms,

A groan of disappointment arose from Ulva, which prompted Astrid to say,
"Sorry Ulva, but the answer is no and that is final",
A little disheartened, Ulva skulked back into bed whilst Astrid glanced at Falbjorn and said,
"Come on young man, back to bed",
"Okay, good night mother, love you", said Falbjorn,
"Love you too my little prince", said Astrid,
After both Falbjorn and Astrid had left Ulva's room, the house became quiet once more, still against the howling gales blowing outside. As the night wore on, Ulva was having trouble sleeping. Despite her efforts, she couldn't get her mind off the wolf stone no matter how hard she tried. Her curiosity was burning and she desperately wanted to see the stone for herself.
Restless and fidgeting under the blankets, Ulva sat up in her bed, contemplating as she heard the wind blowing and the sound of snow pattering against the roof,
"What's the harm in having a quick peek? I'll be there and back before anyone notices", declared Ulva before she leapt out of bed,
Quickly and quietly, Ulva quickly slipped out of her night clothes and into a linen dress, fur trimmed boots, a hooded red cloak and mittens made of white fox fur.
Once she was dressed, she fastened a belt around her waist before she sheathed upon it a small dagger and a brass lamp. Ulva glanced at herself in a nearby mirror before she made her way to the door. She was about to make a swift exit when she suddenly wheeled round and walked over to the bed. She tenderly collected up Valka and hugged her tightly before kissing her gently on the fluffy cheek.
Ulva then placed the doll into bed and placed the blanket over her,
"I won't be long Valka, see you soon", she said,
Pulling up her hood, Ulva snuck out of her bedroom before she crept downstairs and slipped through the front door into the bitter and dark night.

CHAPTER II:
THE WOLF STONE

With cold gales and flurries of snow billowing around her, Ulva ran down the street, careful to avoid the town guards who were wandering about as they patrolled the town. Knowing that the gate into Gormstad would be closed for the night, Ulva made her way towards a small and secret opening that sat at the bottom of the towering wall encircling the town, hidden by some small barrels located behind a dilapidated timber house. After squeezing her way through the hole, Ulva found herself standing out in the open amongst a sprawling grassland covered with pale frost. Shaking slightly from both fear and the cold, Ulva grabbed her lantern and turned it on, illuminating her face with a warm bloom of light.

Holding up her lantern, Ulva stared out into the cold and the gloom, eyeing the dark forest that sat on the edge of town before she suddenly sprinted across the field, being wary not to slip on patches of ice or tumble in the thick blanket of snow beneath her feet. Ulva shivered as bitter winds blew across her face, coughing slightly as her mouth had started to become dry. After following an unmarked path, Ulva climbed up a slight incline before eventually stopping in front of a large and dark forest, its undergrowth permeated with gloom, its towering trees of spruce, birch and pine looming over ominously.

Feeling her heart beginning to race, Ulva nervously turned to face the town before she stared at the forest with nervous trepidation,

"Come on Ulva, you've got this", she said to herself,

Summoning her courage, Ulva started making her way into the forest as the moonlit trees shook against the terrible wind.

Upon entering the Gormwood, Ulva was surprised by how quiet it was thanks to the trees shielding the dark undergrowth from the torrential snowstorm outside. There came the soft sound of whistling wind, the shifting of leaves, hooting owls and cawing crows on the air, but they were faint and gentle.

With tiny snowflakes fluttering down above her head, Ulva glanced around at the trees surrounding her, great, towering pine trees that cast foreboding and sinister shadows that seemed to twist, dance and shift in the lamplight. Ulva looked down at the floor and began to follow the path carefully and cautiously, hoping it would lead her to the wolf stone.

As Ulva walked deeper into the forest and time wore on, the air got colder and the forest thicket became darker with every passing step until the only light that could be seen was the bright glow of Ulva's lamp.

Enveloped by crooked and contorted shadows, Ulva felt her heart beginning to race as she began to pick up the pace. Around her the trees swayed in the wind and after walking over a log bridge that spanned a chasm in the forest floor, Ulva gasped as she was startled by a flash of lightning, "This was such a bad idea", said Ulva before she pulled on her cloak,

Suddenly Ulva let out a yell as a loud and terrific boom of thunder crashed through the forest, sending the poor child rushing through the forest in terror. As Ulva raced down the path, she yelped as her foot suddenly snagged on a fallen branch and she went flying forward, striking the ground painfully, her lantern bouncing across the hard and frosted ground as it left her hand.

Ulva coughed as she pulled herself up, clutching her throbbing chest before she brushed the dirt off her dress and picked up her lamp, which thankfully wasn't damaged, "I can't see a thing", huffed Ulva as she stared around at the surrounding forest,

Suddenly there came a terrible noise as the air was filled with the sudden howl of a wolf. Ulva let out a scream before she blindly ran through the forest as fast as she could.
Leaping over some rocks and fallen logs, Ulva could hear rustling leaves and the pattering of heavy paws nearby, but because it was so dark she couldn't determine where the sounds were coming from, only that they were close behind. The path suddenly shifted up ahead and from the darkness came a sudden burst of moonlight as an opening appeared in the trees.
Surrounded by a ring of trees bathed in cold, silver light, Ulva wheeled round and saw large dark forms running towards her along with several pairs of shining feral eyes that glistened in the shadows, yellow and ravenous. With little time to think, Ulva ran to the left and rushed down the wooded path before she leapt into the air, falling into darkness before she landed in a small quagmire, her legs buckling under the impact.
Hearing snarling and howling accompanied by the sound of trampling, galloping paws, Ulva quickly extinguished her lamp before she ducked behind a nearby tree, holding her breath as a large pack of wolves raced by, kicking up snow as they disappeared into the forest.
When the howling had died down, Ulva sighed in relief before she illuminated her lamp, glancing forward as she spotted a narrow path lined with what looked like carved stones, some of them roughly hewn and covered in runes whilst some of them were shaped like the heads of wolves, "Maybe the stone is this way", uttered Ulva softly before she walked out of the quagmire and back onto the path, this one wider and dimly lit by moonlight filtering through the vast canopy of foliage looming overhead,
Cautiously and at a much faster pace, Ulva quickly followed the path and wandered through the thicket, climbing over steep bumps and under logs, clambering through small tunnels made of dirt and rock and crossing trickling and bubbling streams.

Finally, after what seemed like an eternity, Ulva came to a large and cavernous clearing, a large grove surrounded by crops of stone and a ring of towering trees.
Sitting at the heart of the grove was a tall, rectangular and intricately carved monument made of black stone, its long, dark shadow stretching across the meadow,
"There it is", gasped Ulva as she stared at the wolf stone in awe,
Unable to contain her excitement, Ulva rushed towards it, her footsteps echoing across the stone floor as she ran. Upon reaching the wolf stone, Ulva reached up to touch its smooth and icy skin, admiring its beautiful surface with wide eyes filled with shining wonderment.
At the top of the wall was the large figure of a man. The man had long flowing hair and his arms were outstretched, his face giving off a menacing and wicked grin of delight. Below this figure was a large and monstrous looking wolf, its face twisted into a snarl, its eyes bejewelled with orange stones. From its maw came billowing clouds of smoke and flickering tongues of fire that leapt from its fangs. Surrounding the giant wolf was what looked like werewolves, their faces twisted with horror, rage and despair. Beneath these figures were three wolves attacking some humans, their mouths twisted into horrible smiles, their eyes comprised of shining stones. Standing beneath these wolves were seven figures, a giant man with a flowing beard wielding a great chain, a one-handed man wielding a blade, a small, armoured man wearing an apron over his armour whilst holding a smithing hammer and four animals, two wolves and two ravens.
Lying slain at their feet were the three wolves with the bejewelled eyes whilst the monstrous wolf with the amber coloured eyes had been ensnared by a chain, its writhing limbs and body contorted by a painful embrace of steel,
"It's so pretty", gasped Ulva as she admired the stone,

Ulva spent a considerable amount of time staring at the wolf stone, even managing to read the runes that ran around its edges. The runes spoke of the Saga of the Seven Heroes and how Fenrir fell that dark day.

But eventually Ulva was becoming far too tired and cold to remain any longer, so she decided it was time to leave and head back home before her parents and siblings got wise in noticing her absence. As Ulva turned on her heel and was about to leave the grove, there came terrible howls as several large, shadowed forms leapt from the darkness and landed in the grove, terrifying Ulva as she saw six black wolves with horrible bloodshot eyes rush towards her, their horrible faces locked into vicious snarls, their teeth glistening with spit in the lamplight.

Ulva glanced around in a desperate attempt to find an opening through which she could escape, only to realize that the wolves had encircled her and blocked any chance of escape.

Realizing she was trapped and with tears beginning to run down her pale face, Ulva pulled the dagger from her belt and held it up to the wolves with shaking hands,

"Go away!" she barked,

At that instant, one of the wolves leapt towards Ulva, opening its maw in a great rush of fangs. It was at that moment that a hooded figure suddenly leapt from the darkness and thrust a long dagger into the wolf's skull, causing blood to fly and spray upon Ulva who squealed in terror. The wolf collapsed to the floor and went limp as blood poured from its fractured skull. Seeing its packmate had been slain, the other wolves angrily pounced upon the mysterious figure, their claws extended and their fangs bared in furious anger.

In an amazing show of strength and speed, the figure quickly slammed its fist into one of the wolf's snout, sending the creature crashing to the ground before catching a third wolf by the throat and plunging a dagger deep into its heart.

The figure then spun round and snapped the neck of one of the wolves before swiping a fourth wolf across the neck, cutting its throat. The figure then picked up the wolf that had been punched in the snout and plunged its teeth into the wolf's chest, piercing its beating, quivering heart. The wolf let out a wretched whine of pain before it's still body was tossed to one side in a bloody heap.

The two remaining wolves whimpered before they scarpered off into the night, howling bitterly over the loss of their family. Shaking from fright as she stared wide eyed and unblinkingly at the mysterious figure who had saved her life, she gasped as the hooded entity suddenly turned to face her. It was then that the figure lowered its hood to reveal its face. Much to Ulva's surprise, the figure was a young woman and a beautiful one at that.

She was of average height and thin in stature. Her skin was as pale as snow and flawless like porcelain, her lovely face framed by locks of cascading jet-black hair, which lapped down passed her shoulders. Her eyes were large, asymmetrical and shone with a dim glow, one was as red as wine whilst the other was blue and coloured the shade of frost. The woman was garbed in a black dress embroidered with little red patterns, the hemline of which reached halfway down her legs that were wrapped in high black boots buckled with silver. The top of her arms was sleeved, but the lower part of her arms were bare. On her hands were black gloves whilst over her shoulders was draped a black and red cloak. Around her waist was a leather belt embossed with small rubies, the silver buckle being shaped like that of a wolf's head. The woman wore a small pendant on her slender neck and fastened to her belt was a sheath of leather and a small tin flask.

Shaking and pale with fright, Ulva stared at the woman as she sheathed her dagger before reaching up and wiping the blood that was smeared across her mouth.

Glancing down at Ulva, the woman smiled before she said in a sweet and honeyed voice,
"Hello",
Ulva said nothing as she stared at the woman nervously,
"Are you hurt?", said the woman,
Ulva shook her head,
"Good", said the woman before she tilted her head slightly, her smile widening as she beheld Ulva,
"What a pretty little girl", she said,
"Th…thank you", said Ulva,
"What are you doing out here all alone in the cold and the dark?", asked the raven-haired woman,
"I…I came out here to see the wolf stone", said Ulva,
"Magnificent isn't it?", said the woman before she stepped forward, causing Ulva to back up in fear,
"No one knows how old it is, but they say it is ancient and carved by those whose name has been lost to time", she said,
"My brother Falbjorn said they are many just like it all across Norway", said Ulva,
"Did he now?", said the woman as she stared at Ulva with unblinking, glowing eyes,
"Yes, are you out here to see it too?", asked Ulva,
The woman in black laughed before she said,
"Oh no, I'm looking for a different artefact",
"And what might that be?", asked Ulva,
"Nothing for you to worry about", said the young woman,
"Well I hope you find it and it brings you much joy. Now that I have had my fill of ancient stones and dark forests, I should be going, I'll be in so much trouble if my parents discover that I snuck out", said Ulva nervously,
"Go?", asked the woman,
"Yes, but thank you for saving me, you are so brave and courageous going after those horrible wolves. I hate them so much, nasty, wicked monsters", said Ulva with a trembling voice,

The raven-haired woman's smile faded and her frame had become ridged as she looked taken aback by Ulva's unkind words.
As Ulva sheathed her dagger and began making her way out of the dark grove, she heard the raven-haired woman say faintly,
"Oh no you don't",
It was then that Ulva was suddenly grabbed from behind and was thrown violently across the grove with incredible force. Ulva cried out in pain as she violently struck the wolf stone, her back exploding with pain before she tumbled into the snow, her lantern shattering as it struck the ground.
Ulva began to cry as she felt a terrible pain wrack her small body, her head throbbed and she could taste blood. With blurry vision, Ulva looked up and saw the raven-haired woman walking hastily towards her, her cloak billowing in the wind as lightning began to flash overhead and thunder rumbled.
Ulva could see that the young woman was grinning horribly from ear to ear, her face had been stretched back, revealing a wide, sinister and crooked smile filled with razor sharp teeth, her glowing eyes burning with unhinged madness and delectable malice.
Ulva weakly tried to reach for her dagger, but it was no use as the young woman kicked it away,
"Mommy!", cried Ulva,
"She's not going to save you now", hissed the raven-haired woman,
Ulva spluttered as the young woman suddenly grabbed her by the throat with gloved hands and lifted her up off the floor, her little legs dangling in the air as she thrashed and kicked about.
Glaring at Ulva, the young woman said,
"You think wolves are horrible monsters? Fine, let me show you how terrible we can be",
"Who are you?!", blurted Ulva,

The young woman tilted her head and said in a soft, whispering hiss,

"Hati, the Princess of Wolves",

Ulva gasped in shock as Hati laughed maniacally before she was flung through the air, striking the ground hard. Ulva groaned as she lifted her head up as she felt a stinging sensation envelop her face before she felt blood trickle down her cheek.

Crawling on her belly, Ulva tried to escape as she could hear Hati's laughter ringing out amongst the raging thunder,

"You thought that I was going to just let you leave? Why would I deny myself a good meal and let such a sweet and succulent little thing like you go?", she said,

Ulva groaned as she tried to pull herself up, but her legs gave way and she was in too much pain to stand.

Hearing Hati's footsteps approaching closer from behind, Ulva cried out for her parents,

"Plump as a little piglet and sweet as treacle", said Hati as she grabbed Ulva by the throat and lifted her up so that their eyes were level,

Baring her teeth, Hati licked her lips as saliva spilled over the edge of her lips and ran down her chin and throat.

With her stomach growling, Hati said to Ulva,

"I am so hungry…always hungry. Not to worry though, you shall satisfy my appetite for quite a while",

"You can't be real, you just can't! You are nothing but a character from a story and even if you were real, you are meant to be dead!", yelled Ulva as her body shaked and tears ran down her face as she sobbed,

"Yes, the gods did their best, but sadly for them, I am back and the only one who is going to be dead in this place is you", growled Hati,

"Please, don't eat me, I taste terrible, I'm nothing but bone!", pleaded Ulva,

Hati chuckled and said in a purring voice,

"All the more marrow for me to suck",

Ulva watched as Hati opened her mouth, spreading her jaws unnaturally wide, revealing two rows of sharp fangs dripping with ice cold saliva and blood on account of her diseased, inflamed and red raw gums.
Ulva screamed as Hati prepared to devour her,
"Mommy, Daddy help me!", she cried,
But just as Hati was about to tear poor Ulva apart, there came a sudden whoosh of wind and the sound of clanging metal before a large and sharpened axe flew from the darkness, spinning across the grove before it plunged deep into Hati's back, causing her to emit a piercing scream as she dropped Ulva to the ground.
As soon as Ulva landed, she immediately began to crawl away as Hati thrashed about, flailing her arms as she tried to reach for the axe buried into her flesh.
Ulva glanced up and through the gloom, she saw a figure suddenly emerge from the darkness, it was her mother Astrid, her crimson hair unfurled and despite being dressed in her nightgown, Astrid was wielding a sword and looked every inch a warrior,
"Leave my daughter alone!", roared Astrid,
"Mommy!", cried Ulva as she forced herself onto her feet before she threw open her arms and ran towards Astrid,
Astrid gasped in horror as she beheld her daughter.
She rushed forward and fell to her knees, dropping her sword before embracing Ulva tightly,
"Oh my little lamb, thank the gods you're alive", she said,
"I'm so sorry mommy, please don't be angry", cried Ulva as she wept,
"What were you thinking? I told you this forest was dangerous", said Astrid as she cradled Ulva tenderly,
"I just wanted to see the stone", whimpered Ulva,
"It was foolish of you to seek it out, I thought I taught you better than this", snapped Astrid,

Ulva responded with a little squeak before she buried her face in Astrid's shoulder,
"Come on, we're going home", said Astrid as Ulva wrapped her arms around her neck and clung onto her back whilst her mother collected up her sword,
"No, she's mine!", shouted Hati,
Astrid wheeled round and watched as Hati angrily wrenched the axe from her back, the sound of cracking bone echoing through the grove before she snarled and tossed the axe aside with a clatter.
As Astrid saw Hati's flaming blue and red eyes leering at her, her heart sank as she realized who she was,
"It can't be, you're real?", gasped Astrid,
"Of course, you didn't think I was just a myth did you? Legends are borne from seeds of truth planted many years ago, cultivated and grown by generations of storytellers. The wolf stone itself tells of what happened to me all those years ago, immortalized by those who survived my father's wrath", said Hati,
"But you died, the gods slew you", said Astrid,
"They did and now I have returned, only to find some little mortal intruding on my feast", hissed Hati,
"I'm warning you now, leave now or I will achieve what the gods could not and destroy you", growled Astrid,
Hati chortled with maniacal delight before she suddenly pulled off her gloves and discarded them, revealing sharp black claws,
"Bold aren't we? I'd like to see you try, gods couldn't kill me, what chance have you got?", she growled,
Astrid gasped as Hati suddenly lunged at her with incredible speed, her angry screams echoing through the grove before she sent Astrid and Ulva tumbling to the ground,
"Run Ulva!", cried Astrid,
As Astrid and Hati began to fight, Ulva watched with wide and horrified eyes as she witnessed her mother violently clash with the terrible Princess of Wolves.

Though her mother's words compelled her to flee, she was too frightened to move and was immobilized by fear.
Ulva whimpered and clasped her hands together as she watched Hati tear, rip and slash away at her mother with claws whilst Astrid used her blade to deflect the oncoming blows before stabbing and swinging in retaliation, causing Hati to cry out as Astrid's blade sliced through her flesh.
It was then that Astrid swung her blade and slashed Hati across the face, causing blood to spray across the snow. With Hati crying out in pain, she clutched her bleeding face. Astrid wheeled round and was about to flee when Hati suddenly grabbed her from behind and thrust her fangs deep into her shoulder, crushing flesh and pulverising bone with her powerful bite. Astrid screamed as she felt a burning sensation explode from the wound.
Furious, Astrid elbowed Hati in the stomach and wheeled round before she shouted,
"You bitch!",
Hati groaned as Astrid slammed her fist hard into her face, causing her to collapse into the snow. Clenching her teeth as she struggled against the pain of her wound, Astrid rushed forward and scooped Ulva up in her arms before they both fled into the forest. Ulva shielded her face from the cold as her mother raced through the forest, leaping over stone and wood as she galloped between the trees.
Suddenly there came a horrible, bloodcurdling and spine-chilling scream of anger that echoed throughout the forest, it was Hati and she was incandescent with rage. With the wind howling around her, thunder crashing and lightning flashing, Astrid raced through the Gormwood, squeezing Ulva tightly under her arm as she felt blood running down her chest. The wound was bubbling, bleeding and oozing a foul and noxious stench.
As Astrid ran through a clearing, she could hear tree branches cracking and the sound of rustling leaves before there came the sounds of loud, thundering paws against the ground accompanied by vicious howling and snarling.

It was then that Hati suddenly leapt from the darkness in the form of a giant black wolf with glowing eyes and shining teeth, lunging at Astrid and Ulva as she ripped through the trees and thicket. Astrid quickly whipped round and slashed Hati across the snout with her sword, causing the beast to bellow and howl in rage before she raced after Astrid and Ulva, snapping angrily as she tried to lap up her prey.

With Hati's cold and frosty breath billowing against her back and with Ulva crying under her arm, Astrid summoned up all her strength to get through the Gormwood. After rushing past dozens of trees and unable to shake Hati loose, Astrid came to a sudden halt before she wheeled round and plunged her sword straight into Hati's jaw. Hati squealed in pain before she staggered backwards as a torrent of blood spilled from her pierced mouth.

As Hati was preoccupied with her painful predicament, Astrid quickly fled, her ears filled with a terrible cacophony of crashing thunder and the pained howls from the Princess of Wolves.

CHAPTER III:
POISONED BY A PRINCESS

Despite the wound on her shoulder and her body becoming increasingly weary, Astrid eventually left the Gormwood and hurried back to her house, not stopping until she was back within the safe confines of her home surrounded by loved ones.
Inside the Skarlagen household, Erik, Falbjorn, Thyra, Kjalmar and Wulfric were sitting at the foyer table anxiously awaiting the return of Astrid and Ulva,
"Please let them be alright", said Thyra as she clutched the cat head pendant that was hanging from her neck,
Glancing at his teenage daughter, Wulfric reached out and gently held Thyra's hand,
"I'm sure they will be", he said in a soft and reassuring tone of voice,
"It's my fault, if I hadn't brought up that stupid wolf stone, then Ulva wouldn't have been enticed into entering the Gormwood", said Falbjorn sadly,
"You know that Ulva is a free spirit, she would have probably wandered into the woods eventually even if you hadn't brought it up son", said Wulfric,
"I just feel so guilty and helpless", sighed Falbjorn,
"I know lad, but none of this was you're doing, it just happened", said Wulfric,
Suddenly the front door burst open and Astrid stepped in from the cold, shivering along with Ulva.
As everyone rose from their chairs, Astrid watched as Wulfric stormed up to her and threw his arms around her,
"You're both alive, thank the gods", he said,
"Just barely", replied Astrid,
Ulva squeaked as Falbjorn hugged her tightly before he said,
"I thought something terrible had happened to you",

Ulva said nothing as Falbjorn then angrily snapped at her,
"Don't you ever do that again!",
Ulva whimpered as Falbjorn burst into tears,
"Come on Falbjorn, let's get you back to bed", said Erik as he took his younger brother by the hand and accompanied him into a nearby room,
Folding his arms, Wulfric glared at Ulva before he said in a deep and angry voice,
"Explain yourself this instant young lady",
Ulva anxiously glanced up at her mother as her heart pounded in her chest,
"Don't look at her, look at me", growled Wulfric,
"Come on now my love, she's learnt her lesson and I've already given her enough grief. Let's just sort ourselves out and get some sleep", said Astrid before she looked at Thyra and said,
"Thyra, can you make sure Ulva gets a hot bath and a change of clothes?",
Taking Ulva in her arms, Thyra said,
"Yes mother",
"And once you've tended to her wounds, can you tuck her into bed?", said Astrid,
"Sure, no problem", said Thyra before she glanced down at Ulva and said,
"Come on you naughty pup, let's get you all cleaned up",
After Ulva and Thyra disappeared down a nearby corridor, Kjalmar said to his mother,
"What happened? You look a mess",
"I'll tell you some other time, you go and get some sleep now okay?", said Astrid,
Kjalmar sighed,
"Yes mom", he said,
"There's a good lad", said Wulfric,
As Kjalmar returned to his room, Wulfric turned to Astrid and kissed her gently before saying,
"Thank you for saving our daughter",

Astrid blushed a shade of red before she and Wulfric made their way to the master bedroom.

As Astrid sat herself down upon the edge of the bed, she gently and painfully peeled off her soiled clothes, revealing the awful wound that cut through her shoulder and down to her breast.

After collecting a jug of water and some cloth, Wulfric turned round and gasped as he beheld his wife's injury, nearly dropping the jug of water in his hand,

"Mighty Freyr, how did you get that bite?!", exclaimed Wulfric,

"Sit, I'll tell you", said Astrid,

Wulfric sat himself down next to Astrid before he dipped the cloth into the jug resting upon his lap and began cleaning the angry wound, Astrid mumbling through her teeth as the cold water touched the broken and bloody flesh where Hati had bitten her,

"It looks so painful, what happened?", asked Wulfric,

"I found Ulva at the wolf stone, she was being attacked by a woman", replied Astrid,

"A woman?", asked Wulfric,

"Not just a woman…but a…I can't believe I'm saying this…a monster, Hati, the Princess of Wolves", said Astrid,

Wulfric stared blankly at Astrid before he said,

"What?",

"I know it's difficult to explain, but it's true. She had hair as black as night, skin as white as snow and horrible eyes that shone with fire and frost. She tried to kill Ulva and she nearly killed me when she took a chunk out of me, thankfully we escaped", said Astrid,

Dabbing Astrid's wound, Wulfric said nothing as he struggled to contemplate what his wife had just told him.

After a few moments of silence, he said,

"So you were bitten…by a monster of legend",

Astrid nodded,
"I can't imagine how awful it was for you, I'm just glad you both are safe", said Wulfric as he finished cleaning up the wound,
"She was…more monstrous than anything I could have ever imagined. She treated my daughter like a piece of meat and had no qualms tearing her away from me. I hope to never see her again", said Astrid,
Placing the bloody cloth and jug down upon a nearby table, Wulfric sat himself beside Astrid and gently held her in his arms, allowing her to rest her head against his chest,
"Shhhh, it's over now, let's just get some sleep and sort everything out in the morning", said Wulfric,
It was then that Astrid pushed Wulfric gently away and said,
"Wulfric, I was bitten by Hati…does that mean?",
Wulfric stared at Astrid in confusion before his eyes suddenly widened,
"Gods above", he gasped,
Wulfric inspected Astrid's wound, examining the teeth marks and the deep cuts.
It was then that his nose caught a scent of almonds, a scent that made his heart leap in horrific realization,
"I wonder…", he said before he placed a hand upon Astrid's wound and began chanting a magic spell,
Astrid watched as Wulfric's hand suddenly lit up with an ethereal white light before wisps of magic fluttered and swirled around the wound.
Wulfric stared at the wound, hoping that it would heal thanks to his magic. His heart sank however when the wound failed to close and it just seemed to become more agitated and angrier, flaring and pulsating with venom and blood.
Sighing heavily, Wulfric closed his palm and extinguished the magic circling around his hand, slumping back onto the bed as his fears were realized,
"How long do you think I have?", asked Astrid,
"Hard to say, days, weeks, who knows", said Wulfric,
"Is there anything we can do, is there a cure?", said Astrid,

"I know of a place that might help, but we need to leave now if we are to get there in time. I'll inform my parents and ask them if they are willing to look after the children for a couple of days while you pack some supplies", said Wulfric,
"We have to leave now? Can't we wait until morning? Shouldn't we tell the children?", asked Astrid,
"We shouldn't disturb them, getting them all worked up and worried will achieve nothing. Besides we'll be gone for no more than a week at most, they will be okay, they are good kids", said Wulfric,
Astrid smiled and said,
"That's because they are our kids",
"Yeah", said Wulfric,
Getting up off the bed, Astrid made her way over to the nearby wardrobe and began rummaging around for some clothes whilst Wulfric left the bedroom to inform his parents of their intentions. An hour passed before Wulfric's parents Guthrum and Frigga arrived. In that hour, all the children had returned to their beds for the night, including Ulva, who had been bathed and put to bed in a clean nightgown, her wounds cleaned and dressed.
Once Astrid had changed into some clean clothes and both her and Wulfric had finished packing, they sat themselves down with Guthrum and Frigga and told them everything that happened, from Ulva leaving the house to Astrid learning that she had been infected with the wolfblight. They then told Guthrum and Frigga of their intention to leave for some time and requested that they keep an eye on the children until they returned.
Thankfully they agreed, albeit a little begrudgingly thanks to the untimely nature of the request. Once they were ready to leave, Wulfric and Astrid quietly went into each of their children's bedrooms and kissed them goodnight and goodbye. Once they had seen to Erik, Thyra, Kjalmar and Falbjorn, they finally came to Ulva's room.

Pushing the door open gently, Astrid and Wulfric entered quietly and made their way over to the bedside, staring at Ulva with teary eyes. They saw that Ulva's arm and head had been bandaged, she had a black eye and was sleeping soundly with her arm wrapped around Valka.
With her lower lip trembling, Astrid leaned in close and kissed Ulva on the cheek,
"We'll be back soon little lamb. I love you, always will", she said in a trembling voice,
As Astrid pulled herself away, she watched as Wulfric gently stroked Ulva's head and whispered,
"My wonderful, troublesome little pup, what are we gonna do with you?",
It was then that Wulfric closed his eyes and gently placed his palm upon Ulva's forehead,
"What are you doing?", asked Astrid,
"Shhh, let me concentrate. I won't hurt her, I promise", said Wulfric,
After Wulfric had uttered a spell, Astrid watched as magic flowed from her husband's fingers before the glowing wisps wrapped around Ulva's head and faded,
"There, she will sleep better now", said Wulfric sadly,
"What did you do?", asked Astrid,
"I erased the terrible memories of this night from her mind so they won't trouble her ever again and she won't be tormented by guilt. She will assume that after you told her your bedtime story, she slept peacefully and nothing eventful happened this night", said Wulfric,
"Will it affect her in the long run?", said Astrid,
"No my love, it's harmless magic, but it will do her a world of good", said Wulfric,
Turning to Astrid, Wulfric then said,
"Come, let's go, the sooner we leave, the sooner we can get back",

Astrid nodded before she gave a teary glance at Ulva and left her in peace. Entering the foyer, Wulfric and Astrid both bade farewell to Guthrum and Frigga, thanking them for helping on such short notice.

They then asked one final request, should the children ask of their absence, they were not to divulge the exact nature as to why they left, only that they had to go somewhere in haste and would be back soon. They of course agreed and walked Wulfric and Astrid to the door. Taking each other's hand, Wulfric and Astrid made their way out the front door and into the dark gloom and snow, turning on their lamps as ice and wind billowed and raged around their shadowed forms.

CHAPTER IV:
A GIFT FOR THE GRIEVING

Despite promising that they would return after a few days, Wulfric and Astrid were never seen again. After receiving no word from either of them, a search was conducted and despite everyone's attempts, they had vanished, much to the grief and anguish of their loved ones and were eventually presumed dead.

Twenty winters had come and gone since then and as the bright morning sun began to rear its glowing face upon Gormstad, the town was bustling and the gates were open. Trundling through the crowds wandering outside the gates was a large timber carriage that was being pulled by two horses. In the carriage sat four people whilst a fifth person was sitting at the front, holding onto the reins and sitting cross - footed on a rectangular seat.

Behind him the four people were sitting opposite one another, two men and two women of differing ages and appearances. One of the men was considerably tall, well-built and possessed broad shoulders and a round chest. He was a large man and though he was not obese by any stretch, he was quite generously proportioned in the belly. His face was clean shaven and framed with long, thick locks of dark brown hair. One of his eyes was covered with a black eyepatch, beneath which sat a scar. His one good eye was small, glistening and shaded the same colour as his hair. He was wearing a blue short sleeved tunic, tanned hide trousers and plain black boots. Lining his belt were what looked like small, intricate tools and a pouch. At his feet sat a small and slightly rusted pickaxe. This man was named John Forrester and he was a humble miner by trade.

Next to him was his wife Ulva, now a full grown and beautiful young woman dressed in a blue dress and a black cloak.
Opposite John and Ulva was a man who was grizzled and quite handsome. He was a lot older than John and Ulva and had short, cropped hair that was copper red in colour, the shade matching that of his moustache and beard. He was wearing a dark green tunic over a shirt of silver chainmail. Covering his shoulders and lapping at his feet was a thick fur cloak and upon his lap sat a long and beautifully decorated sword. His name was Einar and he was Ulva's elder brother. Sitting beside Einar was a middle-aged woman whose appearance betrayed an aura of an adventurer. She was wearing shining armour that was coloured a brilliant white and intricately decorated with patterns and images of monsters and animals. Slung across her back was a bag fit to bursting with maps, books and tiny trinkets collected from far and wide. Wrapped around her neck was a beautiful scarf adorned with colourful patterns and flowing Arabian script. Encircling her brow was a beautiful wreath of exotic flowers and hanging from her belt was a pouch full of foreign coins. The woman was of similar height to Ulva, but she was much larger in build, her oval face crowned with silver blonde hair whilst her eyes were shaded a beautiful and vivid shade of purple.
Eyeing the woman, Einar chuckled before saying,
"Why do you wear that armour Eira? You are not a warrior, you can barely lift a sword",
Eira glared at Einar as she plucked a small pipe from her belt and lit it with a strike of a match.
With smoke billowing from her mouth as she breathed in the fumes, Eira said,
"I'll have you know that I wear this armour in reverence of my hero, the great shieldmaiden Torva Thrumgar. It took me months to make and every detail is an exact and perfect replica of the original", she said,

"Very impressive, gods know I wouldn't know how to make such a fine coat of iron", said Einar,
"Thank you", said Eira,
"So what will you do now that you have come home to Gormstad?", said Einar,
"Reopen my antique shop, reorganize the stock and perhaps begin planning my next journey to find more artefacts", said Eira,
"Sounds good, have you recovered anything of interest lately?", said Einar,
"Nothing much, just a few items here and there", said Eira as she puffed her pipe,
"I want to thank you for accompanying me to Hrimgar to collect Ulva and John, it's been a long journey from Northumbria and I think they appreciate the company, especially during such a difficult time", said Einar,
"Oh we do, I can't wait to get settled into our new home" chirped John,
"Don't mention it, I'm happy to help", said Eira who then glanced over at Ulva,
"How are you coping Ulva? I am sorry to hear about what happened, it must have been devastating for both of you", she said,
"It was...I'd...rather not talk about it please", said Ulva despondently,
Eira folded her arms and said,
"Of course, forgive my impertinence, but if you both ever need to talk or just need a friendly face to support you through it all, my door is always open",
"Thanks Eira, that means a lot to us", said John,
"Yes...thank you" muttered Ulva softly before she huddled herself closer to John,
"It's gonna be okay" he whispered to her,
Ulva looked up at John's loving gaze before she rested her head against his shoulder. Seeing this made Eira's heart sink as a tinge of sadness welled up inside her stomach.

She had known Ulva for many years and seeing her so grief stricken was terrible to witness. Some months ago, she was informed that John and Ulva were expecting a child, a baby girl. Eira remembered seeing Einar, Ulva, John and their families being so jubilant and happy at the news. They were going to name her Frigga after Ulva's grandmother, who was a great warrior and a shieldmaiden. But it was not to be, Eira was not told much about the situation other than the child was wrapped in cloth and buried with no more to be said, only silence, flowing tears and broken hearts following in the tragic wake. Little was said as the carriage trundled through the main gate and into town.
As they crossed the threshold into Gormstad, the carriage driver said to John and Ulva,
"Moving to a new home eh? Well I think you two are gonna love it here, peaceful, vibrant and full of friendly people",
As the carriage came to a halt, the driver said with a hearty and gruff voice,
"Here we are, welcome to Gormstad",
Once the driver had stood up and jumped down from his seat, everyone inside the carriage got to their feet and followed suit. Eira and Einar jumped off first whilst John slowly helped Ulva down. The driver unhatched and opened the back of the carriage before he began assisting Einar, John and Eira with unloading their possessions.
As Eira coughed before collecting up her bags, John approached her as Einar talked to the driver,
"Um Eira, I was wondering if I could pay your shop a visit later", he said,
"No problem, but come around midday, I have some errands to run first", said Eira,
"Thank you I appreciate it; I just want to buy something special for Ulva. You know she's been struggling lately and she and I just love antiques, so I think it might cheer her up a little", said John,
"That's sweet, you're a good man John, she's blessed to have you" smiled Eira,

Glancing over at Ulva, John said softly,
"Oh I think it is I who is blessed",
"Indeed, well see you later", said Eira as she collected up the rest of her belongings,
John watched as Eira made her way into the town square and out of sight up one of the narrow streets ahead.
After Einar had paid the driver his dues, he said to John and Ulva,
"Come, let us be off to your new home, it's not far",
Einar slung two bags over his back and with a heave, picked up one of the crates from the carriage,
"Can I have a hand?", he said,
"Sure", replied John,
John went up to the carriage and collected another heavy crate. There were three other bags and two more crates in the carriage, but Einar had informed the driver that they would return for them shortly.
John, Ulva and Einar began making their way through the square as the traders and merchants had gathered to sell their wares to the good people of Gormstad. After pushing through the bustling crowds that had gathered, Einar, John and Ulva made their way down a street on the right, passing many towering buildings that sat on each side of the cobbled pavement.
A few minutes passed before John said to Einar,
"How fares Maud and grandfather Guthrum?",
"Quite well John, coping as one can be expected in such troubling times. I heard cousin Gerdi is performing quite well in his studies and Kara said the other day that she intends to become a shieldmaiden just like grandmother Frigga", replied Einar,
"That sounds like Kara all right, fiery to a point, I think she'll make a great warrior", said John,
"What of our brother Kjalmar?" said Ulva,

"That no good wastrel only went and lost another job just before Eira and I left to come and collect you from the harbour several days ago. He cares more about his drink than keeping silver in his pocket", said Einar,
"Really, what did he do this time?" asked Ulva as a look of concern and disappointment appeared on her face,
"Got frustrated at a customer, they argued about the weight of a cut of meat and there was a scuffle. It was the last straw and Guldar had to get rid of him. Don't know what he is doing now, but I honestly don't care anymore. He's always causing trouble for this family and sullying our good name, he isn't worth my worry", growled Einar,
"Well I hope he sorts himself out, gods know that he needs to step up and be a good father to Kara", sighed Ulva,
"I can talk to him; I mean I can imagine it's been difficult for him since Helga passed away. I think he just needs a helping hand and some guidance in getting him off the drink", said John,
Einar snorted,
"Well he's had way too many chances to better himself, but if you want to help him, go right ahead, I will not stop you", he grumbled,
Eventually Einar, John and Ulva arrived at another town square, a small and cobbled open space enclosed on all sides by timber buildings. In the centre of the square was a large monument, a pillar of inscribed stone. Einar couldn't remember the exact details, but it commemorated those who had died in some battle that occurred centuries ago outside of Gormstad. Adjusting his eyes to the bright morning sun, he guided John and Ulva down the street on the right. It was this street where he lived, with John and Ulva's new home located next door. They had both lived in England for a while, but after the loss of their child, they both agreed to return to Norway to live on a permanent basis,

"So John, Ulva, before you arrived in Norway, I took the liberty of moving all of your possessions into your new house. Maud and Kara meanwhile have been busy filling your pantry and getting everything sorted and tidy", said Einar,
"Thanks Einar, Ulva and I could not have moved here so smoothly and quickly if it weren't for your efforts and that of the family", said John,
"It's quite alright, I wasn't going to leave my brother-in-law and sister to struggle with settling in, especially not at this time", said Einar,
"If you are not busy this evening Einar, would you like to come to dinner?", asked Ulva,
Einar smiled and said,
"Wouldn't miss it for anything",
John, Ulva and Einar soon passed a large house, it was two stories high and constructed from red timbers, its triangular roof was made of green tiles that glistened in the sun, a quaint and charming looking building. A few doors down sat a building of similar size and appearance except the building was brown in colour.
Walking up to the door, John noticed that it was carved with images of beautiful trees, a star-studded sky and unearthly looking creatures dancing in delight. A lot of doors in Gormstad were decorated with such images, many people believed they kept evil spirits from entering their homes. Putting down the crate, Einar pulled a large key from his belt and unlocked the door before pushing it open. John entered first, followed closely by Ulva and then Einar. As they took in their surroundings, John, Einar and Ulva found themselves standing within a large and spacious looking foyer that consisted of a wide, open space sitting before a balcony and two sets of stairs on both the left and right of the entrance. There were two doors on each side of the room leading to other areas of the house. In the centre of the foyer was a long table covered in a long and woven cloth of lightly coloured fabric with three wooden chairs on each side.

Behind the table was a wall that sat just below the balcony, in the middle of which sat a beautiful arched hearth of brick, an alcove containing an empty cauldron and some firewood. Above the hearth hung a large woven tapestry which depicted a cloaked and hooded man standing in a forest wielding a bow, at his feet was chained a wolf with blue eyes baring its fangs.

After setting down their crates, John and Einar cracked them open before John got to work lighting some lamps whilst Einar began lighting a fire at the hearth,

"It hasn't changed much", said Ulva as her mind filled with happy memories of her childhood,

She remembered when she was just a child, carefree and free spirited. She could remember the rainy nights when the air was filled with the cracking sounds of the fire, the torrential rain hammering on the roof, the delicious smells of cooking suppers provided by her uncle Gurlod and the sound of playful sword fights with her brother Falbjorn.

Ulva remembered the days when she would hear wondrous stories from her grandmother, who would tell her of her travels across Scandinavia. She could remember sitting on her grandfather Guthrum's lap, laughing as he told her such funny stories of chasing poultry in the square, playing jokes on bartender Svolnir at the Black Boar tavern and his terrible attempts at wooing the local girls.

Ulva couldn't help but smile as she remembered the songs and rhythms they would sing together, the riddles they told one another and of course the warm hugs they shared. Ulva had fond memories of her grandparents and she treasured them dearly. Harkening back to such happier times made Ulva's heart sink as she gazed around the room.

She whimpered softly as she could feel her eyes welling up as she longed for the comforting presence of her grandmother and her parents, both of whom she missed terribly.

As Ulva wiped the tears away from her face, she was approached by John, who wrapped his arms around her before he gently cradled her and kissed her sweetly on the cheek.
After a moment of silence, Ulva said,
"I should start unpacking",
"Sure", said John,
After watching Ulva collect up a bundle of clothes in her arms before making her way upstairs, John walked over to Einar, who was standing nearby over a nice, hot fire.
With Einar having got the fire going, the room was now lit by a heavenly orange glow from the newly born flames,
"Right, now that the fire's lit, I'll head back to the square and collect up the remaining crates", he said,
"Thank you Einar, I appreciate the help, I really do", said John,
"It's no problem at all John, after the terrible loss you and Ulva suffered, I am glad to help in any way I can. It may not feel like it now, but I think you will come to love Gormstad in time, I cannot think of a better place to start anew", said Einar,
John smiled softly,
"I'm sure we will", he said,
It was then that John placed a hand upon Einar's shoulder and said,
"Know that I am proud to call you my brother",
Einar nodded in response,
"And I you", he said before he walked out the door,
Sighing deeply, John glanced around the room before he collected up some clothes and made his way upstairs, passing through a wide threshold before walking down a long corridor that led into the master bedroom, a large room filled with carved wooden cabinets, tall cupboards and some filled bookshelves. The walls were decorated with lanterns, woven embroideries and colourful shields surrounding a large bed covered with soft white sheets, fur coverings, thick blankets and pillows.

After placing the bundle of clothes he was carrying down upon the bed, John said to Ulva,
"Happy to be home?",
"I guess", said Ulva sadly,
"Here, I'll give you a hand", said John before he began folding some clothes,
"Thank you", said Ulva,
To the sound of crackling embers, the gentle whistling of wind and the low moaning creak of timber walls and floors, Ulva and John quietly began putting their clothes away.
As Ulva was clearing away some tunics and some pairs of socks, she gasped in surprise as she came across a small pair of mittens, brightly coloured and small enough to fit one's palm.
Ulva shakingly picked them up and tearfully eyed them as she realized what they were,
"So tiny", she squeaked,
With her hands trembling, Ulva kissed them gently before she pressed them close to her chest as tears ran down her face.
Seeing his wife upset, John embraced her tightly and said,
"I am sorry Ulva, I know the last few months have been terrible for you, but know that I love you and will be there for you no matter what, as will many others here who will support you always",
Ulva looked up at John before she placed a hand upon his face,
"Thank you for being so supportive, you must think me pathetic and weak to be blubbering like this", she said,
"Not at all, no matter how emotional you get, I would never think any less of you" said John,
"I mustn't forget that this has been difficult for you too", said Ulva,
"It has, but we will pull through, always have, always will", said John quietly,
"Remember the vows we made all those years ago? We are in this together", said Ulva,

"Until the first winds of the Fimbulwinter and the coming of Ragnarok", replied John,
Suddenly, there was the sound of a door slamming shut downstairs. John left to investigate whilst Ulva removed her cloak and continued putting away some more clothes.
Downstairs Einar had returned with the crates along with the carriage driver. After a handshake and a farewell, Einar sent the driver on his way with an extra handful of pennies in gratitude for his assistance in moving the crates.
As they unpacked together, John said to Einar,
"Is that all of them?",
"Yeah", said Einar,
"Again thank you for your help, it means a lot to me", said John,
"Not at all John, happy to help, especially when it concerns family", smiled Einar,
"Will you be okay?", asked John as he noticed Einar's cheery smile had faded into a despondent frown,
"I have to be, for my family, for my wife", said Einar,
"Things will get better Einar, or at least we hope they will get better. That's all we can do in times like this, hope that such dark times are fleeting and that these moments of misery are overcome by newer, better memories", said John,
"You are right John, we all must try and move on, for a man cannot dwell on his tears forever, lest he be drowned by them", said Einar,
"But don't feel compelled to move on too quickly, the loss of loved ones is never easy to overcome and people don't truly recover from it, they just learn to live on with a hole in their heart", said John,
Einar laughed,
"How true", he said,
John smiled before collecting some items up off the floor,
"Right, we better finish putting all of this away. I need to quickly visit Eira and her shop, I want to surprise Ulva with a gift", he said,

"That's sounds lovely lad, in that case why don't you make your way there whilst Ulva and I finish sorting everything out. Once you come back, we can all head over to my place for supper, the others will want to see you both I am sure", said Einar,
"Will Maud and Guthrum be there?", asked John,
"Of course", said Einar,
"And Kara?", said John,
"Not sure, will you be inviting our good friend Brenna?", said Einar,
"I don't see why not; Brenna makes for great company. I could listen to his stories for hours. I'll pop round to see them on my way back and ask if he wishes to attend", said John,
"Excellent, I think this evening is going to bring us some well needed cheer, oh how I have missed it", exclaimed Einar,
"Indeed", said John,
John walked over to the front door and was about to leave when Einar called out to him,
"Welcome home lad, I think you and Ulva are going to like it here", he said,
John said nothing, but he smiled at Einar warmly before he left, closing the door behind him before he made his way down the street. It was bright outside and the air was refreshingly cold, dry and crisp. As John made his way through the streets, he passed by a young girl who was handing out samples of throka, less commonly known as Crystal Mist, a sweet drink made from blackberries that was favoured amongst the Norse.
After being gifted one such bottle, John sipped the drink as he walked through a dark and narrow alleyway before eventually arriving at Eira's antique shop, a small and inconspicuous looking timber building. Above the door hung a large wooden sign that read *'Eira's Antique Treasures and Earthly Delights'*.

John slowly entered, as he did a blast of warm air hit his cold face. The interior of the shop was a large room that was lit by glowing lamps that hung from the ceiling and walls, there were also multiple candles flickering on the shop counter. John noticed upon entering that the air was toasty and pervaded by the strong scent of burning.

John glanced around and could see that the walls were lined with many cabinets, each one filled with all sorts of trinkets and curious treasures. John inspected one of the cabinets, inside he could see exotic and foreign paraphernalia, strange books, dainty little music boxes, weathered maps and some forbidden and unusual looking objects.

As he browsed, there came a female voice,

"John?",

John turned round to see Eira standing behind the shop counter. She was no longer wearing her suit of armour and was now wearing a long purple dress with sleeves embroidered with lace fastened with a belt that was made from what looked like silver scales. She was wearing gloves and on her slender neck was a small necklace with a diamond shaped amethyst.

In the gloomy shadows cast by the candles, torches and lamps, her violet eyes seemed to glow faintly,

"Ah Eira hello, I've come to purchase something for Ulva", beamed John,

Eira grinned,

"Of course, I'll be happy to assist you in finding something special. Follow me, I might have something in the back", she said,

Eira turned and entered an opening standing behind her, John quickly followed, gripping his money pouch as he did. John gasped as he found himself standing in a vast room with a high ceiling that seemed to stretch away into never-ending darkness. As far as his one eye could see, John saw towering shelves and cabinets fit to bursting with antiquities and objects.

Everywhere he looked there was a glint of gold, a shine of silver and a gleaming sparkle of crystal and glass, all seductively winking at him as they glistened in the light, enticing him into making a purchase.

John could not see the floor, for it was drowned in piles of books, there seemed to be books everywhere, some piles several times his height.

John yelped as he nearly slipped on a discarded bottle that was lying on its side, clattering as it rolled across the floor. In fact, he now noticed that there were also mounds of bottles everywhere, all of them empty. As wondrous as the room was, it was untidy and incredibly unkempt, as if it had not been cleaned in years.

As John's sight adjusted to the lamp light and the shining treasure around him, he could see Eira walking ahead through a pathway that had been made through the sea of books that surrounded her.

Following close behind, John said,

"This place is full of treasure, it's incredible",

"It's wonderful isn't it? I have spent years collecting up this stuff, I can't get enough of it", said Eira,

After winding through a maze and labyrinth of highly piled books, Eira and John soon found themselves in a small area that was cleared of junk and litter. Standing before them was a small row of tall wooden cabinets. Eira approached one and before she opened it, she reached for her belt and from it plucked a small round flask. Opening its head, she gulped down its contents, ingesting the horrible and bitter tasting liquid, which made her shiver and splutter in pain.

She then unexpectedly coughed before she belched what seemed like a flicker of fire that badly startled John,

"Odin's beard, what the hell was that?!", he gasped,

"Medicine", replied Eira, her mouth and nostrils slightly smoking,

"For what?!", yelled John as his heart thumped hard within his chest,

"None of your business", snapped Eira,

"Sorry, forget I said anything", said John,
Putting the flask back on her belt, Eira cleared her throat and coughed once more.
She then produced a small key and opened the cabinet with a turn of its crystalline head,
"Do you have any idea what Ulva might like?", she said,
"I know she loves animals, literature and weaponry, her grandmother being a shieldmaiden after all", said John,
Eira inspected the contents of the cabinet before pulling out a hair brooch. It was made of carved wood and was shaped like a doe in a sitting position, with large eyes and a pointed face and ears.
Eira pointed to what looked like a tear just below the doe's eye made from a small sapphire,
"How about this lovely hair brooch, notice the tear here? This piece was inspired by the Saga of the Fawn Princess", she said,
"Ah one of Ulva's favourite stories", said John,
"Not sure of its providence, but I reckon its quite old", said Eira,
John folded his arms as he stared at the piece before he shook his head and said,
"It's beautiful in its craftsmanship, but Ulva has many brooches, I doubt she will want another one, so I'll pass",
Eira placed the brooch back into the display case before pulling out a ceramic vase that was richly decorated with leaves, strange symbols and birds with large plumes and tails,
"How about this lovely piece from the Far East? I bought it off a merchant when I traversed the Silk Road. He didn't tell me where he got it from, but it's definitely beautiful and I can give you a good price for it", said Eira,
"I don't know if she would be interested I'm sorry", said John,

Eira huffed in frustration and placed the piece back into the display case,
"I have thousands of pieces in this room alone. We will be here all day if we inspect each one individually. Why don't you have a look around yourself, perhaps you might find something", she said,
"Very well, I'll let you know if I find anything", said John,
"Splendid, well I'm off for a smoke, call me when you find anything", said Eira,
Lighting her pipe, Eira made her way out of the room back to the front counter outside. In silence, John began to look around and soon started rummaging through the many treasures lying sprawled across the floor.
As time wore on, John had gone through assortments of books, astrological tools, chests filled with shiny junk, stuffed taxidermy, piles of fabrics, carpets and tapestries, colourful vases and an array of armour and weaponry.
Between scouring the shelves, cupboards and mountains of paraphernalia, John would sit for a while, listening to Eira conversing with customers who had entered the shop. Most of the conversations were short and dull, but sometimes a conversation would come up that peeked John's interest.
On one occasion John could hear Eira arguing with a customer, shouting with inflammatory fervour,
"I told you, that's the price I've set, I am not going any lower!", she yelled,
There came a male voice before Eira shouted,
"Because you're an idiot, that's why!"
Suddenly there came the sounds of a scuffle before a loud bang could be heard,
"And stay out!", shouted Eira before she slammed the door shut angrily,
"I swear sometimes these customers have more gold than sense", grumbled Eira,
"Are you okay?", asked John,
"I'm fine, just keep looking", replied Eira,

After finishing his drink, John set the bottle aside before resuming his search, discovering more books, adorable dolls both human and animal and collections of furs, cloaks, coins and walking canes.
With sweat beading his forehead, John groaned as he began to pillage through another pile.
After what seemed like an eternity had passed, John angrily set aside some artefacts as he began combing through yet another assortment of treasures,
"This is taking forever", growled John,
It was then that Eira appeared in the doorway holding a bottle of cider,
"Anything?" she said,
"No, there are so many wonderful things in here and yet I have found nothing for Ulva", said John sadly,
Eira took a gulp of her drink and said,
"Well I think I might have found the perfect thing you are looking for",
John stared at Eira,
"Really, what is it?", he said,
"Follow me", said Eira,
Pulling himself up, John followed Eira to the shop foyer where an artefact was waiting for him.
On the front counter sat a long rectangular box made of old and gnarled wood that was as black as coal, the fine grain speckled red like sprayed blood,
"It's a box", said John,
"Ah but it's what's inside that truly matters", said Eira,
John watched as Eira gleefully opened the box, revealing its contents. John gasped in amazement at what he saw.
Lying on a bed of blood red silk was a long and beautiful silver dagger. Its hilt was as black as night and at the heart of the crossbar was a wolf head, it's eyes red and furious, its mouth open with a lolling tongue sticking out between its fangs. The pommel itself was a round and smooth ruby.

Etched into the dagger were several lines of text in archaic runes, the runes were extremely tiny and were barely readable by the naked eye. They were not of the familiar elder futhark dialect, nor were they Frisian or Saxon futhorc.
If they were, John could have read them with ease, he was after all a Saxon and they were his mother tongue,
"These runes are old, centuries old and are written in a form of Norse that is no longer spoken or written. Luckily however I've been able to roughly translate them", said Eira,
"So you can read them?" asked John,
"Of course I can read them, I wouldn't rightly call myself a scholar if I didn't", huffed Eira,
"Well what does it say?", said John,
Placing an eyeglass to her eye, Eira ran a gloved finger along the lines of runes upon the dagger and said,
"With this frosted fang of darkness cold and iron flesh of aeons old, I plant a kiss upon my breast and pierce my quivering heart. With blood running hot unfurled and upon the turning of dawn against the world, from the gift of the dark wolf I set myself free, thus my soul is unbound of lycanthropy",
Eira then flipped the dagger over gently, revealing on its other side more lines of text.
As Eira began reciting the incantation, John noticed the candles around him were flickering as if caught in a breeze and the lamps of the shop were flashing and dimming, their light pulsating like a heartbeat,
"With this dagger named Vulthur, blessed with the power of Fenrir's Bane, I purge my flesh, quell my blood, purify my tainted soul, cleanse my feral mind and once again make myself whole", said Eira before she removed her eyeglass,
"Well that's what it says, pretty poetic if you ask me", she said,
John stared at Eira with a look of bemusement,
"What the hell does it mean though?", he said,

Eira shrugged,

"I have no idea, perhaps it's powerful magic, perhaps it's garbled nonsense", she said,

"Where did you get it?", asked John,

"I don't know where it came from or what its purpose is, but it has been with me ever since I inherited this shop years ago from my late and dear father. He never spoke of how he obtained it, in fact he didn't speak of it much at all, so I doubt he cared to be honest. However I think Ulva will like it, if not for its mysterious qualities, then most definitely for it's dark beauty", said Eira,

John picked up the dagger and carefully inspected it, it was weighty and ice cold to the touch. He winced in pain as he accidentally cut his finger on the edge of the blade, it was surprisingly sharp.

John placed the dagger back into its box before sucking on his bleeding finger,

"You okay?", asked Eira,

"Yeah, nothing to worry about, anyway how much do you want for it?", said John,

Eira was silent for a moment before saying,

"Fifty pieces of silver should suffice",

"Done", said John,

Eira watched as John unfastened a small leather pouch from his belt and placed it upon the counter.

After quickly counting its contents, Eira pocketed the pennies before she handed the box over to John and said,

"It's all yours",

Placing the box under his arm, John said,

"My thanks Eira, by the way, would you like to come to dinner later tonight? We are having a small feast to celebrate our homecoming",

"Sorry John, but I've gotta keep an eye on the shop and complete some errands, but thank you for the offer, perhaps another time", said Eira,

John frowned with disappointment,

"I understand" he sighed,

"Don't worry John, I will definitely visit as soon as I am able, you have my word", said Eira,
"I look forward to it and thank you again for the dagger, I will relay Ulva's reaction when we meet again", said John,
"So what will you do now?", asked Eira,
"Visit Brenna and his family, ask them if they want to come to dinner", said John,
"Good idea, do send him my regards", said Eira,
"I will", said John,
As John went to leave, Eira said,
"Will you and Ulva be okay?",
"I hope so Eira, I truly do", replied John before he opened the door and left, leaving Eira alone to quietly smoke her pipe,
Outside John noticed that the town was bathed in the warm and orange glow of the low evening sun, it was getting late,
"How long was I in there?", muttered John,
It mattered not, he had what he came for and was about to make his way to Brenna's home when he was suddenly approached by an elderly man. The man was incredibly thin and slightly shorter than John. His long hair and beard were silver in colour and he was garbed in crimson robes. Around his neck hung an ornate necklace lined with precious stones. His tapered fingers were long, bony, pale and adorned with large gleaming ruby rings.

The man was dressed quite luxuriantly, but his face betrayed an aged and creepy ugliness. The man had a pointed nose and a face that was ghostly pale and heavy with creases, scars and marks whilst his lips were thin, pursed and drained of colour. He looked almost like a cadaver and had an unsettling air about him that made John's stomach turn. But what caught John's attention most were the man's eyes; they were deep set into the old man's skull and were glowing slightly with a dark bluish green colour.

The man stared at John with a curious glance before bowing his head,
"Forgive me young man, I understand you might be quite busy, but please allow me a moment of your time", he said,
"What do you want?" said John as he eyed the old man with suspicion,
"Allow me to introduce myself, my name is Vulpes", said the old man,
"Vulpes? As in Vulpes, one of the Godi to Jarl Turold?", said John,
"How very perceptive of you, indeed I am an advisor, record keeper and administrator of wisdom and guidance to his lordship", said Vulpes,
"You look...different from the last time I saw you. I was just a boy then, but I remember you crowning the brow of Jarl Volhath many years ago at the Haustblot festival, you looked more...human", said John,
An amused chuckle rose from Vulpes's throat,
"Age does terrible things to us my dear boy, I am no exception. Anyway, I must ask, who might you be?", he said,
John eyed the spindly creature standing before him and said,
"John, my name is John",
"A pleasure to meet you", said Vulpes,
"What do you want? I am a busy man and I haven't got time for idle chatter", said John,
"Very well, I am here regarding the box you are carrying", said Vulpes,
John's eyes widened, the pit of his stomach suddenly flared with a sickening feeling of worry and dread.
He gripped the box tightly, determined to not let the withered husk of a man take it,
"You are?", he said,
"I recognize the wood that box is crafted from, its unique colour and grain can only be found in a forest located far to the north, a place known simply as Coldwood, or in its more ancient name Jokullholt. Might that box perhaps hold a dagger inscribed in totemic tongue?", said Vulpes,

John's mouth opened slightly in surprise,
"*How did he know about that?*" he thought,
"I don't know what you are talking about", muttered John,
A horrible chuckle left Vulpes's lips,
"Oh come now, I am old, not stupid, I can spy a little lie when I see it, but it matters not, let's just cut to the chase. I would like to purchase it off you and I am willing to pay handsomely for it", he said,
"You do?", said John,
"Indeed, just name your price. Whatever your heart desires, it can be yours", said Vulpes,
John did not say anything as he pondered Vulpes's offer. It would have been a lie if John did not admit that he paused to think about the offer. A mysterious and beautiful dagger of unknown value that would delight his wife or trade it for something that could set him, his friends and family up for life, never to know hardship or misery again. Indeed the offer was tantalizing, but then John thought about Ulva and how wondrous the look on her face would be when she receives her gift. To see her smile again, to hear her laugh again, it was something more valuable beyond any price Vulpes could offer. As John pondered upon his predicament, he began to sweat as his arms and legs turned to jelly.
Eventually, after agonizingly wracking his brain over the situation, John composed himself and said bluntly,
"Godi Vulpes, I truly appreciate the offer, it is indeed very tempting",
Vulpes's grin widened,
"However, I promised myself that I would get the perfect present for my wife and that is what I intend to do. I am sorry, but this dagger is not for sale, at any price", said John,
Vulpes's grin quickly faded to be replaced by a look of genuine shock as he was taken aback by John's answer,
"Really?!" he spluttered,

John nodded in response,
"But, but surely a man such as yourself would greatly benefit from such a generous offer. I wouldn't throw away such an opportunity like this quite so quickly and easily!", gasped Vulpes,
"I am sorry Vulpes and I do appreciate the offer, but I spent a lot of time and effort finding this dagger and I am not willing to go back to my wife empty handed after wasting such time acquiring it", said John,
At this point Vulpes's patience was wearing out as his almost skeletal frame was quivering with rage,
"Are you quite sure? I will not be offering this chance again", he growled,
"Have a nice evening Vulpes, now if you will excuse me, Ulva is waiting for me and I do not wish to keep her waiting any longer than I need to. I wish you luck in your search for another one though. Perhaps you might want to search around town a bit more, I am sure there are plenty more arcane belly stabbers lying about", said John,
John then walked away as he made his way down the street, leaving Vulpes alone and seething with anger.
The old man growled angrily as both his hands were curled into shaking fists,
"A grave mistake my young friend, you will regret it", he snarled,

CHAPTER V: WOLFBITE

As John was making his way to Brenna's house, he could not take his mind off his encounter with Vulpes and was hoping deep down that he had not just made a terrible error of judgement. After walking through several alleyways and passing many houses, John soon found himself standing before a very wide and dark street.

After walking for quite some distance, John soon arrived at a large house. Unlike the other buildings, this one was detached and enclosed around a moderately sized garden, which was colourful and full of flowers, plants and vegetation. There were bushes that were full of small vividly blue and red flowers with tiny petals. There were thickets of blooming wolfsbane and monkshood, strong smelling herbs, tall perennials of bluish nootka lupine and white yarrow.

As John approached the front door, he noticed a faint smell of garlic in the air and could hear the gentle whistling of windchimes. The house itself was a two-storey timber building with tall arched windows and a slanted roof made of slate that was crowned with carved wolf heads. Behind the house, John could see a small, stout tower constructed from timber and hanging from the door he spotted a small flickering lantern.

John cleared his throat and was about to knock when the door suddenly swung open, making John flinch as he nearly tumbled backwards. Out of the shadows stepped a middle-aged man who closed the door behind him.

The man was wearing a shirt of dark grey mail, over which he wore a light blue tunic. Across his waist was a thick leather belt lined with pouches and spread across his chest was a dark blue silk sash embroidered with silver stars.

Pinned to the sash was a large badge of gold, etched into it was what looked like the symbol of a tree with three stars above it.

John recognized it as the symbol used by the Folkmoot of Gormstad. Hanging from the man's belt was a long sword and sat under his arm was an embossed helmet.

The man himself was muscular with a shaved head and a short black beard, his piercing eyes coloured a dull grey.

John recognized the man, it was Hersir Barmund, captain of the Gormstad Guard,

"Excuse me citizen", said Barmund before he walked past John and disappeared out of sight down the road,

Turning back to the door, John gently knocked, hoping Brenna would answer. A moment passed before the door creaked open slightly. Peering through the opening was a face that John recognized, a handsome man with a thick flowing mane of dark blonde hair. The man possessed a thick beard and his eyes were coloured a brilliant emerald green that sat behind round, purple tinted spectacles, it was his friend Brenna. He looked exhausted, a little dishevelled and the skin around his eyes had been rubbed raw.

Brenna's eyes widened upon seeing John,

"John?", he said,

"Brenna, it's good to see you", said John,

"Likewise", said Brenna,

"Why was Barmund in your house?", asked John,

"Nothing for you to worry about, what do you want?", said Brenna,

"Well, I was just passing by and I was wondering if you would like to join us for a little gathering to celebrate our homecoming", said John,

Brenna adjusted his glasses and said,

"Sorry John, but I haven't got time for parties at the moment, got a lot of things on my mind at the moment",

"Like what?", asked John,

"I don't want to talk about it", said Brenna,

"That's fine, but if something is troubling you, then I am willing to listen and help if possible", said John,
Brenna stared at John before he sighed deeply and said, "All right, I'll tell you if you promise not to go around blabbing",
"I promise", said John,
"Well I don't know how to explain this, but there are rumours that a werewolf has been sighted near the town. Barmund wanted some advice on how to approach the situation in the most delicate and tact way possible without drawing unwanted attention. I've been engrossed in my studies as of late so that I may be of some assistance", said Brenna,
"Ah yes I remember now, you study them correct?", asked John,
"Correct", said Brenna,
Folding his arms, John said,
"Not to be rude and I know a man's hobby is his gold, but I've always found your fascination with werewolves to be…well odd. Werewolves are just monsters borne of fairy tales and legends, I have never seen one and as far as I am aware they don't exist",
"Just because you haven't seen one doesn't mean they don't exist. I have had the misfortune of seeing one personally and let me tell you, they are more terrifying than anything out of your fireside fables. For your sake John, I hope that you never do", said Brenna as he glared at John,
"At least we can agree on that", said John,
"Indeed, well if there's nothing else, I bid you farewell. I have some very important research to conduct and I've kept you long enough. Please go and enjoy yourself this evening, don't let thoughts of werewolves and my troubles concern you", said Brenna,
"Okay, but if you change your mind, you know where to find us and if you ever need someone to talk to, our home will always be open to you", said John,

Brenna nodded before he quickly darted back inside and slammed the door shut,

"Werewolves pah, what nonsense", huffed John,

As John made his way back home, night was beginning to descend on Gormstad as the sunset had painted the sky orange and the first stars of the night had begun to emerge. The air was turning colder, the windows nearby had started glowing and the town guards were turning on the streetlamps. It wasn't long before John arrived at Einar's house and as he walked up to the front door, he was startled when it suddenly swung open.

Standing before him was Einar, who looked slightly inebriated as he grinned from ear to ear whilst holding a mug of beer in his hand,

"Ah there you are John, we were wondering where you had gotten to", he said,

"Hi Einar, sorry I took so long", said John,

"Oh don't worry about all that brother, come, come, everyone is waiting", he said as he welcomed John through into the foyer,

As John entered, he felt warm air envelop his body and he could see several people sitting around a large fire pit situated in the centre of the room. Rotating over it on a spit was a large and succulent roast, it smelt divine, its rich flavour wafting heavily through the air.

The first person John laid eyes on was Ulva, who was now wearing a beautiful white dress that was low cut and embroidered with silver thread. She was wearing the silver bracelet that John had bought her on their first date and the slippers that he had gifted her last year for her birthday. She was also wearing a lovely crimson shade of lipstick, which beautifully complemented the scarlet tones of her hair and above her brow sat a lovely white flower.

Sitting next to her was a tall and large woman garbed in a black dress, her beautiful round face framed by long brown hair that flowed down to her waist, her brown eyes shining with delight as she revelled in conversation with Ulva.

Her name was Maud and she was both Einar's beloved wife and a renowned songstress whose voice was celebrated throughout Gormstad.
Sitting next to Ulva in a large rocking chair was an elderly man who was gaunt, small and hunched in stature. His head was completely hairless, but his chin was covered in a long and magnificent beard that sat nestled beneath rosy cheeks. The old man was draped in a red, moth-eaten tunic and he was smiling warmly as he eyed Ulva and Maud whilst he puffed on a long pipe.
The old man glanced up and smiled as he saw John approach,
"It is good to see you young pup, welcome back to Gormstad", he said,
John beamed at the old man's words and said,
"Likewise granddad Guthrum",
Maud gasped as she got to her feet and said,
"John, it's been a while!",
John was about to respond when Maud suddenly ran over to him and squeezed him tightly in a warm hug,
"Maud, it's so good to see you", said John,
Pulling herself away from John, Maud said,
"I heard about what happened to you and Ulva, I'm so sorry",
"Thank you, it has been tough, but we are managing. Anyways I heard about your brother Heidrun becoming a skald to the Highmoot, I can't believe it, you must be so proud", said John,
Maud took a large gulp of her drink before she hiccupped,
"Oh I couldn't be happier", she said as she beamed proudly,
"I'll bet", laughed John,
Einar closed the door before he walked over to Maud and sat himself down beside her whilst John walked over to Ulva, who stood up and allowed John to take her seat.
As he sat down, Ulva curled herself up on his lap,
"Welcome back" she cooed,

John felt his stomach twirl as he felt Ulva run her fingers across his chest, she smelt of sweet alcohol and strawberries mixed with a tinge of perfume that had the unmistakable scent of lavender,
"Thank you my love", said John before Ulva pulled him in close for a kiss,
After turning the spit on the fire, Einar went around refilling everyone's drinks as they waited for the food to cook.
As he filled John's mug, Einar said,
"Where's Brenna?",
"Brenna said he was too busy to attend", said John,
"A shame, but I'm sure he has his reasons", said Einar,
"Speaking of missing people, where's Kara?", asked John,
"Feeling a little unwell", said Einar,
"Well I hope she gets better soon", said John as he took a sip of his drink,
"I'm sure she will", said Einar,
As the night slowly wore on, the air was filled with laughter and merriment as Guthrum, Maud, Ulva, John and Einar tucked into a small, but sumptuous banquet of delicious fruits, hog roast, spatchcocked chicken and creamed desserts with nuts and honey. They all took immense pleasure in idle gossip and indulgent chatter, telling silly jokes and sharing stories amongst themselves. At one point, Einar produced his lyre and began to play.
Not just skilled with a blade, Einar was fond of music and spent much of his time practising and composing delightful melodies and songs upon his lyre, a beautiful and ornately decorated instrument made from reddish brown wood adorned with knotted patterns and images of trees, deer and a bearded figure. This figure was Bragi, the Nordic god of music and poetry.
As the night wore on amongst the glow of the fire pit and the wafting of pipe smoke, everyone began to sing amongst themselves. Maud was the highlight for she was a great singer and it was this talent that drew Einar to her.

They had met at a midsummer festival several years ago, he being a skald and she being a talented songstress, they fell head over heels for one another and the rest was history.
As the fire began to quieten down at the end of the evening, Guthrum, Einar and Maud had retired to bed, leaving John and Ulva sitting by the dying embers.
After talking for quite some time, Ulva finished her drink before she got to her feet and made her way to the door,
"I need some air", she said before she glanced back at John, "You coming?", she said,
"Yeah", said John as he stood up with the box containing the dagger tucked safely beneath his arm,
Taking each other by the hand, John and Ulva made their way out through the door, closing it behind them as they left before they made their way down the street.
Glancing up at the shining moon, John said,
"What a lovely night, I do enjoy our little night-time walks together",
"Me too", said Ulva,
As John and Ulva arrived at the monument sitting in the middle of the quiet and deserted town square, John said,
"Can we stop for a second? I have something I want to show you",
"Really?", asked Ulva,
John nodded as he and Ulva came to a halt at the foot of the towering stone standing before them,
"I...um...got you a present", he said,
Ulva glanced at John with a surprised look as he handed her the box that he was carrying,
"Oh John, you shouldn't have", she said,
Ulva opened it and gasped at what she saw, the dagger glinting in the moonlight.
Picking it up, Ulva stared at it in amazement, her eyes sparkling with wonder and delight at the sight of such a treasure,
"Oh it's beautiful John, it must have cost a fortune", said Ulva,

"The cost doesn't matter, you are worth more than whatever I spent to acquire it", said John,
Beaming, Ulva kissed John on the lips before saying,
"Thank you John, I love it",
"You're welcome, it's been difficult for us both lately, so I thought this might cheer you up", said John,
John grinned as Ulva threw her arms around him and they both embraced.
It was then that John whispered into Ulva's ear,
"Care for a dance my love?",
"Always", said Ulva before her and John walked over to where the moon bathed the square in silver light,
They then put their arms around one another as they slowly danced and stared into each other's eyes with loving adoration.
As they waltzed under the cold glow of the crescent moon, John placed his arm around Ulva's waist and softly hummed Lupa's Lullaby, the sound of which made Ulva smile contently before she rested her head against John's chest. She then closed her eyes as a single tear ran down her face, her mind wandering to memories of the time her parents sung it to her in times of sadness, fear and grief,
"Thank you" she whispered,
John responded by simply kissing Ulva on the forehead.
As they continued to dance in each other's arms, Ulva said in a gentle tone of voice,
"John?",
"Yes Ulva?", said John,
"Promise me everything will be okay", said Ulva,
As John cradled his wife, he said softly,
"I promise",
As they continued to dance, they were both suddenly startled when a sudden and long drawn howl suddenly pierced the air. Feeling a chill run down his spine, John glanced around the square hoping to catch a glimpse of something amidst the surrounding gloom, but he couldn't see anything and that frightened him.

As Ulva huddled close to John with a look of concern etched upon her frightened face, John said,
"Let's get out of here",
Suddenly there came a great and loud thud as something large struck against the cobblestones. John and Ulva looked in the direction of the sound and were horrified to see a hulking figure appear near the entrance of the square as it jumped down from a nearby roof.
The figure was half - human, half – wolf and the fur that covered its entire body was silver in colour. Its legs were like that of a dog and its arms were muscular, attached to which were large paws tapered with sharp claws. The creature had pointed ears, a shaggy mane and a greyish tail. Its wolfish face was fixed into a hideous and furious snarl, its glowing, teal-coloured eyes burning with rage, it was a werewolf.
The werewolf eyed John and Ulva silently before it glanced at the dagger in Ulva's hand. It then roared loudly and raced towards them with great and terrifying speed.
As Ulva let out a scream of terror, John grabbed his pickaxe,
"Run Ulva!" he barked,
As she began to run back to the house, John ran towards the monster and caught the beast in the snout with his pickaxe, sending blood flying. The werewolf snarled with anger and with incredible strength swung its arm. John dodged the blow, feeling a rush of air pass his face. The creature snapped at John as he brought his pickaxe down upon its body. The werewolf then in rage pushed John, who went flying.
John landed with a thud, crying out in pain as he felt his back strike the hard ground.
As pain wracked his body, he weakly and painfully raised up his head, watching in horror as the werewolf ran after Ulva,
"No!", cried John,
Collecting up his weapon, John pulled himself up onto his feet and immediately gave chase. Down the street, Ulva was running with all her strength, she was panting heavily and beginning to sob in terror. She then suddenly tripped over her dress and tumbled to the ground.

She rolled round and watched as the werewolf came up to her and stopped dead in its tracks,

"Give me the dagger", it snarled as it stretched out its hand, As Ulva shakingly held out the dagger to the werewolf, John shouted,

"Ulva!",

Full of rage, John ran over and plunged the sharp end of his pickaxe into the werewolf's back. The monster roared as blood sprayed everywhere. John then pulled Ulva to her feet and ran back over to the werewolf and began brutally attacking it. It was then that the nearby door swung open and a bare-chested Einar appeared holding a blade in his right hand.

Maud was standing close behind him, looking shocked and horrified at the commotion,

"What the hell's going on?!", yelled Einar,

Einar gasped as he saw the visage of the werewolf, who was swinging at John with mighty and vicious claws. Einar raced over to John's side and sliced at the werewolf's neck, whilst John swung at the beast's back. As blood began to seep down its spine, the enraged werewolf bellowed and grabbed Einar by the throat before sending him flying in a great show of strength. Einar tumbled to the floor and was knocked unconscious as his head hit the pavement, causing Maud to cry out in shock before she ran over to his side.

John meanwhile was clashing against the werewolf, swinging wildly as he blocked the beast's vicious claws. The werewolf suddenly swiped at John's hand and knocked the pickaxe from his grasp before John was pushed to the floor.

John watched in horror as the werewolf opened its mouth and was about to bite his exposed throat when Ulva dived in front of him, shielding John from the beast's attack,

"Leave him alone!", she screamed,

John watched as the werewolf sunk its fangs deep into Ulva's shoulder, his heart sank as she let out a piercing scream that echoed throughout the street.

With all the strength she could muster, Ulva took the inscribed dagger in her hand and plunged it deep into the werewolf's right eye, piercing it with a sickening squelch. The werewolf bellowed a bloodcurdling and terrible screech before fleeing into the darkness.

Ulva cried out in pain and writhed on the floor as her shoulder bled profusely and she felt a horrible, blistering, painful and burning sensation race down her entire body,

"Ulva!", cried John as he raced over to Ulva and fell to his knees,

He felt sick and nauseous as he witnessed the horrible visage of Ulva lying on her back, wounded and bloody. Her beautiful dress was soaked with blood and had been torn where the werewolf had plunged its fangs into her flesh.

As she squirmed upon the ground, Ulva gazed up at the sky with horrified and unblinking eyes as she said,

"It bit me John, the monster bit me",

CHAPTER VI: THE FIRST TURNING

"Gods I've been bitten!", cried Ulva,
Shaking as he beheld his distressed wife crying out in pain, John gently scooped Ulva up off the floor before he sheathed her dagger upon his belt and placed his hand upon her forehead. She was cold to the touch, sweating and shivering as her blood began to run down John's arms. There was a foul stench coming from the wound, it smelt like rotting flesh, but also faintly of almonds. He walked over to Maud, who was kneeling next to Einar, she looked worried and was shaking.
Einar meanwhile was groaning as he began to awaken, his vision spinning as his head throbbed with pain,
"Is Einar going to be okay?", asked John,
"He'll be fine", said Maud,
She looked at John and said,
"What the hell happened? I heard screaming",
"It was a werewolf, it bit Ulva", said John,
"What, I thought they were nothing but monsters from bedtime stories?!", blurted Maud,
"So did I until now, it came out of nowhere and attacked us, we are lucky to be alive. Take Einar inside, I'm going to tend to Ulva at our house", said John,
John was about to leave when Maud pulled out of her pocket a small yellow plant,
"This is witch hazel, give it to Ulva, it will stem the bleeding", she said,
"Thank you Maud, I forgot you know quite a bit about healing plants", said John,
"It's no problem, now go and tend to your wife", said Maud,

John slowly and painfully carried Ulva to their home, his breathing heavy, his head throbbing and every inch of his body was painful.

Fighting through the pain, John entered his house and closed the door behind him before he climbed up the stairs and made his way into the bedroom, placing Ulva gently upon the bed.

Seeing his wife writhing as she groaned and murmured in pain, John plucked the witch hazel from his pocket and held it to Ulva's face,

"Okay Ulva, Maud said to eat this, it will make you better", he said,

Ulva grimaced as she took the flower in her mouth and began to chew. She swallowed in disgust, it was bitter tasting and earthy. John then looked in one of the nearby cupboards and found a small flask of water, which he tenderly administered to Ulva, watching anxiously as she gingerly sipped. It provided only a moment of relief before the pain welled up again in her stomach.

She felt hot and itchy all over and she could feel a burning sensation crawling under her skin,

"I'm burning", she groaned,

"I'm here Ulva, it's gonna be okay", said John as he applied a cold flannel to Ulva's forehead,

He then tenderly and carefully removed Ulva's clothes before he tucked her into bed. John then wiped the smeared makeup and flecks of blood from her face and began cleaning up her wound. The wound was ghastly to look at, it was a large and deep bite mark that lined the front and back of her shoulder, two long lines of oozing and bloody puncture wounds.

Shaking with immense pain and wracked by a blistering, stinging sensation, Ulva gritted her teeth and yelled out as John wiped the blood away from the seeping wound,

"Shh...it will be over soon Ulva, just try and bare it", said John softly,

Once the blood had been cleaned up, John placed the bloodied cloth into a nearby bucket and slowly walked over to the bedside table.
On it was Ulva's sewing box, John opened it and found inside a needle and thread. With his hands shaking, he collected them up and went back over to Ulva's side.
When Ulva saw the needle, she knew what he was going to do,
"No John, please don't", she pleaded,
"Ulva, I need to sew up the wound or you might bleed to death", said John in a soft, but affirmative tone of voice,
"I'm frightened", squeaked Ulva,
John sat down next to Ulva and gripped her little hand,
"I know you are, but please let me do this, let me help you. I will be as gentle as possible I promise", he said,
Ulva sighed and muttered,
"Fine, just get it over with",
"Thank you", said John,
Ulva closed her eyes as she could feel the cold pin touch her skin. She then began to hiss through gritted teeth and groan as John inserted the needle into her flesh and began to thread through the wound. She tightly gripped the bedsheets as John sewed up the larger wound marks. It took no more than a minute, but every second felt like an eternity and it was incredibly painful.
Once John had finished his work, he collected from a nearby drawer a small box that he had put away earlier in the day. Inside was a tiny wooden pot filled with herbal cream, he opened it and from it came a pungent and strange medicinal smell. With two fingers, John gently began to apply the salve to Ulva's wounds. Though still in pain and with her skin feeling as if it was burning, Ulva's breathing began to quieten down as her shaking was beginning to stop.
As John finished applying the salve, his mind was heavy with terrible thoughts, where did the werewolf come from and why did it attack them?

It was then that Ulva began to mumble to herself,
"Ulva?", said John,
Ulva continued to mumble incoherently,
"What are you saying?", asked John,
Suddenly, Ulva opened her eyes and stared at John with a vacant and blank expression before she uttered softly,
"Am I going to turn?",
John's blood ran cold as he suddenly came to a horrible realization, Ulva had been bitten, was she going to become a werewolf? If so, then how long would it be before she would turn? He needed answers urgently and he knew exactly the person who would give them to him, Brenna Torstensson. Putting the pot of salve away, John gave Ulva another drink of water before he pulled the sheets up to her chin,
"I don't know, but try to get some sleep", said John in a shaking tone of voice,
John kissed Ulva sweetly on the forehead as she began to drift off to sleep.
Suddenly there came the sound of the door downstairs swinging open followed by the sound of footsteps,
"John?" came two voices in unison, it was Einar and Maud,
"I'm up here", he said, all the while keeping his eye on Ulva, John could hear heavy footsteps coming up the stairs and he soon saw Maud and Einar enter the bedroom.
Einar was holding John's pickaxe whilst Maud was holding the box that Ulva's dagger came in,
"We found these outside and wanted to return them to you, also we wanted to see if Ulva was alright", said Maud,
"Thank you", said John as Einar and Maud put the box and pickaxe to one side near the bed,
They soon turned their attention to Ulva who was sleeping peacefully, the salve was working well and the water was beginning to bring down her temperature,
"I can't believe what just happened", said Einar with a heavy sigh,
"Yeah, I mean, it doesn't seem real doesn't it?", said Maud,
"Are you well?", asked Einar to John,

"Not really, I'm hurting, but don't worry about me, I'll be fine, and you?",
"A bump to the head won't keep this old man down", said Einar,
As Maud and Einar watched Ulva sleep, John went over to the wardrobe and quickly removed his bloodstained tunic before throwing on a fresh one.
He then placed Ulva's dagger into a sheath on his belt before opening one of the nearby wardrobes. John pulled out a cloak and put it on, fastening it at the neck with a brass brooch.
He then turned to Einar and said,
"I need to go and find Brenna, he knows much about werewolves, maybe he can help Ulva. If he doesn't, then he might know who can. Ulva has been bitten, I need to know if she will become a werewolf and if so, we need to find a way to cure her",
"I'll come, my sister will need all the help she can get", said Einar,
John nodded in approval before he said to Maud,
"I am asking much of you Maud, but can you...",
"Say no more, I will watch over her", said Maud,
"Thank you", said John before he glanced at Einar,
"Let's go, we have work to do", he said,
As John and Einar both stepped outside, they noticed that it had begun to snow, the pavements and streets were covered with a light dusting of dry snowflakes. Quickly, they made their way to Brenna's house.
As John knocked on the door, he heard movement coming from beyond the threshold. As the door opened, John and Einar were both surprised to see Eira appear instead of Brenna.
Smoking her pipe, she stared at Einar and John with a surprised look,
"John, Einar, what are you guys doing here?", she said,
"I could ask you the same question young lady", said Einar,
"I came over to see if Brenna was okay, we baked some cakes together and shared some drinks", said Eira,

"Well, where is he now?", said John,
Eira puffed on her pipe as smoke billowed from her mouth,
"He's in his study, pouring over his books trying to make sense of everything", she said,
"Let us in, we need his help", demanded John,
Eira yawned,
"It's late, can't it wait until tomorrow?", she said,
Both Eira and Einar were startled when John suddenly slammed his fist into the door,
"Ulva's been attacked by a werewolf, we need to see Brenna now!", he snarled,
"What?!", gasped Eira,
"Yes, now will you please let us in?", asked John,
"Okay, okay, come in quickly, I'll take you to him right away", said Eira,
Einar and John entered and found themselves in a large room, a foyer with plain white walls. In front of them was a large roaring fireplace, to the left of the hearth was an arched opening that led to other sections of the house and to the right was a tall and narrow bookcase.
On the floor was a great woven carpet and above the fireplace was a large and imposing portrait of Brenna, who was wearing a long, flowing coat of black leather trimmed with fur. He was wearing under this coat a linen shirt and a long red scarf. Brenna was also wearing black leather trousers and boots whilst on his belt hung a shining lamp. Brenna had a serious look on his face and he was holding in his right hand a silver sword whilst under his left arm was tucked a large book.
John and Einar watched as Eira walked over to the bookshelf on the right and grabbed one of the books before pulling it out. John and Einar were surprised to hear a lock click before the bookshelf swung open, revealing a secret doorway and a flight of stairs that led downwards into darkness.
Eira turned to her friends and said,
"This way, watch your footing when you go down",

John and Einar could see Eira make her way through the opening and nervously followed behind.

As they walked through darkness, Einar said,

"What's with the secret entrance?",

Puffing her pipe, Eira said,

"Being a lycanthropist, Brenna has been studying werewolves for many years in the hopes of learning more about them and finding a cure for their venomous bite. He does this in secret, for those with closed minds and fearful hearts might not be so understanding of the work he does for the safety of this land and its people",

After stepping down a steep and dark staircase, John, Einar and Eira found themselves in a large basement that was illuminated by iron chandeliers mounted with white crystal lamps, its stone walls lined with bookshelves fit to bursting with old scrolls and weighty tomes bound in leather and hide.

There were tables, chairs, chains and buckets scattered around the room in an unkempt fashion. Sitting in the left-hand corner of the room were three large and empty iron cages and a table, upon which lay a human skeleton, though its head was animalistic and pointed, its hands and feet ending in sharp claws.

Glancing around the chamber, John and Einar noticed that the air smelt of damp mixed with the faint aroma of blood. At the back of the room stood a hunched figure, his back was turned and it looked like he was tinkering with something on the table before him, it was Brenna.

As they walked towards him, Einar and John glanced over at the long tables running against the nearby wall, staring curiously at the assortment of artefacts that covered their surfaces.

There were large jars filled with embalmed and pickled wolf heads that were contorted into different shapes, glowing bottles containing bubbling, colourful liquids and large bundles of herbs and plants.

There were wooden mortars and pestles, skulls and bones both human and lycanthropic marked with runes, symbols and numbers, strange and intricate instruments of dubious function, bowls filled with teeth, crushed powders, gruesome entrails and silver coins both solid and melted.
On the walls above the tables hung large anatomical drawings of humans, wolves and werewolves as well as some old tapestries. One of the tapestries depicted the Saga of the Seven Heroes whilst the others were of a young woman sitting under a tree looking towards a distant sunset with forlorn sadness and fear, a monstrous werewolf with bulging eyes consuming a hapless victim, a group of people dancing under the moon as their bodies were transforming and one of a large wolf dressed in women's clothing fleeing through a forest in distress.
As Eira, John and Einar walked up to Brenna, they noticed that he was pouring a liquid into the basin sitting before him, John's heart quickened as he realized that it was human blood.
Clearing her throat, Eira said,
"Brenna, John and Einar are here to see you",
As Brenna turned round, John and Einar noticed that he was wearing the exact same outfit from his portrait,
"John, Einar, what perfect timing, you're just in time to witness a little experiment I have been conducting, come have a look, I think you will find it most interesting", said Brenna,
"Forgive us Brenna, but we don't have time", said John,
"It will only take a second", said Brenna,
John sighed and stepped closer as everyone gathered around Brenna, they looked down at the basin in front of him and saw a shallow pool of blood. Grabbing a vial from a nearby wooden rack, Brenna opened it and poured its contents into the basin, a black and viscous liquid.
A familiar scent suddenly caught John's nose, the smell of almonds.

As the black liquid began to mix with the blood, they were all shocked to see the blood begin to fizz and foam furiously, coagulating and congealing, bubbling violently as the two liquids reacted.
With a rather pleased smile lighting up his face, Brenna said, "Remarkable isn't it? What you just saw is what happens when werewolf venom mixes with human blood. I have no actual venom to spare, so I concocted an artificial synthesis to use in this experiment, a facsimile that is remarkably like the real thing. As you can see, the werewolf venom is reacting violently to the blood. Such a reaction might explain why werewolves are so vicious, their blood is literally boiling with fury due to it becoming feral",
As Brenna walked over to the other side of the table and began to write something down in a nearby open book, John slammed his fist down upon the table, which made everyone jump,
"Forgive me for not being so courteous, but I am not here for a study or a lecture, I am here because I need your help and damn it I am not leaving until I get it", said John,
"Then what are you here for exactly?", said Brenna before he began to gulp down some dark cider from a bottle,
"We were attacked earlier this evening by a werewolf, Ulva's been bitten", said John,
In shock Brenna spat out his drink, spraying it over the wall, the sudden noise causing Eira to burn herself on a lit match. Brenna coughed as he adjusted his glasses,
"I'm sorry, I thought you just said Ulva had been bitten", he said,
Einar sighed,
"Yes Brenna, didn't you just hear us?", he said,
Brenna's jaw dropped before he suddenly exploded into a fit of panic. He quickly collected some tools from his desk and shoved them into his pockets.

Papers flew everywhere as he grabbed his leather bag and began stuffing it with books,
"Apparently you know much about werewolves and I was wondering if you might be able to see her, confirm if she is cursed and hopefully tell us if there is a cure", said John,
"Of course I will see her, if she has been bitten, then we might have little time before she turns!", blurted Brenna,
Storming past John and Einar, Brenna yelled,
"Quickly, we need to find her and bring her here immediately without delay!",
Before John, Eira and Einar could say anything, Brenna quickly raced out of the room, his boots thundering against the steps as he rushed upstairs. Without saying so much as a word, John, Eira and Einar quickly ran after him. As they came to the top of the stairs and back into the foyer, Brenna quickly shoved them all out through the front door and slammed it shut behind him. He locked the door before running down the pathway and out into the dark streets.
As Brenna, Eira, John and Einar ran as fast as they could, Brenna turned to John and said,
"I told you, I told you werewolves existed, but you wouldn't listen",
"Yes you were right Brenna, but can you blame me for not believing?", said John,
"No I suppose not, now tell me John, where is Ulva and when was she bitten exactly?", said Brenna,
"She's at our house and was bitten not too long ago", said John,
"Then that means we have some time to act, but we must hurry. When someone is bitten by a werewolf and the venom has seeped into their blood, they are cursed to transform every night into the very same creature that bit them and will not turn back until the following dawn. Did you leave her alone by any chance?", said Brenna,
"No Maud is with her", said John,
"Shit, well let's just pray that Ulva hasn't turned already or Maud might just become Ulva's first victim", said Brenna,

"What?!", cried Einar,
"Calm yourself Einar, it's more than likely she hasn't turned yet, but I don't want to take that chance, let's move, time is of the essence", said Brenna,
"I don't understand, why would Ulva turn tonight? The moon isn't full, don't werewolves usually turn at the full moon?", said John,
Brenna stared at John with disgust as he ran,
"What kind of lunatic told you that?", he said,
"When I was a child, I was told that werewolves only turn at the rise of a full moon", said John,
"Utter nonsense, this my boy is real life. I've been studying werewolves for years and I know for a certainty that the wolfblight is a haematological disorder, it affects the blood and is not invoked by moonlight", said Brenna,
"A what?", asked John,
"It is an affliction of the blood", said Brenna,
"Oh right", said John,
"So you actually study werewolves, it's not just a strange hobby?", said Einar,
"Of course, as a lycanthropist, it's my livelihood", said Brenna,
"Did you decide to study werewolves out of curiosity or was it an encounter with a werewolf that encouraged your interest?", asked Einar,
"It's complicated, now be quiet, I need to think for a moment", snapped Brenna,
The four sprinted down the street before they finally reached John's house. They barged their way in and stormed upstairs, shocked to find the bed that Ulva was sleeping in was empty. Furthermore, both Ulva and Maud were nowhere to be seen,
"Quick, search the house!", barked Brenna,
Immediately everyone began scrambling to look for the two young women, John and Einar searched upstairs, whilst Eira and Brenna checked downstairs.

As everyone was beginning to panic, they suddenly heard a loud clattering of pots and pans from somewhere deep within the house followed by the sounds of screaming.
John turned in the direction of the noise and quickly realized where it was coming from,
"This way, to the pantry!", he cried,
The four raced down the corridor, almost tripping over the carpets. They soon came to a small opening located at the back of the house and dashed inside.
The pantry was a moderately sized room comprised entirely of bare stone walls fortified with timber which were lined by a dozen fat barrels filled with an assortment of foods that were cured, dried, salted and packed with ice.
The group noticed that one of the barrels filled with dried and fresh fruit had been tipped over and was broken, the contents smashed and splattered across the floor alongside pieces of broken wood, iron pots and some blood. In the middle of the pantry stood Maud, who was staring in horror towards the back wall, she was shaking terribly and was as pale as a ghost.
At the back of the pantry was Ulva garbed in her dressing gown rushing about wildly, snarling and growling as she was rummaging through some nearby boxes looking for meat. With bloody hands covered in lacerations, she pulled down large chains of sausages, hocks of salted pork and slabs of raw beef hanging from the ceiling before viciously devouring them, tearing off chunks of dripping and bloody flesh before swallowing them voraciously as she gorged and feasted with ferocious fervour,
"Maud!", yelled Einar,
Maud turned and gasped as she saw Einar, Eira and Brenna standing before her.
Shaking like a leaf, Maud rushed forward and threw her arms around Einar,
"Thank the gods you're here", she gasped,
"Maud, are you alright, what's going on?", asked Einar,

"It's Ulva, she awoke a few moments ago, she was okay at first and we were talking over some tea. Suddenly she got violent, she stormed out of bed and ran down here before she went insane. She broke open a barrel with her bare fists and just started gorging on apples. Then she went after the poultry and began ripping the chickens apart, feathers, skin and all. If all that wasn't enough, now she's going after the red meat. Please stop her, I'm scared she might hurt herself or attack me", whimpered Maud,

As Einar comforted Maud, who was beginning to hyperventilate, Eira, John and Brenna ran over to Ulva and tried to restrain her,

"Stop it Ulva, you're going to make yourself ill!", yelled John,

"Calm down Ulva", growled Eira,

Ulva screamed in anger as she flailed her arms and legs about as she tried to escape, her mouth foaming with blood, her eyes wide and feral,

"It's the first sign of the transformation, immense hunger accompanied by feral rage. Her appetite for flesh has been grossly altered by the venom in her blood. Quickly give her this, it will calm her down and suppress her need to feed", said Brenna as he quickly reached into his pocket and pulled out a small blue flower,

John quickly snatched it and shoved it into Ulva's mouth. After swallowing it, Ulva suddenly stopped thrashing about and began to calm down. Her body stopped shaking, the throbbing veins in her neck disappeared and her eyes that looked so animal and dark were now back to normal. Panting heavily, Ulva lifted her head and glanced around with a frightened and confusion look on her face.

She gasped at the state of the pantry and said,

"What happened, did I do all this?",

"Ulva, you frightened the hell out of us", said John,

"What did you give her?", asked Einar,

"Wolfsbane, does nothing for humans, but it can calm a werewolf and delay the turning process for a brief amount of time. Now quickly, we must get her back to my study, we have much to discuss and I don't know how long it will be before Ulva turns. At the very least, if we can bind her there, she won't pose much of a threat and won't be able to escape", said Brenna,
"Why not just keep her here?", asked Maud,
"Oh I'm sorry, do you have specially prepared chains that can hold down a werewolf?", said Brenna,
Maud shook her head,
"No? Thought not!", snapped Brenna, which caused Maud to flinch a little,
"It's okay Maud, go back to the house and keep an eye on granddad, I'm going with the others", said Einar,
"Okay, be safe", said Maud before she gave Einar a kiss on the cheek,
John gently picked Ulva up in his arms before everyone raced out of the house with Brenna leading the group,
"Sorry for the mess John, I don't know what came over me", said Ulva,
"Don't worry about it, food can be replaced, you can't", said John,
Back at Brenna's house, the group went through the open bookcase in the foyer and down the stairs into the study. Brenna quickly made his way into the chamber and cleared some space, moving a table to one side whilst Eira began lighting some lamps.
Brenna then swiped a nearby chair and placed it down before gesturing John over to it,
"Sit her down", he said,
John gently placed Ulva on the seat, she looked nervous, frightened and was cradling her wounded hands.
As Ulva began tenderly rubbing the sore and throbbing wound on her shoulder, Brenna gave her a drink of water before collecting up a book and a quill.

John sat himself down next to Ulva as Eira, Einar and Brenna collected some chairs and sat in front of her. Once everyone was seated, Brenna cleared his throat and adjusted his spectacles before turning his attention to Ulva, who was now rubbing her belly, her face etched with pain and discomfort. Gesturing to the horrendous wound on Ulva's shoulder, Brenna said,
"Forgive me Ulva, but I will need you to remove your gown. I know it's distasteful to ask, but I will be able to examine you better if you do. Besides once the turning begins, it will be more comfortable for you if you weren't wearing anything",
Ulva glanced at him nervously before turning to her husband,
"It's okay Ulva, just do as he says, I'm sure Brenna knows what he's talking about", said John,
"Of course I do", said Brenna as he glared at John,
Ulva sighed before she hesitantly began to unbutton her gown.
She then nervously pulled it off and allowed it to pool at her feet before placing her arms over her chest to protect her modesty,
"I don't like this, is there no way to stop the turning?", she uttered,
"Other than a cure I'm afraid not, the transformation process has already begun, all we can do tonight is simply wait it out until morning. At least here we can make sure you are safe, comfortable and will not bring harm to yourself and others. Also I can keep an eye on you and gain a greater understanding of your circumstances through observation. This will give me an indication on how much time you have before the change is permanent", said Brenna,
"What?!", gasped Ulva,
"What do you mean permanent?!", blurted John,

Brenna sighed before he said in a gentle but affirmative voice, "Once a person has been bitten by a werewolf, it is only a matter of time before they turn upon the coming of night. One can delay their transformation and lessen their pain and discomfort with wolfsbane. Ultimately though it is inevitable, no matter how one tries to delay it. Based on the victim's vitality and tolerance to pain, the victim will suffer multiple turnings before eventually becoming a werewolf permanently at the completion of the final turning",

Ulva gripped John's hand and began to squeeze it tight, her heart beginning to pound against her chest as she heard Brenna's concerning words,

"I have spent a long time trying to find a cure, but to no avail. But I will not give up in my pursuit for one. I must make you all aware that if we don't locate a cure within the next several days, Ulva will become a werewolf for all eternity and she will be lost to the wolfblight forever, that is if the turnings don't kill her first", said Brenna,

It was then that Ulva began to shake and whimper as her eyes began to well up, she was distressed, as was John, who in shock began to cradle his head in his hands,

"Ulva please calm yourself; I know it's something you don't want to hear, but if you get upset now, you might trigger your turning early", said Brenna,

"No…it…it can't be", uttered John as he shook his head in disbelief,

"I'm sorry John but it had to be said, however I will do everything I can to locate a cure", said Brenna,

Glancing up at Brenna, John said,

"I shall hold you to your word",

"Trust me John, in the presence of all the gods above, I swear I will do all I can to stop the wolfblight from taking Ulva", said Brenna,

"Thank you", said Ulva,

"I can't believe this, first our daughter and now this", uttered John,

"We'll be okay John", said Ulva,

"I hope so Ulva, I truly do", said John,
"Do you two need some time alone?", said Brenna,
"No, we're good", said John,
"Right, now that that's all cleared up, it's time to begin your examination", said Brenna,
"Examination?", asked Einar,
"Yes, it is a necessity I assure you, whilst we search for a cure, I will be examining and monitoring Ulva's mental, emotional and physical health over the next few days so I can determine how far the wolfblight has progressed within her and determine how urgently she needs a cure", said Brenna before he turned to Ulva,
"My dear, do I have your permission to conduct an examination on your person?", he said,
"I guess", said Ulva,
"Excellent, might I have a look at your wound?", said Brenna, Ulva nodded and moved her arm so that her infected shoulder was visible. Brenna leaned in closer and examined the bite, he noticed that it was swollen and was becoming slightly gangrenous despite John's balm. The deep lacerations were a vivid and bright red whilst the surrounding tissue was coloured an angry crimson and green mottled with black and purple. It was an ugly wound and it seemed to be getting worse as time wore on.
After writing down some notes into his book, Brenna then took out a measuring tape from his pocket and stretched it down Ulva's side. Ulva stared at Brenna nervously as he glanced at the tape before he wound it up and shoved it into his pocket before writing something down into his book.
After clearing his throat, Brenna said to Ulva,
"How are you feeling at this precise moment?",
"My entire left side is burning because of my wound, I can also feel a stinging pain run across my chest and neck", said Ulva,
"Anything else?", asked Brenna,
"I feel sick and I can feel this sharp stabbing in my belly", said Ulva,

"What about emotions, are you happy, sad or angry?", said Brenna,
"No just frightened", said Ulva as she sadly glanced down her feet,
Brenna began muttering to himself as he wrote some details down into his book,
"Okay, victim is Ulva Forrester, daughter of Wulfric and Astrid Skarlagen, born in Gormstad, Norway. Height is five foot and seven inches, twenty-six years of age, auburn hair, deep blue eyes and a fair complexion", he said,
As Brenna was writing in his book, Einar, John and Eira were staring in silence as they observed Brenna intently.
After he had finished writing, Brenna then took a small pin from his pocket and said to Ulva,
"Give me your hand",
"Do you really need to prick my finger?", murmured Ulva,
"Sorry my dear, but I need to do this", said Brenna,
Ulva sighed before she anxiously presented her hand to Brenna, who lightly pricked her forefinger. Ulva watched as a few drops of blood oozed from her finger before dripping into a vial of green liquid that Brenna had plucked from his belt. Everyone watched as the drops of blood sunk to the bottom of the vial. For a few seconds nothing happened, but as Brenna swirled the vial round, the liquid inside turned a vibrant purple colour.
Such a sight made Brenna's heart sink,
"Just as I suspected, wolfblight, Sanguinetic Lupinaris, it's unmistakable", he said before glancing at Ulva,
"I hate to say this, but you are definitely in the early stages of your first turning. I estimate we haven't got long before it begins", he said,
Ulva looked at John nervously, who was equally troubled,
Brenna then placed the vial onto a nearby table before he wrote more notes down into his book,
"Okay Ulva, how are you feeling right now?", he said,
"Tired, very tired all of a sudden", said Ulva,

Clearing his throat, Brenna said,
"Okay anything else?",
"I have terrible heartburn, it's making my mouth water and I didn't say anything earlier, but I am itchy all over. I can almost feel something crawling under my skin, like a great horde of ants are running through my flesh", said Ulva,
"Ah, that would be the werewolf", said Brenna,
"Wait what?!", blurted Ulva,
"Well yeah, you don't go from one form to another without the catalyst already being present. The wolf is inside you, dormant, shifting and moving about as she incubates within your flesh, waiting to burst forth when you turn", said Brenna,
Ulva's face went pale as she felt her arms and legs turn to jelly whilst her stomach was doing somersaults.
As John huddled himself closer to Ulva, Brenna leaned in and said to her,
"Open your mouth",
Ulva's eyes widened,
"What?", she said,
"I said open your mouth…please", said Brenna,
Ulva reluctantly compiled and opened her mouth, allowing Brenna to glance down into her throat. After finding nothing out of the ordinary, Brenna scribbled down some notes before he suddenly held his ear against Ulva's chest.
Beyond the erratic beating of her heart, he could hear something coming from deep within her chest, a faint sound that sounded like growling,
"What is it?" asked John,
Brenna remained silent for a moment before he said,
"Thank you Ulva, that concludes my examination for the time being",
"Well?", said John a second time as he was becoming irritated,

"I was just checking something that's all. If you listen very closely you can hear a very faint sound coming from her breast, almost like a soft snarl or whimper. The wolf is desperate to come out, she's hungry and very angry", said Brenna,
John shot a confused and concerned look at Ulva, who responded with a shrug,
"I can't hear anything", she said,
"You doing okay?", asked Eira as she puffed her pipe,
"Not really, I'm hurting and I'm frightened, I mean this is my first time", said Ulva,
Closing his book and placing it upon his lap, Brenna said, "First time for everything my dear",
Brenna glanced over at Eira,
"What time is it?", he said,
"Not sure, I reckon late evening", said Eira,
"Got it, thanks", said Brenna before he smiled at Ulva,
"I'm impressed, I was expecting you to turn earlier than this given how sudden the symptoms appeared after you had been bitten. I am pleased that you are still holding yourself together", he said,
"Thanks I guess", said Ulva despondently,
Before anyone could respond, Ulva suddenly let out a sharp and pained yell, which made everyone get to their feet,
"What is it Ulva, what's wrong?", asked John,
"A sharp pain in my ribs and my skin feels like it's tightening", she groaned,
"Okay, that will be your muscles contracting, I think we are starting to see the next stage of the transformation, acute, intermittent bouts of pain accompanied by spasms of the joints and muscles", said Brenna,
Brenna placed his hand upon Ulva's head and noticed that her forehead was hot to the touch,
"Temperature is quite high, how are you feeling now?", said Brenna,
"I'm burning up, please make it stop", she pleaded,

"I'm sorry, but there's nothing I can do besides offer you support and comfort. Once this transformation has passed however we will start looking for a cure. But for now you just need to ride it out until dawn", said Brenna,
As Ulva closed her eyes tightly, she felt tears begin to run down her face,
"I know you are in pain right now, but can you stand?", asked Brenna,
Ulva weakly nodded,
"Okay, when you are ready, follow me over here", said Brenna softly,
Whilst Brenna walked over to the wall nearby, everyone helped Ulva up onto her feet before she staggered and limped over to his side. Brenna then crouched down and picked up two metal chains that were bound to the wall.
He then cleared his throat and said,
"Right Ulva, I'm going to bind you now, from what I have seen, it's time to do so. Though I know you don't mean to, your transformation will cause you to act violently, therefore this must be done for your safety and ours. I will only remove them when I know the turning has passed and you no longer pose a threat, do you understand?",
"Yes", said Ulva weakly as John applied a damp flannel to her brow,
Brenna opened the silver cuffs attached to the end of the chains before he slid them around Ulva's wrists. Once Brenna closed the cuffs tightly with a click, Ulva sat herself down upon her chair whilst Einar, John and Eira repositioned themselves in front of her.
Looking at the sight of his wife in chains, John angrily shook his head in disgust,
"I hate this, watching Ulva being chained up like this, it's not right and it's not fair", he growled,
Brenna suddenly glared at him with a horrible and accusing stare,

"Oh I'm sorry, would you rather have her tear us all to shreds or would you rather that she breaks loose and goes on a rampage across all of Gormstad?!", he snapped,
John was about to speak when Brenna interrupted him,
"Before you say that any of this is not fair, have a little perspective and more importantly, have some gratitude to the fact that I am doing everything I can to help you and your wife. There are people out there right now suffering the same fate as Ulva, scared, alone and doomed to a nightmarish fate and I cannot help them. But if I could, then I am sure they would be more grateful than you are right now. So you have three choices, you either sit down and shut up whilst I do what I must do, you vacate the room and stay out until morning or you can get out of my house and find someone else who can help Ulva",
Taken aback by Brenna's words, John said,
"Brenna...I...I'm sorry, I...",
Brenna sighed deeply before he removed his coat and placed it behind his chair before he sat himself down,
"I know John, I'm just a little stressed at the moment", he said,
"If this is such a stressful occupation, why do you do it? Why do you subject yourself to such horrors?", said Einar,
"Because I have to Einar, someone must protect the good people of this land from such a wicked affliction and as far as I am aware, I am the only person in Norway who is actively trying to seek out a cure. I have tried searching any other lycanthropists who might be able to assist me, but apart from a few scholars who have studied it in passing, I have found no one else", said Brenna,
"And we all appreciate it, even if it doesn't seem like it at times", said Eira,
"Thank you", said Brenna,
Silently, Brenna stared at Ulva for a moment before he scratched more notes down into his book.

He then placed the back of his hand against Ulva's forehead and noticed that she was getting increasingly hot and was beginning to sweat all over even though her face and body had gone very pale,
"Hmm, high fever, a common symptom of imminent transformation", said Brenna,
"So...what's going to happen to me exactly?", squeaked Ulva,
"I have some idea, but to be honest, I am not entirely sure", said Brenna,
"Not sure?", asked Einar,
"Every turning is different for each person, there may appear some similarities over different transformations, but ultimately no two turnings are exactly alike, therefore I cannot be certain as to what will happen to Ulva other than some premeditated guesses. I do know two things though, the changes depend on the victim's physical and mental condition and that the turning will be painful, beyond anything you have ever felt before", said Brenna,
"Really?", said Ulva,
"I am not going to sugar coat this, it will be brutal and gruelling", said Brenna,
Ulva stared at the floor with a disheartened glance as her mind began to conjure up horrible images,
"I am sorry for the blunt delivery of my words, but I would be doing you a disservice if I used delicate language to convey the seriousness of the situation", said Brenna,
"We'll be here for you though no matter what happens, all of us", said Eira,
Eira's words did not bring Ulva much comfort as her mind raced with many lucid and terrible visions of contorting bodies and breaking bones. She sighed and stretched out her body, sprawling her legs out over the floor.
But just as she was about to relax, Ulva suddenly felt a terrible burning sensation explode from deep within her chest before the skin covering her entire body became incredibly hot and tight.

Ulva began to cough and splutter violently, much to the concern of everyone surrounding her,
"Water, I need water!", she yelled,
Eira quickly collected up a pail that was sitting close by. She then dashed over to a nearby basin and began to fill the bucket with some water as Ulva groaned and clutched her burning chest,
"Hold on Ulva, Eira won't be long", said John,
"It burns, I can barely breath!", cried Ulva,
"What's wrong with her?!", yelled John,
"I don't know", stammered Brenna,
"Here you go", said Eira as she handed the pail to Ulva,
Ulva tore the pail from Eira's hands and quickly dunked her head into the bucket before she began to greedily guzzle down the water, causing some of it to spill out onto the floor,
"Slow down Ulva, you'll make yourself sick", said John,
"Shut up!", snarled Ulva as she wrenched her face away from the pail, her eyes burning with anger as her face, hair and mouth dripped with ice water,
John, Eira, Brenna and Einar stared at Ulva as she slammed her head back into the pail and continued to drink in great and long draughts. Much to their surprise, she drank the entire pail within seconds and once it was empty, she tossed it angrily to one side.
As Ulva tried to catch her breath, she suddenly could feel her skin break out in an intense and terrible itching that was much worse than before. Ulva fumbled and groaned as she began to scratch and claw at her skin furiously. John tried to help by scratching her back, but it was no use, the intense burning was getting stronger. It was then that Ulva ran her hands through her hair, only to realize that as she pulled away, she saw some locks of her beautiful red hair come clean off her scalp and into her palms.
Seeing this, Ulva let out a horrified scream,
"What's happening to me?!", she squealed,

Brenna got to his feet, as did John, Einar and Eira,
"Sweet Freyja, I think it's starting", gasped Brenna as he backed away from Ulva,
Suddenly, Ulva let out a pained yell as her skin erupted into a stinging and painful sensation, it felt like her skin was being scratched viciously by thousands of tiny knives or needles. She spluttered and spat onto the floor as her mouth began to fill with saliva,
"It hurts, make it stop!", she yelled,
It was then that Einar began to panic,
"I'm sorry, I can't watch this", he said before leaving the chamber in a hurry,
"Einar wait!", cried Eira as she ran after him,
Ulva cried out in pain and moaned as she collapsed to the floor before she violently kicked her chair away with a sharp snap of her leg, causing it to smash into the wall with a loud crash,
"It's okay Ulva, you're going to be okay", said John in a vain attempt to calm his distressed wife,
Whilst John was trying to comfort Ulva, Brenna said to him, "It might be best if you went with Einar and Eira, you are not going to want to see this",
"Absolutely not, I am not going anywhere, if she is going to suffer, then I want to be by her side helping and supporting her in any way I can", snapped John,
Brenna rolled his eyes,
"Stubborn fool, alright fine you can stay, but don't say I didn't warn you. Prepare yourself, it's going to be spectacularly horrific and messy" he huffed,
"Come on, how bad can it be?", grumbled John,
"Very", said Brenna sternly,
John and Brenna watched as Ulva began to writhe and squirm on the cold stone floor. She was crying out in pain as she furiously scratched at her skin, so hard and furiously that she was beginning to bleed as her nails dug into her flesh.
As the chains holding her rattled and shook, she suddenly felt a shooting, sharp and intense pain rip down her back.

John watched in horror whilst Brenna took a vial of clear liquid from his pocket and quickly gulped it down,
"What's that?", asked John,
"Something to steady my nerves, trust me, I'm going to need to keep a firm hand whilst I document this. It is not for the faint hearted, so I hope you have a strong stomach", replied Brenna,
"Got anymore?", asked John,
"Sorry, all out", said Brenna,
"Oh gods, make it stop!", screamed Ulva,
She suddenly felt the itching and stinging sensation rush upwards towards her head and suddenly and instinctively, Ulva began to claw at her scalp. As she scratched furiously, her hair began to fall out in strands and clumps. Eventually there was little hair left on her head, just a few tuffs and long strands latched onto her bald scalp.
But the pain was so terrible that Ulva continued scratching and kept going until blood began to seep down her face as she tore into the skin on the top of her head, causing it to become gory,
"May Odin have mercy on her soul", uttered Brenna,
With her head now bloody, Ulva suddenly clutched her chest as an intense electrical pain exploded from deep within her flesh. Ulva cried out in pain as she felt her heart expand in size, thumping away violently like a hammer against her breast.
Seeing Ulva in such pain, John rushed forward to help her, but Brenna stopped him,
"No don't intervene, for her sake we must let this happen, no matter how horrible it looks", he said,
John tried to push Brenna out of the way as he heard Ulva crying out his name, but Brenna overpowered him and grabbed him by the scruff of his neck as Ulva's cries echoed through the chamber,
"Listen to me John, you won't be able to help her, you cannot help her, it's too late, the turning has already begun!", he snapped,

Suddenly, Ulva let out a horrible and sickening scream of terror as she felt something rupture in her chest before her upper body was enveloped in agonizing and excruciating pain. There were cracking sounds of erupting bone and horrible popping sounds as her ribs began to crack and her ribcage split apart.
Her breathing became laboured and pained as she tried to inhale as much air as she could into her swollen, bleeding and haemorrhaging lungs which were now collapsing. Ulva hunched over and opened her mouth, from which came a torrent of gushing blood which splattered over the floor. She could now feel her bowels begin to twist and her legs went numb. With her body now in agony, Ulva felt her mouth suddenly explode with an excruciating pain.
Through some strange and instinctive urge, Ulva suddenly reached up to her mouth and wrenched a large and bloody molar from her mouth with a crunch and then a snap. She tossed it to one side before she began to pull out another. John felt sick as he watched Ulva pick the teeth from her mouth, one by one they snapped as she ripped them out until she was screaming toothless and bloody,
"What is she doing?!", barked John,
"It's not her doing, it's the werewolf, it's taking control and forcing her to mutilate herself so she can prepare the way for its appearance", said Brenna,
As Ulva's body began to shift and grow bigger, she felt her back muscles expand and begin to tear painfully. She watched as from her palms, fingers and feet erupted black lesions forming paw pads that burst through her skin. She felt her fingernails begin to painfully grow and lengthen in size before they became sharp and tapered into a point.
At the same time, her legs and feet began to stretch and elongate, the bones splitting and cracking as they lengthened.

With every inch of her body exploding with pain, Ulva now felt her vision beginning to spin as her eyesight blurred and pulsated with flashing lights, her brain overworking to flood her nervous system and body with natural opioids to try and numb the horrendous pain. Ulva felt sick from the spinning, so she closed her eyes to try and stop the dizziness.

Getting onto all fours, Ulva could suddenly feel the skin of her back begin to swell. She scraped her nails against the floor, digging her sharp claws into the floor as her back began to split open down the middle. She screeched and growled as her back suddenly ruptured, causing blood and spinal fluid to splash onto the floor. John could now see the pulsating muscles of Ulva's back and her exposed spine that was jutting out, quivering and lengthening as it broke apart. From her open back, John and Brenna could see red fur beginning to bloom and grow from her mangled flesh and skin as the sinews began to stretch and pop.

Ulva was now in such immense pain, she could feel and hear every bone in her body breaking and pulling, snapping and contorting.

She suddenly felt the fifth toe on each foot begin to fuse with the fourth and her heels began to stretch back. From the top of Ulva's scalp began to emerge red fur that enveloped her lengthening ears, which were now pointed and wolf - like. Feeling a sudden instinctive urge, Ulva raised her hands up to her face and used her nails to tear at her face, ripping into her skin and tearing it off in strips before pulling off chunks of flesh from her skull. Such a sight caused John to retch and heave as he suddenly felt nauseous and faint. Ulva then tore at her arms, causing red fur to burst from the wounds and scratches. John noticed snow white fur was beginning to push through the skin on Ulva's belly and her hands and feet started to turn white.

Suddenly Ulva could now feel a sharp and intense pressure begin to build from within her skull and behind her eyes.

As her eyes began to swell and bulge, Ulva covered her face with her hands to stop the building pressure, but it was no use, it got more and more intense with every passing second. Feeling another urge overcome her, Ulva then did something that made John faint and lightheaded. Screaming at the top of her lungs, Ulva plucked out her eyes with sharp fingernails, wrenching her eyeballs from their sockets before discarding them onto the bloodied floor.

Ulva then lowered her head, casting her gaze away from John and Brenna as if to spare them from such a horrific sight as blood ran down her face and pattered against the floor.

By now, red fur was sprouting from every inch of Ulva's naked body beneath falling skin and her disjointed spine was now growing in length past her jutting posterior. John noticed that Ulva's hands and feet were now paws covered in white fur, ending in sharp, black claws. Ulva then glanced up at John and Brenna, causing them both to jump back in shock.

Deep set into her eye sockets emerged ice - blue eyes, but instead of human eyes, they were that of a wolf, the irises black and set in a deep shade of blue.

As Ulva's body began its final stages of the transformation, Ulva spat out more blood, before she began to retch and heave violently. She then vomited all over the floor, spewing out blood.

Ulva then reached up to her face and gripped the upper and lower part of her jaw with her claws. John and Brenna gasped as she began to wrench her mouth open, groaning as she pulled her jaws apart to the sickening sound of crunching bone. Her cheeks suddenly split, causing blood to run down her face and neck.

Brenna and John watched in horror as from her gargling and gaping mouth emerged what looked like the snout and muzzle of a wolf, its red fur and shiny black nose damp with blood. As it emerged, you could hear whimpering and growling and you could see rows of sharp glistening teeth and pointed fangs.

As the muzzle fully appeared, Ulva reached up and ripped the remaining skin off her skull, pulling away the last remaining traces of her human face like you would remove a mask or hood, exposing a full face of fur, a head of a monstrous wolf. It was too much for John as he fainted and collapsed onto the floor near Brenna, who was shaking as he ran his quill across his book, filling up the page with lines of ink.

Finally, as the last inch of Ulva's bare skin disappeared under fur, Brenna watched in horror as a thick, long and bushy tail sprouted from behind her and with its emergence, the transformation was complete.

She was just over six and a half feet in height and her entire body was covered in red fur. Her front paws were as white as snow, as were her feet and the lower part of her hindlegs. Her entire belly, throat and neck was also white. The tips of her long and pointed ears were black, which matched the colour of her nose, the end of her tail, her sharp claws and a band of fur that was wrapped around her throat just under her head. Her wolfish eyes were as blue as glacier ice and were glowing. Her arms, waist and legs were thin, taut and muscular whilst the fur of her chest was puffed out and looked incredibly soft.

Staring intently at Brenna, Ulva growled with bared fangs before she threw back her head and let out a long and terrible howl, which sounded like the guttural cry of a wolf combined with the agonized human scream of a woman. She then began to shake her damp fur, causing flecks of blood and bodily fluids to fly everywhere.

With a deep sigh and trembling hands, Brenna finished writing his notes and closed his book.

He looked over to John, who was beginning to stir from his unconscious state. Brenna then sat himself down and stared at Ulva, who was staring back with horrible eyes as a vicious snarl uttered from her lips,

"Oh Ulva", said Brenna sadly,

Suddenly, there came the sounds of footsteps coming down the stairs. At the doorway appeared Einar and Eira. Einar's eyes were bloodshot and teary whilst Eira looked exhausted. As he laid eyes upon his sister, he fell to his knees in shock,
"Ulva...no", he uttered,
"By the gods", gasped Eira,
Ulva glared at her brother intently as Einar stood up and approached her,
"Sister", he said,
Ulva suddenly rushed forward, snapping at them with sharp teeth dripping with saliva. Ulva winced as the chains binding her became taut and wouldn't stretch any further.
She snapped and struggled to try and get free from the chains, but it was no use, they would not break, no matter how hard she tried. Enraged, Ulva retreated and began to lick at her wrists where the cuffs dug in.
Einar covered his mouth in shock, whimpering slightly as he beheld his beloved sibling,
"Never have I seen something so terrible", he uttered,
As Eira and Einar stared at Ulva, Brenna saw John sit himself up, rubbing his throbbing head and groaning in pain,
"John, are you okay? You passed out", he said,
"I think so, I don't know what came over me, I...", said John,
John lifted his head up and he gasped as he caught the sight of Ulva, who was crouching low to the ground. John put a hand to his mouth, his eyes welling up as his heart sank at the sight of his wife.
Getting up off the ground, he stepped closer to Ulva. As he did, she eyed John carefully and growled at him through vicious fangs,
"Ulva?", uttered John,
"John be careful, she's angry and in pain, she is not the wife you know and love in this form", said Brenna,
"Then why hasn't she attacked me yet?", said John as he slowly approached Ulva, holding out his hand as if wanting to touch her,

"I don't know if you can understand me, but let me comfort you, please", he said,
John gasped as Ulva suddenly lunged and snapped at him, nearly taking his hand clean off.
Staggering backwards, John said,
"She attacked me...she...she's become a monster",
Einar hugged John as he saw that he was shaking and beginning to tear up,
"I'm sorry lad, come on, some sleep will do you some good", he said,
"Gods I am so tired", sighed John,
Brenna opened his book and said,
"Well there is nothing more we can do for Ulva tonight. With the transformation complete, Ulva would have usually done what werewolves usually do, hunt, feed, fight, fuck and sleep. Being bound however she can't do much other than growl at us, she may look frightening and intimidating, but she cannot harm us whilst in those chains providing we keep our distance. I would advise you all go and try and get some sleep as we wait for dawn to arrive",
"Can I sleep in here Brenna? I don't want to leave Ulva's side", asked John,
"I'm sorry, but it's a mess in here and you can't do anymore for her than you already have. You were there to comfort her before she turned and you were there for her when she transformed and that is all you can do. So please, go get some food and rest, you'll need your strength for tomorrow", said Brenna,
"What's happening tomorrow?", asked Einar,
"Well Ulva will turn back at dawn and we will need to tend to her when she reverts back to her human form. I will also need to run a general health check on her and once that's done, we can sit down and think about what to do next. So off you all go, there is a guest room upstairs with some beds if you wish to stay the night or you can return to your homes. Either way, I expect you all here around sunrise", said Brenna,

"Thank you Brenna, I will return home and see if granddad Guthrum and Maud are okay. They will be worrying about Ulva and me, not to mention they will want to know what's happened, I think I will stay there tonight", said Einar,
Brenna removed his scarf and placed it down upon a nearby chair,
"Very well if that's what you wish, what about you John?", he said,
"I'll sleep upstairs, I will feel better knowing my wife is close by rather than walking back home to a cold and empty house", said John,
Eira suddenly put her arm around John and said,
"I think I'll stay too; I'm knackered and I can't be bothered to walk home at this time of night",
"That's great, I could use the company of a friend right now", said John,
"Then it's settled, now away with you all, have a good night and I'll see you all tomorrow", said Brenna,
"What will you do?", asked John,
Brenna stretched his arms before he said,
"I'll tidy up and keep an eye on Ulva",
As Ulva rattled her chains in anger, Brenna said,
"Enough of that",
After Einar and Eira said their goodbyes and left the study, John walked over to the foot of the stairs and before he left, he turned and waved at Ulva,
"Goodnight Ulva, I love you", he said softly,
Feeling a single tear run down his face, John reluctantly began walking up the stairs, leaving Ulva and Brenna alone.
Brenna sighed and after writing one more sentence down in his book, he slammed it shut and placed it down upon a nearby table. He then sat himself down in front of Ulva, with enough distance between them so she couldn't reach him. Staring at the werewolf in front of him, Brenna said,
"I'm sorry you had to go through that Ulva, you don't deserve any of this",

Ulva stared at Brenna before she tried to pull on her rattling chains,
"I wouldn't bother, those chains won't break", said Brenna,
Ulva responded to Brenna's words by glaring at him whilst uttering a long and vicious growl,
"Come on now, I had no choice but to bind you, my life, your life and everyone else's in the village would have been threatened if you escaped, this was the only way I could ensure everyone would be safe, including you", he said,
Ulva angrily turned her back on Brenna before she curled herself up on the floor, pouting and growling as she started scraping the ground with her claws,
"Listen to me Ulva, whilst I don't have a cure for you yet, I swear that I will do everything I can to find one. I admit that I haven't had much success in the past, but now that someone I know and love has been affected, I can no longer afford to be complacent and indolent", said Brenna,
Ulva continued to sulk as Brenna stood up and collected a bucket before he filled it with water.
Using a mop from a nearby cupboard, he spent a few minutes cleaning the floor, clearing up any puddles of blood, vomit and traces of skin and flesh that were left over from the turning.
Once the area looked relatively clean, Brenna then put away the mop and bucket before deposing of any soiled cloth. He then sat himself back down in his chair, folding his arms as he relaxed.
With his head getting heavy, Brenna closed his eyes before he said to Ulva,
"Good night my lupine beauty",
Knowing that she was unable to free herself, Ulva resigned herself to her imprisonment and wrapped her tail around her body before she too began to doze off.

CHAPTER VII:
BARENHAUTER

It had begun to rain in Gormstad, the streets and houses were lashed with cold and torrential rain as the wind howled across the town. Though the streets were deserted, at the gates of Gormstad appeared a hooded man. He was wearing a long brown coat over a tunic fastened with silver clasps, black trousers and an embossed belt lined with knives, a silver axe and fat leather pouches. Attached to his back was a thick leather strap that was slung over his shoulder, hanging from which was a magnificent golden sword with a jewelled hilt and a cloth sack filled with supplies. The man was clean shaven and his long hair was light brown in colour, his face hidden by the fur trimmed hood attached to his coat. The man glanced up at the gates standing before him with cold grey eyes before he slammed his fist against them with a gloved hand.
At eye level, a small opening appeared, behind which appeared the eyes of a guardsman,
"Who goes there, what do you want?", came a gruff voice,
The hooded man smiled before he said,
"Guten Abend, may I come in?",
The guardsman glared at the hooded man,
"I'll ask you again, what do you want?", he said,
"My name is Vilhelm Barenhauter, at your service", said the hooded man,
"Never heard of you, are you a traveller, an adventurer?", said the guardsman,
"I am a traveller, adventurer and a hunter of beasts, now will you please let me in? I am soaked through with rain and I'm starving", said Vilhelm,
The guardsman disappeared before the gates swung open with a heavy creak.

As Vilhelm walked through, he shoved a hand into his pocket and tossed the guardsman some silver coins,
"Good boy, go buy yourself something nice", he said,
Entering the lamp lit square, Vilhelm took a sharp turn to the left and made his way down a long, dark and wide street. He soon found himself in front of a door, beyond which he could hear laughing and the clattering of metal. Above Vilhelm was a wooden sign that swung in the wind and rain, it spelt in large black letters, '*The Black Boar*'.
Vilhelm pushed the door open and entered. The inside of the tavern was a large open space crowned by a timber roof that was held together by thick iron bars. Suspended from the roof by black chains were large chandeliers that blazed with a hot orange light. Scattered about were chairs and tables and up against the wall was a stone fireplace, its mouth billowing with the embers of a roaring and toasty fire. Up a few wooden steps in front of Vilhelm sat a wide floor that was enclosed by small alcoves filled with people drinking deeply from large tankards and mugs whilst scoffing down delicious hot food. At the back of the tavern was a large counter, behind of which stood towering oaken caskets filled with all sorts of alcoholic beverages.
As Vilhelm glanced around, he noticed the warm air was thick with the smell of smoke mixed with the faint aroma of chocolate. Vilhelm walked up to the bar at the back of the tavern as some people sitting nearby turned to face him, staring at him with both curious glances and cautious glares. Not only that, but it seemed that he had caught the attention of some young maidens sitting nearby, who were smiling at him seductively as he approached. After flashing a wink at them before blowing them a kiss, Vilhelm sat himself down upon a stool at the counter before he pulled down his hood. When Vilhelm glanced to his right, he caught a man staring at him,
"Keep your eyes to yourself unless you want to lose them", he growled,

The man quickly averted his gaze and continued to drink as Vilhelm pulled off his gloves, revealing his badly mutilated hands. He was missing his pinkie finger and half a thumb on his right hand whilst he only had three fingers on his heavily scarred left hand. Such wounds were shocking, but they were to be expected from his line of work, one does not venture across the land and hunt monsters without returning completely unscathed.

Vilhelm cleared his throat and began to hum, tapping the bar with his hand before he whistled sharply as he summoned the barmaid, a small woman with blue eyes and curled dark hair wearing a brown dress beneath a giant white apron.

As the barmaid was cleaning the inside of a mug with a grubby looking cloth, she asked sweetly,

"Can I help you?",

"Why yes gorgeous, a mug of milk please", said Vilhelm,

The bartender disappeared round a corner before coming back with a luscious tankard of creamy milk, its head topped with a thick vanilla foam. She placed it down before Vilhelm presented her three silver pennies.

Vilhelm then gulped down the milk in great draughts before wiping his mouth,

"Delicious, another round", he said,

The barmaid took away the empty mug from Vilhelm before she refilled it and placed it down in front of him. Vilhelm slammed some coins down upon the counter before he quickly snatched up the mug and with immense delight poured its contents down his throat.

After Vilhelm had ordered and drank his third and final round, he leaned over the counter and said to the barmaid,

"Pardon me, but I've heard that there has been a werewolf sighted within the town, is this true?",

"Aye, is that why you are here?", she replied,

"Indeed, slaying monsters is my speciality", said Vilhelm,

"Well I don't know if the rumours are completely true, but two of my customers say that they spotted a werewolf prowling the town, it was big, monstrous and had terrible claws, teeth and eyes", said the barmaid,

"And where was it last seen?", asked Vilhelm,

"One of them saw it near the monument behind the town hall whilst the other said he saw it run down the road near the home of Einar Skarlagen. I bet you all the money I have that Brenna Torstensson is involved somehow, man always was obsessed with the beasts, never understood why", said the barmaid as she began to scrub down the counter with a cloth,

With a wide grin etched upon his face, Vilhelm said,

"Brenna Torstensson you say…interesting, very interesting indeed",

CHAPTER VIII:
THE FLAYING OF FUR

At Brenna's house in one of the bedrooms upstairs, John and Eira were sleeping to the sound of pattering rainfall. The room in which they laid was small and plain, its timber walls devoid of any decoration. There were two beds covered in thin sheets and some throws with a small wooden chest sitting in between them. Whilst Eira was curled up against the wall and was making not a sound, John was turning and squirming in his bed, his forehead beaded with sweat as his mind was caught in the throes of a deep and troubled sleep.
As his eyesight adjusted to the light, John found himself in a cold and quiet forest, there was no wind or breeze to speak of and there were no sounds of any bird or animal. The ground was soft with snow and there was light fluttering of snowflakes in the crisp and still air.
Surrounding him were rows of trees illuminated by moonlight, their barks were coloured black and speckled with red, the leaves crowning their trunks and branches were coloured a deep dark crimson.
As John gazed off into the distance, he suddenly noticed a shadowed figure wearing a hood and cape, the figure stared at him before it walked away,
"Hello, are you lost?", he said as he called out to the lone and mysterious figure,
Seeing the figure disappear through the trees, John gripped the hilt of his pickaxe before he cautiously began following it, the snow crunching under his feet as he went. As John wandered through the forest, the wind began to pick up, causing the leaves on the trees to rustle and quiver. After quickening his pace, John soon found himself standing in a grove surrounded by trees and wolf - headed totems that stood thrust into the frozen ground.

From their gaping mouths, you could hear the wind passing through their throats, the wind making it sound like they were softly howling.

Stepping down a flight of stone stairs, John could see the figure standing in the middle of the grove with its back to him. Once he came to the end of the staircase, John jumped down onto the white forest floor, surprised to hear a crunch coming from under his foot. It was not crispy like soft snow, but hard and brittle.

Lifting his foot, John noticed to his disgust that he had stepped in what looked like some bones, but he couldn't figure out if they were animal or human. John glanced forward and noticed that the pathway lying before him was littered with gnarled and broken bones all scattered about. As he walked towards the figure cautiously, he noticed several human skeletons sprawled out nearby, their skulls elongated and their open mouths filled with sharp fangs and teeth.

John's heart began to race as he realized what they were, the decaying bones of werewolves, long since deceased. Their ribcages were filled with blooming red flowers, their throats were full of leaves and vines had enveloped and entangled their arms, legs and tails.

As the air filled with the sound of howling wind, John soon found himself standing before the hooded figure.

As he plucked his pickaxe from his belt, he said,

"Who are you, where am I?",

The figure said nothing,

"Damn it, answer me!", barked John,

"You are in a sacred place, a place of darkness where monsters roam", came a female voice,

John's heart sank, he recognized the voice,

"Ulva?", he gasped,

"John", she replied,

Dropping his pickaxe, John held out his arms and went to embrace his wife, when Ulva said in a rasping and horrible voice,

"Don't come any closer",

"Ulva it's me, I was so worried about you. After seeing you turn, I just want to hold you again", said John,
Ulva kept her back turned to John as she said,
"You have failed me",
John stared at Ulva with a confused look,
"What are you talking about?", he said,
"You failed to defend me from the wolfblight and now I am cursed to spend my years hungry, angry and alone", said Ulva,
"You will never be alone Ulva; I will always be by your side no matter what. You are my wife and nothing will change that. I love you and I don't want to lose you. To be without you would be like a night without stars, a forest without flowers, a river without water", said John,
John watched as Ulva turned round to face him, her face hidden beneath her hood,
"No, despite what you promised at our wedding, you have failed to protect me, you failed to defend me from the werewolf's bite", she hissed,
John glanced down and noticed the bottom of a red tail shuffling beneath Ulva's dress.
It was then that Ulva pulled her hood down, revealing her face. She was in her werewolf form, her mouth dripping with blood, her eyes furiously glowing red,
"And for that, you must die", she said,
John screamed in terror as Ulva suddenly lunged at him, burrowing her razor-sharp fangs into his chest before piercing his beating heart.
John shot up in his bed screaming, which startled Eira as she leapt from her bed, slamming her back against the wall,
"John, what's wrong?!", she cried,
John said nothing as he huddled up under the bedsheets, he was shaking and his face was as white as a ghost.
After throwing on a shirt, Eira sat herself down beside John and said,
"Had a nightmare?",

"The worst I have ever had and I think it happened because of what I saw earlier this evening. Seeing Ulva turn like that, seeing her in such pain and agony, watching as her beautiful face and body was transformed into something frightening, something ferocious and monstrous", said John,
Burying his face in his shaking hands, John said,
"I don't think I can do this",
"Come on now, you've got to be strong, not just for Ulva, but for yourself, you cannot let this beat you down", said Eira softly,
"I know, I'm just frightened, so very frightened", whimpered John,
Wrapping her arm around John's shoulders to try and comfort him, Eira said,
"Yes this is all very frightening, I have seen many terrible things in my travels but nothing compares to this",
"Really?", said John,
"I've wandered the frozen coasts of Kelstaag, faced the raven lords of the Dautharos and I nearly died when I was trapped in a tomb for days with nothing to eat but mort moss and some rats. I would face it all again rather than see Ulva go through all of this", said Eira,
"The worst part is that I wasn't able to help her, I could only watch as she became a beast and now I am frightened that I am failing to protect her when she needs me most", said John as he wiped his eye,
"You're not failing her John, she...", said Eira,
Eira was cut off as her and John suddenly heard a loud cry coming from downstairs.
With all haste, Eira and John leapt out of their beds and rushed down into the study, fearful that something bad had happened.
Appearing at the foot of the stairs, Eira and John saw Ulva thrashing about as Brenna was on the floor clutching his arm as it profusely bled,
"Brenna!", cried Eira as she ran over to his side and helped him up,

"I'll be fine, it's just a flesh wound. I underestimated Ulva's reach and she caught me with her claw", said Brenna,
"Come on, it will need dressing", said Eira as she went over to the nearby basin and helped Brenna wash the blood off his arm,
Whilst Brenna's wounds were being cleaned and wrapped up, John walked towards Ulva and stared at her as she flailed and thrashed angrily, screaming and roaring as she tugged and pulled at her chains,
"What did you do to make her so angry?", asked John,
"I did nothing of the sort, she's angry because she will be turning back soon and the wolf that has taken control of her body doesn't want to leave", snapped Brenna,
"Is there any way we can help her?", said John as he watched Ulva slam her fists against the wall and scrap her claws against the ground,
"No, we just have to wait until dawn", said Brenna as he appeared beside John, his left arm completely covered in bandages,
"Poor Ulva, she's so distressed", said Eira sadly as she lit her pipe,
"Like I said, there's nothing we can do about it", said Brenna before he turned to John,
"Whilst we wait, I must warn you, when Ulva turns back to normal, I just want to warn you that she might act a little...differently", he said,
"What do you mean?", asked John,
"She will mostly be the Ulva you know and love, but she might be a little unpredictable. It doesn't always happen, but I just wanted to warn you regardless", said Brenna,
"Will...will she be a different person?", asked John,
No, but just be aware of the possibility of sudden mood swings, sudden urges of lust, violence and hunger, that sort of thing", said Brenna,
"I understand", said John,
John watched Ulva anxiously as she snapped at her chains,
"How was she last night?", asked John,

"She was okay, she slept most of the night", said Brenna, Suddenly John, Eira and Brenna could hear the distant bellowing of a horn, dawn had arrived. Upon hearing the sound, Ulva suddenly became quiet. She then let out a long and terrible howl, a wailing that sent chills down everyone's spines. John watched as she began to violently pull and scratch at her fur, ripping out clumps that came away clean in her palms before tearing off entire strips, revealing bloody human skin underneath.

It was then that Ulva let out a sharp and pained cry as her back suddenly split open just below the neckline, Ulva tried to reach up and pull at the bleeding crack, but she just couldn't reach. To John's surprise, Ulva suddenly walked up to him, whimpering and whining as she stared sadly at him. She then pressed her snout against his hand before licking it gently with a wet and rough tongue,

"What's she doing?", asked John,

"Damn it, she needs to shed her pelt, but she's stuck and is asking for help", said Brenna in an irritated tone of voice, John looked at Brenna with a shocked expression before he blurted,

"What can I do?!",

"Here, I'll do it", said Brenna exasperatedly,

John's eyes widened as Brenna plucked a sharp knife from his belt and walked behind Ulva, who was whining and groaning in pain as blood ran down her back,

"Do what exactly?", said Eira,

"Watch", said Brenna as he gently stroked Ulva's cheek, which was warm to the touch and felt like cotton,

"It'll be okay Ulva, this will hurt, but it will all be over soon", he said before glancing at Eira and John,

"No matter what happens, do not disturb me whilst I do this", he said,

After helping Ulva straighten up as she was slightly hunched and staggering on her feet, Brenna took a deep breath before he suddenly stabbed Ulva just above the spine, causing the werewolf to cry out in pain, much to Eira and John's horror and dismay,

"Don't, you're hurting her!", barked John,

"Relax, she'll be fine, usually werewolves can transform back on their own, but sometimes they need help, especially during their first turning. It might look painful, but Ulva will be thankful for it later", said Brenna,

Wiping the sweat from his brow, Brenna suddenly began drawing the knife down Ulva's back, causing blood to run down onto the floor as Ulva groaned loudly,

"Good thing I have done this before, skinning a werewolf is not the easiest thing I've ever done", grunted Brenna,

After Brenna finished running the knife down to the base of Ulva's spine, John and Eira grabbed each other as Brenna wrenched the knife from Ulva's back before placing it down. Brenna then grabbed the sides of the incision he had made with both his hands and with a heave, began to pull outwards, causing poor Ulva to screech in pain as Brenna ripped her back open.

As he could see pale and unblemished human skin appear before him, Brenna grunted as he then pulled downwards, stripping the fur off Ulva as if removing a coat before leaving it to pool at her feet. Panting heavily, Brenna backed away as he allowed Ulva to finish what he started, watching as Ulva stripped the fur away from her arms before peeling away at her legs, de-gloving and removing the fur from her thighs and calves like slipping off a long sock or stocking. Finally, Ulva then reached up behind her head and tore off her wolfish face before dropping it the ground. She then took Brenna's knife and with one great swipe, sliced her tail off at the base of the spine, sighing in relief as she did.

With her body trembling and dripping with blood and bodily fluids, Ulva dropped the knife as she stared at John, Eira and Brenna.

Holding out her arms, she weakly limped forward and threw herself into John's embrace before she began to sob, exhausted and emotional from the terrible ordeal.
Not caring that his wife was blood-soaked and reeking of terrible odours, John squeezed Ulva tightly, stroking her head as he cradled her gently,
"Someone get me a towel", he said,
As Eira left the study to fetch something to cover Ulva, Brenna quickly scooped up the remains of Ulva's pelt off the floor before placing it into a pile. To John and Ulva's shock, he then struck a match and dropped it, setting the bundle of fur, claws and teeth alight.
As he did, the pelt suddenly squirmed and thrashed about, screaming a sickening and agonized howl as it turned to ash,
"What the fuck was that?!", gasped John,
"The skinned pelt of a werewolf is a dangerous thing; it can live on for some time after it has been removed from its host. If I hadn't destroyed it, it would have tried to attack and bite anyone within the vicinity", said Brenna,
"I heard screaming, is everyone okay?", said Eira as she appeared with a towel in her arms,
"Yes my dear, nothing to worry about", sighed Brenna as he slumped himself into his chair,
After wiping the tears from her face, Ulva took the towel from Eira and threw it around her, coughing and spluttering before she said to Brenna,
"Thank you",
"For what?", said Brenna,
"For being there for me during my first turning and for helping me get through it", said Ulva,
Opening his eyes, Brenna said,
"It's okay Ulva, I wasn't going to let you face this alone",
Ulva then turned to John and said,
"I'm sorry for frightening you",
"Don't be", said John as he smiled in relief,
"John, why don't you run Ulva a bath? She looks like she could use one", said Eira,

"Good idea and thank you Eira for helping us too", said John before he and Ulva made their way upstairs towards the bathroom,
After stretching her arms and yawning deeply, Eira walked over to Brenna and tenderly began to rub his shoulders,
"You did good Brenna, I'm proud of you", she said,
Brenna said nothing before he quickly shot up out of his chair and rushed over to one of the nearby bookshelves.
As he began grabbing some books, Brenna said,
"Now begins the difficult part, I promised John and Ulva that I would find a cure. Now that Ulva's first turning is out of the way, I must focus all my attention on locating one quickly",
"And you believe these books have the answer?", asked Eira,
"I hope so, Ulva only has a few days left at most before she turns permanently and I must find a cure in that time. I have gone over these books again and again and none of them have given me the answers I seek. But perhaps if I go over them one more time, I might find something that I had missed before, something overlooked", said Brenna,
"Do you need a hand?", said Eira,
"That would be great thank you", said Brenna as he opened a large leather-bound book,
As she puffed on her pipe, Eira grabbed a book from the bookshelf standing in front of her and began to read.
Upstairs in the bathroom, Ulva waited patiently whilst John ran her a bath, sitting beside a large tub that sat beneath a small tap jutting from the wall. Once it was filled with warm water, Ulva removed the towel wrapped around her shoulders and lowered herself in, sighing as the water and steam washed over her weary body.
Wiping the blood from her face, Ulva smiled with pleasure as John knelt beside the bath and began to gently massage her back with a soft and wet cloth,
"After all that horror, this is just what I needed", said Ulva as she stretched out her arms and legs,
"Can I ask you something?", said John,

"Sure, what's on your mind?", asked Ulva as she ran her fingers through her hair,
"If you don't mind me asking, what was it like being a werewolf?", said John as he ran the cloth across Ulva's neck,
Ulva said nothing as she pondered John's question,
"Ulva?", said John,
"It was like wearing a very tight, suffocating, confining and damp outfit that sticks to your skin, like walking through ice cold wind whilst wearing wet clothes. I could see and hear everyone, but no matter how hard I tried, I couldn't control my body, I was paralyzed and helpless despite my arms and legs moving about, it was like being a puppet on a string", said Ulva,
As John ran the cloth across Ulva's arms, she said sadly as she stared at the bathwater,
"I saw you standing before me and I was crying out trying to stop myself from attacking you, but no one could hear me, I was powerless, a prisoner in my own body",
"Well I am just glad you are back to normal, even if it is only until tomorrow night", said John,
Ulva fell silent as John placed the cloth down and picked up a small wooden cup, which he used to scoop up some water before he poured it over Ulva's hair, rinsing out the gore and blood. Ulva closed her eyes and began to softly hum to herself as she ran her hands up and down her arms, smiling gently as she heard John hum along with her.
It was then that a growl emanated from Ulva's mouth,
"Ulva?", said John,
Ulva opened her eyes,
"Hm? Sorry I was in a world of my own, the water just feels so good against my skin", she said,
"I'm glad, after what happened last night, it's nice to just spend some time alone with you", said John,
Blushing, Ulva glanced up at John before she tugged on his arm,
"Join me, it's lovely", she said,

"Okay", said John before he stood up and slipped his clothes off,
Feeling slightly aroused, Ulva bit her lower lip as she eyed John's naked body as he lowered himself into the bath. John grinned as he felt heavenly warm water, foaming bubbles and delightful steam wash over his body.
Sitting cross-legged across from Ulva, John stared at Ulva as she ran her fingers through her auburn hair,
"Ulva, I need to ask you something, though I am afraid to ask it", he said,
"You can tell me anything you big softie", she said with a sweet smile,
"Okay well I had a nightmare last night...I was in this big forest and you were there too", said John,
"Yeah?", said Ulva,
"Yeah, but you were not yourself, you were acting strange, hostile and what you said troubles me greatly. You accused me of having failed to protect you from the werewolf last night", said John,
Ulva's smile faded as John lowered his gaze and said,
"Tell me this, if only to put my mind at ease, do you blame me for what happened? Do you think I have failed you as a husband because I wasn't able to stop you from being bitten?",
John closed his eyes as he awaited Ulva's response, praying that she wouldn't react angrily to his words.
He was surprised however when Ulva reached forward and began to gently stroke the back of his neck,
"No John, I don't think you have failed me as a husband because of what happened and I never will. It was unfortunate, but there was nothing you nor I could have done to prevent it other than chasing the monster off. You protected me and I protected you, that's all there is to it", she said softly,

"But I didn't protect you, you jumped in the way of the werewolf to defend me and so you were bitten. I shouldn't have put myself in a situation where you had to do that", said John,

After kissing John gently on the cheek, Ulva said,

"And I would do it again if it meant saving my husband",

Feeling his heart skip a beat, John said,

"Really?",

"Yes, you are good to me John, you have always been there for me and despite what happened last night, I don't think any less of you nor do I question your actions as my husband and my best friend. So please John, don't worry about such things nor question what we have. I love you, always have, always will and no werewolf is going to change that", said Ulva,

"Ulva...I'm...I'm sorry for doubting you", said John,

Ulva smiled before she huddled up close to her husband, causing the water around them to slosh against the sides of the bath,

"Besides, why would I say such things about you? You are funny, sweet, soft hearted and handsome", she said,

"And you are beautiful and charming, even as a werewolf, I still love you", said John,

Ulva giggled before she said,

"Even with all that fur? Even with fangs, claws and a tail you would still find me alluring, your beloved wife?",

With a smile on his face, John said,

"Of course, I would love you in any form",

"Oh John", said Ulva as she rested her head against John's chest whilst he wrapped his arms around her in a loving embrace,

CHAPTER IX:
A CHANCE OF A CURE

As Brenna finished looking through the book sitting in his hands, he angrily slammed it down on the table, frustrated that it contained nothing regarding a cure for the wolfblight, "Damn it!", he growled,
"Don't worry, we'll keep looking", said Eira,
Brenna sighed as he ran his hand through his hair,
"I can't give up, I cannot break the promise I made to John and Ulva", he said,
"Then why did you make that promise in the first place?", said Eira,
"Because they have been through enough already, I wasn't gonna tell them that there is nothing that can be done. I know there is a solution, I just know it", said Brenna,
Placing a comforting hand on Brenna's shoulder, Eira said,
"Come on, sit down and rest while I continue looking",
Brenna sighed as he sat himself down,
"This whole situation is a mess", he said,
As she rolled her pipe in her mouth, Eira stared at the bookshelf in front of her, casting her gaze over some books that she had yet to open. It was then that she saw an old looking book tucked away in the corner next to a large and weighty tome bound in hide. Intrigued, Eira pulled it off the shelf and inspected its cover, it was blue in colour and adorned with a silver crescent moon, its title written in silver words that read, '*The Lore of Jokullholt*'.
Walking over to Brenna, Eira said,
"This looks promising, have a read whilst I make us some hot cocoa",
Brenna glanced up as Eira gave him the book,
"Where did you find this?", he said as he eyed its cover,

"At the bottom of the bookshelf, it was hiding behind a giant book", said Eira,
"I haven't seen this book in a long time, I almost forgot that I had it", said Brenna,
"Well there's no harm in looking at it, perhaps it will hold the answer to your problems", said Eira before she left the study, bumping into John as he came wandering in,
"Hi John, do you and Ulva want some cocoa?", asked Eira,
"Not at the moment", said John,
"Okay, suit yourself", said Eira before she made her way up the stairs,
John glanced over at Brenna before he walked over to where Ulva had been bound, there he picked up Ulva's bed clothes from off the floor,
"Ulva and I are heading back to our house to get some fresh clothes, we'll be quick as we can", said John,
"Okay, but I will need you both back here as soon as possible", said Brenna as he opened the book lying upon his lap,
"Don't worry, we won't be long", said John as he wandered out of the room and disappeared out of sight,
"Go and find Einar while you are at it", said Brenna,
"Got it", said John,
All alone in his study, Brenna flicked through the pages of the book sitting in front of him, eyeing lines of text accompanied by pictures of monstrous werewolves, dark gnarled trees and ancient artefacts. Soon he came to a particular page that caught his attention.
Upon the page was the drawing of a large shrine, an ornate looking throne dwarfed by a large plinth hewn from moonstone and wreathed in ice. Atop the plinth sat a statue with long, outstretched arms ending in sharp claws. The statue had two heads; one was a human face whilst the other head was that of a wolf.
Sitting beside the drawing was a roughly made sketch of a dagger, its blade etched with runes.

As Brenna stared at the page before him, Eira appeared whilst carrying two mugs of steaming hot chocolate. She gave one to Brenna before she sat herself down next to him, glancing at the book lying upon his lap,
"What's that, some kind of chair?", she said,
Brenna laughed,
"It's more than that Eira, it is an ancient artefact known as Fenrir's Bane. It has the ability to cure a person of the wolfblight", he said,
"Then that's it then, the very thing you've been looking for", blurted Eira,
"Unfortunately no", said Brenna sadly,
Eira frowned,
"What do you mean?", she said,
"I know this artefact can cure a person of lycanthropy, I've always known of its existence, I even visited it once a long time ago in my search for a cure. However when I found it, I discovered that a key was needed to activate its power, an engraved dagger with a jewelled hilt, a key that I do not possess", said Brenna,
Pointing at the engraved dagger upon the page, Brenna said,
"I travelled far and wide and spent years in search of this dagger, this key, but after nearly nine long years of questing, I simply could not find it despite enduring much hardship and heartache. With my health endangered and my finances in near ruin, I gave up hope of finding it and using its power. So I instead set my sights on finding other alternative solutions for a cure, forgetting about this book in the process",
After taking another sip of his cocoa, Brenna continued,
"I tried making potions, balms and elixirs, but none of them worked. When I tried magical spells, none of them were of any help. I sought out wisdom from seers, witches, sorcerers and at one point even demons, but none of them could provide a cure. I once tried praying to the gods, but they responded with nothing but silence",
"None of them worked? Like at all?", said Eira,

"Yes, no matter what I did, nothing seemed to work. I read every book I could find on werewolves and the wolfblight, but very few of them talked about a cure and those that did brought me no closer to finding one. I travelled to every library, bookshop and market I could find for a book that might provide an answer, but alas I found nothing truly worthwhile", said Brenna,

Staring sadly at the dagger lying upon the page before him, Brenna said,

"If I could just get my hands on this artefact, then perhaps there might be hope",

"It's a very beautiful piece", said Eira as she stared at the drawing,

Suddenly Eira's eyes widened as her mind tweaked,

"Hold on a minute, I swear I have seen this dagger before", she gasped,

Brenna spluttered as he spat out his cocoa in shock,

"Damn it, why am I always drinking when something surprising happens?!", he barked,

Flashing a shocked look at Eira, Brenna blurted,

"What do you mean you've seen this dagger before?!",

"Wait here", said Eira as she rushed out of her chair before running upstairs with all haste,

After quickly finishing his cocoa and placing both the empty mug and book down upon a nearby table, Brenna stared at the entrance to his study with anxious anticipation for Eira's return.

Eventually after waiting many agonizingly long minutes, Brenna saw Eira appear alongside John, a newly clothed Ulva, Maud, Guthrum and Einar in tow.

After everyone made their way in, Eira said to John,

"Give me the dagger quick",

With a look of confusion etched upon his face, John handed Ulva's dagger over to Eira before she held it up to Brenna,

"Is this the dagger you've been looking for?", she asked,

Brenna gasped as his mouth opened in shock, his hands beginning to shake as his eyes began to tear up,
"It...it can't be", he said,
"Well is it?", said Eira,
"Yes, yes it is", said Brenna as Eira handed him the dagger,
As Brenna ran his fingers across its cold blade, his face suddenly lit up with a smile before he began to laugh loudly and boisterously.
Lifting the dagger high into the air, Brenna cried out,
"By all the gods above the legends were true, it exists, it truly exists! All this time I have searched for it and it was here in Gormstad all along!",
"What is it?", said John,
"Quickly, everyone sit down, I'll explain everything", said Brenna,
John, Ulva, Einar, Eira, Guthrum and Maud all glanced at each other in confusion before they sat themselves down in a circle around Brenna.
Rotating the dagger between his fingers, Brenna said to John,
"This dagger was on your person, where did you get it?",
"I bought it off Eira in her antique shop, it was a gift for Ulva", said John,
"You mean you've had it all this time and you never told me?!", snapped Brenna as he glanced over at Eira,
"I had completely forgotten about it until I rediscovered it a few days ago when I was tidying up. Even if I knew I had it, I wouldn't have guessed that this dagger was the key to finding a cure for Ulva unless you told me. Trust me, I would have given it to you straight away if I knew how important it was to you", she said as she pocketed her empty pipe,
"You mean to tell me that this dagger is actually a cure for Ulva?", said John,
"Yes, this is not just any ordinary dagger, this is Vulthur the Vargslayer, the key to curing Ulva", replied Brenna,
Feeling her heart flutter in her chest, Ulva said,
"You mean we have a chance to rid myself of the wolfblight?",

Pointing at the open page upon his lap, Brenna said, "See this drawing here? It details an artefact known as Fenrir's Bane, located within the dark depths of a forest known as Coldwood. According to this book, we need to take Vulthur there and conduct a ritual. The book states that the afflicted must sit upon Fenrir's Bane and speak the Incantation of Healing inscribed upon Vulthur's blade before plunging it into their heart, this will cure them of the wolfblight",
"So that's what those runes on the dagger were, a spell needed for this ritual the book talks about", said John,
"Exactly", said Brenna,
Feeling nervous, Ulva squeaked,
"I must stab myself...in the heart?",
"That's what it says", said Brenna,
Ulva felt nauseous as she gripped John's hand,
"Gods, that sounds horrible", she gasped,
"Better than being a werewolf for the rest of your life", said Brenna,
"Hm...true", replied Ulva,
"So let me get this straight, the dagger that John bought Ulva is not just an antique, but a powerful artefact that can be used to cure Ulva of her lycanthropy at some ancient throne located in a dark forest by means of a strange ritual?", said Einar,
"Yes", said Brenna,
"Well what are we waiting for? We must get to Coldwood and perform the ritual before it's too late. As you said before, we only have a few days at most before Ulva's transformation becomes permanent", said Einar,
"This Coldwood, is it far?", asked John,
"Not too far, if we keep a brisk and steady pace, we should get there in a few days", said Brenna,
"What about taking a carriage? Surely that would be faster than walking", said Ulva,

"It's early spring, all of the carriages in Gormstad will have been taken to Kristtorndal in preparation for the Eostre Festival happening later this month", said Maud,

"Well in that case, let's get a move on and start packing for the journey, the sooner we leave, the sooner we can get to Coldwood", said John,

"We will need food and water, fresh clothes, healing supplies and some form of protection from both unforeseen dangers and the elements", said Brenna,

"Don't worry about all of that, Guthrum and I can sort it all out", said Maud,

"Indeed, I have several large backpacks you all can have, they have served me well in the past", said Guthrum,

"That would be amazing grandad, thank you", said Einar,

"Let's go Guthrum, we have some work to do", said Maud,

"Right, let us make haste", said Guthrum as he staggered up off his chair,

After Maud and Guthrum had left together, Eira said to Brenna,

"I'm going to my shop to see if I can find anything that might prove useful for your journey",

"That would be great, thank you Eira", said Brenna,

As Eira left the study, Brenna said to Einar, John and Ulva,

"If we are going to do this journey, I recommend you all go and set any affairs you have in order before we leave later this afternoon. We will be gone for several days at the least and it won't be possible for us to return",

"Well in that case, I need to send a messenger to the mine at Ishellir Crossing and inform Felbert that I won't be able to return to work for a few more days due to personal reasons, he'll understand, he's a good man", said John,

"Ishellir Crossing you say? Hmm...now that you mention, we will be passing Ishellir on our way to Coldwood. We can always make a quick detour and inform him on the way", said Brenna,

"An excellent idea Brenna, good thinking", said John,

"I don't need to inform the library, it's currently closed and I'm still on leave", said Ulva,
"And I am semi-retired, so I'm fine", said Einar,
"Good, now off with you all and be ready to leave by midday at the latest", said Brenna,
"Before we go Brenna, I need to tell you something", said John,
"What is it?", asked Brenna,
"Well I don't know if it's important, but when I left Eira's antique shop with the dagger, I was approached by a man, Godi Vulpes. He was interested in the dagger and he offered to purchase it from me for whatever price I named, but I didn't sell it to him", said John,
"Well it's a good thing that you didn't, if you had given him the dagger, we would have lost our only chance of curing me. I am glad you kept it, even if it meant us losing a potentially grand prize", said Ulva,
Brenna scratched his chin and said,
"Hmm...Godi Vulpes, advisor to the Jarl of Gormstad, powerful, wealthy, morally dubious and quite a frightening man, why would he want the dagger? Vulpes is no academic nor is he a collector of antiquities, so why would he be so intent on getting his hand on it?",
"Perhaps he knows of its power and needs the dagger to cure someone he knows. He didn't explain why he wanted it, other than he was willing to pay handsomely for it", said John,
As everyone pondered the situation, Ulva suddenly gasped as a horrific thought entered her mind,
"Wait a minute, what did Vulpes look like?", she said,
"Well, he was an old man with silver hair and a beard of the same colour. His eyes were a horrible greenish blue, like moss in rancid pond water",
Ulva gasped,
"Oh no", she said,
"What is it?", asked Einar,

"I remember now, the werewolf that attacked me. Before it bit me, the werewolf spoke to me and demanded that I hand over the dagger", said Ulva,
"Wait, the werewolf actually spoke to you, as in clear and audible words?", said Brenna,
"Yes and I remember what it looked like, its fur was silver in colour and its eyes were coloured a greenish blue", said Ulva,
"Godi Vulpes had silver hair, green - blue eyes and wanted the dagger, so that must mean...", said Brenna,
Everyone's mouths dropped in shock, in unison they blurted,
"Godi Vulpes was the werewolf!",
"This is highly troubling, if he was willing to attack someone to get the dagger, then he might try and attack us again, he might even have the audacity to kill", said Brenna,
"He could still be watching us, waiting to strike again, either personally or by sending night - knives to finish what he could not complete. Either way, we are all in great danger and we need to leave as soon as we can, I fear we are no longer safe in Gormstad", said Einar,
"Right, whilst I get organized here, you three should get ready for the journey. I do urge that you travel together whilst conducting your errands, there is safety in numbers and there is no telling if or when Vulpes will try and claim the dagger again", said Brenna,
"Okay, what then once everything has been sorted?", said John,
"Once everyone is ready, meet me back here so we can all leave together. Be careful and be swift, we haven't got much time, now go and may Odin watch over us", said Brenna,
Taking Ulva by the hand, John said,
"Come on Ulva, we need to pack",
"I'll come too", said Einar,
As John, Ulva and Einar were about to leave Brenna's study, there suddenly came a loud knock at the door which startled everyone into a panic,
"Wait here, I'll see who it is", said Brenna,

Drawing his sword, Brenna made his way up the stairs before he cautiously opened the door, sighing in relief as he saw Hersir Barmund standing in the doorway looking rather bemused,

"It's alright guys, it's just Barmund", said Brenna as he called down to his friends,

"Apologies for the disturbance Brenna I won't keep you long, I've just come to give you this", said Barmund before he handed Brenna a piece of paper,

"What's this?", he asked,

"Information concerning the curfew", said Barmund,

"What curfew?", asked Brenna,

"There have been reports of a werewolf sighted within the town. This is merely a precaution whilst we search for the creature, but by the command of Jarl Turold and the Gormstad Folkmoot, there is to be a curfew until further notice from sunset till sunrise starting from tonight. No one is to enter and leave the town unless special permission has been granted to them", said Barmund,

Suddenly John blurted,

"Hey, I know who the werewolf is, it's..."

John let out a pained grunt as Brenna suddenly elbowed him in the ribs,

"Thank you for letting us know, we shall be vigilant", smiled Brenna,

"Thank you for your understanding, we don't want to incite a panic, but we want everyone to be aware of the situation. It's rather troubling, there hasn't been a werewolf sighting in these parts for years. I just hope we can find it quickly, the safety of the townsfolk depends on it, anyway have a good day and remember the curfew", said Barmund,

With a bow of his head and a swish of his cloak, Barmund left to join his fellow guards who were issuing out papers to passers-by,

"Why did you do that for? If Barmund knows the werewolf is Vulpes, then he can deal with him right here and now, neither us nor the town will have to worry about him", snapped John,

Brenna glared at John and said,

"Are you mad, do you honestly think Barmund is going to believe such an accusation against a high-ranking member of the town council?! We know that Vulpes is the monster, but we have no actual proof other than our word and showing Ulva's bite as evidence of Vulpes's deed will only end with her being clapped in irons and taken away. No, we need to avoid Barmund and leave as quickly as possible. Now go all of you, I shall see you later",

After Brenna went back inside his home and slammed the door shut behind him, Einar, Ulva and John returned to their homes to prepare for the journey ahead.

CHAPTER X:
A LURKING FOX

Near the town square located in front of the main gate, Vilhelm was talking to a nervous looking citizen, a man with long blonde hair and a golden beard wearing a belted tunic, "And where did you see this werewolf?", asked Vilhelm,
"Well I was out late last night and I was a bit drunk, I was stumbling home when I saw a large, shadowed figure at the end of the street. It was human in shape but covered in fur and had the head of a dog. It was darted away before I could get a real look at it and when I walked past the home of Brenna Torstensson, I swear I could hear the faint sounds of screaming and howling. I don't know if it was the drink, but I swear I had seen and heard a werewolf", said the blonde headed man,
A smile formed on Vilhelm's face,
"Thank you, you have been most helpful, worry not I will have that monster dead very soon", he said,
"Thank goodness, I hope it will be taken care of, a werewolf prowling around Gormstad can only mean trouble", said the blonde-haired man,
Vilhelm laughed,
"Indeed, but do not worry my friend, I shall do everything in my disposal to get rid of it. As frightening as they are, a werewolf is just like any other monster. You cut off its head and pull out their heart and the beast is no more. Now if you will excuse me, I need to go and talk with an old friend", he said,
At Brenna's house, Vilhelm strode up the pathway and stopped at the front door. After clearing his throat he knocked gently, but there was no response. Vilhelm knocked again, this time banging his fist against the door. Eventually there came a rattling before the door swung open, revealing Brenna's face.

With a wide grin, Vilhelm said,
"Torstensson",
Brenna glared at Vilhelm before he slammed the door in his face,
"Brenna open up, I just want to talk, you know, friend to friend?", said Vilhelm,
Brenna pulled the door open and said,
"What do you want Barenhauter? I am far too busy to deal with your shit today",
"Too busy for a chat with an old friend? So what are you studying today? Still worried about werewolves after all these years?", said Vilhelm,
"You know that I am, I said I wouldn't rest until the wolfblight was removed from this land", said Brenna,
Vilhelm folded his arms,
"Don't you think you should give it a rest? You've been chasing this flight of fancy for far too long. Why don't you settle down, get married, have a couple of brats running about", he said as he smirked beneath his hood,
"I am not in the mood Vilhelm, please leave", sighed Brenna,
"Don't be like that, I just need to ask you a question. I am looking for a werewolf that has been spotted lurking within the town. Everyone I have spoken to say that the werewolf has been seen nearby and somehow your name keeps popping up. So my question is, have you seen or heard anything that might help me find it?", said Vilhelm,
"I have heard about this werewolf yes, but I haven't seen it and I am not involved", said Brenna,
"Interesting, I spoke with a man earlier and he said that sounds were coming from inside your home just after he spotted the werewolf, most curious", said Vilhelm,
"I told you, I don't know where the werewolf is!", barked Brenna,

"Very well, I will leave you to your business, but all joking aside Brenna, if you do hear anything please inform me, I would hate to see some innocent people die at the hands of these monsters. Make no mistake though, I will find the werewolf and when I do, I will take its head and mount it on my wall, making it watch as I fuck its widow", said Vilhelm,
"Good day Vilhelm", growled Brenna before he disappeared behind his front door and slammed it shut,
Bemused and smirking to himself, Vilhelm made his way back down the path and out onto the adjacent street, humming and whistling as he did.
As he walked further down the street, Vilhelm could feel the air grow cold as the sun faded behind some clouds. Suddenly Vilhelm heard a voice call out his name, it sounded like a long and sharp hiss and it came from a nearby dark and narrow alleyway.
Vilhelm glanced around before drawing his golden sword,
"All right, who's there? If you want a fight then I shall happily oblige", he said,
An evil chuckle suddenly echoed from the shadows,
"Oh no, not fight, nothing of the sort", came a voice,
Vilhelm watched as an elderly man garbed in crimson robes suddenly emerged from the alleyway, his right eye bandaged tightly with cloth,
"Who are you?", asked Vilhelm,
The figure bowed his head and said,
"Godi Vulpes, it is a pleasure to meet you",
"Shouldn't you be at home with some cocoa old man? It's quite chilly today", said Vilhelm,
Vulpes's creepy grin widened,
"Do not underestimate me young one, you have no idea of what I am capable of", he said,
"Who are you and what do you want? I'm quite busy", said Vilhelm,

"My name is Vulpes of Tarn Gren, Godi and advisor to the Jarl of Gormstad and I know who you are and why you are here. You are Vilhelm Barenhauter and you are looking for the werewolf that has been spotted wandering about. I can help you in this regard, which is why I have come with a proposition", said Vulpes,

"A proposition?", asked Vilhelm,

"Yes, the werewolf has taken something that is very precious to me, an old dagger of immense value. Let us kill two birds with one stone, find the werewolf and kill her, then bring me back my dagger. Do this and you shall be handsomely rewarded and be hailed as the hero who saved Gormstad from a terrible monster", said Vulpes,

"Her?", asked Vilhelm as he sheathed his blade,

With a horrible grin etched upon his face, Vulpes said,

"Yes, her name is Ulva Forrester",

Vilhelm's eyes widened in surprise,

"Ulva Forrester...that name rings a bell, Brenna mentioned once that he had a friend named Ulva, this of course was a long time ago. I knew that Brenna was involved somehow, how else could the screams coming from his house be explained? He's obviously keeping her true nature a secret from everyone so that he can protect her", he said,

"Indeed, so now that you have the identity of your target and the promise of immense riches, tell me Vilhelm, do you accept my contract?", asked Vulpes,

"How do you know Ulva is the werewolf?", asked Vilhelm,

"Because she attacked me and scratched out my eye", said Vulpes,

"Oh", uttered Vilhelm as he stared at Vulpes's bandaged eye,

"Well, do you accept?", asked Vulpes,

With greedy thoughts of gold and fame filling his head, Vilhelm said,

"Sure, I accept your proposition", he said,

"Excellent, I'll be awaiting your return at the Black Boar tavern, I assume you know where it is", said Vulpes,

"Of course I do", huffed Vilhelm,

"Also do not forget the dagger, it is a family heirloom and I wish to see it safely returned to me", said Vulpes,
"What does it look like?", asked Vilhelm,
"It has a black hilt with a ruby pommel. The blade is inscribed on both sides", said Vulpes,
"Okay and what does Ulva look like?", asked Vilhelm,
"Ulva is fair of face and young, her hair is red in colour and her eyes are like ice. More than likely she will be with her husband John, a one eyed brute of a man", said Vulpes,
"Duly noted, now if you will excuse me I'll be off, I've got a werewolf to slay", said Vilhelm,
"Excellent, good luck my friend", hissed Vulpes,
Vilhelm watched as the old man stepped back into the shadows, his pale moon – like face lit up with a frightening grin as he disappeared,
"Creepy bastard", uttered Vilhelm,
As Vilhelm resumed walking down the street, he could feel his belly beginning to rumble,
"I suppose it wouldn't hurt to get some breakfast first, I cannot work on an empty stomach. I hope Vulpes is not lying about a reward, I don't do this just for fun, I have habits and indulgences that must be satisfied and only the gleam of gold can do that", he said,

CHAPTER XI:
OUT INTO THE COLD

As it neared midday, John was finishing packing up the last of his supplies for the journey at his house. Stuffed into his backpack was a considerable quantity of food, largely consisting of cured meat and grained bread alongside some hardy fruits. With Ulva's appetite now much more ferocious than normal, John knew it was better to be safe than sorry and he ensured they both had a plentiful supply of nourishment. Additionally, John had filled the bag with bandages, rope, kindling and flint for lighting fires, several days' worth of clothes and a map. Lining his belt were leather pouches filled with medicine, bundles of blue wolfsbane, as much money as he could carry, his pickaxe, a brass lamp and a dagger. Strapped to his back was a small wooden shield. As he threw on his cloak and fastened it tightly, John could see Ulva coming down the stairs. She was wearing a red dress, black boots over white woollen stockings, a pair of gloves and a long white shawl wrapped around her shoulders. On Ulva's leather belt was sheathed Vulthur next to a crystalline lamp and she wore around her neck a bejewelled black choker. Slung across her back was a brown leather backpack filled with supplies.
She walked over to John before they both looked around the room they were standing in, their hearts filling with sadness. Hoping to have begun a new chapter of their life here, it was painful to know they would have to leave again, it was a sobering thought,
"Will we ever come back?", asked Ulva,
"I hope so", sighed John,
He glanced at Ulva and saw her eyes beginning to well up as she struggled to maintain her composure,

"Hey come on now, it's going to be okay, you'll see. I promise I will get you to Coldwood and back in no time and then we can start a new life here just you and me", said John before he brushed away a tear from Ulva's face with his thumb,
"I love you", said Ulva softly,
"Love you too. Come, Brenna will be waiting", said John,
After leaving the house and locking it behind him, John pocketed the door key before he took Ulva by the hand. Together they then made their way to Einar's house. As they arrived, John and Ulva saw Einar, Maud and Guthrum waiting for them outside. Maud was holding Einar's hand whilst trying to fight back tears. Guthrum meanwhile was openly upset, the poor old man was shaking and wiping his eyes, trying to look brave for his beloved grandchildren. Seeing him in such emotional distress, Ulva walked over and hugged him tightly,
"Take care Ulva, come back to us safe and sound", said Guthrum,
"I will granddad, look after yourself whilst I am gone", said Ulva,
Guthrum glanced over to John before he slowly hobbled towards him.
With a sad smile, he said,
"My boy, you travel with the people I treasure most in this world, Einar and Ulva mean everything to me, watch over them",
John bowed his head and said,
"I will",
"Thank you young pup, that is all I can ask of you", said Guthrum,
As Guthrum bade farewell to John, Ulva and Maud hugged one another, Maud now visibly upset,
"See you soon", she whimpered,
"You too", said Ulva,
After Maud had finishing saying her goodbyes to John, Einar embraced her before they both kissed,
"Hurry home", said Maud,

"I will be counting the days", replied Einar with a warm smile before he said to Ulva and John,
"Ready to go you two?",
"Ready as I'll ever be", said John,
Bidding their final farewells to Guthrum and Maud, Einar, John and Ulva waved goodbye and made their way down the road towards Brenna's house, all three of them emotional as they walked away,
"Farewell you guys, we shall see each other again soon!", shouted Maud,
"Remember, do not fear the night, for it bears the next dawn!", cried Guthrum,
After a short walk, John, Einar and Ulva arrived at Brenna's house, entering quietly before making their way down into the study where Eira and Brenna were waiting for them. Brenna was garbed in his black coat, red scarf and usual attire of a shirt, trousers and boots, a sword and lamp fastened to his belt. He was carrying on his back a large rucksack which was filled with everything he needed for the journey, including some books, strange looking tools and alchemical ingredients. Eira was standing next to him smoking her pipe. To John's surprise, she was not wearing anything warm or practical for the journey and it appeared that she had not packed anything,
"Aren't you coming with us?", said John,
"No", said Eira,
"What?", asked John,
"Though I wish you success in your quest and I look forward to your return, I have a shop to run and I am far too busy to be gallivanting across the land. Besides I can watch over Maud and Guthrum whilst you are gone", said Eira,
Seeing John and the others looking rather disappointed at her decision, Eira smiled and said,
"I do have some things that might help you on your journey though",

Eira walked over to the nearby table and returned holding a leather bag. She then reached in and pulled out a small box, which she handed to Einar.

Einar opened the box to reveal five balls made of glass, each one was topped with a small wooden handle attached to a long wick that sat inside,

"What are they?", asked Einar,

"These are dragon orbs, powerful artefacts of my own design that might prove useful on your journey. How they work is that you twist the handle atop the orb which lights the fuse inside. Once the fuse is lit, simply shatter the glass and the orb will erupt into a ball of fiery destruction. Be careful with them though, they are highly explosive and pack quite a punch. Also please use them sparingly, they are difficult and time consuming to make. Should you use one, make sure you are at a safe distance so you don't get caught in the blast", said Eira,

"What fascinating little trinkets, thank you Eira, I shall use them wisely", said Einar,

Eira then reached into the bag and pulled out a small bracelet which she handed to Ulva,

"This is known as a helbredelse bracelet. It won't stop your transformations at night, but it might make the turnings less painful. The bracelet is designed to release a numbing agent into your body through contact with your skin", she said,

Eyeing the bracelet intently, Ulva slipped it onto her wrist and said,

"It's lovely, thank you Eira",

"Right now that everyone is here, it is time we began setting off. With any luck we should be getting some good miles behind us by nightfall when we set up camp", said Brenna before he wrapped his arms around Eira and said,

"I shall be back soon, watch over the house while I'm gone and look after yourself. I haven't said it much, but you mean a lot to me, you are worth more than all the treasures in your shop", he said,

"Be careful Brenna and good luck", said Eira,

Glancing at her friends, Eira said,
"Come, I'll see you all to the door",
After everyone had made their way outside and said their goodbyes to Eira, John, Ulva, Brenna and Einar began walking down the street with heavy hearts,
"Good luck my friends, keep to the northern road and for Odin's sake come back alive, I don't want to bury any of you!", cried Eira as she waved them goodbye,
"Don't worry, we will!", yelled Brenna,
As everyone made their way down the street, they passed several houses and a row of market stalls before coming to a deserted street lined with cobbled stones.
Knowing that he would soon be leaving the safety and homely comfort of Gormstad, John couldn't help but feel his stomach bubbling with anxiety. Despite having his friends and family at his side, he felt nervous. He was no coward but knowing that he wouldn't see Gormstad for quite some time made him uneasy.
Suddenly John came to a halt as he heard the sound of quickened footsteps coming from a nearby alleyway.
Before he could speak, John watched as Vilhelm rushed out from the darkness, his cloak billowing as he sent Ulva crashing to the ground with a hard kick,
"Ulva!", barked John,
As he, Einar and Brenna drew their weapons, they watched in horror as Vilhelm raised his axe high, ready to strike a blow to Ulva's neck,
"Forgive me", he said,
Ulva let out a piercing scream as she saw the glistening axe come down upon her, only to gasp as John lunged forward and pounced Vilhelm, sending both of them flying across the stones. As Vilhelm and John fought viciously and violently with axe and fist, Einar quickly joined the fray whilst Brenna tried to comfort the shaking and teary-eyed Ulva. John grunted as Vilhelm punched him in the jaw, sending a strong, throbbing pain rushing across his face.

As John fell backwards, Vilhelm got to his feet and pushed Einar back before drawing his golden blade. The street rang out with the sound of scraping metal as Vilhelm and Einar clashed, their blades striking against one another in a shower of sparks. As Einar and Vilhelm parried, John grabbed his pickaxe from the floor and ran towards Vilhelm.

Seeing John coming towards him, Vilhelm bellowed as he swung his axe and caught Einar in the arm just below the shoulder. Einar roared out in pain and crumpled to the ground as his arm began to bleed. John swung his pickaxe, but Vilhelm blocked it with his axe and swung his blade in return, breaking the pickaxe into two. Fragments of wood were sent flying as the metal head of the pickaxe clattered to the ground. Vilhelm then struck John in the face with the hilt of his sword, crushing his nose. With his head ringing with pain, John stumbled and fell to the ground.

His vision then went blurry before he passed out unconscious,

"John!", cried Ulva,

Rushing over to her husband's side, Ulva fell to her knees and began to shake John to try and wake him. Seeing Ulva defenceless, Vilhelm rushed towards her with sword in hand. Suddenly Brenna leapt forward before he engaged with Vilhelm, clashing violently and striking each other with hard and powerful blows as metal rang out. Vilhelm growled as he swung his left arm against Brenna's blade, the metal of his axe screeching as it met Brenna's silver sword.

Brenna swung his fist, catching Vilhelm in the side of his head, which made him recoil backwards. As Vilhelm shook off the pain, he saw Brenna, Ulva and Einar were now encircling him, pointing their blades at his head as they glared at him angrily. Outnumbered, Vilhelm laughed as he dropped his sword and axe, raising his arms above his head in surrender,

"Well played, well played indeed", said Vilhelm,

But just as Brenna was about to restrain Vilhelm, he was suddenly thrown off his feet and sent flying across the street by an invisible and powerful force that felt like a blast of wind alongside Einar and Ulva. Einar and Brenna were immediately knocked unconscious as their heads struck the hard ground whilst Ulva cried out as she rolled across the cobblestones.

Feeling dizzy and tasting blood in her mouth, she saw the figure who had cast the spell appear before her, an old man wearing scarlet robes. The old man stared at Ulva before he walked over to Vilhelm. She couldn't hear what they were saying, but before her vision went black, she could see Vulpes pick Vulthur up from off the ground.

Vulpes eyed the dagger with wonder and glee, his face brimming with delight,

"Vulthur the Vargslayer, at long last it is mine", he hissed,

"Yeah, yeah, fantastic, I would like my reward now, seeing as how I got you the dagger and all", said Vilhelm,

"Of course", said Vulpes before he reached into his pocket and handed Vilhelm a jangling purse of money,

Vilhelm excitedly snatched up the purse and poured its contents into his palm, his smile faded and his heart sank when he counted just twenty pennies of silver,

"Are you kidding me, that's it?", snapped Vilhelm,

"Oh come now, this wasn't exactly a difficult task and let's not forget that you never negotiated an exact price, I promised you a reward and this is it", said Vulpes,

Vilhelm tossed the purse upon the ground, spilling the coins across the pavement,

"Now you listen here old man, I did what I was told and I expect proper remuneration for my work!", he spat,

Vulpes glared at Vilhelm,

"If you weren't aware, you've only completed half the job, Ulva is still alive after all. Also it was I who retrieved the dagger, not you. If I hadn't arrived, you would be in irons right now. As such, you shall not get a proper reward, nor a hero's triumph for your dismal efforts", he hissed,

Seething with rage, Vilhelm collected up his golden sword and stormed over to Ulva's unmoving body,
"Fine, you want a dead werewolf? Well here you are!", he shouted,
Vilhelm lifted his sword up in the air and was about to behead Ulva when an arrow suddenly appeared and flew straight into his hand. Yelling out in pain, Vilhelm dropped his sword with a clatter. Both Vulpes and Vilhelm were shocked to find themselves suddenly caught in a flurry of arrows.
They looked down the street and saw Eira standing at the other end, she was wielding a large bow and firing off arrows towards them,
"Get the fuck away from my friends!", yelled Eira,
Vilhelm watched as Vulpes angrily snapped his fingers before vanishing in a cloak of smoke and fire. Picking up his sword and axe, Vilhelm suddenly fled, sprinting down the street as fast as he could.
Eira ran over to Ulva, Einar, John and Brenna as they all began to regain consciousness,
"Guys, what happened?!", cried Eira,
"We were attacked by a man who tried to kill Ulva", groaned John,
"Not just anyone, Vilhelm Barenhauter, a monster slayer and adventurer", said Brenna as he got up off the ground,
"You know him?", asked Einar,
"We've been acquainted", said Brenna before he turned to Eira and said,
"How did you find us?",
"I was having a smoke outside your house when we heard the screams and the fighting, so I came running as fast as I could", said Eira,
After Ulva was pulled up off the floor by Einar, she rushed over to Eira and hugged her tightly,
"Thank you Eira, if it weren't for you I would have been killed, you saved my life", she said,

"No need to thank me, I wasn't going to let those bastards kill you", said Eira,

"Seriously though Eira, you have my undying gratitude, I cannot thank you enough", said John as he clutched his bleeding face,

"This Vilhelm, did Vulpes hire him to have you all killed?", asked Eira,

"It looks that way", said Einar,

"Why would he attack me?", asked Ulva,

"Obviously Vulpes told Vilhelm what you are and ordered him to kill you. He likely offered Vilhelm some incredible reward for your demise and filled his head with ideas of glory and how he would be conducting a chivalrous and noble act of justice that would have earned him the love and respect of the town", said Brenna,

"Regardless, we need to leave now before either of them try again", said John,

"Before I passed out, I saw Vulpes take Vulthur. He now has the dagger; we must get it back from him. Fenrir's Bane will not work without it", said Ulva,

"Does anyone know where he might have gone?", said John,

Lighting up her pipe, Eira said,

"If he's not in Gormstad, he will have fled to Tarn Gren, his tower residence located within the Gormwood just outside of town",

"What's the quickest route to get there?", asked Einar,

"You could walk through the Gormwood, but I wouldn't recommend it, the forest is dangerous and you could get lost. Instead I would recommend another route, one that is not public knowledge. Under the town there are subterranean tunnels, a network of ancient passageways and chambers that were once used during times of war and crisis to smuggle people and goods in and out of Gormstad. Some of these tunnels are connected to the sewers and I know that one of them goes directly to Tarn Gren", said Eira,

"How would you know about such a thing?", said John,

After blowing smoke into the air, Eira said,
"I like to read old maps in my free time, I remember seeing the tunnels on a map of the town once",
"Can you take us there?", asked John,
"Sure...I'll",
Eira's words were cut off when there came the sound of guards marching towards the street, followed by Barmund barking orders,
"Quickly, let's go before Barmund gets dragged into all of this. I don't think he'll believe us when we say we were attacked by a mad wizard because Ulva is a werewolf and possesses a magical dagger", said Eira,
With the sound of thundering boots getting louder, Eira and her friends slipped into a nearby alleyway and fled before Barmund and his guards could arrive to investigate.
After walking through several streets, John, Brenna, Ulva, Einar and Eira eventually arrived at a small garden that was hidden at the end of a narrow street sitting under one of the town's towering stone walls.
The garden itself was enclosed by an iron fence and gate, it was unkempt and overgrown with wildflowers, weeds and dry gnarled roots. At the centre of the garden sat a large and dilapidated well, a circular hole with cracked stone walls that was missing a bucket and rope.
Everyone walked over to the well and peered inside, seeing nothing but gloomy darkness as their ears were filled with the sound of howling wind coming from deep within the well.
After knocking the ash out of her pipe and pocketing it into the pouch on her belt, Eira said,
"Right, this is the entrance to the tunnel you will need to traverse, climb down and you will come to a small chamber with an opening. Follow the tunnel until you come to a trapdoor, it will lead you to Tarn Gren",
"Seems simple enough", said Einar,

"Now pay close attention to what I am about to say, many of the tunnels have been abandoned and have fallen into ruin, flooded, collapsed or might be inhabited by creatures, so please be careful and watch yourselves", said Eira,
"Got it, thank you Eira", said Brenna,
"Now is there anything you need to do before you leave?", said Eira,
"Not that we know of", said John,
"Good, well best of luck you guys, may the gods watch over you", said Eira before she turned on her heel and walked away, wiping the tears from her face as she left,
Turning to Brenna, Einar and Ulva, John said sadly,
"Well, let's go",
After exchanging nervous glances with one another, John and his friends slowly and carefully stepped into the well, grabbing onto the bars of a small, iron ladder that stretched down into the earth.
As darkness enveloped him, John felt his heart beginning to pound in his chest as he slowly climbed down,
"Farewell Gormstad, we shall return", he muttered under his breath as his body began to shake with fear, anxious at what awaited him and his companions down in the tunnels, anxious that their journey had now well and truly begun,
Odin help them all.

CHAPTER XII:
THE KING OF WOLVES

Far to the north of Gormstad, there was a vast valley of ice and snow, a tundra surrounded by towering hills and rocky outcrops. At the heart of this bitter and frigid expanse stood a large and foreboding structure wreathed in great snowstorms and rings of fire and choking smoke. The structure was mighty in size, a sprawling collection of looming towers, walls and halls constructed from dark stone, black crystals and gnarled old wood laced with shimmering veins of rubies and moonstone. This was Ulfholl, the dreaded fortress where Fenrir and his forces held dominion. It was here that the seven legendary heroes cornered Fenrir and used the chain Gleipnir to bind and imprison him deep within the underworld.
The inside of Ulfholl was just as frightening as its exterior, a hulking, wretched and towering construct full of dark, winding and labyrinthine stairs, tunnels, corridors and rooms that twisted within crooked walls beneath ceilings illuminated by dimly lit lamps of crystal and glass.
For many centuries, people avoided Ulfholl in fear of disturbing the ghosts of Fenrir and his three children, who many believed haunted its empty and hollow towers. But in truth, if the foolhardy, the adventurous and the downright stupid dared to venture into the towering monstrosity, they would have found nothing more than a ruinous hill of decay and darkness full of rubble for the heroes had demolished it with righteous fury after sentencing Fenrir to the cold shadows of Niflheim. But that was a long time ago, now the fortress has been rebuilt by those loyal to the dark wolf, his followers known as the Cult of Fenris. Thanks to their efforts, its once silent halls were now filled with many different sounds and smells as the cult preoccupied themselves with all manner of work.

Outside Ulfholl stood Garm Fenrirsson, a very handsome and thin man who had long dark grey hair and a beard, his eyes were coloured gold and were piercing and wolf – like. He was wearing black bejewelled robes with intricately ornate iron pauldrons and a breastplate made of black steel. Garm stared out at the desolate frozen wasteland before him, watching intently as howling winds and snow swirled around him.

Garm suddenly heard the long and mighty howl of a wolf before he saw two giant wolves emerge from the snowstorm with snow billowing behind them, one black with blue and red eyes and one with blood red eyes and a heavily scarred body covered in cuts, gashes and bloody marks. It was his brother and sister Skoll and Hati. They were larger than any normal wolf would ever grow to be, from a reckoning they were roughly five meters in height.

Garm watched as his siblings suddenly came to a halt in front of him before they were enveloped in light and transformed into their human forms, Hati being garbed in black linen and furs whilst Skoll was wearing an ornate suit of white armour that was frosted with silver and encrusted with rubies.

Upon a glance, he looked remarkably like his brother and was physically imposing. He was very tall, muscular and had long brilliant white hair. Unlike his brother though, Skoll was clean shaven and his skin was covered with scars.

As Skoll and Hati approached Garm, he said,

"Hail my dear brother and sister, how fared the hunt this morning?",

"Dismal, the snowstorms are truly biting for we found no game within the foothills of the valley", growled Skoll in a deep and guttural tone of voice,

"Oh well, there will be more opportunities I am sure", smiled Garm,

"I hope so, running around does give one an appetite", said Hati,

"Has there been progress regarding the preparations for the resurrection ritual?", asked Skoll,

"Indeed, after twenty years of work, the ritual chamber has finally been fully rebuilt and restored. I just need confirmation on when we will be able to begin", said Garm,
"Excellent, I look forward to seeing our father's glorious return from the depths of Niflheim", said Skoll,
"Come let us head inside", said Hati,
Skoll, Hati and Garm made their way inside the fortress, the door closing behind them as they entered. Before them stretched a long and dark hallway lit by glowing white lamps hanging from the walls, which were made of shining black stone enveloped in twisted wooden branches and covered in glowing eyes and horrible crystalline faces both human and wolven frozen into permanent screams, cries and groans.
As Fenrir's children walked down the corridor, everyone who was present lifted their heads and stared at them with faces of both delight and trepidation,
"The children of Fenrir have returned, hail the Princes and Princess of Wolves!", came a voice,
Deeper inside the hallway, Hati, Skoll and Garm were soon greeted by two individuals.
One of them was a young man wearing a suit of black armour that was beaten and covered with dents and scratches. His gauntlets were shaped like claws and he was clutching a helmet that was shaped like the head of a wolf. His belt was encrusted with red diamonds and on his right arm was fitted a red armband adorned with a black symbol, a fearsome wolf head wearing a crown.
Such a symbol seemed to be everywhere, it adorned the banners and flags draping the walls, it was stamped and tattooed upon the armour and flesh of the cultists and even the servants wore it in the form of a necklace or badge.
The man had short black hair and was clean shaven with small red eyes and above his wiry and pale lips sat a thin moustache. His name was Raud and he was the fearsome Drottingr, the commander of the Ulfhethnar and Skoll's second in command.

The other man was tall, burly and bearded, his small eyes and long hair coloured a deep dark brown. He was wearing red robes fastened with a thick leather belt whilst a sash of fur ran across the width of his monumental body. Around his thick neck hung a large, ornate and heavy looking silver chain and collar bearing a symbol identical to the one adorning Raud's armband, the crest of Fenrir.

The man was Godi Haldor, a sorcerer of great renown and leader of the Goddar of Ulfholl,

"Godi Haldor, it is good to see you, how soon we will be able to begin the ritual?", said Garm,

"We should be ready within the hour", said Haldor as he bowed his head,

"Excellent we must not delay in returning our beloved father to this world so that we may begin the commencement of his plans", smiled Garm,

"Drottingr Raud, how fares the Ulfhethnar?", growled Skoll,

"My prince, training is going exceedingly well. The berserkers are honing their skills as we speak and we have swelled our ranks triple fold, I am personally overseeing their progress myself", said Raud,

"Good, keep up the good work, I want the Ulfhethnar to become an unstoppable force", said Skoll,

"Yes my lord", said Raud as he thumped his breastplate with an armoured fist before he left the hallway, his footsteps thundering against the stone floor,

Garm turned to Haldor and said,

"Once the preparations are complete, summon the Goddar for the ceremony",

Godi Haldor smiled and said,

"At once your royal highness",

After Haldor had left, Skoll said,

"We have an hour to kill, I am going to inspect my warriors",

After Skoll had stormed away, Garm glanced at Hati and said,

"I'm going to assist in the ritual preparations, what will you do in the meantime?",

Hati's face lit up with a horrible grin,
"Feed", she said as her mouth began to salivate,
Garm rolled his eyes and made his way down the hallway, people bowing their heads as he passed.
When Garm vanished from view, Hati walked over to one of the nearby servants, a young girl with braided hair who was wearing a simple cotton dress and an apron,
"Summon a prisoner, bring him to my quarters", she said,
"At once my lady", said the servant in a soulless and emotionless tone of voice, her eyes wide and vacant,
Hati made her way down the corridor, listening to the sounds around her as she went, the sound of chattering mouths, the clanging of metal and a low rumbling mixed with the howling of wind. At the end of the hallway, she passed two giant wolf statues wearing crowns before she came to a large gate that was sealed. Hati then turned to the left and made her way up a flight of stairs before eventually arriving at her room.
The room was built in the same fashion as the rest of Ulfholl, it's walls were crystalline and black in colour whilst being adorned with some banners, horrifying stone faces and lamps that glowed an ominous red colour.
To the left-hand side of the room was a large four posted bed covered with thick black sheets and blankets, a row of bookshelves and some large cabinets that were gilded with silver and made of burnished black wood. From the ceiling hung a massive chandelier adorned with white glowing crystals.
Hanging from the right-hand side wall was a towering and beautiful mirror, in front of which sat a chair and table.
Hati slowly walked over to the bed and sat upon it, smiling at the touch of the soft blankets beneath her.
After removing her cloak, boots and gloves, Hati walked over to the mirror and glanced upon the table sitting before it.
There she spotted an ornate wooden box, which she opened to reveal a beautiful crown frosted with silver, its jagged points encrusted with diamonds and rubies.

The crown was a magnificent piece, how it shone in the lamplight, it looked like it was made of ice.
With a delighted grin, Hati took it and placed it upon her head before she admired herself in the mirror, giggling as she felt her heart fill with joy,
"I am beautiful", she said,
Suddenly there came a knock at the door. With a spring in her step, Hati stepped over to it and pulled it open.
In the doorway stood the servant she had talked to earlier alongside a large man with short dark hair wearing a white shirt, brown trousers, a waistcoat and small leather shoes. His brow was sweating slightly due the fact that his face was flush from the warmth of the air and that he had demolished a heavy meal earlier in the day. As the man was glancing around nervously, the servant next to him bowed before she left him and Hati alone.
Hati's eyes widened as she looked upon the prisoner. She began to feel her mouth water and her stomach was beginning to growl with hunger as she stared at him.
Leaning herself against the doorway and folding her arms, she said in a honeyed and sweet voice,
"Well what do we have here, a handsome young man come to visit his princess?",
The man sheepishly rubbed the back of his neck as he said,
"You wanted to see me your royal highness?",
Twirling her hair through her fingers, Hati's grin widened as she bit her bottom lip,
"Yes, I have had a rather hectic morning and I wanted some company", she said,
"Company?", asked the man as he began to blush,
"Do come in", said Hati sweetly,
The man smiled before he said,
"Thank you, your royal highness",
Hati gestured the man inside before closing the door behind her with a kick. As the man was gazing around the room, Hati unfastened the top button of her dress, allowing her cleavage to become more exposed.

She then walked over to him, wiping the saliva from her mouth as she did. She then took the man by the hand before they both sat themselves down upon the bed.
The man nervously shifted his hands on his lap as Hati wrapped her arm around him and said,
"And what is your name?",
"Hans...my lady", replied the man,
Hati licked her lips,
"Hans, how lovely, thank you for seeing me, it gets so lonely here. Tell me, are you enjoying your time in my beautiful home?", she said,
"It's...cosy", said Hans, his voice slightly slurred from the intoxicants flowing through his blood,
Despite feeling a little uneasy, Hans made no attempt to question his circumstances or flee as he had been drugged beforehand. It was the way of the cult, all prisoners and servants were routinely given a cocktail of toxins and poisons which would make them more susceptible and agreeable to the words, commands and actions of the royal children.
It also made them less likely to attack or escape their overlords,
"You are too kind Hans, tell me are you comfortable, have you eaten well?", said Hati,
"Oh yes, very well", said Hans,
With sharp, black fingernails, Hati gently scratched Hans's arm,
"I am glad, I wouldn't want any of my beloved subjects to go hungry. No one likes to be hungry", she said as saliva began to seep from the corner of her mouth, her red and blue glowing eyes growing larger at the sight of the fat and slovenly peasant,
Noticing its shimmering beauty, Hans glanced up at the crown that Hati was wearing and couldn't help but stare at it in admiration.
Noticing that Hans was looking at her headwear, Hati said,
"Do you like my crown Hans? It belonged to my mother",

"It's very beautiful, I have never seen anything like it before", he said before smiling softly,
"Yes, my mother was said to have looked radiant in it, but I wouldn't know, she died when I was just a child", said Hati,
Hans frowned,
"I'm sorry to hear that, how did she die?", he said,
"By giving birth to me and my siblings, the pain was too much and her heart gave out. My brother Skoll has never quite gotten over it, his heart is filled with so much rage and grief", said Hati,
Seeing Hati frown, Hans placed a comforting hand on her leg before he said,
"It will be okay",
Hati smiled before she huddled up closer to Hans and said,
"You are sweet Hans, tell me, do you have a special someone in your life? Surely such a dashing and kindly young man such as yourself must have caught the eye of many lovely maidens",
"I'm afraid not my lady", said Hans,
Hati tilted her head and said,
"Really, how come?",
"I don't know, maybe I'm not their type, maybe it is because they think I am dim and ugly, lacking in both money and charm", said Hans sadly,
Hati chuckled softly before she said,
"Money isn't everything and it's not what you look like that matters, it's the quality of your character. For example, I judge a man not by his appearance, but by his...taste",
"Pardon?", asked Hans,
"You know, his hobbies, choice of literature and music, that kind of stuff", said Hati,
"I wish other girls felt the same way", said Hans sadly,
Staring straight into Hans's eyes, Hati said in a purring voice,
"Well I am not like other girls",
Getting a little flustered, Hans said,
"Yes...you are special",

It was then that Hati gently perched herself upon Hans's lap, positioning herself comfortably as to sit directly above Hans's growing bulge,
"So you think my crown is beautiful, do you think I'm beautiful?", she said as she fluttered her lashes seductively at Hans,
"Yes...you are beautiful, I have heard people saying that you are not human and that you are actually some kind of wolf in disguise, a hellhound, a monster, but I disagree, you are very beautiful and nice to talk to", he said slowly as the lower half of his body began to tingle with pleasure whilst his heart began to race,
It was then that Hati gently ran her hand across the side of Hans's face before she pulled him in closer,
"Come here", she purred,
To Hans's surprise, Hati suddenly kissed him passionately and forcefully, growling softly from deep within her throat as she pressed her lips against his, her long tongue rolling around the inside of his mouth. As they kissed, Hati could feel Hans run his hand up her thigh. It was then that Hans yelped as Hati nipped at his lip, drawing a slight trace of blood.
Licking her salivating lips, Hati began to laugh before she said,
"Come Hans, I must give you a reward for being such a gentleman. Get on the bed, take off your shirt", she cooed,
Feeling his face begin to glow with a welling up of warmth, Hans laid himself down on the bed and quickly removed his shirt. He couldn't believe his luck, no girl had ever been so forward with him before, especially not one as beautiful as Hati.
He watched as Hati joined him as she crawled up to his side,
"It's getting hot in here", she said,
Hans watched with wide eyes as Hati suddenly ripped open the top of her dress with a soft and playful moan, causing buttons to pop and go flying as she exposed her breasts.

Brushing her unfurled hair back, Hati leaned in and nuzzled Hans's chest and neck before she lightly licked against his skin. Hati squirmed with delight as she could feel the veins in Hans's neck quiver with blood. Hans watched with immense pleasure as Hati then slipped her dress off, the only thing she left on was the crown upon her head.
Hans eyed every inch of Hati's naked body with delight as she seductively removed his trousers and underwear, exposing his erect penis,
"Well, what do we have here?", she purred,
She playfully grabbed it and gave it a few tugs before licking up and down the shaft from the base to the tip.
Hans clenched his teeth and dug his fingers into the bed as Hati rolled her tongue over and around his penis, his body blooming with heat and pleasure as Hati began to suck gently.
When Hati was finished playing, she crawled over him and began to gently kiss his neck. Rather pleased with himself, Hans smiled as Hati caressed and kissed his chest.
It was then that Hati's stomach growled, which made Hans chuckle,
"Hungry are we?", he said,
"Oh yes, I am very hungry, always hungry", said Hati with almost a growl,
Hans was about to say something when Hati put her finger up to his lips,
"Shh...close your eyes, I have a surprise for you", she said,
Hans closed his eyes, grinning from ear to ear,
"Alright my princess, I await your surprise", he said,
Hans beamed with delight as he imagined what the surprise could be, something exciting he hoped, perhaps some racy lingerie or an erotic novel they could read together.
After a few seconds of silence from Hati, Hans said,
"Everything alright?",
"Give me a minute", sung Hati,
Hans waited impatiently as the seconds wore on, it was then that Hati said,
"Okay, you can open now",

Hans then opened his eyes, eager for his surprise. But as his eyesight adjusted to the light, he saw that Hati's face had changed and shapeshifted into a wolf's head, her black fur glistening with sweat, her red and blue eyes burning with excitement, madness and hunger as her muzzle was dripping with ice cold saliva.
She grinned at Hans, baring her fangs and stretching her pointed face into a crooked and twisted smile before she said with a horrible tone of voice,
"Kiss me big boy!",
Hans let out a piercing and horrified scream as Hati lunged at him with razor sharp teeth and extended claws. Some of the cultists heard the screeching and quietly fled. Accompanying the screams was the sound of tearing and scraping, the splashing of blood as it spilled onto the floor, the sound of gnawing and gnashing of teeth, the gargled cries punctuated with the sounds of snarling, the pulling of flesh and the cracking of bones.
Suddenly the screams fell silent, the only thing that could be heard was the horrible sounds of chewing and slurping.
After some time had passed, Skoll appeared as he stormed up the stairs, his armour rattling and his boots thundering against the floor as he approached the door to Hati's room.
Slamming a bloodied fist against the door, Skoll barked,
"Hati get yourself ready, the ritual will be starting soon",
"Come in my darling brother", came a voice,
Skoll pushed the door open and entered the room, coming to a standstill as he saw a most horrific sight. Though it didn't faze him in the slightest, to a mortal man of weak constitution, it was enough to make one heave.
The bed was soddened with pools of blood, upon it lay Hati, her skin was blood-soaked and she was squirming with delight as she chewed upon a raw and bloody bone. Next to her lay the mutilated corpse of Hans.

There was little of him left, he had been disembowelled and torn apart, his steaming entrails were strung across the blankets, his chest and ribcage had been forcefully ripped open, his limbs were stripped of flesh and most of his head was missing.
Hati's face was now human again, but her teeth were still sharp and gory. As she gorged herself on bloody raw meat, she glanced over at Skoll.
With a big and satisfied grin on her face, she adjusted her crown and said,
"Welcome brother, help yourself to leftovers",
"What are you doing?!", growled Skoll,
Hati rolled herself onto her stomach as she began to chew on some sinews and stomach lining,
"I was hungry and I needed to feed. I love fat people, especially fat boys, so plump, so porcine, their bellies are so soft and succulent. Not to mention their bones are fit to bursting with juicy marrow, their livers slick and greasy with fat like rich pâté and their hearts, oh their hearts are the best, ossified with fat, their arteries are clogged so when you bite them, they burst with heavenly cream", she said,
Licking her bloody lips, Hati continued to feed, causing Skoll to slam a fist down upon the nearby table with such force that it made the mirror shake and nearly cracked the table.
Seeing Skoll glare angrily at her, Hati lifted herself off the bed as she picked her teeth with a sharp bone,
"I'd appreciate it if you didn't destroy my belongings", she said,
"Look at the state of you, you are a mess!", snarled Skoll,
Hati scoffed,
"Oh calm yourself brother, I'll be ready for the ceremony I promise", she said,
"You'd better be, I will be damned if I have to postpone the resurrection just because you're being a gluttonous bitch!", spat Skoll,
"Relax, I'll quickly wash and be down as quickly as possible", said Hati,

"Good, remember Hati, you are the Princess of Wolves, it's time you started acting like it", snarled Skoll before he left and slammed the door behind him,
Hati smirked as she threw herself down upon the bed, flexing her fingers and stretching out her body as she squirmed in the blood and gore.
Turning to Hans's corpse, Hati said,
"I'd better be going now, thank you for such a lovely meal",
After kissing what was left of Hans's face, Hati ran her hand across his broken trunk, playfully wrapping some veins and arteries around her fingers,
"It was nothing personal, I just can't help myself, a girl's gotta eat after all and I do enjoy playing with my food", she said,
Hati stared at the corpse lying beside her for a moment before her smile widened and she said,
"Why Hans, you've lost weight",
Suddenly Hati burst out laughing, giggling and chuckling sinisterly to herself as she laid herself flat upon the bed and howled with maniacal laughter.
Suddenly there came the sound of a loud and deep howl which resonated throughout Ulfholl, it was a cry summoning the cultists to the deepest and darkest part of the fortress, the ritual chamber which sat in the dark bowels of Ulfholl.
Hati lifted her head up before she sighed and got off the bed, making her way towards a nearby door as she started preparing herself for what was soon to come.
The ritual chamber was dark, cavernous and bitterly cold, its walls were towering and it's ceiling seemed to stretch eternally into shadow.
The chamber was lit by hundreds of glowing crystals and at the bottom of the chamber was a great stone circle carved into the floor and divided into rings. The outer rings were carved with large runes whilst inside the inner rings were carved an intricate series of symbols that interwove with one another. The circle was gigantic and dwarfed the crowds standing around it.

Standing before the circle was a raised dais, a large stone platform decorated with red flags bearing the black crest of Fenrir. In the centre of the dais was a podium which was sitting before a long and narrow walkway that stretched over the edge of the circle. At the end of this walkway was a small pedestal topped with obsidian glass that was moulded and cut into a wolf's head with an open maw and glass eyes.
Surrounding the edge of the circle were rows of figures wearing red robes and hoods, their heads bowed in reverence and respect, these were the Goddar, the treacherous wizards and sorceresses of the Cult of Fenris.
Beyond these mages were huddled men and women of differentiating appearance, all of them wearing the same attire, suits of steel and leather armour adorned with the crest of Fenrir. Some of them were bare headed whilst some of them were wearing or holding wolf - headed helmets. These were the cultists of Fenris, supporters of the dark wolf himself.
Behind them stood more armoured figures, but these ones were wearing suits of black steel armour and red cloaks. These figures were the Ulfhethnar, berserkers and warriors who made up Fenrir's royal guard and the elite fighting division of the army, a frightening and powerful force to be reckoned with. Unlike the other cultists who were cheering, yelling and giving off an air of childish exuberance and excitement, the Ulfhethnar were standing silently in the darkness, their red eyes glowing from within their helmets, their bodies swaying and their feet shuffling in a restless and agitated manner.
Standing upon the dais in the middle of the cavern were three figures, Drottingr Raud, Godi Haldor and a small, thin and wizened old woman with silver white hair that was styled into a bun. She looked like an old vulture, a featherless new-born chick. Her face was ghostly pale and was perched upon a tall and very thin neck. Her eyes were cold and shaded blue whilst her nose was pointed like an arrow.

She was wearing a blue dress and a silver cloak that shimmered like webbed frost. This woman was Packmaster Daghilda, Lady Superior of the Cult of Fenris who served as their leader and representative. Though she looked like a weak, small and ugly crone, she was greatly respected as a powerful witch, earning even the admiration of Fenrir himself.

The chamber seemed to be relatively quiet until the air suddenly erupted with the sound of thundering drums that boomed alongside the moan of a great horn which bellowed with a tremendous howl. It was the Augarhorn and with its roar appeared the children of Fenrir as they emerged from the entrance gate.

Skoll and Garm were wearing white and dark grey suits of armour respectively beneath black cloaks. Behind them was Hati, she was wearing a black and red dress alongside a red cloak fastened with a ruby brooch. All three of them were wearing crowns, Hati was wearing her silver crown whilst Garm was wearing a simple yet beautiful golden coronet decorated with red stones. Skoll was wearing his white wolf-headed helmet, his brow nestled by a black crown adorned with sharpened points.

The chamber echoed with the almost deafening roar of the drums, the cries of the Augarhorn and the fanatical cheers of the cultists as the children of Fenrir approached the dais. Haldor, Raud and Daghilda turned and bowed their heads as they watched Garm, Hati and Skoll take their places behind the flag draped podium. The cheers from the crowds grew louder and more intense as Skoll walked up to the podium and stared out at the adoring crowds, a rare smile appearing on his face as he raised his hand to silence the entire chamber.

To the quiet howling of wind, Skoll cleared his throat and began to speak,

"Cultists of Fenris, loyal and beloved companions all, after many centuries of wallowing and waiting in the shadows, I Skoll Fenrirsson, Firstborn of the Ironwood, Lord Imperator of the Ulfhethnar and Prince of Ulfholl announce that today, we shall finally free the King of Wolves from his prison within this very chamber!",

A jubilant roar arose from the crowds,

"With the resurrection of our exalted father, he will guide us towards glory, victory and revenge!", roared Skoll,

"Hail Fenrir, hail the King of Wolves!", cried the crowds of enraptured watchers,

Skoll and his siblings walked over to Godi Haldor, Packmaster Daghilda and Drottingr Raud before they were each presented with a long dagger made of obsidian glass. Once Haldor, Raud and Daghilda bowed and stepped back, Skoll, Hati and Garm made their way past the podium and towards the pedestal on the edge of the walkway.

The drums began to rage again, filling the air with a heavy rumbling sound. When all three of them came to a stop in front of the pedestal, the drums fell silent and the Augarhorn blared one more time before it too was silenced.

Hati, Garm and Skoll then removed the gloves from their hands before they raised their daggers above their heads,

"It was our blood that forged Gleipnir, now it will be our blood that will break the bonds that bind our father Fenrir, freeing him from this very chamber where he was sealed by Tyr and Viddar so long ago!", cried Skoll,

The crowds cheered as the children of Fenrir sliced their palms with the daggers and watched as the blood dripped into the open maw of the glass wolf statue, its mouth closing once its thirst for blood had been slaked.

The crowds watched in amazement as a steady river of blood began to flow from the dais. The blood seeped onto the circle and began to run across the floor, flowing through the rings and symbols on the floor.

It was then that Skoll glanced up at the cultists and bellowed, his voice reverberating throughout the cavern,
"Cultists, prepare yourselves for the return of your master!",
Skoll watched as the Goddar put on black wolf masks whilst the cultists put on their helmets. Together they all began to chant and sway in unison, filling the chamber with the echoes of ancient and archaic words and the sound of a terrible and blasphemous song. As they did, the drums began to thunder as the blood flowing within the circle suddenly caught fire, lighting up the entire cavern with a warm red glow.
As the cultists lifted their voices, the fires rose higher until they became towering pillars of raging flame, a mighty, swirling vortex of intense fire,
"Arise dark wolf, return to us now, return to the dominion of man!", roared Skoll,
Skoll, Hati, Garm and the Cult of Fenris watched in awe and fear as a wolf shaped shadow suddenly emerged from the fire, stretching itself over the crowds and bathing them in darkness. It was then that a creature cloaked in smoke, shadow and flame rose from the circle. Behind the towering wall of fire, the cultists could now see the dark form of a colossal, infernal and demonic wolf with long horns twisted into the shape of a crown, its orange eyes burning like rings of fire, its mouth glowing brightly against its black fur. It was Fenrir, freed from the cold depths of Niflheim.
Suddenly the flames dissipated and all the lights within the cavern went out, plunging the chamber into absolute darkness as the chanting ceased and the drums were silenced. Suspended above the circle were two flaming and piercing eyes that leered down at the frightened and awed cultists. There was the sound of heavy breathing accompanied by a deep growling and a rustling of monumental chains,
"My children…after many centuries of imprisonment, I have returned", came a booming and demonic voice,

CHAPTER XIII:
ROTTA

"It feels like we've been in these tunnels forever", grumbled John as he turned a corner, his lamp flooding the tunnel stretching before him with a warm glow,
"Don't worry, I reckon we'll be at Tarn Gren soon enough", said Einar,
"I just hope we don't bump into anything down here, I don't have a weapon", said John,
It was true as his pickaxe was destroyed by Vilhelm and he had given his dagger to Ulva in which to defend herself,
"Here, take this", said Einar as he unstrapped a sword from his back and handed it to John,
"Thanks", said John before he eyed the blade in his hand,
The sword that Einar had given him was simple in design and devoid of any decoration. Its hilt was wrapped in frayed leather and the crossbar was slightly dented, it wasn't the most grandiose of weapons, but it was comfortable to hold and would do for now.
As John, Brenna, Ulva and Einar continued making their way cautiously down the tunnel, they were startled by a loud and sudden bang that seemed to come from the other end.
With everyone drawing their weapons, John whispered,
"What the hell was that?",
"I dunno, wanna have a look?", whispered Einar,
"Fine", grumbled John,
John glanced upwards as he passed through an opening at the end of the tunnel before he found himself standing in a small stone chamber, its walls covered with dripping water and cobwebs illuminated by a slither of daylight filtering down from a crack in the ceiling. Suddenly John let out a yell as he felt something touch his bottom, nearly jumping out of his skin in fright.

The sound startled Einar, who staggered backwards and crashed into Brenna, sending them both tumbling to the ground with a metallic clatter,

"The hell?!", yelled John,

Suddenly he could hear Ulva giggling to herself,

"Goddamn it Ulva, now is not the time!", barked John,

"Sorry, I couldn't resist", said Ulva,

John sighed and rolled his eyes,

"Can you wait until later?", he said,

"I'll try, but I make no promises", said Ulva as she beamed from ear to ear,

Brenna got to his feet before helping Einar up off the floor,

"Guys, can we quit with the games? This isn't the place nor time for jokes, it will be nightfall soon and we don't have time to mess about", he said,

"Sorry, I was just having a bit of fun", said Ulva,

"Ulva with all due respect, we are not here to have fun, we are on an important mission to save your life", growled Brenna,

"Well excuse me for wanting to try and lighten the mood, Odin knows we could do with a bit of it", said Ulva,

"You can have all the fun you want once you've been cured, let us just focus on the task at hand", said Brenna,

As he walked forward, Brenna could suddenly hear Ulva huffing in anger,

"What was that?", he responded,

"Nothing, I just don't understand why you can't just have a laugh. I thought John's reaction was funny", said Ulva,

"There is nothing funny about all of this, grow up!", snarled Brenna,

"Hey, don't talk to my sister like that!", barked Einar,

"Please, your threats are empty, you'll do nothing to me because you know that I am the only one who can help save your sister", spat Brenna angrily,

"You wanna bet?!", roared Einar,

As Einar, Brenna and Ulva began to argue amongst one another, John yelled,
"Guys, be quiet! Can't you hear that?!",
Everyone fell silent and glanced around as they could hear the faint sound of chewing, the breaking of bones and a low growling sound coming from down the adjacent tunnel,
"What is that?", asked John,
"I don't know, but everyone stay on guard", whispered Brenna,
As John, Brenna, Einar and Ulva walked into the tunnel standing before them, they could hear scratching and the sound of chewing getting louder and louder.
Eventually the light of their lamps caught something up ahead, a small wooden door covered in scratch marks and cobwebs.
What startled everyone though was the unexpected sight of dusty human bones lying propped up against the corner of the door alongside a rusted weapon and a small palm sized journal,
"Is that...a body?", said John as he shuddered with fright,
"It looks like it", said Einar,
Keeping his eyes locked upon the bones in front of him, Brenna stepped forward and gently picked up the journal lying upon the floor. Brenna placed his lamp down upon the ground before he inspected the journal in his hand, its cover worn with age,
"It appears this person kept a journal", he said,
"What does it say?", asked Ulva,
With Einar lifting his lamp so that Brenna could see properly, Brenna opened the journal and began to read its contents, just able to make out the barely legible handwriting which had been scrawled down roughly with considerable haste owing to its untidy nature,
'Damn Olaf to hell, he said there would be treasure in these tunnels, but we have found nothing. Not only that, but Tarn Gren is completely empty and devoid of any riches. It is with a heavy heart and a trembling hand that I write this.

I lost Gorvik further down the tunnels and with my leg badly fractured I cannot go back to find him nor can I go any further. I am so tired and in so much pain, I was able to hide from the monsters that lurk down here by sheltering behind this door.
By remaining silent in the darkness, they lost sight and interest of me and left. If anyone finds this, please tell my beloved husband, Dangeir of Gallerheim that I love him and that I am sorry for leaving him and the children alone. May we one day be reunited in Valhalla – Abbi Fanvolkull.
"How tragic, the poor girl", said Einar,
Stuffing the journal into his bag, Brenna said,
"If we ever get to Gallerheim, I am sure this Dangeir would appreciate hearing about his wife's fate",
"Must have been terrible for her, down here all alone and afraid. I hope she found peace", said Ulva,
"What did she mean by monsters?", said John,
"I don't know, but we should keep moving, there's no point further dwelling on it here", said Brenna before he slowly and cautiously opened the door in front of him,
As John, Brenna, Einar and Ulva wandered into another chamber that looked exactly like the one that they had just left, they could see where the sound of the scratching and chewing was coming from. In the middle of the room was a cat, a tabby with golden fur and stripes. It was eating and playing with what looked like some dead rodents.
As John entered the room first, the cat looked up and began to purr as it noticed John and his friends. Flicking its tail, the cat stepped forward with little padded feet and stared at them curiously,
"Don't worry guys, it's just a little kitty", said John,
Suddenly everyone let out a terrified yell as something leapt from the darkness and pounced the poor cat. The cat let out a piercing screech before it was torn to shreds by some horrible creature. The creature hissed and spat as it tore bloody chunks of flesh off the screaming feline.

As the cat's squeals died down, the creature turned to face John and his companions. It was a black rat, but unlike normal rats, this one was over twice the size of the cat it had attacked. The rat glared with white and monstrous eyes and let out a nasty and revolting hiss before it suddenly leapt forward with sharp claws and large yellow teeth.
John yelped as the rat struck the side of his sword with a clang. The rat scuttled backwards, shaking its head as its mouth foamed with blood. The rat then struck again, but this time John caught the vile creature with the tip of his sword, slicing its throat open.
The rat hissed before it bled out upon the floor and expired, "Is it dead?", gasped Ulva,
Lightly tapping the rat's body with the tip of his sword, John said,
"Yes, it's dead",
Suddenly there came a loud hiss as another rat suddenly emerged from a nearby hole. The rat glanced at Ulva before it lunged at her.
Ulva screamed as it hooked onto her arms with clawed feet before it tried to take a bite out of her face,
"Get it off me!", cried Ulva as she tried to rip the creature away from her chest,
Einar quickly rushed forward and snatched up the rat, holding it as it thrashed and squirmed about before he slammed it hard against the wall, the rat squeaking as its skull cracked upon impact.
Panting heavily, Einar dropped the rat before he said to Ulva, "Are you okay?",
Brushing her hair back as she shook with fright, Ulva said, "Yeah, yeah I think I'm okay",
"Were you injured?", said John,
Ulva shook her head before Brenna said,
"Come on, let's...",

Suddenly there came angry hisses as several giant rats rushed out of the nearby hole, growling and arching their backs as they glared at John, Einar, Brenna and Ulva,
"Run!", yelled Brenna,
As the rats lunged at them, John, Einar, Ulva and Brenna fled down the nearby tunnel, running as fast as they could whilst their lamps swung in the dark. To the sound of footsteps and scurrying feet, Einar, John, Ulva fled down another dark tunnel before they found themselves standing in another chamber.
It looked exactly like the previous two, but this one was much larger and there was a small stream of water trickling through the centre of it,
"Where do we go now?", said John,
"Over there", said Brenna as he pointed towards a dark opening that sat on the other side of the chamber,
Suddenly there came a scream of terror from Ulva as hordes of giant rats suddenly began pouring out of the walls through cracks and large holes. Like a great flood of fur and scurrying claws, the rats rushed forward with their teeth glistening and their eyes glowing against the lamplight,
"Hurry, let's go!", cried Einar,
Einar, John, Ulva and Brenna raced out of the chamber as the rats scurried after them, squeaking and hissing menacingly as they gave chase.
As John's eyes adjusted to the darkness ahead of him, he gasped as he saw a large door emerge,
"Quick, through here!", he yelled,
After John quickly pushed the door open, Brenna, Ulva and Einar dashed through before John looked back and saw hundreds of rats rushing towards him with bared teeth and lolling tongues, their beady eyes glistening in the gloom as their claws scraped against the stone floor. As the rats lunged forward, John slammed the door shut and locked it tight.

The air was filled with the sound of loud thudding and scraping claws as the rats slammed their bodies against the door and scratched at the wood. John, Einar, Brenna and Ulva watched anxiously, hoping that the rats wouldn't get in. Suddenly the scratching, hissing and screeching fell silent and for a moment, John, Einar, Ulva and Brenna thought that the rats had fled.

Unfortunately there was a loud crash as the door suddenly exploded into a shower of splinters, the air filling with the sound of shrieking rats as they burst forth through the broken door and rushed forward as fast as their little legs could carry them,

"Shit!", barked Brenna before him and his friends hightailed it down the tunnel with all haste,

After running through darkness for what seemed like an eternity, John, Einar, Brenna and Ulva suddenly noticed light at the end of the tunnel illuminating what looked like a ladder,

"Look, a way out!", shouted John,

"Hurry!", cried Einar,

John quickly climbed up the ladder and as he got to the top, he saw the bottom of a trapdoor. John pushed it open with a hard thrust, causing light to burst from above. John grunted and strained as he pulled himself up out of the hole before he began helping up Ulva, Brenna and Einar as the sound of hissing and scurrying rats filled his ears.

Once everyone was safely pulled up through the trapdoor, John, Einar, Ulva and Brenna watched as the rats rushed the ladder and began to climb it, snarling as they clambered upwards,

"What are we going to do?!", cried Ulva,

Einar quickly grabbed the edge of the trapdoor and slammed it down before locking it. John, Einar, Brenna and Ulva watched nervously as the rats pounded and thrashed against the underside of the door, causing it to rattle loudly as it bounced on its hinges.

Eventually though the sound of angry rats faded away as the horrible rodents scarpered and fled, much to everyone's relief,
"Oh thank the gods", sighed Brenna,
Feeling cold wind blowing against their faces, John, Einar, Ulva and Brenna turned round to find themselves standing in a large and cavernous chamber with towering stone walls. As they glanced around, they spotted a most curious sight, rows of red barrels daubed with white paint that were stacked high towards the ceiling,
"Where are we?", asked John,
"Tarn Gren", said Brenna,

CHAPTER XIV:
TARN GREN

Before anyone could say anything, a loud and sudden thud struck the bottom of the trapdoor, causing Ulva to let out a scream as the noise startled her.
Suddenly there came a gruff sounding voice from the top of some nearby stairs,
"Is anyone there?",
"Quick, hide", whispered Brenna,
Extinguishing their lamps, John, Einar, Ulva and Brenna quickly dived behind some barrels and peered through the small gaps between them. As John huddled close to one of the barrels, he could smell the scent of rusted iron and could taste copper upon his lips as he inhaled the aroma.
Glancing curiously at the barrel sitting before him, John suddenly felt a chill run down his spine as he realized what the barrel contained,
"Exploding powder, here?", he said,
As John pondered upon the implications of such a volatile and dangerous subject being stored beneath the Gormwood, he noticed a shadow appear down the nearby stairs. At the entrance of the chamber stood a man wearing a suit of leather and steel armour, across which was fastened a black leather strap attached to a belt. Across his right arm above the elbow was a red armband adorned with the black crest of Fenrir. The man was also wearing a helmet shaped like a wolf head and around his neck was hung a pendant that looked like some sort of strange symbol. The man walked slowly into the chamber, his breathing heavy and muffled by the helm he was wearing.
As the man walked through an opening between the stacks of barrels, John could hear him inhaling deeply as he scented the air,
"I swear I heard something", said the man,

John quietened his breathing as he could feel the man's presence. The wolf – headed man suddenly came to a halt and glanced around with cold, unblinking eyes as he tried to locate the source of the mysterious noise. Much to John's relief however, the armoured man walked away and stomped over to the trapdoor.

Staring forward, Brenna noticed the symbol on the man's arm, a symbol that filled him with dread,

"Oh no, the Cult of Fenris", he uttered in shock,

Suddenly there came the voice of a woman as another figure appeared near the stairs wearing the same uniform, helmet and pendant as her male companion,

"Olaf, what are you doing?", she said,

"I swear I heard something down here Sibbi, almost like a scream", said Olaf,

"Well you can investigate later, come on we need to go, Godi Vulpes is about to make an important announcement and we don't want to be late", said Sibbi,

"Fine, but I swear I heard something", said Olaf,

"You sure you are not drunk?", laughed Sibbi,

"No, I know what I heard", growled Olaf,

As Sibbi and Olaf left, John and his friends cautiously crept out from their hiding places.

Adjusting his purple tinted spectacles, Brenna said in a hushed tone of voice,

"Right let's go but we need to be careful, if we are caught, the chances of us getting out of here with Vulthur are very slim",

"Who were those people? They look rather menacing", asked Einar,

"Yeah and did anyone notice the armband they were wearing? It looked like some sort of symbol, a wolf wearing a crown", said Ulva,

"I saw it too, what was it?", said John,

"The crest of Fenrir, it is a symbol worn by the followers of Fenrir. It means that this fortress is home to the Cult of Fenris", said Brenna,

"The Cult of Fenris?", asked Ulva,

"They are the fanatical followers of Fenrir, they are losers, terrorists, murderers, anarchists, lunatics and twisted deviants. It is believed that they have been hiding in the shadows waiting for their master to return to Norway. Little is truly known about them as they are secretive, even I'll admit I don't know a lot about them and for a long time I thought they were just a myth. But considering they are inside the home of Vulpes, I bet he is involved with them somehow, we just need to find out why", said Brenna,

"Why would people ally themselves with the monster that cursed this land with the wolfblight?", asked John,

"I am not sure, but whatever the reason, we need to be careful, these people are dangerous and they have no qualms about brutally murdering innocents", said Brenna,

"So what's the plan?", asked Einar,

"We find Vulpes, retrieve Vulthur and leave as quietly and as quickly as possible, we don't want to stir up the cult", said Brenna,

"So the Cult of Fenris worship and follow Fenrir, does that mean they are werewolves too?", asked Ulva,

"I don't know, but if they are, then that means Tarn Gren is full of them and that means we are in more danger than I thought", grimaced Brenna,

"Come let us be off, we are wasting time standing around here", said John,

"Indeed, our first step is locating some disguises and finding out where Vulpes is, perhaps one of the cultists can tell us", said Brenna,

"Sounds like a very difficult and taunting task", said Einar,

"I know...but we have no other choice", said Brenna sadly,

Summoning up their courage, John, Brenna, Einar and Ulva quietly snuck past the barrels and crept up the stairs, keeping an eye out for any cultists that might appear. With their weapons drawn, they came to a long corridor with high stone walls decorated with large red and black flags bearing the crest of Fenrir.

After glancing around, John, Einar, Ulva and Brenna quickly made their way down the corridor.
But just as they were about to turn the corner at the far end, they came face to face with Olaf and Sibbi,
"Intruders!", barked Olaf,
Before Olaf and Sibbi could react, Einar and Brenna pounced on them with a crash.
With a heave, Einar grabbed Olaf by the neck and violently twisted it with a crack whilst Brenna cut Sibbi's throat, silencing her cries before she bled to death.
As Brenna and Einar got to their feet, two more cultists appeared,
"What's going on here?!", barked one of the cultists,
John quickly punched the cultist in the face, sending his helmet flying with a crash. He then quickly and deeply stabbed him in the stomach and chest, causing the cultist to collapse to the floor in a pool of his blood.
Meanwhile Ulva stabbed the other cultist in the heart, puncturing his armour and killing him instantly,
"Quickly see if their uniforms fit, we'll need them if we are to get around Tarn Gren undetected", said Brenna,
Brenna, Ulva, John and Einar immediately began to strip the uniforms from the dead cultists and spent a few minutes trying them on to see if they fit. Ignoring the smell and the fact the armour was blood-soaked, they were just able to squeeze into the uniforms. Placing on their wolf - headed helmets, everyone collected up the dead bodies off the floor and carefully hid them amongst the barrels in the basement. Realizing there was quite a bit of blood marking the floor, John, Brenna, Einar and Ulva wasted no time in hanging about and hastily made their way down the corridor. Turning the corner, they came face to face with a large foyer area. To the left was a massive gate with large locks between two cloaked guards.
On the right was an archway which led to a large hall where uniformed cultists were gathering. On the other side of the foyer sat a large staircase that led to other parts of the tower.

As John and his friends stepped into the foyer area, they were met by a cultist who said,
"Olaf, Sibbi, Thorkeld, Gorvik, did you find the source of the noise in the basement when you went to check?",
None of them answered and simply glanced at each other nervously,
"Well?", barked the cultist, his voice resonating against the inside of his helm,
"Um...we think it might have been a hobgoblin, but we found nothing", grunted John,
"Good, now get your asses into the hall, Lord Vulpes is about to deliver some important news and it is of the highest priority that we hear it", said the cultist,
"Yes, right away", said John,
John and his companions made their way through the archway and entered the hall, which was a long chamber illuminated by flaming torches, the walls were lined with red banners and at the back sat a large flag - draped stage and a podium. As the cultists quickly rushed in to fill the space, John noticed that the back of the hall was the first to be filled as the cultists were hesitant to stand at the front.
Walking to the front alongside Einar, Brenna and Ulva, he observed the men and women standing around him. He noticed that some of the cultists were tall and thin whilst some of them were short and potbellied, their faces ranging from handsome and beautiful to ugly, grotesque and ghoulish. Despite the varying differences between them however, the cultists all had three things in common. Firstly, all of them were wearing the same attire, brown and black uniforms made of both leather and steel.
Secondly none of them were wearing any footwear or gloves and finally, all of them had an intimidating air about them, there was something off about them and neither John nor his friends could understand why.

Perhaps it was the malicious attire they were wearing, perhaps it was their wolfish eyes, their sharpened teeth or unnerving behaviour. Whatever the reason, it made John and his friends uneasy.

It was then to everyone's surprise that Einar suddenly walked towards one of the cultists and tapped him on the shoulder, "What are you doing?!", gasped Brenna,

"Gonna learn a bit more about who we are up against", said Einar,

The cultist turned round and said in a muffled voice, "Yes, can I help you?",

"Excuse me, but I am new here, I'd like to know more about the Cult of Fenris", said Einar,

Laughing from beneath his helmet, the man said boisterously, "Ah hello there, my name is Jormund and may I welcome you to Tarn Gren and to the Cult of Fenris. Well to answer your question, the Cult of Fenris is more than just a group or an organization, we are a family, a fellowship comprising of those who follow Fenrir. We carry out his will to ensure his plans come to fruition", said Jormund,

"Plans?", asked Einar,

"Oh yes, the dark wolf has plans for this world, plans that will change this land forever and for the better. We not only support his cause, but we all joined for personal reasons", said Jormund,

"Such as?", said Einar,

Jormund silently pointed at a man nearby, a tall man with short tufted blond hair,

"See Arnskr over there? Was bullied for most of his life and got no respect or affection from anyone, not even his own family. Now he has both love and respect from all his brothers and sisters, he's never been happier", he said,

Jormund then pointed at a nearby elderly couple who were roaring with laughter as they talked to one another,
"Over there is Bertrygg and Gitta, they both suffered greatly from poor health due to their age and found it difficult to do anything. Now thanks to the cult and the wolfblood flowing through their veins, they are healthy and fighting fit. It is as if they are thirty again", he said,
Jormund then glanced towards four teenagers standing near the wall in a huddled circle.
There were two boys and two girls all chatting away together and looking rather content in each other's company,
"Those kids over there are Ari, Bjork, Runar and Hemming. Ari was a farmer's son, he found farm life tiresome and wanted to travel the land experiencing endless thrills and adventure. Hemming and Runar were orphans who spent many years outside in the cold, unloved and forgotten", he said,
"How awful", said Einar,
"But we took them in when no one else would and we gave them a home and a family. Bjork meanwhile belonged to a noble family bearing an ancient bloodline of mighty warriors. Despite her lineage, Bjork was born lame and could never meet the expectations of her peers and family. Bjork wanted to overcome her weakness and become more powerful than any of her ancestors ever were. Now the wolfblood has empowered her, allowing her to cast off her disability and shine like a true warrior. You see my friends, we all joined Fenrir and his cult out of wanting a sense of purpose and belonging, to take revenge against a society that has rejected and hurt us. We are the forgotten, the rejected and the deviant. Where we were homeless, we now have a home, where we were once shunned, we are now embraced and where we were wanting of happiness, companionship and power, we have it all and more", said Jormund,
"And you?", asked Einar,

"I joined many years ago because I lost my wife, my son, my brother and my father in a werewolf attack, the same attack that inflicted the wolfblight onto myself and my two daughters. Knowing we wouldn't find a cure in time, we decided to join Fenrir so that we would be able to control our turnings rather than lose our humanity to the terrible disease. It is the unfortunate and tragic case for many of my brothers and sisters here", said Jormund,
Einar's eyes widened,
"Wait a minute, you are...?", he said,
"Yes I am a werewolf, just like everyone else here. Arnskr became more confident thanks to his newfound strength and Bertrygg, Bjork and Gitta are healthier and more active thanks to the wolfblood running through their veins. We are stronger than we have ever been and the best part is that our humanity and minds are kept intact, only our bodies are changed by lycanthropy", said Jormund,
"So you are a werewolf who can shapeshift at will?", asked Ulva,
"Yes, I realized that if you can't beat them, join them. I came to understand that there is no cure to this wolfblight and eventually it will infect everyone throughout all of Scandinavia. So instead of trying to run from it, my family and I joined this cult because at least now I can control myself and protect the ones I love from destruction. Instead of being bitten against our will by some mindless monster, we found a different way. By surrendering ourselves to the wolfblood, not only can we transform at will, but in both forms we retain our minds and our humanity. We can also change at any time; we don't have to wait until nightfall. In this we are not helpless victims of a disease, we are instead liberated from the fear of the wolfblight", said Jormund,
Everyone's blood ran cold with dread,
"You said that Fenrir had plans for this world, what are they?", asked Einar,

Jormund folded his arms and said,
"You should know, he wants to finish what he was sent out to do all those years ago, gift everyone in Norway with the wolfblight and begin making this world a better place for all. Anyway I should go, Vulpes will be here soon and I don't want to miss his speech",
As Jormund walked away, Einar said,
"Well at least now we know what the cult is, why it exists and why people join Fenrir",
"What Jormund said does indeed explain a lot and now we know that Vulpes is indeed in league with the Cult of Fenris, there is no doubt about it", said Brenna,
"But it still doesn't answer why Vulpes wants Vulthur", said John,
"Perhaps we will find out in a few moments, it sounds like Vulpes is going to make some kind of announcement", said Ulva,
"So what do you guys think?", asked Einar,
"Well, from what Jormund was saying, they believe that joining the cult is their best chance of survival against the wolfblight and that membership gives them fulfilment. It's illogical thinking influenced by fanatical lunacy and paranoia. But then again, I have seen some truly horrible turnings in my time and I have seen a lot of good people lost to the wolfblight. If I knew that there was another way to live instead of suffering from such an awful affliction, I would at least consider it", said Brenna,
"I think it's all ridiculous, Jormund talked like he was brainwashed, no normal human being would ever think that any of this was good or normal. It's madness to think that the best option to save themselves from the wolfblight is to surrender to it. Worst part about this is that they are idolizing the very being that brought it here in the first place. Fenrir is evil and will always be evil, it is in his nature to be wicked. No good can come from following him", growled John,
"What do you make of all of this Ulva?", asked Einar,

"Being able to control the wolf within me does sound like a good idea. I remember back to my first turning and it was horrible. I wouldn't wish that pain and suffering on anyone, so at least being able to shapeshift without pain whilst keeping myself in control does sound tempting and strangely comforting", she said,
"You can't be serious", said John,
"However you are right John, we are humans, silly, fallible, scared, amazing humans and we do not need this power. We are strong enough to survive and thrive without the wolfblight and we will one day overcome it together. We do not need such an affliction and we certainly do not need Fenrir, his children or this stupid little cult", said Ulva,
"I have no real comment regarding the situation, this is all complicated and I care little for these cultists, I only care about curing my sister", said Einar,
"It's a good thing everyone around us is too wrapped up in their own lives to pay attention to us. If they heard what we were saying, we would be in real trouble for spouting such blasphemies", said John,
"Thankfully we haven't raised any suspicion yet, so we should count ourselves lucky and just focus on the task at hand", said Brenna,
"I think it's because they are a bit stupid in the head, being warped and brainwashed will have that effect", huffed John,
Suddenly John, Einar, Ulva and Brenna were startled as the doors behind them slammed shut now that the hall was completely full,
"I don't like this at all", uttered John,
The lights suddenly began to dim as the cultists glanced at the illuminated podium standing before them. Becoming increasingly frightened, Ulva grabbed John's hand and held it tightly. Einar and Brenna huddled closer too, nervous at what might happen next. It was then that the air was filled with the sound of applause and cheering as a figure appeared on stage. The figure that stepped up to the podium was Godi Vulpes, gleefully smiling from ear to ear.

As Vulpes outstretched his arms, the cheers got louder before Vulpes raised his hand to silence the cultists,
"Brothers and sisters, I thank you for your attendance this evening, I welcome you all wholeheartedly on this momentous day. With pride and joy in my heart, it is here and now that I make this announcement, the fires of Ulfholl have been relit and our exalted father Fenrir has returned!", he cried,
Brenna, Einar, Ulva and Einar stood aghast at Vulpes's words, their stomachs churning and their bodies beginning to quake in fear as rapturous cheering rang out around them,
"Hail Fenrir, hail Fenrir!", cried the cultists,
"In addition to this most wondrous news, we finally have Vulthur the Vargslayer in our possession!", barked Vulpes, who then held up the glistening dagger to the crowd, driving them wild with delight,
"There it is", whispered John,
"But how do we get it?", replied Einar,
"I don't know, but let us wait and see what Vulpes does next", said Ulva softly,
Brenna did not respond for he was trembling with anger and was struggling to contain his emotions,
"You know what this is don't you my brothers and sisters? It is an artefact of great power that can cure a person of lycanthropy", said Vulpes,
John and his friends were startled when the cultists suddenly began to boo, jeer and utter angry cries and howls, enraged by Vulpes's scathing words,
"This dagger has the power to ruin Fenrir's plans of spreading the wolfblight across Norway and finishing what he started all those years ago. We cannot allow that to happen, which is why Prince Garm himself is coming here to personally collect the Vargslayer and take it with him back to Ulfholl where it will be destroyed", said Vulpes,
"So that is why he wanted the dagger, he wants to destroy the only thing that can purge this land of the wolfblight, the one thing that can save Ulva", gasped John,

"Once Vulthur and Fenrir's Bane have been destroyed, our father Fenrir shall initiate the final stage of his plan and bring glory to the cult. But for now do not let that concern you my brothers and sisters. As we await the arrival of Garm, we shall celebrate and enjoy this victory and make ourselves merry with cheer and joy!", yelled Vulpes,

As the hall erupted with more applause, howling and cheering, John and his friends watched as Vulpes made his way off the stage and disappeared out of sight amongst armoured guards.

Now feeling calmer and more in control of his emotions, Brenna turned to his friends and said,

"So now we know why Vulpes wanted the dagger, this revelation is more frightening than anything I could have imagined. I thought initially that Vulpes was a mere collector, then I thought he was a man wanting to cure his lycanthropy. Now we know the truth, he is one of the thirteen Lords of the Cult of Fenris, more specifically the Lord of Clan Gren. Not only that, but Vulpes is serving an ancient monster that I thought was sealed away centuries ago by the seven heroes of legend. This goes beyond wanting to help Ulva, the very kingdom is in grave danger",

"The thirteen Lords?", queried John,

"I don't know much about them, heck I don't even know their names, but according to my research, the Cult of Fenris is divided into clans or packs and each one is ruled by an elected leader", said Brenna before he glanced at Ulva,

"My dear, I promised you that I would get you to Coldwood and cure you of your affliction, but years ago I also promised myself that I would not only rid the world of the wolfblight, but I would also stop Fenrir if he ever returned. Once we have secured you a cure, I must ensure that his plans do not come to fruition, whatever they may be. I cannot allow him to spread the wolfblight further and allow years of hard work to be undone", he said,

Turning to his friends, Brenna then said,
"But I cannot do this alone, that is why I am asking you all for your help. Will you all assist me in stopping Fenrir from carrying out his malicious plot?",
"Of course I will, I don't know how much help I'll be, but I will do everything I can to save the people of this kingdom and the land that I love. You are going to help me, so it is only fair that I help you in return", replied Ulva,
"Count me in, I do not wish to experience the unending nightmare of a world ruled by Fenrir and his monstrous werewolves", said Einar,
"I guess I'll help too, I mean helping Ulva has been and will continue to be my priority, but Norway needs help and I for one will not run away in fear nor stand by whilst these monsters threaten to ruin more lives. Fenrir and his followers have cruelly desecrated my wife, igniting her blood with flame and filth and now they threaten everyone and everything I love, I will not stand for it", said John,
"I...thank you my friends, it is a lot to ask of you I know, but from the bottom of my heart, thank you. We shall see to it that Fenrir is thrown back into the void from whence he came and all the monsters that follow him shall be destroyed. Ulva will be cleansed of the wolfblight and the land shall be saved", said Brenna,
"It sounds like a tall order, so what's our first move?", asked Einar,
"Retrieve Vulthur and set off for Coldwood with all haste", said Brenna,
"And then what?", said John,
Brenna shrugged,
"I don't know how we are going to get rid of Fenrir, but let's just take it one step at a time and focus on curing Ulva for the time being", he said,
Brenna turned round to face the door as the cultists were slowly making their way out, laughing and talking as they did,
"Let's go", he said,

John, Brenna, Einar and Ulva slowly and carefully moved through the crowd and walked back into the foyer area, which was now buzzing with activity. Some of the cultists were now clutching drinking horns and were drinking in great draughts sweet mead, cherry cider and spiced blood wines. Pushing their way through the hordes of celebrating cultists, they saw a flight of stairs nearby and began to make their way up, hoping it would lead them deeper into the tower and closer towards Vulpes,

"Right, let's look around and find out where Vulpes went", said Brenna,

After climbing the stairs, Brenna glanced around to find himself standing in a long corridor. Nearby were some wide-eyed servants with vacant and blank looks on their faces. Walking up to a young girl garbed in a plain dress, Brenna asked in a gentle tone of voice,

"Excuse me young lady, but I have some urgent information for the Godi, where might I find him?",

"Lord Vulpes? I am not sure; he was meant to be downstairs making an announcement. If he's not there, then he's either in the council room or in his bedroom", said the girl,

Brenna reached into his pocket and handed the girl two silver pennies,

"My thanks child", said Brenna before he turned back to his friends,

"Right, if we split up, we can cover more ground in a quicker amount of time. Ulva, we'll check Vulpes's bedroom, John and Einar, you investigate the council room", he said,

"Right, let's go Einar", said John,

"Good luck everyone", said Einar,

After planting a kiss on Ulva's iron cheek, John made his way down the corridor with Einar in tow before they both disappeared out of sight,

"I don't like this Brenna, I have a feeling that something bad is going to happen, the atmosphere of this place feels wrong", said Ulva,

"It's probably nothing to worry about, now let's go, time is short", said Brenna,
After everyone had split up, John and Einar found themselves at the end of a corridor lit with sapphire lanterns. Coming to a tall and arched doorway, they slowly reached for their weapons and opened the door before peering through. They saw in front of them a large and dimly lit room with a ceiling that seemed to soar high above their heads. In the centre of the room was a large and circular stone table with ten empty chairs.
Standing behind the table was Vulpes who had his back turned. He was looking at a giant mirror that was suspended in front of him, a mirror that had been hewn from a sparkling white crystal. The mirror was massive and shone with a blazing, glistening light. With his face lit up with delight, Vulpes raised his arms and began speaking an incantation in a language neither John nor Einar could understand.
John and Einar watched in awe as the surface of the mirror suddenly began to shimmer and ripple before a face appeared in the fractals of the crystalline mirror.
The face was of a man with a chiselled and bearded chin, thick soot grey hair and yellow wolfish eyes, it was Garm,
"Godi Vulpes, it is good to see you, how fares the pack of Gren?", he said,
"Quite well my prince, they are jubilant in hearing of your father's return and eagerly await your arrival", said Vulpes,
"Tell me Vulpes you cunning fox, do you have Vulthur the Vargslayer?", said Garm,
Vulpes pulled the dagger from his pocket and held it up before the mirror, a sight which made Garm's smile widen,
"Excellent, most excellent, my father and siblings will be thrilled. I shall inform them at once. Tell your followers that I shall be there with all haste, I look forward to meeting them", he said,
"It shall be done", said Vulpes,

To the sound of distant and rumbling thunder outside the tower, Garm silently stared unblinkingly at Vulpes before he frowned and said,
"Vulpes, there is something I must ask you",
"Anything", said Vulpes,
"When you tried to get Vulthur, I heard that you attacked a young woman...is this true?", he said,
Vulpes's smile faded,
"Yes, I had hoped that my appearance would have compelled her to hand over the dagger without bloodshed, but things went sour", he said,
"Is she and her companions dead?", growled Garm,
"No my prince, last time I saw her she was in Gormstad. That fool Vilhelm failed to have her killed and before either of us could finish the job, we were forced to flee", said Vulpes,
"What was her name?", said Garm,
"Ulva Forrester, a librarian and wife of a miner named John", said Vulpes,
"So she is still alive? This is not good news and not good for you. Our mission involves a great deal of secrecy and we cannot afford to let people get wind of our plans and our existence, at least not until Vulthur and Fenrir's Bane have been destroyed. You should have made sure Ulva and any witnesses were killed before claiming the dagger without a fuss, but instead I find out that they are still alive. They might learn of what you are, who you work for and even might end up finding out about our plans. Our secrecy has been potentially compromised by your actions", said Garm,
"Forgive me your highness please", begged Vulpes,
"It is disappointing that you have made such a grievous and foolhardy mistake. You know that failure will not be tolerated and you know the price of failure don't you?", snarled Garm,
It was then that Vulpes put his hands together and began to plead,
"Please no, I am sorry, I will fix this, I promise!",

Garm snarled suddenly at Vulpes, his eyes glowing with rage as a sudden boom of thunder crashed outside,
"See that you do Vulpes, once our conversation here has concluded, return to Gormstad, find the girl and kill her. If she has any friends or relatives that are aware of what happened, eliminate them by any means necessary, leave no trace of your deed intact. When I come down there in a few days' time, I want their corpses presented to me, bloody and lifeless, am I clear?", he growled,
"Yes most omnipotent and great prince of wolves", said Vulpes, his hands shaking in fear,
"Good to know that we have come to a mutual understanding. Fail this Godi Vulpes and I will have to reconsider your position within this organization", growled Garm,
Vulpes bared his teeth and clenched his fists,
"I will not let you down, I swear it", he hissed,
Garm scowled at Vulpes and said in a gravelly tone,
"Good, in the meanwhile see that the tower is ready for my arrival, enjoy your evening Vulpes, do not fail me",
The mirror suddenly flashed before going silent and dark to the sound of ominous thunder as the frightening visage of Garm vanished, leaving Vulpes alone and shaking with fear,
"If I don't find them soon, I am a dead man", uttered Vulpes,
"So what now?", whispered John,
"We sneak up behind him, cut the bastard's throat and take the dagger", whispered Einar,
John nodded in agreement and both him and Einar slowly and carefully crept towards Vulpes, drawing their swords as they did. As they moved towards Vulpes, they noticed the old man begin to sniff the air. As they got closer and closer, John and Einar slowly lifted themselves from their crouched positions and as they got within striking distance of Vulpes, they lifted their weapons, ready to deliver the killing blows.

Suddenly Vulpes wheeled round and blasted them off their feet in a rush of wind, sending John and Einar flying across the room before they landed with a crash, receiving a glancing and painful blow from the floor. John winced in pain as his vision spun and his side erupted with pain. He turned to see Einar was groaning and clutching his chest as he coughed violently.

John glanced forward and saw Vulpes walking towards him, his face contorted into a furious look of disgust,

"Well, well, well what do we have here?", he hissed,

Pulling the helmets off John and Einar and tossing them aside with a clang, Vulpes's eyes widened as he looked upon their faces,

"So it's you two, came all this way to get Vulthur back? Well that is not going to happen, I will make sure that you and your little friends trouble me no more. I cannot and will not fail Prince Garm again. He will kill me for failing to deliver the dagger to him and eliminating all suspects to my deeds. You have seen and learnt too much and thus you must be erased", he said,

John glared at Vulpes,

"You bastard, you think you have won? I will be leaving here with that dagger, mark my words!", he snarled,

"Oh I think not and I will make sure that you die most painfully", said Vulpes,

As John groaned in pain, Vulpes lowered himself down, bringing his face closer to John's as his ghoulish eyes glared menacingly at him,

"You know it didn't have to be this way right? You could have just simply given me the dagger and none of this would have happened. Not only would you now be richer and happier, but you wouldn't be here bleeding and your wife certainly would not be under the influence of the wolfblight", he said,

As Vulpes straightened his back, he said to John,
"This is your own doing, you thought you would be a great husband by giving your wife a gift, well look how that turned out, your folly will cost you your life and that of your loved ones",
Before John could respond to Vulpes's scathing words, he saw Einar pass out from the pain,
"Einar!", he gasped,
Suddenly a small group of cultists emerged through the doorway, their armour rattling as they ran into the room.
As the cultists encircled John, he watched with fading vision as Vulpes backed away, allowing the cultists to move in,
"Throw them in the holding cells until I figure out exactly how to deal with them", he ordered,
As the cultists slowly approached, Vulpes said,
"Nighty night little hero",
One of the cultists then stepped over to John and stamped down hard onto his face, knocking him unconscious.

CHAPTER XV:
A FRIEND IN DARK PLACES

Elsewhere in Tarn Gren, Brenna and Ulva approached a small timber door and cautiously opened it. Peering inside they spotted a large and spacious bedroom with plain walls. To the left of them was a large arched window which looked out into the dark forest outside the fortress, its glass panes running with lashings of rain. There was a large and richly furnished bed pushed up against the back wall covered with fine fabrics of red and gold with matching pillowcases. Near the bed was a row of wardrobes made of a light brown coloured wood and up against the side wall were some bookshelves and a glowing fireplace.

For such a powerful figure of immense influence and wealth within the Gormveld, Vulpes lived rather modestly, for the room was devoid of any semblances of proper luxury other than the bed. As Brenna and Ulva entered and gazed around, they could hear footsteps echoing nearby, the spitting and crackling of the embers within the fireplace and the sound of rainfall against the window mixed with the distant booming of thunder.

Their hearts sank when they realized that Vulpes was nowhere to be seen,

"Damn, he's not here, he must be in the council room", said Brenna,

"Okay, but let's quickly look around first, there might be something here that might prove useful to our journey", said Ulva,

"Okay but we shouldn't dally for too long, we should be swift before people start getting wise", said Brenna,

Removing their helmets and placing them down upon the bed, Brenna and Ulva began looking around. Ulva scanned through the wardrobes and found rows of hanging clothes, primarily luxurious and exquisitely crafted robes coloured in many different shades and made from an array of different materials, from linens and cloth shaded in a rainbow of hues to cashmere wool, delicate cottons and beautiful furs and silks. Beautiful pieces to be sure, but nothing of significant interest or practical use. Closing the wardrobes, Ulva walked back over to Brenna, who had finished looking through the side dressers near the bed. He had found little of interest apart from a few coins and some jewellery, which he had no scruples about pocketing. They then both walked over to the bookcases and began to browse their contents.

Most of the books were of little use, from mundane titles detailing politics and history to rudimentary accounts pertaining to cult finances, expenditure and organization. The only two books however that piqued Brenna's curiosity was one detailing the history of the Cult of Fenris and a general tome about werewolves and lycanthropy written by members of the cult itself. Brenna quickly snatched up the tomes and shoved them into his bag before closing it.

As Brenna threw his rucksack onto his back, he walked over to the bed and collected up the helmets that laid on the sheets, he handed Ulva hers before saying,

"Right, let's go",

Suddenly, they heard the door swing open before a female voice called out, which made Brenna and Ulva freeze in fear, their hearts leaping in fright,

"You two, drop the helmets and turn around", came the voice,

Brenna and Ulva raised their hands above their heads in surrender, dropping their helmets with a clatter. With their faces frozen in horror, they turned round to see a short, young woman standing near the door.

She was a teenager by the eye's reckoning, her face was as pale as snow, which contrasted beautifully with her turquoise blue eyes and long, straight hair that was raven black in colour and streaked with white.

Both Brenna and Ulva saw that the girl wasn't in the best of health, she was rather thin and small in stature, indicating that she was malnourished. She also possessed some rather worrying physical qualities, she had dark circles under her eyes, of which the pupils were of unequal size indicating head trauma. The entire length of her left arm was completely bandaged whilst her right arm was covered in scars and scratches. Brenna and Ulva noticed that, unlike the other cultists, she was wearing boots and she wasn't wearing any armour, instead she was wearing a short sleeved and loose fitting hooded black tunic that came down to her waist, black linen trousers that fitted tightly across her legs and a leather belt with a silver buckle. She was also wearing black velvet gloves and curiously she had a collar made of black leather fastened around her neck, hanging from which was a small and rusted iron ring.

Eyeing Brenna and Ulva suspiciously, the young woman said, "I haven't seen your faces before, you are not members of the cult, who are you and what are you doing in Godi Vulpes's room?",

As Brenna and Ulva exchanged nervous glances at one another, the young woman snapped at them,

"Well? Speak up!",

Suddenly Brenna drew his sword and angrily rushed towards the young woman. Before she could react, Brenna grabbed her by the throat and pushed her up against the wall. Wrapping his hand around the girl's neck, Brenna pointed his sword at her stomach as she squirmed and thrashed about, kicking her legs as she was held off the floor by Brenna's outstretched arm,

"I'd like to ask you the same questions", said Brenna,

"Put me down!", snapped the dark-haired woman,

"I can't do that, how do I know you won't call for someone the minute I release you?", asked Brenna,
"Because if you don't, I will bite your hand off!", barked the young woman,
"Brenna, let her go", said Ulva,
"Not unless she promises to not blow our cover or get in our way", said Brenna,
"I won't I promise, just get off me", said the dark-haired woman,
Brenna released the woman from his grip and sheathed his sword as he saw the young woman rubbing her neck where his fingers had squeezed and made some slight marks on her skin,
"How do you know we are not part of the Cult of Fenris?", asked Brenna,
The woman glared at Brenna and said,
"Because I recognize the stench coming off you, you do not smell like the cultists, you smell human, at least one of you does. Also I have been here long enough to recognize every face that there is in this shithole and I have never seen your faces before, so I will ask again, who are you two?",
"We'll tell you our names if you tell us yours first", said Ulva,
"Very well, my name is Kittra, but you may call me Kit", said the young girl,
"Don't you have a last name?", asked Ulva,
"No, just Kit, the daughter of Vulpes", said Kit,
"Well my name is Brenna and this is Ulva", said Brenna,
"Charmed", said Kit as she folded her arms,
"Wait, you're Vulpes's daughter?", said Ulva,
"To my shame", said Kit in a sad and soft tone of voice,
"Does that mean you are a member of the Cult of Fenris?", asked Brenna,
A look of disgust suddenly appeared on Kit's face,
"Fuck no, I am not a part of that ridiculous little group you call a cult. I do not follow their beliefs nor do I support their insane goals!", she said angrily,
"Neither do we", chimed Ulva,

"Ah a fellow werewolf that doesn't believe all of the bullshit that comes from my father's mouth, that is good, I thought I was the only one", said Kit as the anger faded from her face, "So if you are not part of the cult, then how are you a werewolf? I thought every cultist had lycanthropy and gained it through taking part in a secret and forbidden ritual, were you bitten just like Ulva here?", said Brenna,
"I wasn't bitten, nor have I ever taken part in any kind of crazy ritual, I was...simply born this way", said Kit,
"What, how is that possible?!", gasped Brenna,
"I thought you knew everything about werewolves", smirked Ulva,
"Well clearly not everything!", blurted Brenna,
"Well if you must know I was born with my powers. I am able to change forms at will not because of some disease or some inane ritual, but because my conception was the result of my father brutally assaulting an innocent woman eighteen years ago", said Kit,
Brenna and Ulva's mouths dropped in shock as they stared horrified at Kit before she turned her back on them and said, "I never met my mother and I know nothing about her, not even her name. All I know is that she was a Saxon and that she gave birth to me in a ruined stone barn one stormy night, alone, starving and afraid. According to my father, she perished giving me life",
"Gods above, how terrible", said Brenna,
"Yes and I would rather not speak further on the subject, it's too painful", said Kit,
Ulva and Brenna watched as Kit raised her head and said, "Ever since then I have been locked in this tower, neglected and abused by my cruel father. I hate the man for what he has done to me and what he did to my mother",
"If you hate Vulpes so much, why haven't you escaped?", asked Ulva,

"You don't think I've tried already? I've tried to flee on many occasions, but the cultists have always managed to find me no matter how hard I tried to cover my tracks. They somehow always caught up to me and dragged me back here, sometimes awake and kicking, sometimes unconscious when I don't come quietly and sometimes in a muzzle and chains. Oh and if you are wondering why I haven't cut my father's throat in his sleep, it's because this tower is full of assholes who care more about him than me. I would be slaughtered by the cultists if I tried to harm him, he is their master after all. In short, I am a prisoner here, this fortress is my own personal cage of stone", said Kit,

With heavy hearts, Brenna and Ulva sadly watched as Kit walked over to the window and stared out into the darkness and the rain.

Kit sighed heavily before saying,

"Oh how I long to be free of this hellish place. How I wish to run free through the Gormwood and amongst the beautiful fields and fjords beyond the forest, to lose myself in the splendour of nature. How I long for the happiness, comfort and freedom I have been denied for so many years",

"I am sorry you have had to go through all of this", said Ulva sadly,

Turning round, Kit folded her arms and said,

"So now we have been introduced, I must ask, why are you here?",

"We are here because Ulva was bitten by your father during his initial failed attempt to steal Vulthur away. He succeeded on the second try and fled to this tower, we followed him and now we plan to take it back, for without its power, we cannot cure Ulva at the forest of Coldwood using the magic of Fenrir's Bane", said Brenna,

"That would explain why my father somehow found it despite it being lost for centuries. If you know of all this, then I trust you know what he intends to do with that dagger. If you want to get it back, perhaps I can help", said Kit,

"Really, you would help us?", said Ulva,

"Yes, I will help you recover Vulthur and assist you in escaping, but I want something in return, I do not do this purely out of the goodness of my heart", said Kit,
"Okay, what do you want?", asked Brenna,
"I wish to be free of this wretched place, my father and my lycanthropy", said Kit before she glanced at Ulva,
"We both understand what it is like to have the wolfblight coursing through our veins, it's like a fire that never stops burning, like wasps crawling within your chest, like knives been drawn across your flesh. It is a curse that was forced upon me against my will simply because some monster wanted to slake his lust. It is a legacy that I inherited from my father that I wish to destroy. So here is the deal, I will help you get Vulthur back, but in return I ask that you allow me to accompany you to Coldwood so that I can be cured. I want the chance to have a happy and normal life, a chance to start anew as a free woman. Please I beseech you both, I cannot bare to stay here for another night longer", she said,
After pondering to himself, Brenna said,
"If we agree, will you also help us stop Fenrir and the machinations of his evil cult?",
"Of course, I have no desire to see this land ruled by the dark wolf and his insane followers. They have hurt me, so I will do everything in my power to ensure they pay for what they have done to me and Norway. I don't want the good people of this land to suffer under the wolfblight and I certainly wouldn't want their only hope of a cure to be taken away from them", replied Kit,
"Very well Kit you can come with us, I wholeheartedly welcome your help if it means helping you, Ulva and all of Norway", smiled Brenna,
Kit gasped before she rushed forward and tightly hugged Brenna, much to his surprise,
"Oh thank you, thank you so much", she said,
Pulling Kit off himself, Brenna said,
"You're welcome",
"So what happens now?", asked Ulva,

"Before we leave, I will need to pack some supplies, I shall be as quick as I can. Meet me in the foyer downstairs in a few minutes and I will help you get Vulthur back", said Kit,
As Kit left the room, Brenna and Ulva collected up their helmets and put them back on,
"We need to find John and Einar and tell them of our newfound friend and of our new plan", said Brenna,
"They were going to the council room, we should look for them there then meet Kit in the foyer", said Ulva,
"Okay, let's go", said Brenna,
Brenna and Ulva made their way out of the room, nearly jumping out of their skins in fright as a group of cultists suddenly appeared in the corridor. Fortunately they took no notice of Brenna and Ulva as they simply marched past without so much as a weary glance.
Brenna and Ulva walked down a winding staircase nearby and rushed through some narrow hallways before they eventually came to a corridor that was lit with an ethereal blue glow.
In front of them was an archway that led to a room with a round table and a giant mirror, it was the council room.
As they walked inside, they were disheartened to find there was no sign of John, Einar or Vulpes,
"Where is John and Einar? I thought they would be here. Did they find Vulpes, did they find the dagger?", said Ulva.
Suddenly without warning, a dozen cultists appeared in the doorway behind Brenna and Ulva and rushed inside before they surrounded them, their faces locked into angry snarls, their eyes glowing from deep within their helmets.
As they encircled Brenna and Ulva, Brenna drew his sword and prepared to defend himself and his friend. With the cultists stepping forward menacingly, Brenna raised his sword over his head.

It was then that Vulpes appeared in the doorway, grinning from ear to ear with delight,
"Well isn't this a surprise. After John and Einar came here, I had a feeling you two wouldn't be far behind. Good thing I waited around to see if you would show up and lo and behold, here you are", he said,
"Where's John and Einar, what have you done with them?!", shouted Ulva,
"Oh they are alive…for the moment, but for how long is up to me. Do not worry, you will be joining them pretty soon", said Vulpes before pointed at Brenna and Ulva,
"Seize them", he said,
Brenna and Ulva watched as the cultists suddenly reached out to grab them, but Brenna ran forward, stabbing one of them in the chest before kicking another to the floor,
"Run!", he cried,
As Brenna and Ulva stormed past Vulpes, they almost knocked him to the ground as they fled,
"Get them!", roared Vulpes,
Brenna and Ulva suddenly raced down the corridor as fast as they could. As they fled, they could hear behind them the sound of roaring and howling as the cultists began to transform. Brenna could see more cultists appearing around the corner, but he was able to barge through them before they could react.
As they ran, Ulva glanced behind and saw a dozen werewolves chasing after her and Brenna. Curiously they were still armoured and it seemed that their uniforms had not torn during their turnings. The werewolves were snarling and sprinting on all fours, their tails whipping the air as they chased down the intruders. Brenna and Ulva were almost flying as they dashed down a flight of stairs before running into the foyer, coming to a halt as they realized that Kit was nowhere to be seen. Brenna and Ulva tried to make a run for the front door, but some guards stopped them from leaving.

They then tried to run towards the cellar, but the werewolves chasing them suddenly and with great speed encircled them, blocking off their escape. Brenna and Ulva huddled together as the werewolves glared at them.
As Brenna and Ulva raised their weapons up in preparation for a fight, they were suddenly thrown upwards by a powerful force before hitting the ceiling hard and painfully.
Brenna and Ulva cried out with panicked voices as they were suddenly sent back down to earth, striking the ground with a painful thud. Brenna groaned as he felt his head and chest throb with pain and every breath he took was sharp and painful. He turned his head and saw Ulva was trying to crawl away, but the werewolves stopped her from escaping as one of them had pressed down upon her back with a large paw.
It was then that Vulpes appeared at the foot of the stairs, his hands shrouded with shining wisps of magic that danced around his fingers,
"You know you are really starting to annoy me, not enough that you had to take half my sight and threaten my plans, but you had the gall to murder my siblings and sneak around my tower. I shall make sure you pay for such impudence", he growled before he turned to one of the werewolves standing nearby,
"Sister Runa, take them to the holding cells, I will deal with them later", he said,
Brenna and Ulva watched as the werewolves around them began to change back into their human forms, their fangs and claws retracting, their tails vanishing beneath their armour as their legs and arms contorted along with their faces.
One of the cultists then stepped forward and removed her helmet, revealing herself to be a young girl with wavy blonde hair and green eyes,
"You're coming with us", she said,
As the cultists grabbed them by the legs and began to drag them across the floor, Brenna and Ulva slowly passed out.

As they were being taken down into the basement, Kit appeared at the foot of the nearby stairs carrying a small backpack fastened with a silver buckle.
She gasped as she saw Brenna and Ulva being dragged down the stairs on the opposite side of the foyer,
"What's going on, where are you taking them?", she said,
"We have captured some intruders and Garm has commanded that they must die, his will shall be done", said Vulpes,
"Let them go, too much blood has been spilled here today. If you release them, I will make sure that they do not talk about anything they have witnessed here", said Kit,
Vulpes laughed,
"Oh I think not, these thugs not only broke into my tower, but they have killed several of our fellow cultists and have conspired to steal from me. The bodies of our brothers Olaf, Gorvik, Thorkeld and sister Sibbi were found hidden in the basement, their corpses had been stripped of their uniforms. I imagine the four intruders snuck in here, murdered them and disguised themselves to try and retrieve Vulthur without my knowledge. I will make sure justice is delivered for such heinous crimes", he said,
"You can't do this!", barked Kit,
"I can do whatever I want whenever I want. I am the Lord of Tarn Gren and I have complete dominion over this entire tower and all the hearts and minds within its walls!", snapped Vulpes,
"You think everyone here is bound to you? Well there is one person here who possesses a heart and mind that shall never be yours no matter how hard you try", growled Kit,
"And who might that be?", said Vulpes,
"Me, I have been tolerant of your abuse for many years but now that I have finally discovered a way to be free of you and this place forever, I will no longer stand for it. I promise you now father, if you do not release them, then bad things are going to happen to you and this clan, mark my words!", snapped Kit,

Kit squeaked as Vulpes suddenly slapped her across the face, causing a mark to form upon her pale cheek,
"Watch your tongue child or I shall tear it from your mouth", spat Vulpes before he summoned two cultists to his side,
"Brothers, please take Kit back to her room and keep her there. I will come and collect her once I have taken care of our unwanted guests, then her insolence will be punished", he said,
Kit glared at Vulpes as the cultists grabbed her by the arms and escorted her up the stairs back to her room. As she trudged up the stairs, Kit's mind wandered to thoughts of Brenna and Ulva and how she might free them from the clutches of her father.
With their appearance in Tarn Gren, she knew that they were her only chance of escape, her only chance of being cured of her lycanthropy and her only chance to experience a free and happy life far away from werewolves, diseases, cults, rituals and the grotesque glorification of demons and monsters.
At the top of the stairs, Kit whispered softly under her breath,
"Sit tight guys, I will get you out...somehow and by the gods, I cannot afford to fail",

CHAPTER XVI:
THE SECOND TURNING

Hours passed before John began to stir from his unconsciousness state. As he opened his eyes and wearily glanced around, John realized that he was lying on his back inside a prison cell with a barred iron door. John sat up and glanced around the dark, cold and dry cell he found himself in. He then looked down and noticed that the armour he had wearing had been stripped away, his attire left untouched. Turning round, John saw his rucksack sitting in the corner of the cell. Crawling on his knees, John shuffled over to the bag and opened it, peering inside to discover his food had been taken, much to his disheartening dismay.
Thankfully the rest of his possessions were left untouched. John reached in and pulled out his cloak before he threw it on to try and warm himself.
Suddenly he heard a familiar voice call out to him,
"Hello, can anyone hear me?",
John looked round the cell and noticed that the voice was coming from beyond the wall on the right, it was Einar and he too was sitting inside a prison cell,
"Einar, is that you?", called John,
"Yeah it's me lad, are you okay?", said Einar,
"I'm cold but unharmed, how are you feeling?", asked John,
"I'm in pain, but I'll survive, it's Ulva I'm worried about though. I don't know what time it is and I fear she will turn soon", said Einar,
Realizing that Ulva was nowhere in sight, John cried out,
"Ulva, where are you?!",
"I'm here", came a soft voice,
John shuffled over to the wall on the left and placed his hand upon its cold surface,
"Ulva, oh thank the gods, are you okay? Did they hurt you?", he said,

"They did but I'll be alright, Brenna's still unconscious though, he hasn't woken up in hours, I'm worried about him", said Ulva,
"Is he breathing? Can you hear him?", asked John,
Ulva placed an ear up against the wall of her cell and listened out for any noise. Because of the wolfblood running through her veins, her hearing was now sharper.
Past the sound of the howling wind, she could just hear the faint sound of breathing, Brenna was alive, much to her relief,
"He's still alive, but I cannot get to him to see if he needs healing", said Ulva,
"What about you Einar?", asked John,
"No I'm good", said Einar,
"Have any cultists come down here since we were imprisoned?", said John,
"No it's been quiet, I've been hearing some distant voices, but nothing other than that", said Einar,
"We need to get out of here before they come back", said John before he eyed the bars of his cell and began forcefully slamming his foot against them,
"Don't bother John, I've tried that already and so has Ulva", said Einar,
In frustration, John slammed the door one more time before he punched the wall in anger.
Sighing deeply before he pressed his back up against the wall, John whimpered in despair and covered his face with his hands,
"This is all my fault, Vulpes was right, it's because of me that all of this has transpired. If I had simply given him that stupid dagger, none of us would be here right now. We would be at home curled up around a toasty fire eating delicious caramel puddings whilst listening to Brenna weaving one of his wondrous stories", he said,
"No John it's not your fault, you were just getting a gift for Ulva. You had no idea things would turn out as they have so don't go beating yourself up", said Einar,

"Einar's right John, you are not to blame, no one except Vulpes, it all just happened you know?", said Ulva,
John sighed and stared at the cell door in front of him. He then grinned as he thought of something funny,
"Hey do you guys remember that one time when we all went ice skating at Saergrind?", he said,
John could hear both Ulva and Einar laughing softly as they remembered back to that day,
"Yeah I remember, didn't we all get drunk?", said Einar,
"I slipped simply putting on my damn skates", said Ulva,
"I'll never forget the moment when we all crashed into each other and we all went stumbling. The look on Maud's face was priceless, I'll always remember it for as long as I live", laughed Einar,
John laughed softly before his thoughts began to wander back to Gormstad and of home, his smile faded as his heart filled with sadness,
"But now because of my actions, I've not only put everyone in harm's way, but I have sent us to our deaths. Guys, for what it's worth I'm sorry, if we don't get out of this situation alive, I just want you all to know that I am sorry for everything that has happened. I let stubborn pride get in the way, I should have taken Vulpes's dirty money and ran. But I guess I was an idiot in believing I could make things better", he said,
John suddenly jolted as he heard a loud bang against the cell wall as Ulva struck it in anger with a curled fist,
"John, I am trying everything I can to keep my emotions in check right now so I can hold back the next turning for as long as I can, but you spouting such nonsense is not helping. It makes me emotional and it makes me angry. Pull yourself together and stop feeling sorry for yourself", she said,
"What?", said John,

"How many times must I repeat myself? You are not to blame for this or anything that has happened to us. It might have been fate, coincidence, prophecy or fucking whatever, but all of this was not your fault. You have done all you can in these circumstances, now enough!", snapped Ulva,
John was taken aback by Ulva's tone of voice. Ulva rarely shouted, so whenever she did it would be startling, like a sudden flash of lightning. John gazed at the floor and sat there contemplating to himself.
As Ulva's words ran through his head repeatedly, the more they made sense,
"You're right Ulva, of course you're right. I shouldn't blame myself nor should I dwell on what has happened, the past is the past and I cannot change it. Thank you for making me see sense, sometimes with all that is going on, it can be hard to think and I let my emotions get the better of me, does that make sense Ulva...Ulva?", said John,
Ulva did not respond, instead John could hear her softly whimpering and groaning in pain as she fell to her knees, gritting her teeth as pain enveloped her body,
"Ulva, what's wrong?", said John,
Ulva spluttered as she struggled to get her words out for her throat was beginning to tighten,
"It's...it's starting again", she winced,
John felt his heart leap as the blood drained from his face,
"Einar, what time is it?!", he snapped,
"I told you I don't know, why do you ask?", said Einar,
"It's Ulva, I think she's in the early stages of her second turning",
A sickening feeling welled up in Einar's stomach,
"Gods above, is Brenna awake?", he said,
"Brenna, can you hear me?!", yelled John,
There was no response, Brenna was still out cold,
"Shit, he's still unconscious and we can't reach him", growled John,
"And Brenna is the one with the chains in his bag, that means...", said Einar,

As a horrible wave of dread washed over him, Einar moved over to the nearby wall and said,
"Ulva, is there anything in your bag that you can bind yourself with?",
There came no response before Ulva's voice called out,
"No Einar, nothing", she said,
"Damn it!", shouted Einar as he slammed the door of his cell in anger,
In response to Einar's outburst, Ulva said,
"Guys listen to me…I won't be able to hold off the transformation for much longer, I just hope this cage holds fast. But there is something that might stave off the turning for a little while longer. Talk to me guys, talking seems to get my mind off the pain if not for a moment",
"Um, what should we talk about?", asked John,
"Anything, just do it!", barked Ulva as her body began to shake,
"Okay um…remember that one time when we were up on the Kulaberg mountains one autumn? We went skiing, I think it was our fourth date and we were staying in a lodge", said John,
"Yeah…I remember, it belonged to a man named Olvigsson if I remember right", said Ulva,
"I was just thinking back to the time when we tried climbing the Kedderkuljorn. When we got to the summit, we were so exhausted that we both collapsed on top of one another. I remember how warm and soft you were because you were wearing your fur coat and how beautiful your eyes were as I gazed into them", said John,
"Our first kiss", said Ulva,
"You were wearing cherry lip balm, how sweet it tasted on your lips. I will always remember how wonderful that day was, how we visited Brunda's lodge and enjoyed some venison steaks and his famous hot chocolate, the best I ever tasted", said John as he smiled warmly,
Turning to the nearby wall, John called out to Einar and said,
"Hey Einar, do you remember Brunda?",

"You mean the reindeer herder from Hringdal? Yeah I remember him, such a happy and bright chap. His cocoa was legendary, do you guys remember what made it taste so good?", said Einar,
"It was Samit reindeer milk, he used to mix it into his drinks", said John,
"That stuff was so rich and creamy that you only needed a spoonful, it was...wonderful", sighed Ulva,
"More talking, it's helping immensely", she said,
"All right, what are you going to do once this is all over?", asked Einar,
Ulva suddenly groaned as she felt a sharp pain shoot through her chest whilst she simultaneously felt a creeping sensation crawl across her back.
Feeling a headache beginning to form within her head, Ulva said,
"I don't know...I haven't thought about it",
Suddenly Ulva began to violently cough as blood began to well up and foam deep within her throat. She then spat out a large stinking globule of blood onto the floor.
As blood began dripping from her mouth, Ulva suddenly felt something begin to claw at her chest as she struggled to breath,
"Guys...please talk to me", she begged,
It was then that John began to panic, usually him and Ulva would have much to talk about and would spend hours just chatting to one another. But for some strange reason, at that precise moment in time, he didn't know what to talk about. Searching his mind for some topic to discuss, he could hear Ulva shuffling about in her cell, moaning in pain and gargling up blood which she then spat onto the floor,
"Somebody say something!", roared Ulva,
"I...I...", stammered John, his mind going blank as his forehead began to bead with sweat,
Ulva let out a pained moan before she wearily began to undress as her skin began to tighten and flare up with a terrible and hot itch.

Squirming out of her clothes, Ulva shivered as her naked body sprawled out onto the cold dungeon floor. With her heart pounding in her chest and the blood rushing around her skull, Ulva collected up her clothes and pushed them through the gap between the iron bars standing in front of her,
"Keep them safe for me", she said,
John leaned forward and took the bundle of clothes before shoving them into his bag.
He then laid himself flat on his stomach and reached out for Ulva's little hand before gently and affectionately caressing her delicate fingers,
"John...it won't be long now; I won't be able to control myself when I have transformed. When I was in Brenna's study, I was chained up and posed no threat to you or anyone. But now the only thing between me and you are these bars. I hope they hold, but if they do not, then I want you to kill me should I attack you. If you somehow escape, then I want you to run, run as fast as you can and do not look back", said Ulva,
"But...", whimpered John,
"No buts John, I won't have you wasting your life like this, please just do as I ask", said Ulva,
"I...yes Ulva", said John sadly,
"No matter what happens tonight, know that I love you", said Ulva,
"I love you too", said John as he felt a tear run down his face,
"Guess I'll see you soon, unless one of us dies tonight", squeaked Ulva before she retreated to the back of her cell and curled herself up against the floor,
John's heart sank as he could hear Ulva begin to sing softly to herself. As she sang, John could hear Einar singing along with his sister, his voice weary and gentle. Listening to the beautiful music, John whimpered as he held back tears. For a moment, Einar and Ulva sung together as John was pressed up against the cell wall struggling to keep himself together. Suddenly he was startled by a sudden cry from Ulva as she staggered onto her knees and hands.

Starting to feel lightheaded, Ulva grunted and groaned in pain before she began to retch and heave as she could feel something solid beginning to move upwards from deep within her throat. With a shaking hand, Ulva slowly inserted two fingers into her bleeding mouth and pushed them past her tonsils. It was then that she could feel something soft yet firm sitting wedged in her throat. Trying not to puke, Ulva pressed against it and felt wet fur and a spongy black nose sitting on the tip of a wolf's snout.

Realizing what she had just touched, Ulva suddenly began to vomit violently, spraying the walls and floor of her cell with copious amounts of blood. She then began to scream as her arms and legs exploded with agonizing pain, as if knives were burrowing and twisting into her flesh.

Covering his ears to block out the screeching, John began to rock back and forth against the wall of his cell, murmuring to himself as he heard the heart-breaking cries of his wife calling out his name,

"Brenna, wake the fuck up!", barked Einar,

Brenna could not hear him; he was now conscious but his head was spinning, his hearing was blurred and he was slurring his words as he mumbled to himself. In the cell next to him, Ulva was screaming in agony, her skin pulsating as the werewolf was trying to tear herself free from beneath Ulva's flesh. Ulva suddenly and instinctively began to scratch at her arms with her sharp nails, causing her skin to bleed profusely as she tore it away, revealing damp red fur underneath. As the skin on her back began to split open and bleed, her ears started lengthening into furry points whilst her mouth ruptured with an electric pain as her teeth began to stretch and sharpen into fangs. Ulva squealed as every bone in her body was beginning to change shape, cracking, lengthening, splitting and contorting. As her spine began to lengthen, Ulva arched her back before she clutched her breast, groaning as a painful popping sensation erupted from within her stomach and chest.

As the pressure building against her skull began to worsen, Ulva pressed her bloody palms up against her face to stop the pain but it was no use. She then let out a piercing scream as she could feel her face began to stretch forward, the skin splitting whilst the muscles of her face began to pull and break apart. Instinctively, Ulva suddenly began scratching her face violently, shrieking as she tore at her skin until the face of a wolf emerged.

Once her face had completely changed, Ulva began pulling at her skin with razor sharp claws, allowing fur to burst forth from the wounds she drew across her body. At this point her tail was now visible and the upper part of her body was now fully transformed, but the lower part of her body and legs were still human. However that changed as Ulva slashed at her waist and legs until fur covered her entire body.

In her new form, Ulva let out an angry scream before she rushed forward and immediately began pounding and slashing at the cell door, thrashing about as she went berserk. John watched as two cultists suddenly emerged outside the cell door,

"What's going on in here? I heard screaming", said Runa, Seeing Ulva rampaging about inside her prison cell, Runa shouted,

"She's already turned, inform Vulpes!",

As one of the cultists ran off, Ulva suddenly stopped flailing about and angrily glared at Runa who was staring back at her,

"Stay away from her!", yelled John as he rushed forward and grabbed the bars of his cell,

As Ulva and Runa stared at each other, Ulva sniffed the air and let out a howl before she began pounding her fists furiously against the cell door until one of the bars broke and landed on the floor with a loud clang.

Seeing this, Runa angrily tossed her sword aside as she felt her rage beginning to well up inside her,

"Oh no you don't", she snarled,

As Runa began to change form, Ulva ripped apart the prison door before she stepped out, snarling and hissing as she watched Runa complete her transformation. Einar and John watched as the two werewolves suddenly began circling one another, their tails lashing the air angrily as they growled at each other. Runa suddenly sprinted towards Ulva and began slashing her across the face and catching her snout with sharp claws. The air was filled with the sound of screeching metal, horrible growling and the snapping of jaws as the two werewolves viciously fought one another.

John and Einar watched in horror at the sight of the two she-wolves clashing together, biting, scratching, punching and kicking as blood sprayed across the ground,

"What's going on?", murmured Brenna as he sat himself up,

"Brenna, it's about time, Ulva's already transformed!", barked Einar,

"Transformed...transform...",

Brenna's eyes widened,

"No, when?!", he blurted,

"Literally a moment ago, look at her!", snapped John,

Brenna peered through the cell door and gasped as he saw Runa slamming Ulva into the wall before Ulva spun round and punched her hard in the throat,

"Fuck, I didn't expect her to turn so soon, we need to get out of here, where's Kit?", said Brenna,

"Who?", asked Einar,

"Vulpes's daughter, she said she was going to help us escape and get Vulthur back. Have either of you seen a young girl with dark hair and blue eyes?", asked Brenna,

"No", said John,

"Damn it, where the hell is she?", huffed Brenna,

It was then that Ulva slammed her fist into Runa's jaw with a crack, sending some teeth flying before she plunged her fangs deep into Runa's golden furred neck, puncturing a deep vein which caused blood to burst from her throat. Clutching her bleeding neck, Runa groaned before she fell dead to the ground with a thud.

After Ulva crouched down and lapped up some blood with her long tongue, she lifted her head as she saw some cultists emerge from the nearby corridor. Seeing their sister lying dead at Ulva's feet, the cultists angrily transformed before they rushed forward. Ulva raced towards them and suddenly decapitated one of the cultists, knocking his head clean off his shoulders before she punched straight through the armoured belly of his companion, disembowelling him as his blood, bile and steaming guts spilled out onto the ground. She then grabbed the third cultist by the leg and swung her round before launching her through the air towards a wall, the werewolf howling before she struck the stone, her head splitting open upon impact. The fourth and final cultist then had his head bitten off with one single bite before Ulva rushed down the corridor, roaring in anger as she went.
John, Einar and Brenna could hear horrible screams of terror as Ulva began rampaging through the tower, ripping through cultists and servants alike before she fled deeper into the fortress to conduct some gruesome carnage.
It then went eerily quiet before there came the sound of soft footsteps as a figure emerged before the prison cells, it was Kit and she was holding a set of keys in one hand and a bloody axe in the other,
"Kit, over here!", shouted Brenna,
Seeing Brenna standing behind a barred door, Kit raced over to the cells and quickly began to open them one by one before Brenna and John grabbed their bags and slung them across their backs with Einar collecting up both his and Ulva's,
"Thanks Kit, are you okay?", asked Brenna,
"I'm fine, but Ulva has unleashed utter chaos within the tower. I was able to get down here without her spotting me as she was too busy ripping apart some guards", said Kit,
"What took you so long and where is Vulpes?", asked Brenna,

"I am sorry that I kept you waiting, believe me I tried to reach you sooner, but the guards had me drugged and I didn't awaken for hours. I was only able to escape after I had found an axe and killed the guards whilst they weren't looking. My father is in the council room and he has Vulthur in his possession", said Kit,
"We also need to find Ulva, I won't leave without my wife", said John,
"Ulva's your wife?", asked Kit,
"Indeed, my name is John Forrester and this is Einar Skarlagen, a fine swordsman and an even finer brother and friend", said John,
"So you must be Kit, it's nice to meet you", smiled Einar,
Kit's eyes widened and her heart began to flutter as she gazed upon Einar, her face becoming flushed as she admired his handsome features,
"Wow", she gasped,
"Brenna said Vulpes is your father, so why are you helping us against him?", said John,
Kit was silent for a moment before she snapped back into reality and said,
"Because we share a common goal, I too want to escape and just like Ulva, I want to be cured. My father sullied me just as he sullied Ulva and so I want to help you guys in whatever way I can",
"So you're a werewolf too?", asked Einar,
"Yes, but we can exchange pleasantries and talk more about it later. For now we need to move quickly, I fear we have shaken the hive", said Kit,
"Right, to the council room", said Brenna,
Brenna, John, Einar and Kit quickly made their way down the corridor before they came to a flight of stairs.
After quickly rushing up its steps, they found themselves in the basement of Tarn Gren. After passing the barrels, they rushed up another flight of stairs before they arrived in the foyer area, gasping in horror at what they saw.

The floor was awash with blood and littered with many corpses, their clothes and armour shredded, their bodies mangled, crushed, torn, bitten and dismembered. Einar, Brenna and John suddenly drew their weapons as they suddenly heard footsteps approaching.
They turned to see some cultists rush down the nearby stairs, they were bloodied, wounded and terrified, their armour damaged and their helmets missing,
"Damn werewolf is out of control, we can't stop her!", cried one of the cultists,
The cultist standing at the front of the group suddenly glanced over at Brenna and his friends before pointing at them,
"You, you are the ones who let her out!", he snapped,
"We did nothing of the sort!", barked Einar,
"Kill them all, then go after that crimson beast and kill her too!", cried the cultist to his armoured companions,
The cultists snarled and growled as they transformed before John, Einar, Brenna and Kit's eyes,
"Incredible, the transformation was almost instantaneous", gasped Brenna,
"Yeah yeah fantastic, terrific, can we just focus on the task at hand?", growled Kit,
"Get ready guys, here they come!", yelled John,
The cultists dashed towards John and his friends on all fours. John, Einar and Brenna yelled in anger as they raced forward to meet them and all at once a fight broke out. John, Einar and Brenna angrily attacked the werewolves, swinging and stabbing violently as they sliced and plunged their shining silver swords deep into flesh, bone and skin. John retrieved the shield from behind his back and placed it in his left hand. He then dodged a few blows from one light brown werewolf before leaping forward and taking the beast's head off with a swipe of his sword. Brenna grunted and growled as he struggled to defend himself against one particularly large and brutish werewolf who had a scarred eye.

He looked over to see Kit was standing nearby, watching them fight with worry and fright,
"Hey Kit, I could really use a hand over here!", cried Brenna,
"But I can't fight", said Kit nervously,
Brenna winced as a claw suddenly caught the side of his shoulder, slicing through the leather of his coat and scratching him,
Brenna retaliated by swiping the werewolf in the snout, causing him to back off,
"What do you mean you can't fight?!", he yelled,
"I just can't, no one ever taught me", said Kit,
Brenna slammed his fist into the jaw of the hulking werewolf that was trying to bite him, causing the creature to cry out in pain,
"You're a werewolf, shapeshift or something!", barked Brenna,
Kit began to shake as she felt her stomach sink,
"I'm sorry Brenna, but I promised myself I would never turn, I took a personal oath that I would never take the form of my father, the form he took when he savaged my mother", she said,
"Are you serious?!", snapped Brenna before he angrily deflected a blow from the werewolf's claw and plunged his blade deep into the creature's chest, piercing its heart before it collapsed onto the floor,
Einar punched the werewolf that he was clashing with in the snout, the creature retaliated by swiping at him with a terrible rushing of claws. Thankfully he was still wearing his chainmail shirt under his tunic, thus most of the blows were deflected in a ringing of steel.
While Einar and Brenna were preoccupied, John deflected some blows with his shield before he swung his blade, cleaving the skull of the werewolf standing before him in two. Einar meanwhile let out a roar as he finally killed the werewolf that had been relentlessly trying to end his life, the she – wolf gargling blood as Einar lodged his blade deep into her throat.

With the final cultist slain, John, Einar and Brenna glanced down at the dead werewolves as Kit walked over to them and said,
"Are you guys okay?",
"Yeah, no thanks to you", growled John,
"I'm sorry John, but I would have been of little use to you going up against a group of vicious werewolves", said Kit,
"But you are a werewolf damn it, your strength would have been useful. If you had helped, I wouldn't be in so much pain and Brenna wouldn't be injured!", snapped John,
Kit sadly lowered her gaze and glanced at the floor before she said softly,
"I'm sorry...this is just so overwhelming...I...",
Seeing Kit's eyes beginning to tear up, Einar said,
"Okay John that's enough, you heard that she didn't want to use her power and we cannot force her to do something that she doesn't want to do",
"But surely she can use an axe though and we need people who can fight. If you want to help us, then help us", spat John,
"I have helped you, I freed you from your cages didn't I?", said Kit,
"Yes, but if you can't fight, then you will need to learn how and if you cannot or will not, then you will have no choice but to use your power of lycanthropy, whether you like it or not", said Brenna,
"I told you, I don't want to shapeshift because if I do, I end up like my father, I end up looking like him, like a monster!", yelled Kit,
"So is that why you won't transform?", asked Brenna,
"Yes!", cried Kit,
Before anyone could say anything, there suddenly came the sound of screaming and howling from higher up,
"Come on, we can talk about this later when we are all out of danger", said Einar,

As John, Einar, Kit and Brenna were about to make their way up the stairs, a large horde of armoured werewolves appeared from the nearby meeting hall, there were at least two dozen of them,
"Damn, more cultists!", huffed Brenna,
As Brenna, Kit and John backed off as the werewolves approached, Einar suddenly had an idea,
"Guys, start running up the stairs", he said,
"Why, what are you going to do?", asked John,
"No time to explain, just do it!", barked Einar,
As John, Brenna and Kit ran up the stairs, they watched as the werewolves in the foyer area rushed towards Einar. It was then that Einar reached into his bag and pulled out two dragon orbs. Quickly twisting their handles, he watched as the balls suddenly glowed brightly.
He then kissed them both before he lobbed them towards the werewolves,
"Run for it!", yelled Einar,
As Einar and his companions ran out of the foyer and up the stairs, the orbs went flying before they struck the ground, shattering into a shower of glistening glass fragments. John, Einar, Kit and Brenna watched in horrified awe as the orbs suddenly exploded in a terrific explosion of immense heat, light and noise, engulfing the entire horde in flames. The air was filled with a loud boom as a pillar of fire rose from the explosion, sending body parts and organs raining down upon the ground, splattering the walls with gore.
The explosion also blew the front doors off their giant iron hinges, causing them to crash deep within the Gormwood. After the dust had settled, John, Einar, Brenna and Kit peered down the stairs and saw that the floor of the foyer was blackened and littered with flames, twisted, scorched armour and bloody body parts covered in burning fur,
"Wow, what the hell was that?!", gasped Kit,
"Dragon orbs, highly explosive, I am now only down to four so I need to use them more sparingly", said Einar,

"Come on, we need to find Ulva and the dagger", said Brenna,
Summoning their courage, everyone ran up the stairs as quickly as they could, unaware of the flickering embers that were beginning to rise from the foyer floor. As they fluttered upwards, they brushed against hanging flags and timber beams on the ceiling, causing them to catch fire. Racing through the corridor that sat on the top of the stairs, John and his friends smelt the scent of blood and burning in the air as screaming echoed around them. They saw cultists and servants running past them, fleeing as they tried to escape. There were bodies in the corridor and blood was splattered across the walls where Ulva had attacked them.
As the group ran past some corpses, Brenna stopped dead in his tracks as his eye caught the sight of a familiar looking body. His heart sank as he beheld the young servant girl he had encountered earlier in the day. She had been disembowelled as her entrails were strewn across the floor. Brenna crouched down and gently closed the girl's eyes with a brush of his fingers,
"I'm sorry", he said,
Brenna then got to his feet and went to join his friends further down the corridor. As they ran, they noticed the smell of burning was getting stronger, there was smoke in the air and it seemed the tower was beginning to burn as fires were breaking out. On their way to the council room, John and his friends ran through multiple corridors passing many bodies and pushing past both injured and fleeing cultists. Additionally they also fought and slew a few enraged werewolves who were not so keen to flee.
Eventually Brenna noticed the glow of sapphire lanterns, indicating that the council room was nearby, much to his relief. As they ran down the hallway, they could hear the distant sound of breaking glass, the bellowing of thunder and the howling of wind outside as a storm was now directly over the Gormwood.

When John and his friends came to the doorway of the council room, they could see an intense orange glow coming from inside the chamber. The smell of burning and smoke was now intense and they could hear the roaring of fire. Just as they were all about to enter, John, Brenna, Einar and Kit jumped in fright as a large stone table was thrown through the doorway, breaking into pieces as it struck the adjacent wall.

As John, Einar, Brenna and Kit rushed into the council room, they were stunned by what they saw. The walls were engulfed in towering flames whilst the air was hot and thick with choking smoke. The flags draping the walls were burning, the crystal mirror had been cracked and the chairs were in disarray.

In the centre of the room, Vulpes and Ulva were fighting one another. Ulva dashing and leaping around the room as she tried to dodge the fireballs that Vulpes was shooting from his left hand. Sitting in Vulpes's right hand was Vulthur, which he was using to try and stab Ulva whenever she got close enough. On his face was a grim snarl, his eyes locked into a glare of rage. His face was speckled with blood and his robes had been torn where Ulva had clawed him. John noticed that Ulva's fur was dripping with blood, her soft snow-white belly, neck and paws were soddened with blood. Across her body she had some visible scratches and claw marks where she had been attacked.

As Vulpes fired off another fireball, Ulva ran forward before lunging at Vulpes, sending him crashing to the ground causing Vulthur to be sent flying from his grasp. With his mouth open in shock, John raced forward and dived for it, sighing in relief as he caught the dagger in his hand.

He then quickly stood up and sheathed it onto his belt, "No, Vulthur is mine, you shall not take it from me!", barked Vulpes,

It was then that Vulpes fired a stream of blue lightning from his hands, striking Ulva in the stomach and sending her tumbling to the ground as she screamed in pain before collapsing,
"No!", cried John,
Vulpes stood up and said,
"Finally",
He then turned to see John, Brenna, Einar and Kit standing before him,
"Now it's your turn, I was going to have my werewolves tear you all apart, but now that you are here and my patience has reached its end, I will execute you all myself", said Vulpes,
"Let Ulva go!", yelled Einar,
"Never!", snapped Vulpes,
"Father stop!", came a loud and sudden voice,
Vulpes gazed forward and was surprised to see Kit standing beside Einar, Brenna and John,
"What is the meaning of this?!", he barked,
"I'm leaving father and this time there is nothing you can do to stop me. I'm going with my newfound friends and I'm taking Vulthur with me, even if we must kill you to claim it back. I want nothing more to do with you or this damn cult, Fenrir and his lot can have you, but neither they nor you will keep me in this cage any longer!", shouted Kit,
"I had hoped that you would one day become my heir and succeed me as the Lord of Clan Gren, but it seems that you are a lost cause. You are too human for my liking and too much like your weak and defiant mother to truly take my place. If you attack me here and now, I shall not hesitate to kill you and your newfound allies. The purpose of the cult transcends your worth and I will make sure that you will not leave this tower alive", said Vulpes,
"Not if we kill you first", said John,
"We shall see", growled Vulpes,

It was then that Vulpes began to transform, his red robes began to tear as his body grew larger and more muscular. His hair grew into a flowing mane and from his entire body grew silver fur. His ears and face then lengthened before a tail emerged from behind him. As the transformation finished, Vulpes let out a great and mighty howl.
As Vulpes stepped forward, Kit suddenly rushed towards him with her axe in hand,
"Kit no!", cried Brenna,
John and his friends watched as Kit raised her axe and was about to strike Vulpes when he grabbed Kit by the throat and lifted her off her feet, causing her to drop her axe. Vulpes then glared at Kit before throwing her across the room, causing her to go flying before she struck the floor with a thud.
As Kit cried out in pain, everyone ran over to her and helped her up onto her feet,
"What were you thinking? You could have been killed!", said Brenna,
After spitting out some blood, Kit flashed a grin at Brenna and said,
"Well you did say I needed to fight more",
"Hm, I guess I did say that didn't I", said Brenna,
"Enough!", roared Vulpes before he rushed towards Kit, Einar, Brenna and John,
Seeing Vulpes sprint towards them, Brenna said to Kit,
"Kit, I know that I asked you to fight, but for this one I want you to stand back and keep your distance, this is going to get messy",
Kit watched as John, Brenna and Einar ran towards Vulpes, yelling with anger as they began attacking him with furious swords. As John ran round the beast and stabbed him in the arm and thigh, he glanced over to see that Ulva was still lying on the floor, whimpering, whining and clutching her chest.

As Vulpes was busy fighting Einar and Brenna, John ran over to Ulva, dropping his shield before falling to his knees,
"Ulva, listen to me, I know you are hurt, but you've got to get up", he said,
As he ran his hand through her soft mane, Ulva glanced back at John and growled at him,
"Don't take that tone with me young lady now get up; we need to leave. This whole place is on fire and it's gonna blow once the flames reach the basement", snapped John,
Ulva angrily pushed John away before she tried to stand up, but despite her efforts, she just couldn't do it. Her arms were weak, her wounds were bleeding and her body was shaking with pain. Though he was in pain, John tried with all his might to pull her up, but it was to no avail as she was just too heavy.
As John tried to get Ulva off the floor, Einar and Brenna were busy fighting off Vulpes. Despite them both being seasoned warriors, they were having great difficulty trying to bring down Vulpes. Vulpes bellowed as Einar thrust his sword into his leg and twisted, opening a grievous wound. As blood dripped down his leg, Vulpes screeched in pain before he grabbed Einar by the throat. Einar spluttered and coughed as he was lifted off his feet by Vulpes's powerful grip.
The werewolf then threw him through the doorway of the council room. Einar cried out in pain as he struck the wall outside with a bang and slumped onto the ground. Seeing Einar injured, Kit ran over to aid him as Brenna slashed Vulpes across the chest. Brenna and Vulpes then exchanged horrible and violent blows against one another, Brenna rolled, ducked and dodged Vulpes's terrible claws and fangs whilst Vulpes held firm against Brenna's quick and painful sword strikes. Vulpes suddenly punched Brenna in the gut, causing him to fall to his knees in pain as his belly erupted with pain. Brenna coughed and spluttered as he clutched his stomach. Vulpes then raised his claw and was about to decapitate Brenna when suddenly a voice called out to him from behind, "Hey Vulpes!",

Vulpes turned round to see John standing with his sword and shield in hand,

"Leave him alone!", he yelled,

Vulpes snarled angrily at John and ran towards him as Ulva pushed through the pain and quickly got to her feet before fleeing. John then raised his sword up in readiness to face Vulpes before they suddenly clashed against one another, exchanging and glancing blows as terribly hot flames billowed around them. Suddenly Vulpes swiped at John and knocked his shield away before pushing him to the ground.

As John groaned in pain, Vulpes grabbed him by the throat and held him up at eye level. John thrashed about and tried to free himself from the werewolf's grip, but it was no use. John tore at Vulpes's large and furry arm with his fingernails, he saw a grim smile appear on Vulpes's face as he could smell the sickening stench of rotting flesh upon the werewolf's breath, a noxious scent that made him gag,

"And now that I have you little man, you shall die", growled Vulpes with a horrible, guttural tone of voice,

Through watery, stinging eyes, John watched as Vulpes opened his jaws and was ready to bite his head off when there came the sound of sprinting and heavy paws.

Suddenly Vulpes was struck from behind, causing both him and John to go flying, striking the ground hard and painfully. Gritting his teeth, John pulled himself up and saw Ulva was slashing and tearing into Vulpes, snarling and roaring with pure, unbridled rage.

John picked up his sword and ran over to Brenna, Kit and Einar as Vulpes and Ulva tussled and fought one another with biting fangs and sharpened claws. Vulpes struck Ulva in the face, drawing three long and painful claw marks down her muzzle. Ulva leapt backwards, crying out in pain and shaking her mane as the blood dripped down her face and onto the floor. She snarled at him as Vulpes got back to his feet.

Now the two werewolves were circling one another, growling at each other venomously and staring back with hatred and loathing for one another.

Vulpes and Ulva clashed as fire raged around them, the screams of the fleeing cultists echoing around them as Tarn Gren was slowly getting enveloped in flames.

Ulva yelled as Vulpes bit her arm, he roared in pain as she rushed round and snapped at his tail, biting through fur and bone. Vulpes swung his arms and claws repeatedly, Ulva dodged, rolled and ducked as he sent a barrage of unending blows, trying to break her bones.

Finally after what seemed like a relentless assault on her body, Ulva suddenly surprised Vulpes by jumping backwards before running forward.

She raced past him and latched onto his back before sinking her claws into his flesh, causing Vulpes to cry out in pain. She then tore into the back of his head with her snout and bit down hard, severing his spinal cord.

Vulpes was horrified to feel his body suddenly go numb as he lost all sensation in his limbs. Unable to stand, he collapsed to the ground with a thud, Ulva leaping off his back as he came crashing down. With Vulpes lying on his back, he watched as Ulva clambered onto his chest. He was powerless to stop her as he had become paralysed and couldn't move an inch, the only thing he could move was his eye, which darted around frantically inside his skull in terror as Ulva leaned in close.

Vulpes could only watch in horror as Ulva snarled at him, baring her red gums and bloodstained teeth. It was then that she sunk her teeth into his shoulder before she tore out a massive strip of flesh, causing him to scream in pain. She then burrowed her snout deep into his one healthy eye before wrenching it out with a sickening quelch followed by a popping sound.

With Vulpes blind and screaming in agony, Ulva suddenly clamped down upon his neck with her fangs, crushing his vocal cords before tearing out his throat in a shower of blood. Vulpes clutched his neck as it poured with blood before he fell silent and expired, uttering a long and deep moan as the last gasp of life left his body.

Victorious over her foe, Ulva consumed the flesh hanging from her mouth before letting out a great and triumphant howl that rang out through the entire chamber. She then leapt off Vulpes's corpse and landed softly in front of John, Brenna, Einar and Kit. It was then that Ulva was about to attack her friends and family when part of the ceiling nearby collapsed, sending stone, timber and dust flying.
Noticing this, Ulva got on all fours and raced out of the room and down the corridor,
"Ulva!", cried John as he ran after his wife through billowing flames without thought or hesitation,
"John, wait!", cried Brenna before he chased after his friend, Einar and Kit followed and it was fortunate that they did, for as they ran through the doorway, the roof above them collapsed, sending masonry crashing down that crushed the crystal mirror and Vulpes under a hail of burning stone.
Before she ran after her friends, Kit glanced back and said, "Goodbye father",
John could see Ulva in front of him, she was running on all fours and was racing down the corridor, ignoring the cultists that were running past. John and his friends raced through burning corridors, trying to keep up with the crimson-coloured werewolf in front of them.
John felt his chest tightening as he leapt over dead bodies and dodged burning pieces of ceiling mortar falling on top of him. Screams of pain and the sounds of people crying out for help echoed around him, the air was filled with the roaring of burning fires, the shattering of glass and the tumbling of falling stone. John raced past a nearby room, he watched in horror as the floor of the room collapsed, sending several servants and cultists falling to their deaths as they screamed. Ahead Ulva pushed through a group of cultists and raced round a corner. As John neared the end of the corridor, he gasped as part of the floor collapsed, sending a torrent of fire rushing upwards from the wide cracks.

John ran past the column of fire and dashed around the corner, coming to a corridor that was engulfed in flames, through which he saw a few cultists panicking,
"The tower is falling, run for your lives!", cried one of the cultists,
John watched as the cultists suddenly ran towards him,
"Get out of the way!", one of them yelled,
John watched in horror as the wall to the left of the cultists suddenly exploded, burying them all in rubble, their screams of terror quickly extinguished as their lives were snuffed out like candles. John leapt over the great mound of rubble in front of him, followed closely by his friends.
Arriving at yet another corridor, John saw Ulva running down this one, ignoring the fire and the collapsing walls around her. John immediately rushed after her, dodging more masonry and more fallen bodies that had been crushed. There came the sound of a distant explosion and the whole corridor suddenly shook and vibrated, nearly throwing John and his friends off their feet as the earth quaked.
Eventually, after racing through what seemed like an endless number of corridors, Ulva dashed through a nearby door and into Vulpes's room, it too was on fire. The window nearby was lit up by great flashes of lightning. John watched as Ulva shattered the glass of the window, causing torrential rain and howling wind to suddenly rush inwards, pelting Ulva, John and his friends with ice cold and lashing rainwater.
Outside were towering and dark pine trees that were shaking and creaking in the wind, their lumbering forms disturbed by the chaos of the storm. It was pitch-black outside and there were more screams coming from deep within the Gormwood. John gasped as Ulva leapt through the window and fell into the darkness. John ran over to the window and saw Ulva land onto the deep snow below and with a howl, she ran off into the depths of the Gormwood and out of sight.

Without thinking, John jumped out of the window after her, his mind clouded by emotion and worry for the safety of his beloved wife,
"Ulva, wait!", he yelled,
"John no!", cried Einar,
Einar, Brenna and Kit watched in shock as John fell several stories before tumbling onto the snow below. Grabbing his sword and shield, John quickly got to his feet as his entire body throbbed with pain, hunger and exhaustion.
Wiping the ash and dust from his smoke blackened face, John coughed and spluttered as icy air entered his lungs.
Checking that his bag was firmly fastened onto his back and ensuring Vulthur was safe and secure on his belt, John tightened the clasp of his cloak and ran after Ulva, fleeing into the stormy forest, his figure illuminated by silvery strikes of lightning,
"Damn boy is going to get himself killed!", huffed Brenna,
"We have to go after him!", cried Einar,
"Right!", said Kit,
Holding their breaths, Brenna, Kit and Einar all jumped from the window and landed onto the snow below. It was fortunate for them that there was snow, for it cushioned their fall and ensured they were not injured from such a high jump. Had there had been nothing but hard ground beneath them, they would have at least broken some bones, perhaps their legs, at worse, they would have been killed on impact.
With the wind howling around them and the trees shaking and shifting whilst casting horrible shadows, Kit sniffed the air as she could smell the scent of Ulva and John on the wind,
"They went this way, come on!", cried Kit as thunder boomed and lightning flashed around her,
Kit ran further into the Gormwood with Brenna and Einar running close behind, illuminating the lanterns attached to their belts as they went. As all three of them came to a dark and frozen pathway, Kit sniffed the air again and followed the scent of charcoal and almonds down through the trees, over bumps and steep embankments.

As Kit came to a stop, she was about to say something when suddenly a huge and fiery explosion erupted from nearby. It startled Kit and her friends as their ears were filled with a mighty tremor. They watched in horror through the gaps in the trees as Tarn Gren exploded, engulfing the entire tower in a dazzling light and roaring flames.
Past the noise of the explosion, you could just barely hear the faint and panicked screams of people as the tower collapsed. As Tarn Gren came crashing down, its walls sundered and cracked as the ground quaked and flaming debris rained down upon the forest. Just as the noise began to quieten down and the screams began to die out, more explosions burst forth from the fortress, reducing it to nothing more than a smouldering hill of burning stone and ash, entombing hundreds of people.
Still shaking from the shock of the explosion, Kit gasped, "What the hell was that?!",
"The barrels under the fortress must have ignited", said Brenna,
"Forget about all of that, we need to find John and Ulva before they both end up hurt or dead", said Einar,
"Which way did they go?", asked Brenna,
Kit inhaled deeply, filling her lungs with cold air as she could smell the damp of the undergrowth moss and the rainfall, the smell of burning from the ruins of Tarn Gren and the rich scents of pine, wild garlic and earthy soil. She tilted her head and moved her neck around, trying to locate John and Ulva. Finally she caught their scent and opened her eyes,
"This way", said Kit as she pointed down a nearby path,
Kit began to run down the narrow pathway and into the darkness, with Brenna and Einar running close behind,
"I just hope they are okay", sighed Brenna,

CHAPTER XVII:
ULVA UNLEASHED

Some distance away, John huffed and groaned as he was out of breath. He sheathed his sword and strapped his shield onto his back. He pulled his lantern from his belt and turned it on. Holding up the lantern with a trembling hand and with his heart pounding fast in his chest, John looked around at the trees surrounding him, light bouncing off their dark, thick and towering trunks. The rain was thankfully no longer torrential and had calmed down to a hazy drizzle, but it was still windy and there was still the occasional sounds of booming thunder and the odd flash of lightning, which made John jump in fright. As he glanced round at the forest surrounding him, John realized that his friends were no longer behind him and Ulva was not in front of him. Amidst the chaos of Tarn Gren's destruction, everyone had been separated. John was hit by the sudden realization that he was all alone in the Gormwood and that frightened him greatly. Shaking with fear, John slowly and cautiously began to walk down a nearby dirt road. He didn't know where he was going or where Ulva was, but he had to find her, he just had to. Despite being frightened, wounded, alone, exhausted, hungry and greatly wanting of water and rest, John was determined to find his loved ones.

As he began his walk, he started calling out for Ulva and his friends, trying to ignore the ominous howling of wind and the rustling of leaves around him, as well as the occasional cawing of crows and the hooting of owls amongst the trees.

Somewhere deep in the Gormwood, Ulva found herself at a small and shallow stream, a babbling brook that wound its way through the undergrowth of the forest. As she stepped forward, Ulva was bathed in moonlight as there was an opening in the trees above her.

She sat herself down near the river and dipped her front paws into the cool and crisp water, shivering as it washed over her painful skin. She then washed the blood from her hands and inspected the deep gashes covering her hands and arms. Shaking as her body was wracked with a dull and throbbing pain, Ulva then dipped her feet into the water and allowed the blood and dirt to wash away from the soft paw pads beneath the toes, arch and heel of each foot.

After that was done, Ulva began washing herself down with river water and began drinking from the stream in long and deep draughts. Once she was cleaned of blood, dirt and ash, Ulva then began to tenderly lick the wounds on her belly, paws and arms.

As she tended and nursed herself, Ulva glanced up as she suddenly heard a twig snap behind her and as she turned round, she saw a figure emerge from the shadows.

It was Vilhelm, who waved at her as he grinned maliciously, "Hello there Fräulein, it has been a while hasn't it?",

Ulva glared at Vilhelm and growled at him with bared teeth and fangs,

"Oh don't be like that, it was nothing personal, I was just following Vulpes's orders. If I had known he was going to pay me such a paltry sum of silver for your death, then I wouldn't have bothered at all", said Vilhelm as he began to pace in front of Ulva,

"I suppose you are wondering how I got here after our little scene back in Gormstad. After I gave the guards the slip, I saw you all climbing into a well and so I gave chase, traversing through filthy and dark passageways until I came upon Vulpes's little tower. I saw the barrels in the basement and after seeing the spreading flames, I knew the tower was gonna blow itself sky high, so I hightailed it out of there. I must admit, I am surprised that you survived, but it doesn't matter though, you will die by my hand, right here, right now", he said,

Ulva got to her feet and snarled at Vilhelm, arching her back and flaring her tail in a threatening manner, which made Vilhelm chuckle with amusement,

"Little puppy's in a foul mood, very well then, if it's a fight you want, then it's a fight you will get. I mean after all I didn't come all this way to exchange pleasantries", he said as he unsheathed his golden sword,

Seeing Ulva snarling at him, Vilhelm's smile faded as his heart sank, he couldn't help but feel a little remorseful over what he was going to do next,

"I am terribly sorry you know; I understand the pain and anger you are going through for I too have seen many good people brought down by this vile curse. When Brenna and I were the best of friends, we both promised each other that we would rid this land of the wolfblight together. But we both had a falling out over the manner of how we would do this. He wanted to cure the afflicted and educate people about the wolfblight and how to avoid it. I thought this was too slow and too ineffective, so I chose to deal with the wolfblight in the quickest and most efficient way possible, kill the afflicted and bring an immediate end to their torment and suffering. Forgive me, but this must be done, auf wiedersehen and goodbye", he said,

With terrifying speed, Ulva ran forward and began swinging her arms at Vilhelm. The werewolf was taken aback when Vilhelm quickly deflected her blows with considerable ease. With her blood boiling with rage, Ulva attacked Vilhelm again, who chuckled as he dodged the second blow. It was now his turn to attack, Vilhelm spun as he slashed at Ulva, catching her in the arms and chest with the tip of his sword. The two clashed violently against one another, exchanging blows whilst dodging and ducking,

"Not bad Fräulein, not bad at all", laughed Vilhelm,

Ulva roared as she swung her claw at Vilhelm, she winced as Vilhelm brought his axe up to his face, deflecting the blow and crushing her paw with a metallic ding.

Ulva then jumped backwards and circled Vilhelm whilst he was clanging his sword and axe together. Ulva suddenly rushed at him, trying to bite his throat. Vilhelm stabbed Ulva in the thigh, causing her to flinch in pain.

Ulva ducked as Vilhelm swung his golden sword, nearly decapitating her. She retaliated by slashing him on the arm, causing him to drop his sword. In anger, Vilhelm lunged at Ulva, knocking her off her feet and sending her onto her back. He then began punching her hard in the snout repeatedly, causing her to cry out in pain.

Vilhelm then picked up a stone from the forest floor and tried to lodge it deep within her throat as he pried her jaws open. Ulva however kicked Vilhelm off by raising her hindlegs and thrusting them deep into Vilhelm's chest, knocking the wind out of him and sending him flying.

Ulva ripped the stone out of her mouth and discarded it before rushing towards Vilhelm. Vilhelm groaned as he pulled himself up, he glanced around and picked his sword off the ground. But before he could react, Ulva snatched the sword away and tossed it into the thicket nearby.

Enraged at this, Vilhelm began swinging at Ulva with his axe, the werewolf leaping backwards as she tried to dodge the axe's sharp head.

She yelped as she miscalculated a step and felt the axe slide across her arm, splitting the skin and allowing blood to run down her fur. Clutching her arm, she began to feel weak as the constant fighting was beginning to take its toll on her health. Having just fought Vulpes and his minions, she was ill prepared for an encounter with Vilhelm. After being struck in the back, Ulva wheeled round and saw Vilhelm raise his axe, it was then that as it came down, she grabbed the axe by the shaft before ripping it out of Vilhelm's grasp and tossing it aside.

Vilhelm's mouth dropped aghast as he realized that he was defenceless, he stared at Ulva before quickly fleeing into the forest,

"Fine you win, leave me be!", he yelled,

Ulva did not listen and immediately chased after him. Vilhelm cried out in terror as the werewolf pounced him, sending him crashing onto his back.

Vilhelm looked back at the wolf face leering at him, her eyes fiery with rage as saliva was dripping from her mouth down onto his face.

Seeing this, Vilhelm put his hands up to shield himself, "Wait, don't kill me!", he cried,

As Ulva was about to bite his throat, she heard wolves howling nearby. Lifting her head up, her nose caught the scent of something delicious. Ulva glanced back at Vilhelm and brought her head down to bite his neck. It was at that moment when Vilhelm suddenly rolled onto his side, crying out in pain as Ulva sunk her sharp teeth deep into his arm. She then leapt off Vilhelm and ran into the night to pursue the smell that had caught her attention earlier. Vilhelm squirmed and clutched his arm as it began to flare up with a horrible burning sensation. He cried out as pain began enveloping his entire body and he noticed a foul and bitter smell in the air.

Down the pathway, Ulva was running on all fours. She eventually came to a clearing that bathed in moonlight. There she saw a small pack of wolves circling the freshly slain corpse of a sheep. The sheep's shaggy white wool was blood-soaked and its head had been partially torn from its body. The scent of the raw mutton was intense and made Ulva drool, causing her stomach to rumble.

As she stepped forward, the wolves noticed her presence and arched their backs, snarling and growling to try and intimidate the werewolf away from their kill. But it was no use, Ulva stood on her hindlegs and let out a great and long howl. The wolves whimpered in fear and ran away, but not before one of them grabbed one of the sheep's legs in its mouth and chased after its pack mates. Ulva calmly walked over to the sheep and began to feast, burrowing her snout deep into the sheep's stomach, ripping pieces of fatty flesh from its bones and snapping them up.

Ulva stripped ribbons of meat from the sheep's body and consumed them, pulling out organs and swallowing them down. For a while, she gorged herself on the carcass until there was little left. As she finished feeding, Ulva noticed a purple butterfly hovering nearby. She growled and began chasing it, swiping the air with her paws as she followed the butterfly deeper into the forest and away from the beaten path.

Elsewhere in the Gormwood, John weakly cried out for Ulva. His clothes were damp, his hair was dripping with rainwater and he was shivering. Feeling his legs beginning to give way, he stumbled over to a nearby tree and slumped himself down, putting his back up against the thick, cold trunk. The ground beneath him was cold but dry and at least under the branches of the tree, he was sheltered from the elements. He reached into his bag and pulled out a small round and purple coloured fruit topped with a small green leaf. He slowly ate it, feeling the sweet juice running down his throat. As he felt cold air on his face, he pulled his cloak over his body to try and warm himself. For a while John stayed awake, but as the night wore on, his eyes got heavier until he drifted off to sleep, too tired to carry on,

"Damn it all!", cried Kit as she came to a stop,

"What is it?", said Brenna with a concerned tone of voice,

"I've lost the scent, I cannot smell either Ulva or John anymore", said Kit,

"How can you lose the scent? People don't stop smelling suddenly!", yelled Brenna,

"I don't know, stop shouting at me!", cried Kit,

"Guys relax, we haven't lost them yet, we'll just have to keep searching the forest for them for as long as it takes", said Einar,

"Fine, but before we move on, can we stop for a moment and have something to eat?", asked Kit as she felt her stomach beginning to rumble,

"We don't have time for a picnic", said Brenna,

"It's okay, we can eat whilst we walk", said Einar,

Feeling a little embarrassed, Kit said,
"Um Einar, I know I was the one who asked if we could eat, but I actually don't have anything on me. Would it be okay if I...I mean...might I share some of your... um",
Laughing softly, Einar said,
"Yes Kit, you can have some of my food",
Blushing slightly and grinning softly from ear to ear, Kit said,
"Thanks, I don't mean to be a nuisance",
"Nonsense, it's fine, you just have to ask", said Einar as he pulled out an apple and handed it to Kit,
Feeling her mouth beginning to water at the sight of the enticing fruit, Kit quickly gobbled it up, pulverising it into a sweet tasting pulp with her sharp teeth. Whilst Brenna, Einar and Kit made their way deeper into the forest, they shared amongst themselves some apples and some lumps of cheese as they walked together.
Seeing Kit voraciously gobbling up every piece of food given to her, Einar said,
"Slow down, you're gonna make yourself ill eating like that",
Wiping her mouth of crumbs and juice, Kit said,
"Sorry, I haven't eaten in days",
As a look of concern appeared on his face, Einar said softly,
"How come?",
"I...don't want to talk about it", said Kit as she looked down at the ground with a downhearted glance,
"Okay if that's what you want", said Einar,
After they had finished eating, Brenna, Einar and Kit carefully tread down a slope before they came to a long and winding path that snaked its way around the towering trees,
"I hope they are okay, the Gormwood is dangerous this time of night", said Brenna,
"Why did John simply run off like that? Why couldn't he have waited until we were all together?", said Kit,
"Because when it comes to Ulva and ensuring her safety and comfort, John can sometimes be irritatingly selfish, stubborn and dumb, sometimes all at once", said Einar,
"Really?", asked Kit,

"Yes, but that is only because he loves her, perhaps fanatically so. There are times where he doesn't think straight and usually runs headfirst into dangerous situations to keep Ulva safe, as you have witnessed first-hand. There are times where he only cares about her and no one else, but that's because he's afraid of losing her and is always focusing on ensuring that doesn't happen. I mean considering what he has been through in the past, I can't blame him for thinking and acting in such a way", said Einar,

"You shouldn't enable his behaviour Einar", said Brenna,

"No, but anyone would do anything to protect the ones they love, even terrible things", said Einar,

"What has he been through?", asked Kit,

"Sorry Kit, but I don't think John would be happy if we talked about him behind his back", said Einar,

"Fair enough, I suppose loyalty is a noble and admirable trait, I just wish we had all stayed together", said Kit as she scoffed down another apple,

"We'll find them, the Gormwood may be big, but I imagine they can't have gone too far, I mean where would Ulva go?", said Einar,

"Gormstad perhaps?", said Brenna,

"Good point, I just hope she stays away from the town. In any case, we need to hurry our steps", said Einar,

"What are we going to do after we find her and John?", asked Kit,

"We can talk more about that later", said Brenna,

As Brenna, Kit and Einar began making their way down the nearby path, they began calling out for John and Ulva, their voices floating through the dense forestry around them as they went. However, despite their cries and efforts, Brenna, Einar and Kit spent the entire night walking around the forest, searching in vain for their lost friends.

Not too far away, John was still asleep and was huddled up under the tree. With the cold wind on his face, John began to stir as he slowly opened his eyes and yawned deeply before he stood up. He glanced around at the forest surrounding him before he turned off his lantern.
Collecting up his rucksack, John slowly walked down a nearby snowy slope as he rubbed his eyes. He felt more refreshed and more alert, but he was sore and hungry, his throat was dry and his arms ached. As the first light of dawn appeared in the sky, John could hear chirping birds as sunshine was beginning to peer through the trees.
John walked through some shrubs and wild overgrowths of plants and vegetation before he suddenly heard a voice calling to him,
"John, Ulva!",
John perked up as he recognized the voice, it was Brenna. Following the voice, John ran through the forest as fast as he could, jumping over logs and ducking through groves of garlic and wildflowers. As Brenna's voice became louder and more distinct, John jumped through a green thicket of bushes before finding himself on a dirt path.
He turned round to see Brenna, Einar and Kit were behind him,
"John!", they cried in unison,
"Brenna, Einar, Kit!", he yelled,
John ran over to his friends and hugged Einar tightly,
"Oh thank the gods, we've been wandering the forest all night looking for you, I'm so glad you are safe lad", said Einar,
"I'm sorry for running off, I...",
Before John could finish his sentence, Brenna suddenly punched him square in the face, causing pain to erupt across his mouth,
"What the hell Brenna, I said I was sorry!", yelled John,
"Don't you ever run off like that again, I don't care if it was for Ulva, I do not want to go through all of that again, we have been worried sick about you!", spat Brenna in anger,

"I'm sorry, I don't know what came over me. I just wanted to make sure Ulva was safe", said John,
"Yeah well next time consider how your actions affect your friends", said Brenna,
"I will try", said John,
"But at least you are unharmed that's the main thing", said Brenna,
"We were worried John, there were times where we thought we might never see you again, that Ulva might have attacked you and fled the forest", said Kit,
"Well I appreciate the concern, for what it's worth", said John,
"Did you find Ulva?", asked Brenna,
John shook his head,
"No, I tried to find her, but I needed to rest, I couldn't stay awake any longer", he said,
"Damn it, well we need to get a move on then. There's no telling where she might be by now or if she's hurt anyone", said Brenna,
"Dawn has come and she will likely be turning back by now, if she hasn't already", said Einar,
"Do you guys have any idea where she might be?", said John,
"No, but she can't be far, let's try the northern road and see if we have any luck there. If she's not there, then we'll try the southern road", said Brenna,
As quickly as they could, John, Einar, Kit and Brenna made their way down the path, feeling the morning sun on their faces, the golden rays a welcoming sight after such a tumultuous night.
Near the northern road, Ulva awoke to the sounds of trees swaying in the breeze and the sounds of cawing and rustling leaves. She yawned deeply, stretching out her body and tail, her fur fluffing up as she felt the cold air on her face.

As she got to her feet, she slowly made her way past some bushes and continued walking until she came to a small clearing amongst the forest, a wide and open space surrounded by trees. In the middle of the clearing was a small two-storey timber building.
It was simple in design, rectangular and had several open and glassless windows lining the outside walls, the chimneys were smoking and there came the smell of cooking food wafting on the wind. Feeling her mouth salivating, Ulva crept over for a closer look. It was then that she saw something curious. Near the building were dozens of small deer, tawny and brown in colour, their little backs speckled with white fur. They were galloping about and tenderly playing with one another, their little hooves clopping as they ran, their fluffy tails wagging with happiness. The young bucks and does were being watched carefully and with adoration by three larger deer, two of them were large stags with magnificent antlers and manes.
Licking her lips Ulva crouched down, observing them for a moment before she rushed towards them. The little fawns noticed the werewolf rushing towards them and they let out little bleats of terror as they ran, trying to flee the monster that was chasing after them. The two larger adult stags ran towards Ulva as the adult female tried to huddle the infants together as they cried with fear. The two stags fought valiantly and they were able to wound Ulva in the chest, but they were no match for the might of the werewolf. The two stags were gorged and torn to shreds by a rush of fangs and claws, their blood spilling out onto the ground. Seeing this, the female deer urged the little ones inside as Ulva ran to meet her. The deer yelled out and tried to headbutt Ulva to keep her away from the infants, but her efforts were in vain. Ulva swiped at the female deer and knocked her head clean off her shoulders with one fell swoop, sending it flying before it hit the wall of the cabin with a gory thud.
Ulva then began chasing after the baby deer nearby and made light work of them.

She picked some of them up and tore them in half with a sickening snap. She then ripped off their heads and sliced up the poor creatures. The deer could do nothing but scream and cry as she devoured them, consuming their flesh and blood with gluttonous rage, pigging out as she feasted on the blood of the tender innocents.

After she had killed all the deer that were outside, she raced into the building and systematically began hunting down the rest. Some of them were trying to hide inside wardrobes and under beds, but she found them easily, tearing them from their hiding places before devouring them in a horrific scene of slaughter. They squirmed and screamed as she crushed their skulls inwards and broke their bones, slamming their bodies against the walls and dashing out their brains. She raced into the kitchens and grabbed a large female deer by the throat before slamming her into the ground so hard that her belly split open and her internal organs ruptured. Ulva mopped up the entrails before seeing more baby deer running out through the front door. Furious and blood-soaked, Ulva gave chase. She leapt through the door and quickly finished them off. After gorging on their bodies, Ulva glanced around and realized that all the deer were now dead, their bloody and broken bodies lying scattered across the greenery.

Ulva glanced around before she walked forward. She was about to leave the clearing when she froze and fell to her knees.

Ulva groaned as felt her skin suddenly tighten around her body, squeezing her limbs and suffocating her. Ulva then let out a terrible cry before she clutched her head with bloody paws and collapsed to the ground. As Ulva was enveloped in morning light, her fur started to melt, running off her body and pooling at her sides as it turned to liquid. Ulva's muzzle then began to fall off her face, revealing fresh and young human skin underneath. As the last aspects of her wolfish visage melted away, Ulva slowly opened her eyes as she found herself lying on her stomach.

She could hear John, Brenna, Einar and Kit calling out as they ran towards her. As they got closer, her friends suddenly stopped and gasped in unison. Kit let out a scream of terror whilst Einar started to heave. Brenna covered his mouth in horror with a shaking hand as he stared wide eyed at Ulva. John staggered backwards, his mouth hanging open in abject disbelief at what he saw.

Ulva pulled herself up onto her knees as she glanced at her friends, wondering why they were staring at her with expressions of horror and shock, speechless and frozen with fright,

"Guys, what happened? Where am I?", she said,

"Odin's mercy Ulva, what have you done?", gasped John,

Ulva blinked in confusion,

"What do you mean?", she asked,

"Turn around", uttered Einar,

Ulva turned round and gasped at what she saw. On the greenery were scattered bodies, the broken and mutilated corpses of dozens of dead children, human children. Horrified, Ulva put her hand to her lips and wiped blood off her mouth. She then glanced down and saw that her body was covered in blood. Ulva looked forward and saw the bodies of three adults lying near the building sitting amidst the clearing. She saw two men and a headless woman sprawled out by the front door. Ulva looked up and noticed there was a wooden sign sitting above it which simply read, *'Gormwood Orphanage"*.

Ulva's eyes widened before she held out her bloody hands in front of her face and began to tremble with horror at the realization of what she had done. She inhaled deeply and let out a piercing scream followed by bloodcurdling wailing as tears began to flow down her pale face. She fell to her side and began rocking back and forth as she cradled her head in her hands, crying loudly as her friends tried to calm and comfort her.

CHAPTER XVIII:
AN OMINOUS ANNOUNCEMENT

As he carried a small bundle of cloth that was moving slightly in his arms, Skoll made his way down one of the great corridors of Ulfholl before he climbed some stairs and arrived at the door that led to Hati's room.
Clearing his throat, Skoll gently knocked on the door before he heard a voice coming from inside,
"Enter!",
Glancing down at the cloth huddled in his arms, Skoll entered and saw a large pile of bloody bones heaped up in the middle of the room, lying on top of which was Hati. She was wearing her crown, a simple black dress and a leather collar embossed with iron. In one hand she was holding up a book and was reading attentively. In her other hand she was holding the end of a long metal chain. At the end of the chain sat a large woman who was busy gorging herself on cream cakes, humming in delight as she filled her mouth with delicious, creamy treats, her mind drowning in a potent cocktail of drugs and narcotics that were dulling her senses and making her blissfully unaware of the danger she was in.
Engrossed in her book, Hati licked her bloodstained finger before turning a page, unaware of Skoll's appearance at the door. It was one of her favourite novels, an epic story of a Norseman named Vilkun the Voyager who would set out on many incredible adventures across Scandinavia. Hati especially enjoyed the character of Valka, the malamute companion that accompanied Vilkun on his travels, his closest and dearest friend.
Sighing deeply and contently, Hati glanced down at the woman on the floor and said,
"Bryga my dear, have you ever read the stories of Vilkun?",
"Can't say that I have your highness", said Bryga as she finished her plate,

"Such wondrous tales, you'll have to read them one day", said Hati,
"Yes my princess", said Bryga,
Hati wriggled with glee on her bone pile as she came to her favourite chapter, the part where Valka meets Dornir, the canine companion to the royal guard Svelnari. Just as Svelnari would fall in love with Vilkun, so does Valka for Dornir. Brimming with delight as her heart fluttered with joy, Hati said,
"Oh Bryga, how I long for a mate of my own, someone to share my life with. But who could love such a monster like myself? Who could tolerate my grotesque appetites and still look upon me with adoration befitting a royal princess?",
"I'm sure you'll find someone your highness", said Bryga as she began eating through a second helping of desserts,
Walking up to the bone pile before coming to a halt in front of Hati, Skoll said,
"My sister, I need to talk to you",
Hati did not respond,
"Hati", growled Skoll,
Once again Hati remained silent as she continued reading her book,
"Hati!", barked Skoll,
Hati sighed before she lifted her head so her gaze met Skoll's flaming red eyes,
"What is it brother, can't a girl have some time to enjoy some light reading? I only have a short amount of time to finish this chapter before I must go and ensure the holding pens are secure and induct some people into the cult. After that I have a hunt and a most relaxing bloodbath scheduled with the girls", she said,
"I wanted to apologize for my temper the other day, my mind was not in a good place at the time", said Skoll,
Hati scoffed,
"Oh is that why you are disturbing me, to beg for my forgiveness? Dear brother if you want my forgiveness, you will have to get on your knees and earn it", she said,

Before Skoll could respond, the door swung open and a young servant boy appeared in the doorway,
"Your royal highness? There are some men here to see you", he said,
Hati gasped with excitement,
"Excellent, my boys are here, send them in", she said,
The servant bowed his head and through the door entered three large, handsome and muscular men.
They walked over to Hati and sat themselves down beside her on the pile,
"Hello boys, welcome to my humble and cosy lair, come, come, your princess needs some attention", said Hati,
One of the men began running his fingers through Hati's long black hair whilst the second gently caressed and kissed her arms and legs. The third man meanwhile read poetry to her and spoke honeyed words of fanatical devotion to the Princess of Wolves, praising her physical and personal qualities whilst showering her with all manner of adulation that made Hati blush and squirm with joy.
"Hati I am serious, I spoke out of line, I have just been so stressed lately building our forces", growled Skoll,
Hati placed her book down and collected up a nearby goblet filled with wine which she began to chug down greedily. As some of the red wine began running down her chest, one of the men pulled himself close to Hati and began lapping it up gently with his tongue, causing Hati to giggle with amusement.
Once she had finished the goblet, she tossed it aside with a clatter and said,
"Skoll if you want to kiss my ass, you will have to get in line and wait",
Seeing Skoll glance down at the floor looking rather dejected, Hati sighed and rolled her eyes,
"Oh very well, I accept your apology", she said,
Skoll perked up,
"Really?", he said,

"Really, now get out, my boys are going to shower me with love and it is rather awkward having your older brother watching you like some gross pervert", said Hati,
It was then Hati's smile grew wider,
"Unless you want to join us for some fun", she purred,
Skoll shook his head,
"No thank you, I have important matters to attend to. But before I go, as a gesture of goodwill, I have brought you a little gift", he said,
Hati glanced at the bundle in Skoll's arms, realizing what it was, she perked up and pulled herself off the bone pile, causing some bones to spill from the horrible hoard.
She walked over to Skoll, staring at the bundle as he passed it to her,
"Be careful with it, I went to great lengths to procure it", said Skoll,
As Hati held the bundle in her bloody arms, she felt something small and warm inside, it was moving about and making noises.
She gently unwrapped the bundle and gasped at what she saw. Inside the bundle was a baby, a human baby, no more than several weeks old. He had his eyes closed, his head was round and delicate, his puffy cheeks were rosy and his body was small and free from any marks,
"Oh he's beautiful, thank you my brother", said Hati,
"I knew you would like such a treat. Anyway I will let you be, I need to find Garm. He has received some news that requires my attention", said Skoll,
Skoll watched as Hati began talking sweetly to the little infant and began stroking its tiny head with black sharpened fingernails before she sat herself down on the bone pile, her boys crowding around to catch a glimpse of the tiny and tender new-born. As everyone was preoccupied with the baby, Skoll grinned as he left the room.
Staring down at the small baby in her arms, Hati said,
"Such an adorable little thing aren't you? I bet your mother misses you terribly",

It was then that Hati could feel her mouth beginning to water,
"And she will", she said,
As he came down the stairs, Skoll could see Garm standing at the bottom with his arms folded,
"You have news Garm?", growled Skoll,
"Yes, but you are not going to like it", said Garm,
"Try me", said Skoll,
"Very well, Godi Vulpes is dead", replied Garm,
Skoll blinked in disbelief,
"I'm sorry what?", he said,
"Are you deaf meathead? I said Godi Vulpes is dead, Tarn Gren is a ruin, most if not all of the Gren pack are dead and Vulthur has been taken", said Garm,
Skoll stared unblinkingly at Garm before a horrible and outraged snarl formed on his scarred face,
"What, how, who?!", he bellowed,
"We don't have all the details, but my spies have reported that last night, a werewolf escaped and attacked the fortress, destroying Vulpes and taking Vulthur", said Garm,
"And you only tell me this now?!", barked Skoll,
"I needed confirmation of the incident and I think I now know who is responsible", said Garm,
"Whoever it is, I will rip out their throats, I will flay them alive, I will break every bone in their bodies!", roared Skoll, his red eyes glowing with fury,
"Calm down Skoll, it was Ulva Forrester and her little friends, they stole the dagger and destroyed the tower in revenge. Apparently Vulthur was originally in their possession and after Vulpes took it, they went after him to get it back", said Garm,
"Seriously?", said Skoll,
"That's not all, according to my spies, they are on their way to Coldwood and they plan to use the dagger to cure Ulva. We also have learnt that one of our own has betrayed us, Kittra Vulpesdottir, she helped them escape", said Garm,

"Tell me where they are, I will send a detachment of my berserkers and have them destroyed, then I will claim back the dagger!", yelled Skoll,
"First things first, I will need to gather the high delegation and inform them of the situation, Packmaster Daghilda will want to know of her brother's demise. Secondly I must ensure that the other twelve packs are safe. Thirdly, I will need to send some siblings out to the Gormwood to locate any survivors that might still be in the forest. Fourth and finally, I will need to inform father", said Garm,
"Then can I unleash the Ulfhethnar and tear them asunder?!", snapped Skoll,
"Let us wait and see what father has to say about all of this first", said Garm calmly,
"Fine, but I have a bloodlust that needs to be sated", grumbled Skoll,
"Relax you great brute, your thirst for blood will be slaked yet, just have some patience, skin a few of the prisoners if you need some release for all I care", said Garm,
Skoll angrily glared at Garm as he watched his brother ponder to himself.
It was then that Garm said,
"Now that I think about it, perhaps them escaping Tarn Gren might work in our favour",
"What do you mean?", said Skoll,
Garm smiled maliciously and said,
"I have a plan, but it will require that you restrain yourself Skoll for the time being",
"Fine", growled Skoll,
"Come, let us discuss it over some frosted wine", said Garm,

CHAPTER XIX:
INVOKING THE PAST

Along the northern road outside Gormstad, Brenna, Einar, Kit stood and stared sadly at Ulva as she was standing at the edge of the road. She was hunched over and was violently vomiting, John was standing behind her and gently rubbing her back as she heaved up the contents of her stomach, which was a mixture of vomit, bile, blood and chunks of flesh and broken bone,
"Feeling better Ulva?", asked John,
Ulva coughed and spat onto the ground as she tried to get the horrible taste out of her mouth,
No...I am not feeling better", she groaned,
"Brenna has some flywater, that might make you...",
"I just ate the flesh of children John, Brenna has nothing that can make me feel any better!", shouted Ulva,
"I'm sorry Ulva, it was just a suggestion", said John,
"I don't need suggestions, I need a cure!", barked Ulva,
"Ulva!", snapped Brenna,
Ulva glared at Brenna as he said,
"I know you are upset right now, but don't take it out on John, he's only trying to help. You have suffered I understand that, but so have we all, we are all exhausted and shouting won't make the situation any better. We want nothing more than to locate and secure a cure for you, but it will take time, so in the meanwhile I want you to try and control your temper and I want you to understand that what happened was not your fault. It was tragic, it was horrific, but it was unintentional and was beyond your control or anyone else's",
"He's right Ulva, what happened to those poor children was unfortunate and nothing would satisfy me more than to turn back the clock and stop it from happening, but what's done is done, nothing can be done about it now", said Einar,

"Ulva please, we're just thinking about your health", said John,

Ulva sighed,

"I know, I'm sorry, it's just the guilt...it's eating away at me and I don't know if I will be able to forgive myself for what I have done", she said,

Covering her face as she began to tear up, Ulva said,

"Do I even deserve forgiveness? Perhaps it would be preferable if I were dead so justice would be served for the lives I have taken",

"Don't say that", said John,

"But it's true, I'm a monster, I have committed horrible acts of atrocious slaughter and it will only get worse the further this disease seeps deeper into my blood and bones!", cried Ulva,

John and his friends could now see visible tears running down Ulva's face,

"Seeing what I did...knowing what I did, it will haunt me for the rest of my life", she said,

Suddenly John stepped forward and without saying a single word, threw his arms around Ulva and pulled her in close,

"You are not a monster, you are a friend, a sister and my wife and nothing you say or do will ever change that", he said,

It was then that Ulva buried her face in John's chest and began to cry, sobbing loudly as she shed bitter tears,

"That's right Ulva, let it all out, let the grief, anger and sorrow pour from your heart, keeping it locked away will only poison you", said Kit before she glanced at Einar,

"Releasing your emotions now and then ensures you don't become twisted by melancholy, drowned by your emotions and suffocated by your dark thoughts", she said,

"Hm, that's quite profound", said Einar,

"It's how I have managed to keep myself intact throughout the years. My body might have been imprisoned at Tarn Gren, but I would never allow my mind to be imprisoned, not for one second. So instead of bottling up my feelings, I would release them from time to time", said Kit,

"That takes a lot of courage and strength of character Kit, I'm impressed", smiled Einar,
Kit said nothing, but she did smile sweetly at Brenna and Einar.
When Ulva calmed down, John said,
"It will be okay Ulva, you're just tired and in need of rest...here",
Kit, Einar and Brenna watched as John scooped Ulva up and cradled her in his arms,
"Try to sleep Ulva, it will do you some good", said John,
Ulva weakly nodded before she closed her eyes and rested her head up against John's chest, yawning as she was lulled by John's gentle heartbeat,
"Come on let's go, we have a long journey ahead of us", said Brenna,
With Ulva in his arms, John began moving forward with Einar, Kit and Brenna walking close behind. Heading away from the Gormwood, everyone looked forlorn and despondent. Though they now had Vulthur back in their possession and were now properly on their way to Coldwood, no one was in the mood to celebrate or conduct themselves in a jovial manner as the sight of the massacre at the orphanage had sullied their spirits.
Instead they simply walked in silence over rough terrain and small hills as they followed the path northwards. They were all exhausted and greatly wanting of some rest. But they all knew they had to keep going, for time was against them and it was dangerous to be lurking near Gormstad in the presence of two werewolves.
As everyone was making their way down the path that lay ahead of them, Kit was glancing over at John and Ulva.
She noticed that John was silently watching Ulva sleep with a soft and weary smile on his face as he cradled her in his arms,
"So how did you two meet?", said Kit,
"Pardon?", said John,

"Back at Tarn Gren, you said you were Ulva's husband, so I can assume you are both married. I am curious, how did you both meet? We are finally out of danger, so now is a good time to get to know one another if we are to travel together", said Kit,
"It's a long story", said John,
"Oh go on I'm curious, I've told you all a little about my past, so it's only fair that you reciprocate", said Kit,
"Well it was twelve years ago when we first met, I was living in my hometown of Bamburgh in the Kingdom of Northumbria", said John,
"So you are not from here?", asked Kit,
"No, I hail from the north of England, the land of the Saxons", said John,
"Interesting, you don't look like how I imagined you to look", smiled Kit,
"Really?", said John,
"From the stories I've heard about England being a wild and wicked land full of monsters, witches, sorcerers and powerful kings and clerics, I thought you would have looked a bit different, with glowing eyes, horns and scales", said Kit,
John laughed and said,
"Sorry to disappoint you, but I had them removed a long time ago, they were proving troublesome",
Kit laughed,
"Really?", she said,
"No I'm just kidding; we are mostly just humble farmers and churchgoers. It's funny though that you should mention it though, before I met anyone from Scandinavia, I thought the exact same thing you did. I thought that the Norse were strange beings who worshipped shapeshifting demons and nightmarish monsters whilst conducting pagan rituals of blood and darkness in the forests. We thought you mindless barbarians drunk on butchery, but meeting Ulva and Einar, I learnt that I was wrong...on a day that I will never forget", said John,
"What happened?", said Kit,

"I had just completed my basic education and was setting out into the world of work. I had chosen to become a miner and so I travelled a short distance from my hometown to the priory of Lindisfarne to collect some books that might assist me in my newfound career. I went to the library there and found a book on excavation techniques. In my haste to grab it, it fell to the ground and as I went to pick it up, someone else went for it", said John,

Kit grinned,

"You met Ulva?", she said,

"I glanced up and saw a young girl of fourteen staring back at me. She was carrying a pile of books and looked a little flustered. From that moment I laid eyes on her, I was smitten. She was so beautiful, how her long, luscious hair shimmered like fire, her blue eyes shining like winter frost and how her face was lit up by her cute little smile. I explained that I needed the book and after an awkward introduction, she assisted me with taking it out with permission from the head librarian Hethward. We got to talking and agreed that once her work for the day was complete, we would go to the tavern for a drink together and get to know one another", replied John,

"How lovely, it sounds quite storybook, like the beginning of a beautiful romantic novel", said Kit,

"It would have been a memory filled with nothing but heart fluttering bliss, but then the raid came and sullied it forever with memories of terror and fear", said John,

Kit frowned,

"The...the raid?", she said,

John looked down sadly at Ulva as she slept soundly and said, "Before we left, the priory came under attack from vikkar raiders from Denmark and Skaneland. They attacked the priory because it was famous for being a beacon of wealth and knowledge, its riches immense and its wealth immeasurable, both literary and material.

The raiders pillaged the priory and slaughtered dozens of monks and nuns. I lost friends in the ransacking, even archbishop Higbald himself was injured",
"How awful", said Kit,
"It was terrible, I can still hear the screams of terror and the howls of pain over the tolling bells as the entire monastery was ravaged by fire and smoke", said John,
"And where was Einar?", asked Kit,
"I was travelling west towards Iceland as part of an expedition", said Einar,
"Okay so what happened during the raid?", said Kit,
"When the raiders attacked the library, Ulva and I tried to flee, but we were trapped as the entrance was swarming with invaders. We knew at that moment that the only way we were going to survive was to hide and wait until the raiders left. Luckily we managed to find a bookcase and were able to conceal ourselves behind it. For what seemed like an eternity, Ulva and I remained hidden, making as little sound as we could. Eventually when most of the raiders had left, we seized the opportunity to escape and were able to get to the entrance of the library when one raider spotted us and attacked", said John,
Kit gasped in shock, her eyes shining with fear as she stared at John,
"I fought with the raider when he tried to attack Ulva. He mistook her for a Saxon acolyte and wanted to take her back to Denmark and make her his thrall and slave. In my rage, I slew him and ended up breaking my arm. Ulva and I then snuck out of the priory and we walked across miles of horrible marshes and grim bogland during a violent storm. We trudged through darkness and cold rain before arriving at my home in Bamburgh. There we both got ourselves cleaned up and threw on some fresh clothes before Ulva tended to my arm. Together we then made ourselves toasty and warm as we enjoyed a small supper of apple pie and cocoa", said John,

"When my family and I had found out what had happened, we were horrified, but also grateful that Ulva was alive and unharmed. Thanks to John's sword – arm and Ulva's courage, they both lived to tell the tale and John had earned the respect and gratitude of both myself and the rest of the Skarlagens for saving my sister", said Einar,

"I should think so, you nearly died", said Kit,

"As such I was welcomed into their fold as a friend and from Ulva, I gained her affection and friendship that ultimately grew into love", said John,

"Wait a minute, but doesn't your story prove that the vikkar of Norway were nothing but mindless barbarians drunk on butchery? I mean they attacked the priory, slaughtered peaceful monks and even tried to kill you and Ulva", asked Kit,

"You might think that, but Ulva was no barbarian and after meeting her brother and the rest of the family, my stance changed, especially as I got to know them more over the years. Now I realize that it was wrong to generalize an entire people for the immoral actions of a few and sometimes you shouldn't believe what people tell you about others", said John who then glanced at Einar and smiled warmly,

"Who would have thought that the ones I would call family would come from a people I once believed to be evil. Despite sharing no blood, I am closer to the Skarlagens than my own kin", he said,

"And I wouldn't have it any other way", said Einar as he beamed heartily,

"And that's how we met and over the course of several years we travelled back and forth between England and Norway, staying close through thick and thin. Two years ago I proposed to Ulva under an apple tree outside Gormstad and we got married in a beautiful grove amongst a horgr of frozen stone and mistletoe crowned by a starry sky", said John,

Kit blushed slightly as a smile formed on her face, the cockles of her heart blooming with happiness, the first she had felt in quite a while,

"Such a beautiful story and to think the best is yet to come", said Kit,
"What do you mean?", asked John,
"Well you are both married, so I assume you will have children of your own one day", said Kit,
John was silent for a moment before he then said softly, "Yeah…I guess",
Trying to break the awkward silence that followed John's words, Einar said to Brenna,
"Are you okay Brenna? You've been awfully quiet",
"Hm? Sorry I was just deep in thought. A lot has happened since we left Gormstad and I am just trying to process it all and muse upon the revelations we discovered within the tower of Tarn Gren", said Brenna,
"And what have you come up with?", asked Einar,
"Only that we have made a powerful enemy and we were lucky to survive. If Ulva had not transformed there and then, we would have been executed, our chances of escape were practically non - existent. We need to be more aware of the dangers that lie ahead of us and we need to be more prepared, we cannot afford to fail, not even once", said Brenna,
"We'll just have to be more careful from now on, but for now Brenna why don't you relax a little and just take a moment to enjoy the peace while it lasts?", said Einar,
"I guess so, worrying about what has happened and what is yet to come won't help us in the slightest", said Brenna,
"So remind me, what is our first destination?", asked Einar,
"Our first destination is Ishellir Crossing, it is a considerable distance away, but we should be there in a few hours give or take", said Brenna,
"Ishellir Crossing, what's that?", said Kit,
"I work there, it's a small mine, we just need to tell the foreman there that I need a few more days leave", said John,
"What's a mine?", asked Kit,
"You don't know?", said John,

"I've been in Tarn Gren since I was very young, I wouldn't know", said Kit,
"It's a deep hole where we dig up coal and precious metals and bring them to the surface. Anything we find is then used for various purposes", said John,
"I see and work you there?", asked Kit,
"Yes, I am also a gemcutter, I collect and keep any waste stones or gems that I find in the mine. I then clean, cut and polish them before carving little shapes, images and words into them. After that, the stones are threaded onto string and made into bracelets and necklaces. It has become tradition for Ulva and me to make a bracelet for each other whenever we mark a special occasion. Sometimes we make them for friends and family and if money is tight, we sell them at the market in Gormstad", said John,
"Could you show me some of your work one day?", asked Kit,
"I don't see why not", said John,
"Thank you, that would be lovely", said Kit,
"Forgive me for diverging off topic, but I must ask you Kit, you are a werewolf yes?", asked Einar,
"Yes I am, why do you ask?", said Kit,
"Am I correct in assuming that you can transform and shapeshift at will, you don't need to wait until nightfall to turn?", said Einar,
"That is correct", said Kit,
"So I must ask, what is the difference between you and Ulva? I mean you are both werewolves, but there is something different about the way you turn. It is quieter, bloodless and more controlled", said Einar,

"Well I was born with the power to shapeshift whilst being able to maintain control over my mind. Ulva on the other hand has no control over her crazed and feral state, she is what we call a pureblood werewolf. Born from a single bite, purebloods are the most dangerous, vicious and powerful of all lycanthropes, for the venom flowing in their blood is the most potent. The cultists you faced in Tarn Gren meanwhile were granted their powers through a ritual. They can shapeshift in the same way I can, but they were not born with such powers", said Kit,

"A ritual?", said John,

"The Blodsykning, it is how the cultists gain their lycanthropy", said Kit,

"What is the Blodsykning?", asked Einar,

"Why do you want to know? How could such knowledge benefit you?", asked Kit,

"Because as a warrior, I want to know all I can about who we are up against. A man can master a sword, but what good is a swordsman if his mind is not as sharp as the blade he wields? If there is any knowledge out there that might aid us in our journey, then I must have it, not just for my sake, but for Ulva as well", said Einar,

"You have a point, very well I'll tell you as much as I know, but to be honest I know little about the ritual. First the person involved partakes in a special diet, which they must consume over the course of a fortnight, during which they cannot eat or drink anything else. The diet consists of moonberries and wolf milk. This diet is supposed to be what they call the purification stage. The cult believes that the diet purifies the body and the soul. The mind is tapered by patience, the body is moulded by restraint, the blood is cleansed and the soul is purged. Once the purification is complete, the person is taken to a chamber known as an Ulfhov. I've never been in one and I couldn't tell you what goes on inside, only that the participant partakes in an ancient and dark ritual. Only those within the higher ranks of the cult would know more", said Kit,

"Is this shapeshifting ability permanent?", said Einar,
"Yes, it is permanent, only with the power of Vulthur and Fenrir's Bane might it be reversed. For the cultists, such a power is awe – inspiring, but to me personally, it is a constant reminder of how I am nothing more than the creation of a monster", said Kit,
"You are wrong, you are more than that", said Einar,
"I..I am?", squeaked Kit,
"Of course, I mean I have known you for only a short amount of time, but in that time, I have found that you possess a good heart", said Einar,
"I do?", said Kit,
"Put it this way, if you were truly a monster, would you have chosen to help us get out of Tarn Gren?", smiled Einar,
Kit blushed a bright scarlet red as she stared at Einar with shining turquoise eyes, her heart fluttering deep within her chest as her blood ran hot. After walking some distance, John, Einar, Ulva, Kit and Brenna arrived at the edge of the Gormwood and were now standing in the fields that sat outside Gormstad. Before them stretched an open road that snaked over vast green fields peppered with patches of snow and flourishes of luscious spring flowers.
As they walked, Ulva suddenly awoke, opening her eyes and yawning deeply as she gently squirmed in John's arms,
"Are we at Coldwood yet?", she moaned softly,
"No my love, we haven't even left the Gormveld yet", said John,
Ulva sighed before she slipped out of John's arms and staggered onto her feet,
"I think I'll walk for a little while", she said,
After Ulva had brushed down her dress and adjusted her shawl, she took John by the hand and followed Einar, Kit and Brenna as they resumed their journey northwards, unfortunately ignorant to what was to come next.

CHAPTER XX:
THE HORROR OF ISHELLIR CROSSING

With flocks of pigeons, ravens and seabirds soaring high in the sky above their heads and with the strong morning sunlight glaring in their eyes, John, Ulva, Brenna, Einar and Kit climbed a rather steep and grassy incline before they found themselves standing before a vast expanse of luscious green fields and moors peppered with snow, brightly coloured wildflowers, the fractured remnants of burial mounds, stone ruins and the lone shells of abandoned structures for as far as the eye could see.
Such a beautiful sight caused Kit to gasp as she stared with awe and wonderment. She covered her mouth in shock with a shaking hand before saying,
"So...this is the world outside the Gormwood",
"Indeed, Norway in all its untamed glory", said Einar,
His smile faded as he noticed Kit was becoming teary eyed,
"Hey, are you okay Kit?", he said gently,
"Yes, it's just so...so beautiful", said Kit,
Watching Kit beginning to whimper, Einar walked over to her and said,
"It's okay Kit, take as much time as you need to take it all in",
Wiping the tears of happiness from her eyes, she then breathed deeply, savouring the fresh and crisp air that rushed into her lungs.
It was then that she began to laugh loudly and joyously,
"Freedom!", she cried,
Everyone watched with surprise as Kit suddenly ran forward as fast as she could through the fields, her arms spread outwards as she yelled and laughed with unrestrained delight and blissful euphoria, her face lit up by a jubilant smile,
"The wind, the sun, the beautiful blue sky, the sights and sounds, it's all so wonderful!", cried Kit ecstatically,

Kit then threw herself into the tall grass and beautiful crimson flowers, laughing with unbridled happiness as she rolled around.

Seeing Kit leaping through the flowers and rolling around in the grass, Brenna smiled and said,

"Look at her, so happy, after what she has gone through I don't blame her for acting in such a way. To be trapped all your life like a bird in a cage and to be denied real companionship, love and care, just running through the grass must feel so liberating for her",

"Kit did say she had a bad childhood when we were in the Gormwood, so I completely understand her need to celebrate her newfound freedom", said Einar,

"A bad childhood…that's an understatement, I imagine she has suffered years of neglect and abuse both physical and emotional, the scars visible across her body are testimony to it all. Those are not wounds inflicted through mere accident, those are marks made intentionally by monsters", said Brenna,

"Yeah not to mention she barely blinks, has a slight limp and sometimes makes wolfish noises instinctively. Such characteristics are indicative of someone who has suffered a lot of pain", said John,

"Guys stop talking about Kit when she's not around and stop commenting on her appearance and behaviour like she's some freak or animal. She's a poor girl who has endured much hardship and I don't want us judging her behind her back. If you guys have something to say about her, have the decency to say it to her face", snapped Ulva,

Einar sighed,

"You're right Ulva, of course you are", he said,

"Indeed, I am glad to have her here with us", said Brenna,

"Me too", said John,

"What you guys talking about?", came a voice,

Brenna, John, Einar and Ulva turned to see Kit standing before them, grinning sweetly as her shirt was covered in petals, seeds and tiny heads of pollen whilst resting on her head was a wreath of colourful and pretty wildflowers,
"Nothing Kit, everything's fine", said Einar before he smiled,
"Had a good time?", said John,
"Oh yes, the flowers smell fantastic and the air is so fresh and crisp, I love it. I can't wait to see more wonders on this journey", said Kit,
Brenna chuckled with amusement,
"Well I'm sure we will see and experience many more wonders on our quest. Come let us be off, the day won't last forever and we need to get Ulva somewhere secure by the time dusk arrives", he said,
"Of course", said Kit,
With Kit joining their side along the beaten path, Brenna, John, Ulva and Einar began making their way northwards away from the fields of flowers and towards the vast grasslands of the Gormveld that whistled with the gentle sound of blissful zephyrs.
It would be a while before they all finally arrived at Ishellir Crossing. There was a path that winded itself away from the northern road just past some rocky cairns near a wooden faded sign standing crooked in the ground.
As they walked up the pathway, they caught sight of several buildings made of timber and stone. All the buildings were clustered around a large hillock of grass. Sitting at the foot of this hill was a cavernous entrance that went deep underground. Crowning the top of the hillock was a large timber tower, attached to which was a winding wheel that was capped with a flag. There was a chain going down the centre of the tower and in front of the entrance was a simple metal track, upon which sat small timber carts.
Scattered about the ground were mining tools, rope, pickaxes and barrels filled with powders and liquids used in the extraction of coal.

As the group approached the mine entrance, they noticed a worn sign nearby that read '*Ishellir Crossing Mine*'.
John suddenly stopped and glanced around, eyeing his surroundings with concern and trepidation,
"John, what's wrong?", asked Ulva,
"Can you hear that?", he said,
Everyone fell silent as they looked around, they could hear nothing except the whistling of the wind,
"I don't hear anything", said Einar,
"That's what I mean, it's quiet, far too quiet for my liking. Usually there would be miners out here either working or enjoying some time off. The air would be filled with the sound of clanging hammers and pickaxes, carts trundling upon the rails and a cacophony of laughter, shouting and chatter. But now there is nothing but silence and that frightens me", said John,
"Well perhaps it's a holiday and the mine is currently closed", said Ulva,
"No, this mine is always operational, we never shut, not even for the seasonal festivals", said John before he turned to Brenna,
"Brenna I know this is not imperative to our journey, but I ask that we investigate this. I need to know that my friends are safe before we move on", he said,
Brenna stared at John through shining spectacles for a moment as he pondered to himself.
After a moment of silence, Brenna said,
"Very well, if it will give you peace of mind",
"Thank you Brenna, thank you", said John,
Turning to his companions, John said,
"Guys, have a look around, I'm gonna check over here",
With no time to waste, John, Einar, Ulva, Brenna and Kit quickly scattered and began investigating the area.
After extensively checking the nearby buildings, everyone soon gathered back at the mine entrance, each of them looking rather disappointed by there being no sign of any living miner within the vicinity,

"Find anyone?", asked John,
"No, the sleeping quarters were empty", said Einar,
"Same for the kitchen and the recreation rooms", said Brenna,
"There was no one in the outhouses and the storage huts were deserted", said Ulva,
"I had no luck either, this place is devoid of life", said Kit,
"Then they must be underground then, where else would they be?", said John,
"Perhaps they found or saw something startling and they fled in terror", said Kit,
"Maybe, but we won't know the truth unless we investigate the mine fully. Are you guys ready to enter the mine?", said John,
Everyone nodded in agreement, though they looked worried and anxious. With John at the front of the party, everyone walked over to the mine entrance and peered in, hearing nothing but the sound of gently blowing wind.
As everyone turned on their lanterns, John said,
"Right guys, be careful as you go in, the ground is not stable and keep an eye out for any pits, slopes, falling rocks and sudden drops",
Carefully and cautiously John and his friends huddled themselves together and began walking down into the mine. As they walked deeper into the bowels of the earth, the air seemed to become colder and darker. Approaching the end of the tunnel, Einar, John and Brenna drew their swords. Realizing that Ulva and Kit did not possess any means of defence, John unsheathed Vulthur and handed it to Ulva while Kit was told to stand between Einar and Brenna so that they could protect her from any unsuspecting dangers, Kit still stubbornly unwilling to turn should the occasion arise. As he came to the end of the tunnel, John could feel hard stone and loose coal beneath his feet as the ground began to level off. Glancing forward, John noticed a column of faint light coming from a hole in the ceiling.

Upon closer inspection, John saw the light illuminate a large wooden structure that sat flat upon the floor and was attached to a thick chain that stretched upwards through the roof. It was the coal lift and when activated, it would go up through the opening and towards the winding tower outside. After passing the coal lift and making his way further down the dark tunnel, John said,

"Something is definitely wrong here, we should have encountered someone by now or at least heard the miners working, but yet again, there is nothing, not a single sound, where is everyone?",

"Maybe they truly did leave in a hurry", said Ulva,

"But what could have possibly scared them? We miners are pretty fearless, it would have taken something truly horrific to drive my friends away", said John,

"That's what I am afraid of", said Kit,

"We'll know the truth soon enough", said Brenna,

As he turned a corner and entered a tunnel located on the left, John was become increasingly frightened and worried. Even the presence of his friends or wife wasn't calming him down.

Suddenly John saw something catch the light of his lamp. There was a barrel standing near the wall beside some iron tracks and a beam of timber that was supporting the roof just up ahead.

Upon the barrel lay an abandoned book and sitting up against the barrel was a sword that glistened in the lamplight.

John walked over to the barrel and picked up the sword before handing it to Kit,

"Here take this, if you won't transform to protect yourself and your friends, then at least use this", he said,

"How?", asked Kit,

"Just swing and stab with it, it's not difficult", said John,

Einar couldn't help but laugh as Kit rolled her eyes,

"Not to worry, I'll teach you how to use it, perhaps even show you a trick or two", said Einar,

Turning back round, John lifted his lamp and glanced down upon the book sitting before him. Eyeing its cover, he picked it up and began inspecting it, noticing that the pages inside were dishevelled and speckled with dirt.
In golden writing upon its cover was the title of the book, *'Logbook of Miner Roan Ragnirsson of Ishellir Crossing',*
"Is that a book?", asked Brenna,
"Yes, it is a logbook, every miner that works here owns one, even I have one. These logbooks are important as they serve as our own personal journals and work records. What I don't understand is why Roan would leave his book here in such a manner. Losing or mistreating your logbook can lead to you being punished or fined", said John,
"Read it, it might provide some clues as to where everyone has gone", said Ulva,
John opened the book and began to read, flicking through pages filled with useless lists of names, images and numbers. However near the end of the book were a few pages of a journal which chronicled Roan's daily life within the mine up to a few days ago,
"Moonsday the fifth of Goa - Received a delivery of more food today, mostly coarse grains, milk and salted game. Godric says we need more lumber to bare the weight of the fifth tunnel, told him I will put in an order later today.
Tyrsday the sixth of Goa – Today something attacked Felbert, we were able to wound it, but we couldn't kill it, instead it fled and skulked back down into its lair. Felbert said it looked like a man with the head of a dog. I think he's been drinking too much, there is no such thing...Lunchtime today and Felbert had to resign to his quarters for some rest...wasn't feeling well. Suppertime and Felbert awoke, complaining about feeling itchy and hot all over. He was famished, consumed a whole cut of lamb, four quarters of veal and half a dozen tankards of ale. Valdr was not happy about this and when he confronted Felbert, Felbert lost his temper and nearly beat Valdr to death. Foreman Raben has taken command whilst Felbert and Valdr are being treated by our healer.

Odinsday the seventh of Goa – Last night Felbert vanished as did Valdr, what the hell is going on? First his gluttony, then the mood swings and now he has disappeared. I've sent some men down into the mine to find them, I don't like this..By Odin's mercy! Shock and horror! Valdr was found dead in one of the tunnels, he had been mauled and partially eaten by something, still can't find Felbert. All miners have been ordered by Raben to stay inside the living quarters until morning.
Thorsday the eight of Goa – Felbert was found this morning, he said he had no recollection of the previous night and had woken inside one of the mine shafts. Foreman Raben has ordered Felbert to take some time off. Felbert was not happy at all.
Freyjasday the ninth of Goa – I cannot believe what is happening, last night the miners doing the night shift were attacked, they are all dead! I can't...we need to...",
John noticed that the final page was damaged and the words upon it were illegible.
Putting the book back down upon the barrel, John turned to his friends and said,
"It all makes sense now, the sudden and ferocious appetite, the changes in mood, a man with a dog's head, Felbert was attacked and bitten by a werewolf. I...I think Felbert attacked and killed my friends",
"But it still doesn't explain where everyone is now. We should continue onwards and see if we can find anyone, hopefully someone who is still alive", said Brenna,
"I hope you are right", sighed John,
Glancing into the tunnel up ahead, John began calling out to his friends,
"Godric, Cuthbert?",
Stepping forward, John shouted,
"Aud, Roan, Edmund, where are you guys?!",
There was no response, just silence.
Suddenly there came the creaking of metal and a rumbling noise from deep within the tunnel as something large began trundling towards John and his friends.

From the darkness appeared a long train of mine carts fastened to one another, racing down the tracks with terrifying speed,
"Look out!", cried John,
Seeing the carts rushing towards them, John, Einar, Kit, Ulva and Brenna quickly dived out of the way, just barely dodging the mine train as it sped past them and continued barrelling down the adjacent tunnel.
The wagons continued hurtling forward until they struck the end of the tunnel, derailing with a loud crash before spilling coal everywhere whilst filling the tunnel with dust.
After everyone had helped each other up off the floor, John glanced over at the broken train and said,
"Those carts were incredibly heavy, there was no way they could have simply moved on their own. Someone or something deliberately pushed them, that means there might still be someone alive in the mine",
"John, I think we should leave, we know what happened to the miners, let's just go whilst we still can", said Ulva,
"I'm sorry Ulva, but we are not leaving until I know for certain what happened to my friends", uttered John,
"John we are in danger, we were nearly just killed!" blurted Ulva angrily,
"My friends could still be alive, I can't just leave them here to die!", shouted John,
"And if we stay here we could die!", snapped Ulva,
"Guys enough! We'll go further down and see if we can find something, if we don't find anything then we will leave. Just be on your guard and watch where you step", said Einar,
John and Ulva silently glared at each other whilst Brenna, Kit and Einar made their way back down the tunnel.
As they went deeper into the mine, they could hear the faint sound of footsteps and the crumbling of falling coal,
"Hello, is anyone there?", said Brenna,
There was silence, however as they kept walking forward, everyone suddenly heard a weak and faint voice calling out from a nearby opening,

"Guys, did you hear that?", asked John,
"Through here, I can smell blood", said Kit,
Kit pushed herself through the hole in the wall, sniffing the air as she followed the scent. Her friends followed her in and they all trudged through the darkness until came to a wall. Sitting up against the wall was a hunched and bloodied figure, an elderly man with soft brown eyes and a silver goatee beard. His tunic and trousers were torn and his chest had been ripped open, next to his left hand lay a small and twisted knife.
John gasped,
"Cuthbert!", he cried,
John dropped to his knees and placed a comforting hand on Cuthbert's cheek as his friend coughed violently, his breathing strained and weak,
"Is that you John?", said Cuthbert,
"Yeah it's me, what the hell happened?", said John,
"It was Felbert, he was bitten by a monster. He was fine at first, but then he went crazy and turned into a beast before he killed the miners working the night shift. He then started attacking people above and below ground indiscriminately. Many of the miners were slaughtered like cattle, Aud, Roan, Gunnar, all dead. I tried to fight him off, as did the few surviving miners, but he was just too powerful. Though I was gravely wounded, I was able to crawl away and hide in here. I have spent the last two days sitting here in darkness, hearing Felbert's heavy footsteps and beating heart. He has been walking back and forth within the tunnels dragging bodies into his lair located further down within the mine", said Cuthbert weakly,
"Cuthbert, can you walk? We need to get you out of here", said John,
Cuthbert gently pushed John's hand away and said,
"No my friend, it's too late for me. My spine has been shattered and my legs are broken. I...I have lost a lot of blood and I am so sleepy...so tired",

"No Cuthbert, you're going to be okay. We'll get you to a healer and you'll be fine!", snapped John,
Cuthbert shook his head before he coughed up some blood and weakly said,
"Get out of here John before he comes for you too, save yourself...save...your...",
Cuthbert let out a groan of pain before he closed his eyes and exhaled his final breath,
"No, no, no, no he can't be dead!", gasped John,
"I'm sorry John", said Brenna,
"We should heed his words and go before things get worse than they already are", said Ulva sadly,
"Yes...let's go, I've seen enough", said John,
As they comforted John, Einar, Ulva, Kit and Brenna left the tunnel and started making their way back to the entrance. But as they were ascending the entrance shaft, they all gasped in horror as a shadowed figure appeared standing in the entrance, it was a werewolf. The werewolf let out an angry howl before he picked one of the nearby timber carts and hurled it towards John and his friends, who were just able to dodge it before it crashed into a broken heap.
But the werewolf then suddenly threw another cart, which went flying before it struck one of the beams holding up the roof.
Suddenly John and his friends could see small pieces of stone and rock begin to fall from the ceiling accompanied by a low, rumbling sound,
"Run!", cried John,
In a panicked rush, John, Einar, Brenna, Ulva and Kit raced back into the tunnel as the walls around them began to shake and crumble. Suddenly the tunnel roof behind them collapsed, causing the walls to cave in with a mighty and roaring tremor as clouds of dust and sharp splinters of fractured rock and coal were thrown up. John, Einar, Brenna, Kit and Ulva ran past the hole where they found poor Cuthbert and came to a halt as the rumbling had stopped behind them and it became quiet once more.

Turning round, they saw nothing but a wall of rock, the entrance had been blocked off and they were trapped,
"Shit!", barked John,
"Looks like we can't go back that way", said Kit,
"Well that's just great, now we're trapped. We wouldn't be here if people had just listened to me. We should have left after that mine train nearly ran us over", growled Ulva,
"Well I'm sorry but I had to see where my friends had gotten to!", snapped John,
"Guys please!", cried Kit,
"Why didn't you listen to me, did you want to be a hero and rescue everyone, is that it?", snapped Ulva,
"What? No! I mean maybe", said John,
"Because you're doing a grand job of that", said Ulva,
"Why are you talking like all of this is my fault?! I didn't bring down the roof!", blurted John,
"No, but if you had listened to me, we wouldn't be here!", shouted Ulva,
"I had to find out what happened to my friends Ulva, I have known some of these people since childhood, would you have done the same if they were your friends?", said John,
"Well yes, but these miners are not my friends are they?!", blurted Ulva, her face etched into a snarl,
"Oh so it's okay for you to save your friends, but it's not okay for me to save mine? Would you have preferred it if I let them die instead?! Oh forget Cuthbert and Roan, we must save Tora and Dalla from the book club!", yelled John,
"All right that's enough from both you, no one is to blame for our circumstances and we will get out of this, one way or another", said Einar,
"I certainly hope so", growled Ulva,
"Shut up, now I want you both to apologize to each other so we can put all this behind us and move on before Felbert finds us", said Einar,
Ulva folded her arms and said,
"I'm not apologizing, why should I? I didn't get us into this predicament",

"Neither am I; I will not be blamed for something I am not responsible for", said John,
"Whatever I don't care, either way we need to keep moving", said Einar,
As John and Ulva glared at each other angrily, Einar, Brenna and Kit made their way down the tunnel in front of them, leaving them both to sulk as they followed closely behind, their faces turned away and their gazes averted from one another,
"If we find Felbert, I'm going to kill him, friend or no, he must pay for what he has done", said John,
"Hopefully he hasn't turned permanently and is still in control of his body and mind. There might be a chance to save and cure him if we take him along with us to Coldwood", said Brenna,
"But it's been a long time since he was first bitten, I doubt that he's still the same person I remember him being", said Einar,
"Either way he dies", growled John,
"Only if the wolfblight has fully claimed him John. It would be wrong for us to kill him otherwise. If Ulva was in the same situation, you would do everything to save her and you certainly wouldn't condemn her to death", said Brenna,
"But he killed my friends!", snapped John,
"And Ulva has killed plenty of people too. Felbert is deserving of help just as much as she is", said Brenna,
"I suppose", said John,
"Let's just hope we can get out of here without having to deal with him. After facing my father and his minions, I'd rather not tangle with another werewolf right now", said Kit,
"Same here lass", said Einar,
After walking through lamplit darkness, John and his companions soon came to a black wall of glistening coal and uncut diamonds. There were three coal wagons sitting nearby on the tracks, it was here that the train had been uncoupled and sent racing forward.

Turning to the right, John, Einar, Kit, Brenna and Ulva entered a nearby opening and began making their way down another narrow and gloomy tunnel. Eventually everyone found themselves standing in a large cavern, its high ceiling sparkling with the gleam of bright stones, the coal shining like stars against a clear night sky.

After adjusting the brightness of his lamp as he entered, Einar stepped in with his friends following close behind.

Gazing around, Einar suddenly noticed something standing amongst the rocks nearby, the black outline of some shadowed figure,

"Who's there? Show yourself!", he demanded,

As Einar went to investigate, he was surprised to find that there was no one there, the entity had vanished in a burst of light that bounced off nothing but large crops of stone,

"Guys I don't think we are alone in here", whispered Einar as he felt a chill of dread run down his spine,

As soon as Einar finished his sentence, he suddenly heard a stone being thrown.

It startled everyone and upon investigation, its source could not be located,

"Let's...let's continue", said Einar as his heart began to race, Einar glanced at John and said,

"You lead the way, you know this mine better than anyone of us",

John nodded and traded places with Einar before Kit, Ulva, Einar and Brenna followed him close behind. As Einar stood beside his sister at the back of the group, there came what sounded like a soft moan, gentle, but audible enough to send everyone rushing out of the cavern with all haste, screaming in terror as they heard footsteps coming up behind them.

After running blindly into a nearby opening and through a narrow tunnel, they soon found themselves standing in another cavern, this one very similar to the first, but the air was filled with the sound of dripping water from the ceiling.

John walked forward before coming to a halt as something caught his eye, something that made him drop his sword in shock. Brenna covered his mouth in horror, Einar and Ulva huddled up against one another and Kit stared with her mouth hanging open as they all stared mortified at what they saw. The cavern floor was littered with the corpses of dead miners, all of them mutilated, broken and disembowelled. John felt sick to his stomach as he recognized some of them, Aud, Roan, Foreman Raben, little Ragna, Groffr Geirbjornsson and Droldur to name a few, their frozen faces ghostly in the darkness, their eyes staring back with lifeless stares.

Feeling nauseous, John suddenly fell to his knees before he hunched over and vomited upon the floor as his belly churned with disgust and revulsion,

"Well at least we now know what happened to them", said Kit sadly,

"They didn't stand a chance", said Einar,

John coughed before he vomited again as his nose caught the scent of rotting flesh,

"I knew them all, every single one of them", spluttered John before he gagged and vomited a third time, his body shaking as he groaned and heaved,

Seeing her husband in such a state, Ulva crouched down and gently rubbed his back before helping him up,

"I'm sorry John", she said,

"You're sorry?", growled John as saliva ran down his chin,

Grabbing a tin flask from his belt, John chugged down some cold water before he inhaled deeply and spat onto the floor as he rinsed his mouth out,

"Yes I'm sorry for what happened to your friends and I'm sorry for shouting at you earlier. I'm letting my anger get the better of me and I don't know if it's the wolfblood or not. You didn't know this was all going to happen and to be honest, it was quite noble of you to think about the safety and wellbeing of your friends without thinking of your own", said Ulva,

John put the flask back onto his belt and picked up his sword,
"These guys helped me through some of the darkest times in my life, I would have done anything for them", he said sadly, Struggling to hold back the tears, John glanced over at his friends and said with a quivering voice,
"Not that it matters now, all I want now is to just get out of here",
John glanced at Ulva and said,
"Just want you to know that I am sorry too, you were just looking out for me...for Brenna, Einar and Kit, it's just another testimony to your large heart",
Ulva smiled at John, who responded in kind.
Suddenly before they could say anything, there came a noise from deeper inside the cavern, the sound of moving footsteps. Such a sound made everyone jump and without a second thought they all unsheathed their weapons and dashed over to the source of the noise,
"If anyone is there, show yourself!", barked John as his entire body trembled,
"Hello?", came a voice,
John gasped, he recognized the voice,
"Godric, is that you?", he said,
"John?", came Godric's pitiful voice,
John and his friends watched as from behind a nearby stone appeared a person, a clean shaven and bald man who was stout in stature, his clothes dirty, ragged and bloodstained. Clutching his wounded ribs, Godric gasped as he saw John. Grunting through the pain, Godric quickly limped towards him. John was horrified to see that Godric was covered in deep cuts across his face, arms and side.
John rushed forward and hugged Godric who responded in kind,
"Thank the gods, I thought I would never see a friendly face again. Please John, help me...make it stop", he said in a weak and coarse voice,
"What do you mean, what happened to you?", said John,

Godric whimpered as he tenderly cradled his wounded arm, "When Felbert attacked, I survived though I was bitten. He killed everyone and those he hadn't killed were taken away to the deepest chamber in the mine. I don't know what he has done to them, but I have been hiding down here for days in absolute darkness listening to screams that would curdle your blood. John, I am frightened, I can hear voices in my head and I am in constant pain", he said,

"Have…have you turned yet?", asked John,

Godric sadly nodded and said,

"The pain was unbearable, I remember desperately feasting on the flesh of my dead friends, even poor Ragna who I loved with all my heart. We used to bake cakes together and revel in each other's company, now she's dead along with everyone else. I am so ashamed of what I have done",

Sighing before he wiped his mouth, Godric said,

"My mouth is so dry…I'm so thirsty",

Without hesitation, John plucked the flask from his belt and handed it to Godric, who gratefully took it before gulping down most of its contents. Godric coughed and took in sharp breaths of air before he handed the flask back to John,

"Thank you John, to taste water again and not blood is nothing short of a blessing", he groaned,

"It's no trouble Godric, now let's get out of here and get you to someplace safe. Then we can look to getting you cured", said John,

"Cured?", asked Godric,

"Of course, I'm not gonna let the wolfblight take you", said John,

"Okay…I'll…",

Suddenly Godric let out a pained cry as he felt a sharp pain erupt from his side,

"Godric?!", gasped John,

"No not again!", cried Godric before he grabbed John by the hand and squeezed tightly,

"Please John end my life, I can already feel the beast welling up from beneath my skin. Please kill me before I turn, I don't want to hurt you and your friends and I will not go through all the pain and torment again", begged Godric,
Before John could speak, Godric suddenly let out a pained gasp as he felt a sharp and terrible pain explode from deep within his chest before it rippled across his back and down his limbs,
"I cannot hold it in much longer John, just please…end my misery. I wish to sleep in peace, I wish to see my friends again so that I can tell them I'm sorry for what I did", he groaned,
"I…I can't Godric, you are my friend, I can't bring myself to do it", said John,
Godric grunted and growled as he could feel his throat burning up.
He spat out blood as his teeth suddenly started lengthening and sharpening into points,
"If you won't, then I will!", he snarled,
As Godric could feel his face beginning to change shape, he raced forward and snatched up John's sword before running the edge of the blade across his throat. John let out a horrified yell as blood gushed from Godric's open neck before it ran down his chest and onto the floor. Dropping John's sword, Godric fell forward, grinning as he felt his entire body go numb and cold. John quickly caught Godric in his arms before gently laying him down upon the floor, his bloody hands shaking as he cradled his friend.
Smiling wearily as blood bubbled from his throat, Godric looked at John and whispered,
"Sweet release…thank you",
Godric then expired upon the floor of the cave, his body going limp and lifeless.
Staring wide eyed at Godric as tears fell down his cheeks, John shakingly picked up his sword, his face frozen in horror,
"I…I",

Placing a comforting hand upon John's shoulder, Einar said,
"There was nothing you could have done lad, at least you tried",
John lowered his gaze and whimpered before he wiped the tears from his face. It was then that Einar noticed John's form go rigid as his hands became clenched.
Gritting his teeth, John glared up at Einar and said,
"He shall be avenged, they all shall be avenged",
Carefully not to tread on the bodies that littered the floor, John, Einar, Brenna, Kit and Ulva made their way quickly out of the cavern as they could hear sounds coming from behind them, the faint noise of shuffling and movement against the sound of faint blowing wind,
"Brenna, can I ask you something?", said Ulva,
"What is it my dear?", said Brenna,
"There's something that's been troubling me. Before he ended his life, Godric was about to turn, but that makes no sense, it's still daylight outside, don't people only turn into werewolves at night?", asked Ulva,
"A good observation, Godric experienced what is known as a noon turning. When the werewolf venom is so overwhelming and the victim is so weak and unstable, they can no longer control themselves and so the wolfblight overcomes them during the day. Godric would have been starving, thirsty, mentally, physically and emotionally broken and exhausted so it's no wonder he transformed when he did", said Brenna,
"Could it ever happen to me?", asked Ulva,
"Possibly, there's a chance it might happen to you the longer the wolfblight remains in your body, but you are younger, healthier and you are in the company of supportive friends, so I don't think you will experience what poor Godric did", said Brenna,
"I hope not", said Ulva,

In silence, John, Einar, Brenna, Ulva and Kit continued making their way through the mine until they found themselves standing within a large and well-lit chamber illuminated by daylight pouring down from cracks and holes in the roof.

To the right of them was an opening that led to a tunnel that went up to the surface and in the centre of the chamber was a large circular pit.

Inside the pit were wooden wheelbarrows, discarded mining equipment and, much to everyone's horror, a large, rotting pile of corpses. The corpses were bloody, pale and starting to turn gangrenous, giving off a dreadful and pungent smell. Cuthbert was right, it seemed that the entire mining crew had been slaughtered before being collected up by Felbert and placed in the pit for him to gorge on.

Stepping forward with their weapons drawn, John, Einar, Brenna, Ulva and Kit noticed a dark and hulking figure sitting hunched over inside the pit.

It was a large creature and it was greedily devouring the body of one very unfortunate miner, snarling as it feasted on blood and bile, it was Felbert,

"Damn it, he's turned and it seems like it's permanent", whispered Brenna,

"Looks like I'll have my revenge after all. Okay guys, get ready for a fight", whispered John,

"Are you crazy?! He's huge!", gasped Brenna,

"Yeah, wouldn't it be easier if we just make a run for the exit?", said Kit,

"No, he slaughtered my friends, they must be avenged lest their souls haunt this hellhole forever", said John,

It was then that John suddenly stormed towards the pit, his eyes locked upon Felbert as the werewolf pigged out in his gruesome nest of flesh and bone,

"John come back!", yelled Einar,

John didn't listen as he shouted,

"Hey Felbert!",

The sound of John's voice made Felbert rear his head and turn around. John and his friends gasped as they saw Felbert's face. His fur was iron grey in colour and his back, arms, head and chest were covered in streaks of black fur, the black encircling his eyes like a mask. His mouth was heavy set and full of long bladed fangs, his snout long and pointed. His eyes were small and deeply set into his massive skull, two beady pinpricks of light that glowed with the colour of red wine. As Felbert eyed John and his friends angrily, John stepped forward and pointed his sword at him,
"Felbert, it's me John, we used to work together remember?", he said,
Felbert dropped the corpse in his hand and shuffled his body round to face John properly,
"After seeing Cuthbert and Godric die, I said that you would pay for what you did. Even though you had no real control over what you did, you killed many of my friends, people whom you too once loved dearly. I am sorry Felbert, but I'm here for revenge and to end your pain", said John,
Felbert snarled at John before he jumped out of the pit and landed in front of John and his friends, letting out a massive roar that made the cavern echo with a tremendous, earth-shaking bellow. John, Einar, Kit, Ulva and Brenna gasped as they beheld Felbert's colossal and lumbering form. He was enormous and thrice the size of Ulva and Godi Vulpes. His body was bulging with throbbing muscle and his paws were gigantic, all four of them ending in sharp bloodied claws. His ridged spine was jutting out of the skin running down his back and embedded deep into the top of his skull was the broken head of an axe.
Suddenly Kit snarled at Felbert and cried out,
"I'm not afraid of you!",
Seeing Kit run towards Felbert with her sword in hand, Einar shouted,
"No Kit!",

As Felbert swung his fist, Kit dodged it and began stabbing at Felbert's feet, causing the monstrous werewolf to roar out in pain and anger. Spurred by Kit's courage, Brenna, Einar and John ran forward and began swinging and stabbing at Felbert's legs. As they did, Ulva stared at Felbert, frozen in fear by the sight of such a terrifying beast.

Einar rolled under Felbert and stabbed his blade deep into the monster's crotch, causing blood to spray as he pulled his sword away. Enraged, Felbert swiped at Einar and sent him tumbling to the floor. Brenna felt wind blast against his face as Felbert missed him by inches. Suddenly Felbert slammed his fist against the ground, causing the floor under Brenna to crack, sending him tumbling. Felbert snapped his jaws and roared as Kit jumped up and clung onto his back before she sliced down his spine.

Felbert raised his arms in the air and shook Kit off, sending her flying before she slammed hard into the nearby wall,

"Kit!", yelled Brenna and John,

As Brenna quickly got to his feet and ran over to see if Kit was alright, Einar and John both charged at Felbert. Ulva was still standing nearby, too scared to move. It was a far cry from her attack on Vulpes at Tarn Gren. As a werewolf, she was fearless, but here she was petrified. Felbert roared as Einar and John repeatedly stabbed him in the arms and legs. Felbert swung his arm and sent John crashing to the ground, knocking the wind out his lungs.

He glanced up as Felbert grabbed Einar and opened his mouth, ready to bite his head clean off,

"Don't you dare!", cried John before he grabbed his sword from off the ground and threw it like a javelin at Felbert's head,

The sword struck through the side of the werewolf's large head, piercing his jaw. Felbert screamed in pain, dropping Einar to the ground. He flew into a rampage as he struggled to get the sword out of his mouth. As the werewolf flailed his arms in pain, John used this opportunity to stab at Felbert's legs and try to bring him to his knees.

Though John was able to land a few blows, Felbert got angrier with every stab. Felbert swung his hand and caught John in the side, sending him crashing to the ground near Einar. Felbert snarled as he wrenched John's sword from his mouth and tossed it to one side. As Felbert slowly began walking towards John and Einar, Ulva saw Brenna running towards the werewolf, his sword held high above his head. Brenna was able to stab Felbert repeatedly in the back and the side, but was felled by a painful swipe of the werewolf's tail,
"Ulva, we need help!", cried Einar,
Ulva glanced at the dagger in her hand and then looked back at Felbert as the werewolf raised his arms up in the air, ready to bring them down upon Einar and John and crush them. Seeing this, Ulva ran forward and slashed at Felbert's hands as they came down. As Felbert roared in pain, Ulva leapt onto Felbert's back, clinging onto his fur as he began thrashing about to try and get her off. As she clutched onto Felbert's shaggy, warm fur, Ulva glanced up at Felbert's head. Realizing where she had to strike, Ulva placed Vulthur sideways in her mouth and began to climb up Felbert's back. Felbert flailed about as he tried to grab Ulva, but she was much smaller than him and he couldn't reach. Felbert began running backwards and slammed his back into the wall nearby. It was fortunate that Ulva had just managed to climb onto his shoulders or she would have been crushed right there and then.
Suddenly Ulva squeaked in shock as Felbert shook his head and flexed his shoulders, which jolted her and caused Vulthur to fall from her mouth and land beside John on the ground with a clatter,
"No!", cried Ulva,
Felbert laughed menacingly as he watched the dagger fall from Ulva's person. He then suddenly began thrashing about, nearly sending Ulva flying off his back. As Ulva clung on dear life, she glanced upwards and suddenly noticed the axe jutting from Felbert's scalp.

As Ulva desperately reached out to try and grab the hilt of the axe, Einar, John, Kit and Brenna suddenly raced towards Felbert, all of them aiming for Felbert's legs and together they swung with all their might as they tried to bring Felbert down. Summoning all her strength, Ulva was able to clamber onto Felbert's shoulders.

With both hands, she grabbed onto the handle of the axe and tried to wrench it out. She struggled and pulled as hard as she could, but it would not budge. Felbert smashed his fists into the ground and charged at John and Einar, rushing them off their feet, leaving Brenna and Kit to distract him. As Ulva's heart pounded in her chest and her vision began to spin, she screamed in rage and pain as she wrenched the axe out.

As blood splattered over Ulva, Felbert let out a terrifying and inhuman screech. Ulva then raised the axe above her head and screamed in anger as she slammed it back into Felbert's skull, piercing his brain. Felbert suddenly fell silent before his eyes rolled back into his head. He then collapsed to the ground with a mighty thud.

As Felbert fell, Ulva was thrown from his shoulders before she rolled across the floor and came to a stop.

After everyone got up from the floor, John suddenly rushed towards Ulva and threw his arms around her,

"Ulva you did it!", he cried,

"No we did it", said Ulva,

"Don't be so modest, that took incredible courage and strength", said John,

Brenna groaned as he stretched his arms,

"That was rough", he said,

As John and Ulva collected up their weapons, Einar stepped over to Kit and said,

"You okay?",

"Yeah, yeah I think I'm good", replied Kit,

"I'm proud of you", smiled Einar,

"What for?", asked Kit,

"You charged towards Felbert with all the courage of a vikkar, your bravery reminded me of some of the finest shieldmaidens I have ever known. I knew you could fight; you just needed a little encouragement. Trust me, we'll make a warrior out of you yet", said Einar,
Kit sheepishly grinned as her face went flush and red with embarrassment.
"Right, let's get out of here before anything else happens", said Brenna,
Brenna's words were proven premature as to everyone's surprise, Felbert began to shift slightly. The werewolf weakly lifted his head and let out a long and mournful howl that resonated throughout the cavern before he fell silent.
Suddenly the air was filled with the sound of horrible howling and screaming accompanied by the scurrying of paws, an erratic shuffling of large bodies and the sound of snarling and snapping jaws.
John and his friends turned to face the tunnel behind them and saw many different coloured eyes emerge from the gloom, all of them glowing with rage alongside glistening fangs,
"More werewolves?!", gasped Ulva,
"Felbert must have bitten a few of the miners, they have heard the call of their creator and now they seek revenge for his demise", said Brenna,
"Run guys!", cried Einar,
John, Einar, Kit, Brenna and Ulva ran as fast as their legs could carry them as the werewolves bellowed and cried in anger. Kit was first to enter the nearby opening, followed by Ulva, John, Brenna and finally Einar. They ran through the exit tunnel until they were forced to stop.
Instead of finding a tunnel that led straight to the surface, they came upon a large wall made of mud, broken stone and coal which sparkled in the lamplight.

The tunnel had collapsed and the only way through was a small hole sitting in the middle of the wall, just big enough for them to crawl into,
"Quickly get inside!", barked Brenna,
"Are you serious?!", blurted Kit,
"Just do it!", snapped Brenna,
Kit was the first in, followed closely by her friends. Together they all began to climb up the slope, crawling on their bellies against the wet and cold ground beneath them.
As they continued to climb, everyone suddenly stopped as they realized that the way ahead had been sealed by a collapse of stone and earth, they were trapped,
"What are we going to do?!", gasped John,
Brenna pondered for a moment before he said,
"Kit, start digging",
"What?!", blurted Kit,
"You're a werewolf, use your paws and claws, it's the only way out", said Brenna,
"I can't, I gave an oath that I would never transform", said Kit,
"Look, I know you don't want to and I know that you think being able to shapeshift into a werewolf makes you a monster, but you have to transform or else we will die in here. It isn't something I would ask of you if there wasn't any other way", said Brenna,
Kit said nothing as she whimpered, her mind rushing with the images of her father tormenting her in his werewolf form, his wicked laughter ringing in her ears,
It was then that John shouted,
"Kit please, transform now or we're going to die!",
"Hurry!", cried Ulva,
"You can do it lass, I believe in you", said Einar softly,
As the sound of angry screams and howls got louder, Brenna, Ulva and John began pleading with Kit,
"Do it, do it now!", came the cries,

With her heart pounding in her chest and the pleas from her friends bleating in her ears, Kit gritted her teeth as she closed her eyes, trying in vain to block out the noise.

As the noise became unbearable, Kit let out a scream before she suddenly began to transform. Kit groaned in discomfort as she felt her body, legs, ears and face stretch and contort as they became elongated. Her gloves tore as her fingernails sharpened into claws and her hands turned into paws, all the while her leather boots ruptured as her feet became too large and wolven to be contained.

John, Einar, Brenna and Ulva suddenly heard stretching fabric and the sound of snarling and growling as Kit completed her transformation, Ulva spluttering as her face was smacked by a long and furry black tail.

John, Einar, Brenna and Ulva stared in shock as they saw that Kit was now a werewolf with glistening silver claws and fangs. Her body was covered in jet black fur, but her belly, throat, face and snout were coloured a shade of pure white. Unlike Ulva, Vulpes and Felbert, Kit was still wearing her clothes, albeit pulled and stretched to fit her new form and she was surprisingly not a great deal bigger in size than she was before she transformed,

"Well done Kit, now go!", cried Brenna,

With her chest throbbing with pain and with her eyes welling up with stinging tears, Kit furiously began to claw at the dirt wall in front of her. As she did, a swarm of werewolves suddenly burst into the cavern behind her. Some of them were naked whilst some of them still had pieces of fabric attached to their bodies where their clothes had torn, the remnants of their now lost humanity.

With dirt showering down upon them, John, Ulva, Brenna and Einar began to crawl on their hands and knees as Kit burrowed upwards with all her might to the sound of screaming, roaring and howling. Suddenly as John reached up and grabbed the walls running alongside him, he gasped as he felt his lamp slip from his belt.

It bounced past him, Brenna and Einar before it landed at the bottom of the shaft, shattering into many pieces.

It was then that the pursuing werewolves suddenly rushed into the tunnel below, sending up a whoosh of cold air that extinguished everyone's lanterns, plunging the tunnel into complete darkness, causing everyone to cry out in terror,

"I can't see a thing!", gasped John,

"Just keep going up!", yelled Brenna,

As Kit dug through the dirt and stone, everyone behind her could feel the air getting hotter and more stifling as dirt and coal rained down on them.

At the bottom of the tunnel, Einar was fending off the werewolves as best as he could as they began crawling up the tunnel,

"Einar!", cried Brenna as one of the werewolves caught his friend by the ankle and began to drag him down and out of the tunnel,

Before the werewolf could snap him up, Einar rolled himself onto his back and stabbed the werewolf in the hand and was able to free himself.

As Kit dug further and further, the tunnel began to get narrower as she went upwards. John coughed and heaved as choking dust and coal fumes began to fill his lungs. Through watery, bleary eyes he looked up and could just make out the dark outlines of his wife and Kit. More werewolves began to enter the tunnel behind them and were quickly closing in, swarming the tunnel opening below,

"Faster Kit!", yelled Ulva,

She winced as she felt Kit sharply kick her in the face with one of her back legs. Kit dug and dug, faster and faster, as fast as she could. Einar gasped as one of the werewolves nearly bit him on the foot, in response he swung his sword to keep them at bay as they continued crawling upwards. Kit was struggling to breath as she continued to dig furiously, all four of her paws becoming painful and sore. She winced and whined as she clawed at the dirt in front of her, trying hard to ignore the pain running through her muscles.

Further down the tunnel, Einar and Brenna furiously stabbed at the werewolves with their swords, trying to keep the werewolves away as the beasts swiped with a flurry of claws and snapped with hungry jaws,
"How long is this tunnel?", coughed John,
In front of him Ulva was spluttering and clutching her chest as the air was running out, her head was getting heavy and her vision was beginning to spin,
"John I can't go on, there is no air in here and the earth is suffocating", she groaned,
"Keep going Ulva, we are nearly there", said John, his hot and stinging face burning and dripping with sweat,
Ulva groaned as she forced herself up the tunnel, her arms and hands aching as she climbed. Einar cried out in pain as several claws swiped at his leg and dug into his flesh. In retaliation Einar thrust his sword into the mouth of a werewolf that was crawling inches away from him.
The creature spluttered before collapsing in a heap,
"That should buy us some time", spat Einar as he noticed that the dead werewolf's body was now blocking the tunnel behind him,
John, Einar, Brenna, Ulva and Kit continued crawling up the tunnel as fast as they could, dragging themselves through cold darkness and entombing stone as the sound of screaming and howling bleated in their ears.
Suddenly there came the sound of gruesome tearing as the werewolves crawling behind their dead packmate burst through his body, spraying blood as they chewed, gnawed and ripped their way through the corpse blocking their path, their bloody snouts poking through torn flesh and broken bone,
"Quickly guys, they are coming!", cried Einar,
Glancing back and seeing furious eyes glowing in the dark behind him, Einar pushed against Brenna, forcing his friend to go faster up the tunnel,
"Stop it!", barked Brenna,
"Then move it!", shouted Einar,

Einar's mouth dropped in horror as he saw the werewolves getting closer and closer, one by one they climbed, shuffling on their bellies as they crawled towards him and his friends. Einar reached out and quickly sliced at one of the werewolves, cutting her across the face. It wasn't much, but it bought him and his friends some more time to escape as the she - wolf writhed in pain. However just as the situation looked hopeless, Kit breached the surface of the mine with her snout.
She burrowed upwards and clawed her way out, howling in pain as her head and torso burst through the earth, her vision filling with bright and almost blinding sunshine, her lungs filling with cold fresh air. Kit pulled herself out before getting onto her hindlegs. She then grabbed Ulva by the arm and helped her out of the hole, pulling her away from the earth, her body bruised, wounded and covered in dirt. John was next to come out, gasping as he took in great draughts of air. He pulled himself from the hole and with his legs weak and wobbly, he fell forward and tumbled into the grass. Brenna was next to emerge, coughing and spluttering, his face covered in coal dust, his body shaking as he got to his feet. Finally there came Einar, who groaned and grunted as he pulled himself up. He yelled in shock as the werewolf behind him rose from the hole and snapped at him, just missing him as he ran forward.
Helping John up off the ground, Einar joined Brenna, Kit and Ulva as they all fled as fast as they could across the field, panicking as the werewolves burst from the ground with horrifying speed, ripping up soil and grass as they tore themselves from the choking confines of the tunnel shaft. The werewolves sprinted after them, their blood-soaked pelts covered in coal dust and dirt. John and his companions watched in horror as they saw the werewolves begin to circle them, howling and barking as they ran round them and blocked off their escape. Seeing the werewolves closing in, Einar quickly rummaged through his bag and pulled out a dragon orb.

As he ran, he turned the handle at the top of the orb, illuminating it with light before wrapping some salted meat around it. Kit let out a yelp as one werewolf lunged at her, luckily she dodged the creature before she swiped at the beast with her claw, causing the werewolf to flee.

John, Einar, Ulva, Kit and Brenna suddenly came to a halt as the werewolves suddenly encircled them, their jaws salivating at the prospect of a good meal.

Standing back-to-back, John, Einar, Kit, Ulva and Brenna stood frozen in fright as the werewolves slowly began walking towards them,

"We don't stand a chance", said Brenna,

"But we have a werewolf on our side", said Ulva as she glanced over at Kit,

"There's too many of them, sheer numbers would eventually overwhelm us even if we managed to kill a few", said John,

"Gods, I don't want to die!", gasped Kit,

"We won't, watch this", said Einar,

It was then that Einar held up the meat wrapped dragon orb in his gloved hand and shouted,

"All right, you brutes want some flesh to chew? Then chew on this!",

The werewolves watched with hungry eyes as Einar threw the orb as high and as far as he could. To everyone's surprise, the horde of werewolves suddenly sprinted after the flying piece of meat, tempted by the irresistible looking cut of beef.

Suddenly the orb struck the ground and shattered, exploding in a towering column of fire and light. The werewolves had no time to react as their bodies were blown apart, their bones stripped of fur and flesh before disintegrating into clouds of ash.

As disturbed earth, flecks of bone and splatters of blood rained down upon them, John, Einar, Kit, Ulva and Brenna stared out in shock as the entire horde was enveloped in flame. A wave of awed silence washed over them as they gazed blankly at the destruction, their senses numb to the awe-inspiring sight.

After the initial shock had faded, there suddenly arose a great cheer from everyone as they realized that they were alive, injured but breathing,
"You did it Einar, you saved us!", cried Kit as she rushed towards Einar and threw her arms around him, transforming back into a human as she did,
"You're welcome little wolfie", said Einar before he laughed boisterously,
"That was incredible", said John,
"What a stroke of luck, I completely forgot we had the orbs", said Brenna,
"I guess you could say Eira is the one we should be thanking", said Einar,
"Still we owe you our lives", said Brenna,
"Don't mention it, I wasn't prepared to let those monsters slaughter us", said Einar as he hugged Ulva,
"So what happens now?", asked John,
"We carry on with our journey of course, just because we have escaped the mine doesn't mean we should get complacent. There is a town named Grontorp located some distance away, we shall spend the night there", said Brenna,
"Wait a minute, I will turn again come nightfall, won't it be dangerous for us and others if we make camp there?", asked Ulva,
Placing his bag upon the floor, Brenna said,
"Not if we have this",
John, Einar, Ulva and Kit watched as Brenna pulled out of his bag a small and frosted bottle filled with a dark red liquid. Straightening his back, Brenna held up the bottle for all to see,
"This is a bottle of Vokvir, liquid tranquillity. I bought it with us just in case we needed it. Drinking this concoction will suppress the werewolf within Ulva and allow her to maintain her human form for one night. If Ulva drinks this before tonight, then she will not turn whilst we are in Grontorp, giving her and us some well needed respite", he said,

Ulva stared at the bottle in awe as Brenna handed it to her and said,

"Now listen closely Ulva, this is a complicated potion to put together and I don't have the time nor ingredients to make another one so we must make it count. This bottle has enough liquid inside to stave off your transformation for two nights only and it is the only one I have so make your next and final dose count",

Glancing up at Brenna, Ulva said,

"I...I don't know what to say, only thank you",

"You're welcome", said Brenna,

"Hold on, you've had that thing on you since we left Gormstad. Why didn't you let Ulva drink it whilst we were at Tarn Gren? It would have saved her a lot of pain and torment", said John,

"Because I did not expect us to remain in Tarn Gren come nightfall and we need to use the bottle sparingly if we can", said Brenna,

"Fair enough, but why didn't you let Ulva drink it before she first turned?", asked John,

Sighing in an exasperated tone, Brenna said,

"Because it was too late by the time you brought her to me, does that answer your question?",

John folded his arms and said,

"I suppose, thank you Brenna, this means a lot to me...to us",

"Oh don't get sappy on me now just because I gave your sweetheart a pretty bottle. I didn't really want to use it unless it was an emergency. But since we have gone through a lot lately, I figure a night of rest won't harm. Anyway we should get going, the sooner we get to Grontorp, the better", said Brenna,

"Do I drink the potion now or later?", asked Ulva,

"Whenever you fancy, so long as you drink it before sundown", said Brenna,

Pocketing the potion, Ulva walked over to Kit and said with a cheery smile,
"By the way Kit, that was amazing what you did in the mine, turning into a werewolf to save us, you're our hero",
Kit stared at Ulva blankly before her eyes widened in shock as a horrible realization struck her. She glanced down at her hands and stared at them before she suddenly and unexpectedly burst into tears.
To the surprise of her friends, she suddenly fled down the road at incredible speed,
"Kit wait!", cried Ulva as she chased after her friend,
"What's wrong with Kit?", asked Einar,
"I don't know!", yelled Ulva,
As Ulva and Einar began chasing after Kit, Brenna was about to run after them when he turned round and glanced back at John, who was now staring at the nearby hillock with a forlorn gaze,
"You coming John? We need to go after Kit", he said,
"Yeah, let me just say a few words first", said John,
"Okay, but make it quick", said Brenna before he ran down the road after Kit, Einar and Ulva,
Lowering his head, John said in a gentle and sombre voice,
"In the name of the Allfather, may my friends find comfort and solace in the autumnal wealds of Helheim",
Wiping his eye, John said softly,
"Goodbye guys, I'm sorry I couldn't protect you",
John quickly turned on his heel and ran after his friends, his heart heavy with sadness and regret as he left Ishellir Crossing.

CHAPTER XXI:
SOLACE UNDER THE SUN

"Let's just talk!", cried Ulva as she ran after Kit,
Behind her Brenna, Einar and John were sprinting down the road, their faces etched with looks of confusion and worry,
"I'm sorry if I said anything that might have upset you!", yelled Ulva,
Kit did not respond as she suddenly veered off the road to the left and raced into a nearby field filled with luscious and colourful wildflowers.
Seeing Kit dash through the field at incredible speed, Einar said,
"Damn she's quick",
Ulva, Einar, John and Brenna stopped at the edge of the field as they realized Kit had gone too far ahead for them to keep up with her. On the other side of the field were dotted a few small burial mounds, some of which were capped with pointed stones etched with the names of the dead.
Glancing ahead, Einar noticed that Kit had climbed up onto one of these mounds and sat herself down atop its peak, her hood pulled over her head as she stared out over the vast emerald acres of the Gormveld.
With a sad expression on his face, Einar turned to his companions and said,
"Wait here, I'll be back in a minute",
"You sure you don't want us to come with you?", said Brenna,
Einar shook his head,
"I appreciate the help, but I think it's best if you all stay here whilst I go and talk to Kit", he said,
"Why is she upset all of a sudden?", asked John,
Einar looked towards the field and said,
"I don't know, but I'm going to find out",

"I hope you can talk some sense into her, I hate seeing her like this", said Ulva,
"Me too Ulva, me too", sighed Einar,
With the sun in his eyes, Einar held up his arm to shield his face as he made his way into the field and towards the mounds. To the distant sounds of blaring sheep, whistling wind and the herding calls of the young shepherd girls summoning their flocks to feed with rattling bells and ethereal, melodious cries, Einar traversed the field until he came to the foot of the mound upon which Kit was sitting. He noticed that she had her knees folded up against the front of her body and her arms were wrapped around her legs. Sighing heavily, Einar climbed up the side of the mound and sat himself down next to Kit, who was silently gazing out at the grasslands as the sun lit up her face with a golden glow. Einar's heart sank when he noticed the shining glint of tears running down Kit's pale face,
"Hi", said Einar softly,
"Go away, I want to be alone for a moment", replied Kit,
"Are you alright? Everyone's worried about you", said Einar,
"I'm fine, just leave me alone", whimpered Kit,
"You're not fine Kit, I know it and so do you. Did Ulva say anything to upset you?", asked Einar,
"No", said Kit,
"So how come you ran off like that and frightened the living daylights out of everyone?", said Einar,
"I was just overwhelmed", said Kit,
"Overwhelmed?", asked Einar,
Kit nodded her head and wiped the tears away from her face with her arm,
"Overwhelmed by the realization that I broke my oath to never use my power", she said,
"I know you didn't want to turn, but if you hadn't then we all would have perished in Ishellir", said Einar,
"That's why I did it, even though I swore I would never turn, I did it because I didn't want to die and I didn't want my friends to die either", said Kit,

"And we will never forget your heroic deed, you saved us all, you are a hero", smiled Einar,
"I'm not a hero, I'm a monster", said Kit,
"Why do you think that when your actions have proven otherwise? Why did you create that oath in the first place and why do you treat yourself with such self-loathing?", asked Einar,
Kit turned to face Einar, she stared at him before turning back towards the golden sun,
"Because every time I turn I take the form of my father, every time I turn I see him reflected within myself, every time I turn I am reminded of all the terrible things he had done to me and what he did to my mother", she said,
"What terrible things?", asked Einar,
Kit sighed,
"When I was just a child, he would get drunk and would transform into a werewolf. He would then chase me around the tower and scare me for his own sick amusement. There were nights when he would rush into my bedroom and frighten me, if I wetted the bed out of terror then he would beat me. Because of this, I had trouble sleeping for years out of fear that he would appear in the night and scare me. Eventually he stopped tormenting me and over time I was able to just barely sleep again, but I will never forget the times when he frightened me so badly that I would spend entire nights crying alone in the dark. I would cry for hours and no one would come and comfort me", she said,
Einar stared at Kit in disbelief as she continued,
"Whenever I was able to find a book to read, they would always depict werewolves as horrible beasts. The first time I saw a werewolf, it scared me so much that part of my hair turned white and it has been that way ever since. It was worse still when I discovered that I was an actual werewolf. I didn't realize I was one until I was thirteen and during the night of my first transformation, I was so confused and horrified that I tried and failed to take my own life. When Vulpes found out, he didn't comfort me in any way.

He didn't talk to me about what I was going through nor did he try to help me understand what I was experiencing",
"What did he do?", asked Einar,
"You can pretty much guess what he did, he was furious that I had made such a mess of my room in a fit of rage and was disgusted that I got blood on the floor. As punishment, he confined me to my room for days without food and that only made me feel worse. It wasn't until a few years later that I found out why I was a werewolf and that made me more hateful of what I was and more hateful of him. When I was finally able to control myself and my turnings, I vowed that I would never take such a form again", said Kit,
Einar stared at Kit with a look of horrified sadness as she buried her face in her lap,
"So now you know why I took such an oath and why I am full of such self-loathing. I was surrounded by hatred and fear and it moulded me into who I am. How could I see myself as anything else other than a monster when there was no one around to say and treat me otherwise?", she said,
After a moment of silence, Einar said,
"No",
Kit lifted her head and glanced at Einar as more tears ran down her cheeks,
"What?", she said,
"I said no, you are not a monster and you should not only be proud of who and what you are, but you should be proud to possess such power and you should love yourself", said Einar,
"How can I love myself when I was never shown any love my entire life? I've spent so long being surrounded by people who didn't care about me that I cannot think of anything good about myself", whimpered Kit,
"I can think of a few things", said Einar,
"Yeah, like what?", huffed Kit,

"Think about this, despite everything you have gone through and despite all the misery, cruelty and fear you have been shown, you still became an intelligent and kind -hearted woman who possesses a strong moral character and a fiery spirit. You could have become a psychopath or a sadist with a murderous and violent streak, but instead you chose a different path whether you knew it or not. You grew into a charming young woman whom anyone would be proud to call friend", said Einar,

"Really?", said Kit,

"Of course, I don't see a monster at all and despite yourself thinking or saying otherwise, you never were one nor did you become one. Because despite what you went through, you never allowed it to change you into something you are not. You never used your father's behaviour and actions as an excuse to act in an equally evil and terrible way", said Einar as he warmly smiled,

Kit stared at Einar with a surprised look as he put his arm around her shoulders and said,

"If you come away from here remembering one thing, I want you to remember this, you are not your father, werewolf or not",

Before Kit could respond, Einar said,

"Hold on, I'm not finished, you might possess the same powers as him and you might be his daughter, but you were never like him and will never be like him. He was a monster because he acted like one, you are not a monster because you don't. I don't know if he was abused by his father, but in the end, he chose to treat you the way he did, he chose to be a monster. You chose to help us escape Tarn Gren, you chose to come along on this adventure to help us stop Fenrir and despite your heart telling you not to, you chose to turn in the mine to save us. Like I said a while ago near the Gormwood, would a monster have done all that?",

"I guess not", said Kit,

"And regarding your werewolf power, just because your father used it for evil doesn't mean you should. You don't have to turn ever again if you don't want to, but maybe you could consider using your power for good. Prove to everyone that a werewolf doesn't have to be the monster of dark bedtime stories. It is up to you what you do with your powers and it is up to you if you want to keep them or not. It is your choice and your choice alone, no one should tell you how to act or think based upon their own perception of you. In other words, just because they see a werewolf as evil, that doesn't mean you should be evil or think yourself as such", said Einar,
Kit turned towards the sun before she glanced down at the grass beneath her, her mind racing as she reflected on Einar's words,
"I will...think about what you have told me today, you have given me much to think about", she said,
To Einar's delight, Kit then grinned slightly,
"Thank you", she said,
"For what?", said Einar,
"For listening to what I had to say, for understanding what I went through and most importantly for treating me like an actual person", said Kit,
"You're welcome Kit, that's what I am here for after all, to deliver bad jokes and to put a little happiness into the lives of those I love", smiled Einar,
It was then that Kit suddenly hugged Einar, who silently reciprocated in kind, his face illuminated by a soft smile and the warm light of the midday sun.
As they pulled away from one another, Einar noticed the collar around Kit's neck.
Frowning at the sight of it, Einar said,
"Is that a collar around your neck?",
"It is", said Kit,
"I don't mean to pry, but why are you wearing it?", said Einar,

"My father forced me to wear it, I would be punished if I didn't", squeaked Kit,
"Why would he demand that of you, did he think of you as a pet?", asked Einar sadly,
"No, he saw me more as a possession than a pet. I was only forced to wear this so that he could chain me to the walls whenever I was being naughty or rebellious", said Kit,
Einar blinked in disbelief,
"I'm sorry what?", he gasped,
"Did I stutter? I said he used it to chain me to the wall", said Kit,
With a look of revulsion on his face, Einar growled,
"It is a shame that I wasn't the one who had the chance to kill him for I would have done way worse than what Ulva did to him",
"Believe me, I am disappointed that I didn't get to kill him myself", said Kit,
"Well he's gone now and that's all that matters", grinned Einar,
"Yeah", said Kit,
Leaning closer to Kit, Einar reached up towards Kit's throat, which made her flinch a little as she saw his hand come close to her neck,
"It's okay, I'm not going to hurt you I promise", said Einar in a gentle and reassuring tone of voice,
"Sorry I'm just not used to people touching me", said Kit,
"Here, this will make you feel a little better", said Einar,
Carefully reaching behind Kit's neck, he unfastened and removed the collar, Kit mumbling in pain as Einar peeled the strap away from her throat before tossing it to one side. Rubbing her tender and painful neck, Kit said,
"Thanks, I've been waiting for so long to have that damned thing removed",
"You'll welcome, you're not some damn dog on a leash and your father doesn't have any power over you anymore", said Einar,

"Yeah...well I guess we should get back to the others", said Kit,
"Before we go, would it be too much to ask for one thing?", said Einar,
"Depends on what's being asked", said Kit,
"I want to see you", said Einar,
Confused, Kit said,
"What do you mean? You're looking at me right now",
"I want to see you as a werewolf and I didn't get a proper look at you in Ishellir, show me the other side of Kittra", said Einar,
Surprised and a little taken back, Kit glanced down at the floor as she mulled over Einar's request,
"I...um...", mumbled Kit as she began to tremble,
"You don't have to if you don't want to", said Einar,
"Just this once", said Kit,
Pulling her hood down, Kit sighed deeply before she closed her eyes and began to concentrate. Einar watched in awe as Kit's face began to change and within the blink of an eye, her face had become that of a wolf covered in black and white fur, her teary eyes shining brilliantly as she stared silently at Einar,
Seeing her wolven eyes, Einar smiled and said,
"Your eyes, they are beautiful",
Einar frowned as Kit suddenly squeaked in shock before she covered her eyes and turned away, whimpering as she blushed,
"I'm sorry Kit, I didn't mean to embarrass you or put you on the spot", said Einar gently,
Kit said nothing as she whimpered and whined as tears ran down the length of her snout. Einar noticed that she was rocking slightly back and forth as she continued to cover her eyes, her breathing stuttering as her body trembled.
It was then that Kit felt Einar's warm hand reach up and touch her furry cheek before he gently rotated his thumb, stroking her face tenderly to try and calm her down. Kit stared at Einar as he smiled back at her.

Brushing her tears away with his thumb, Einar said, "I see no monster, just a beautiful creature both inside and out, how could anyone not love you?",
Kit smiled as her face turned back to normal,
"Come, the others will be waiting", said Einar,
After Kit and Einar got up off the mound, they both began making their way back towards the road where John, Brenna and Ulva were waiting,
"You know I'm proud of you Kit, you are stronger than you give yourself credit for", said Einar,
"Thanks, I think you're pretty strong too", said Kit,
"Oh I can swing an axe and wrestle a bear, but it takes a special type of strength to endure what you went through. In that regard, you and Ulva are stronger than me", said Einar,
"I disagree, I think you are just as strong, I mean you are a warrior, that means you must have seen your fair share of horrors", said Kit,
Einar frowned,
"Yes, yes I have", he said,
"You know I am surprised at you Einar", said Kit,
"Yeah?", said Einar,
"I imagine you grew up hearing all sorts of stories about how bad werewolves are. I am surprised that, despite being told such things when you were a child, you would treat me with such kindness and respect despite knowing what I am", said Kit,
"That's because like you, I don't allow my upbringing to influence how I treat others. I judge people by the quality of their character and I don't generalize. You are a werewolf, but that doesn't mean I'm going to treat you any less because of that. Your actions have shown me that you are worthy of both my friendship and respect", said Einar,
"That's good to know", said Kit as her face lit up with a pleasant smile,

"Besides as a werewolf, you kinda remind me of a husky I once knew and she was the best companion a man could ever ask for. It's kinda hard not to love someone who looks like that", said Einar,
Einar and Kit stared at each other before they both burst out laughing.
As they came to the road, John, Ulva and Brenna couldn't help but smile as they witnessed Einar and Kit looking rather amused,
"What's so funny?", asked Ulva,
"Nothing it's fine", chuckled Einar,
"So I take it everything's okay now?", said John,
"Yes I think everything's going to be okay", said Kit,
"Good, now that everything's been sorted, we really should be going now", said Brenna,
"Of course", said Einar,
Stepping back onto the road, John, Brenna, Einar, Kit and Ulva walked side by side as they continued their journey northwards. As they walked, Kit glanced over at Einar as her heart fluttered with happiness. It was a nice and comforting feeling and for once in her life, she wasn't angry, upset, confused or fearful, she felt calm and content, something that she had not felt in many years.

CHAPTER XXII:
A MOMENT OF REST

With the noon sun hanging above them painting the sky with a lovely yellow glow, John, Brenna, Einar, Ulva and Kit continued their way down the northern road, passing many sprawling fields and rocky outcrops of dark stone and snow. As they wandered, their eyes would always catch something of interest, from stone bridges spanning small winding rivers that bubbled and ran with sparkling blue water to half buried ruins that in some distant time would have been called home by people who now bear no name within living memory. They spotted herds of lumbering cows, white sheep with their new-born lambs and rugged goats with curved horns wandering the fields. In the air were many seabirds and hawks soaring overhead. Now and then their paths would cross fellow travellers.

As it neared lunchtime and everyone was getting peckish, John and his friends decided to rest for a while and eat under the shadow of a large stone column that was standing a few yards away from the edge of the road. The column was made of black stone and carved with many images and runes. It was another wolf stone, though this one was much smaller than the one in the Gormwood.

Upon its surface were the familiar faces of the heroes of legend accompanied by the grim and haunting visages of Loki and his children. Sitting themselves down, everyone threw off their bags and began to relax and unwind. Brenna reached into his bag and pulled out his journal and began to write while Ulva had curled herself up next to John as he sat himself up against the column.

They both kissed before indulging in bottles of throka and sweet pastries with a buttery crust. Kit and Einar meanwhile shared some sandwiches that Maud had prepared.

Whilst Einar ate them slowly and daintily, Kit was snapping them up, her face lit up with delight as she savoured the flavours of pork, spiced apple stuffing and soft homemade bread,
"Hungry?", laughed Einar,
Kit wiped her mouth,
"I would be lying if I said I wasn't", she said,
"Well we all need our strength", said Einar before he took another bite,
Einar couldn't help but laugh as he saw Kit hastily gobble up a small cake that John had given her,
"Be careful you don't get a stomach ache, I don't want you to get sick from wolfing it all down", he said,
"Sorry I'm just so hungry, I haven't eaten properly in a long time", said Kit,
"Did you get my pun?", asked Einar,
Kit tilted her head as she stared at Einar with a confused look on her face,
"What's a pun?", she said,
"Ah never mind", said Einar before he chuckled to himself,
As she ate, Kit looked over at John and Ulva and smiled as she watched them talking and laughing together,
"They look so happy, I hope one day to experience such joy in my life", said Kit to Einar,
"Yeah, it's heart-warming, there was once a time when I didn't know if they would ever smile again", said Einar,
"It must be nice always being with someone you love", said Kit,
"I'm sure you will find your own happiness one day Kit. You are young and from now on I believe things will get better for you, the worst is behind you, the best is yet to come. I bet one day someone special is going to come into your life and make you the luckiest wolf, um…I mean girl there has ever been", said Einar,
"Yeah, here's hoping, I just hope there is someone out there who will accept me for who I am", said Kit,
"I'm certain of it", said Einar,

As Kit stretched out her arms and legs, Einar reached into his bag and pulled out two bottles of cider, one of which he gave to Kit.
Cracking the cap, he raised his bottle in the air and said, "Here's to a bright future, may it bring us the happiness we deserve",
"Indeed, skal", said Kit,
Einar and Kit then tapped their bottles together and began to drink. After taking a few gulps, Einar glanced down and noticed something that shocked him. He saw that Kit's hands were not only cut and bruised from where she had been digging, but on both hands she was missing a finger. Her legs and feet were also lined with painful looking cuts covered in dirt,
"Gods above Kit, your hands and feet look very painful, not only that but you are missing a finger on each hand, why?", said Einar,
Kit swallowed a large gulp of cider and said,
"When I was in Tarn Gren, I used to read a lot to escape reality. But when my father learnt that I was reading mostly fiction and fairy tales, he ordered the cultists to stop giving me such reading material, stating that such books would fill my head with nonsense. One night I was bored so I snuck into my father's room to have a look at his collection. When he had discovered that I borrowed a book from his library, he took one of my fingers and said it was the punishment of thieves",
"Odin's mercy, what the hell was wrong with that man?", said Einar,
Kit shrugged,
"It's something I have been trying to figure out all my life and will spend the rest of my life doing so", she said,
"What about the other hand?", asked Einar,
Kit took a few more sips before she said,
"He caught me a second time, I stopped going into his room after that. He threatened that if I was caught a third time, he would take my left hand",

Einar swallowed down more of his drink and said,
"I am so glad that bastard is rotting in Niflheim right now",
Kit raised her bottle and said,
"I'll drink to that",
After Einar and Kit tapped bottles and took a swig of their drinks, Einar said,
"Can you walk okay?",
"I can walk well enough and to be honest the pain doesn't bother me much, I've gained quite the tolerance", said Kit,
"That's no excuse, as soon as we make camp, we're getting you cleaned up and those wounds are gonna get treated. Also, you need a new pair of boots, I've only now just realized that for the last few miles you have been walking along the road with nothing to protect your feet", said Einar,
"Very well", said Kit,
"Do you want to borrow a pair of mine?", said Ulva,
"No I'll be fine, I've suffered worse", said Kit,
"Plus that bandage on your arm will need changing, it's starting to turn colour", said Einar,
Kit glanced down at her arm and said,
"Must it? I don't really want to show you what's underneath",
"Kit if you don't want me to see anything you don't want me to then that's your choice. But you risk your arm getting infected if you leave it like that", said Einar,
Kit sighed,
"Okay, but at least let me change the bandages alone", she said,
"That's no problem at all, also we will have to get your trousers fixed", said Einar,
"What do you mean? My clothes are clean enough", said Kit,
"You have a tear in your trousers", said Einar,
Kit reached down and placed her hands behind her waist. To her surprise Einar was right, there was a large tear where her tail had pushed through when she turned,
"Damn it, these are my favourite pair", she grumbled,
"Not to worry, I'll repair them later tonight, I'm quite good at sewing", said Ulva,

"Good, these clothes are special and are not easy to come by", said Kit as she folded her arms,
"How so?", asked Einar,
"This outfit I am wearing has been made specifically so it will fit me when I am both a human and a werewolf. It can both stretch and shrink, the Cult of Fenris created such outfits after they got tired of constantly having to change their torn clothes every time they transformed", said Kit,
"How fascinating, it's a shame that such ingenuity is being used by such evil people. Perhaps when this is all over, you could consider a venture in tailoring", said Einar,
"I am not one for commerce", said Kit,
"Well that's your decision, but you might make some serious money. You could make so much that you won't even need to get a job", said Einar,
"A job?", asked Kit,
"Well yeah, I don't know what you plan to do with your life once our adventure is over, but you will have to earn a living just like the rest of us", said Einar,
"Really?", said Kit as she glanced down at the floor,
"Yes", smiled Einar before he suddenly tapped Kit on the arm and said,
"Hey! How about a shepherd? You could run around and herd the sheep into their pens",
Kit responded by punching Einar in the arm, causing him to flinch before he laughed,
"Okay so no herding, how about a town guard?", said Einar,
"Oh ha, ha, very funny, a guard dog how original, it's because I am a werewolf isn't it?", grumbled Kit,
"No, no, I'm serious, I could ask Barmund to consider you for a position in the Gormstad town guard. You would get good pay, a very generous pension and fresh new uniforms annually", said Einar,
"Thanks but I have spent most of my life wearing a uniform and living a sheltered and regimental existence", sighed Kit,
"Okay then, so what do you want to do one day?", said Einar,

Kit yawned and stretched herself out, smiling as she felt a refreshing and cool breeze on her face,
"Something nice and quiet, perhaps fishing or gardening", she said,
"Really? I didn't think you the type", said Einar,
"I love them both, when I was young, I would sneak out at times and make my way to the tower ponds. I would fish there and try to catch something. Sometimes I landed a fish, sometimes a frog and sometimes I would hook something horrible and ugly. But I always enjoyed it, it was so relaxing and tranquil. Every evening I would walk amongst the tower gardens and tend to the flowers growing there. On occasion, I would scatter some seeds and when they would eventually grow into lovely little berry bushes, I would pick the fruits and take them to my room and secretly gorge on them", beamed Kit,
"How lovely", said Einar,
It was then that Kit frowned and said,
"It was one of the few things I genuinely enjoyed that wasn't tainted by my father. But even then, he would still find a way to upset me. I once came across this most beautiful rose patch and I plucked one, a sensual and beautiful red rose, the most wondrous I had ever seen. I thought it went well with the colour of my eyes, so I wore it in my hair",
"Let me guess, Vulpes didn't like that either", said Einar,
"When my father found out, he took the rose and crushed it in front of my eyes, saying it was not the way of the cult to worry about appearances and fancy, frivolous things. It broke my heart to see that poor flower getting crushed, but I never stopped going to the gardens. I kept telling myself that if I looked after the flowers and grew some of my own, perhaps something good, pure and wholesome would come from a monster like myself and just maybe…I wouldn't hate myself so much", said Kit,
Einar frowned,
"Oh Kit, you shouldn't think of yourself that way", he said,

Kit closed her eyes and said,
"I know Einar, but it will just take a long time for me to think otherwise",
"Please take as long as you need", said Einar,
"Thanks", said Kit as she fidgeted to make herself more comfortable,
As Einar and Kit sat quietly as they took in the beautiful scenery around them, Ulva plucked from her belt the bottle that Brenna gave her,
"You gonna drink it now?", asked Brenna,
"Yes, I am exhausted and I am not willing to go through another transformation just yet. I want this upcoming night to be one of peace, fun and relaxation. Besides we need to rest so we are better prepared for our upcoming venture. After what we have been through, we need this, not just me, but all of us", said Ulva,
John, Einar, Kit and Brenna watched as Ulva placed the bottle to her lips before she drank, allowing half of its contents to run down her throat. It tasted sweet yet slightly sour and it burnt the inside of her mouth. After a few seconds, Ulva could feel the tingling under her skin fade away as her heartbeat slowed down and a wave of calm washed over her.
Feeling much better, Ulva sighed before she slumped out onto the grass, stretching out her arms and legs as she felt more relaxed,
"That's better", said Ulva,
Grinning from ear to ear, John leant over and whispered something to Ulva that made her blush,
"Yeah?", said Ulva softly,
"Yeah", said John,
After everyone had finished their lunch and had enjoyed some rest, they got to their feet and collected up their bags and possessions before they were back on the northern road.

With the warm sun and cool wind on their faces, it was quite pleasant for once to not worry about things like curses, werewolves, ancient forests and magical shrines and it showed on their faces, everyone looked rather calm and happy.
John and Ulva were holding hands side by side and Brenna was humming to himself a merry tune whilst he was reading. Einar and Kit meanwhile were simply looking around admiring the lovely scenery,
"Such a beautiful day, I'm sure Eira, Maud and Guthrum would have loved it if they were here, we could have had a picnic together", said Einar,
"Who are they?", asked Kit,
"Eira is a friend of the family, she's a scholar and merchant of antiquities. Guthrum is my grandfather on my father's side and Maud is my beautiful wife back in Gormstad", said Einar,
The smile from Kit's face dropped,
"Wife?", she uttered,
"Yes, been married fifteen years come winter", said Einar,
Kit glanced down at the ground with a disheartened and disappointed look before she sighed and pulled on the straps of her bag,
"She's a very lucky woman", said Kit softly,
"She is", said Einar,
Glancing at Kit, Einar noticed the solemn and crestfallen look on her face,
"Hey, are you okay?", asked Einar,
Kit glanced up and said,
"I'm okay, it's nothing, nothing at all",
"Good", said Einar,
Kit sighed sadly before looking over to Brenna, who had put his book away and was now staring at a map,
"So remind me again, what's our next destination?", said Kit,
"Grontorp, it's a tiny hamlet not far from here, we should be there by sunset", said Brenna,
"It will be strange, being around people other than the cultists", said Kit,

"It'll be fun I promise", said Einar,
"I hope so, the last few days have been absolute hell", said John,
"Indeed, we all deserve a rest before we carry on with our little adventure", said Brenna,
As everyone travelled northwards, the clear, blue sky began to turn colour as the day wore on, becoming streaked with beautiful shades of pink and orange as the sun began to set behind the distant mountains, bathing the fields in a warm golden hue.
From the path, John, Einar, Brenna, Kit and Ulva could see some small stone arches lit by candles standing at the side of the road, little shrines to guide lost spirits that might be haunting the Gormveld moors. In addition, they could also see some farmsteads, cottages, burial mounds and windmills in the distance. At one point Kit ran through the nearby fields to blow off some steam and get some stress off her chest, but she requested that she run alone.
After some time running through the grass of the beautiful tundra, Kit returned to her friends,
"Feeling better?", asked John,
"Most definitely", said Kit,
"Hey guys look", said Ulva,
Brenna, Einar, John and Kit glanced ahead to see Ulva standing a few yards in front of them looking northwards. Everyone walked over to Ulva's side and gazed out to see what she was looking at. They could see the road wind its way over some bumps and hills before curving down into the valley below them.
Beyond that, they could see the flickering and twinkling of lights amongst a huddle of buildings in the distance.
It was the hamlet of Grontorp, a quaint and quiet place where little happened and was otherwise only on the map for being a great place for stargazing.

To Grontorp's residents, it was considered boring and dull, but consequently the hamlet was peaceful and far removed from the troubles of the world.

As the air was getting colder and a veil of stars began appearing amidst the evening firmament, John, Ulva, Einar, Brenna and Kit started making their way down towards the village, content in the knowledge that they would soon enjoy some much-needed comfort and rest.

CHAPTER XXIII: GRONTORP

The town of Grontorp was quite small, consisting of no more than two dozen timbered buildings with horse headed gables and thatched roofs all encircled within a stout stone wall. On the eastern edge of the hamlet was a wooden bridge that arched over a wide and slow-moving river that glistened in the fading glimmer of dusk. The hamlet itself was quiet and homely, a far cry from the busy streets and bustling crowds of Gormstad.

In the middle of the hamlet was a large stone well that sat before a quaint two storey tavern, its open windows glowing with a warm and inviting yellow light. Attached to the side of the building was a small, sheltered stable filled with hay. Above the door was a sign swinging in the breeze that read, *'The Weary Traveller'*.

To the right of John and his friends were some gardens and several rows of timber houses of varying sizes whilst on the left was a pathway that led down a road lined with many different shops.

Walking up to the door of the inn, Brenna said,

"Right everyone, I want you guys to go in and rent a room for the night whilst I head to the market and pick up some food and supplies, I won't be long okay?",

"That's fine, we'll get comfortable in the meanwhile", said John,

"Good, once I come back, we can freshen ourselves up and get ready for the night", said Brenna,

"Any plans for the evening?", asked Einar,

"Yeah, I thought we could enjoy a nice supper and a night of drinks together, sound good?", said Brenna,

"Sounds great" said Ulva,

Einar and John nodded in agreement, Kit said nothing as she stared off into the distance silently,
"Splendid, see you all in a moment", said Brenna,
As Brenna turned and made his way down the nearby road, John, Ulva, Einar and Kit entered the inn before closing the door behind them.
The inside of the inn was large and spacious, the air was toasty and filled with the sounds of people talking and laughing, the ringing of coins on tables, the tapping of footsteps and the shuffling of chairs against the wooden floor. Looking around, John and his friends noticed that there were many ornately decorated wooden tables of different shapes scattered about. Sitting up against them were men, women and children. Most of them were drinking from large foaming tankards, hot steaming mugs and overflowing horns filled with an assortment of both frosted and hot drinks.
Some of them were eating hale and hearty meals whilst some of them were challenging one another to arm wrestling matches, flyting contests, riddle competitions and games involving tokens, dice, cards and coins.
Walking up to the bar at the back of the room, Einar couldn't help but smile as he glanced around at the sights and sounds of the tavern.
He noticed however that Kit looked a little uneasy, her eyes were darting around quickly and nervously at the tavern patrons,
"What is it?", he asked,
"So many smells and sounds, it's overpowering, I can't concentrate", said Kit,
"Don't worry, you'll get used to it", said Einar,
"Really?", said Kit,
"Yes, but let me know if it becomes too much for you okay?", said Einar,
"Okay", said Kit,

Behind the bar stood three people, two women and a man. One of the women was portly and round faced with short brown hair and clothed in a long blue dress with white sleeves and an apron. She possessed a pleasant smile and was talking cheerfully to some customers whilst pouring some beer. The other woman was young and had long braided hair as white as snow. She was wearing a dress that was coloured a dark grey and white with long sleeves. The man next to her was lanky, very tall and quite old, his long face was gaunt, shrivelled and peppered with grey stubble. He had short silver hair that was slicked back and was wearing a stained tunic under an old and moth-eaten apron. The old man was writing with a quill into a large book that was lying in front of him upon the counter.

John stepped up to the bar and placed a hand on the counter, the old man responded by glancing up at him with a scowl of indifference.

Slowing closing the book and clearing his throat, the old man said,

"Good afternoon, my name is Wyland, I am the innkeeper here and have been for three generations, how can I help you?",

"Yes, we would like to book a room for five people", said John,

The old man stared at John without blinking before he sighed,

"There is one such room available that can accommodate five people. But I will need the money up front and it can only be leased for no longer than four days", he said,

"Excellent, we only need it for one night, how much?", asked John,

"Twenty-five silvers", said Wyland,

John reached into the pouch fastened to his belt and pulled out some pennies before handing them over to the sullen innkeeper.

Wyland counted them before pocketing them in a pouch that sat on the front of his apron,
"Very well, give me a moment", he said in a rather disinterested tone of voice,
Wyland turned to a clean page in his book before he pushed the quill on the counter towards John and said,
"I'll need your full names, places of residence and a signature from each of you",
After John, Einar and Ulva wrote down and signed their names, Einar handed the quill over to Kit. To everyone's surprise, Kit anxiously stared at the page before her, her wide and unblinking eyes staring at the book with a look of confusion, her hand slightly trembling as she kept the quill motionless upon the parchment.
As Kit stared at the visitor book, Wyland said,
"Is there something wrong? Write your details down and sign the book",
"I...I can't write", whimpered Kit,
"Really?", said Einar,
"I have trouble spelling and I find it difficult to form words. I can read, but I can't replicate what I see on paper", said Kit,
Einar's heart sank,
"You never learned?", he said,
"No one ever taught me, I was only just able to teach myself to read because books were my only means of escape from reality", replied Kit,
Taking the quill off Kit, Einar said,
"Here, I'll write down your details",
Einar wrote down Kit's name before he turned to her and said,
"Do you know where you were born, did Vulpes ever mention a location?"
"No, I was born in a barn in the middle of nowhere", said Kit,

"You will need to be more specific than that I'm afraid. In accordance with the ancient laws of the Taverners Guild, I need to know exactly where every customer comes from should they wish to rent a room and that they must sign the book, for matters of insurance you understand", said Wyland,
"I'm sorry, but I don't know", said Kit,
"Oh come on, surely you must have some idea", grumbled Wyland,
"I don't know alright? Stop asking me such stupid fucking questions!", snapped Kit,
"Kit calm down, it's okay", said Einar,
"I can't calm down, I can't hear myself think, there's too much noise!", barked Kit before she began to mumble to herself,
Einar quickly wrote into the book and said,
"Let's just put down Tarn Gren",
Einar then handed the quill back to Kit,
"Okay, now you just need to sign",
"I told you I can't write", growled Kit,
"I know, but it doesn't have to be fancy, just put a mark down", said Einar gently,
Kit glanced at the book before she looked over at the ink pot next to Wyland's hand. She reached for the pot and dipped her finger into it before tracing her nail over the page next to her name, scratching down a roughly drawn and awkward looking line with her left hand.
Looking across the counter, Kit noticed there were people looking at her with disconcerting and judgemental stares,
"I suppose that will have to do, I have customers that need serving and I can't be waiting all night for miracles", said Wyland as he glared at Kit,
Feeling embarrassed and humiliated, Kit stepped back from the counter, putting her hand up to the side of her face before she began running an ink covered fingernail softly across her blushing cheek.

As Kit began to mutter what sounded like a countdown, Ulva and John looked on with concern as Kit grimaced at the floor, biting her lower lip as her eyes darted quickly inside her head,

"Kit?", asked John,

"I'm fine", uttered Kit softly,

Before Wyland could close the book, Einar said,

"I should also make you aware that the fifth member of our party has yet to return, his name is Brenna Torstensson of Gormstad",

Wyland nodded before jotting down some words into his book, which he then slammed shut.

He then reached for his belt and plucked an iron key, which he then pushed across the counter towards John,

"Before you go up to your room, I need to explain some rules of this establishment. Firstly you may come and go as you wish, but you must check out by early afternoon tomorrow if you are only staying for one night. Secondly please be mindful of other guests and be aware of your behaviour whilst staying at the Weary Traveller. Third and lastly, no violence or abuse will be tolerated towards guests or members of my staff. Anyone caught being abusive will be arrested by the town guard, am I clear?", said Wyland,

"Yes", said John,

"Good", said Wyland who then turned to the two women standing next to him,

"These lovely ladies are Yrsa and Jetta, should you need anything during your stay, they will provide assistance and help in any way they can", he said,

After John took the key from the counter, Wyland said,

Your room is number four just up the stairs, do enjoy your stay here at the Weary Traveller",

As Wyland walked away to assist more customers, John said,

"Let's go guys, remember room four",

John, Ulva, Einar and Kit made their way up some nearby stairs that brought them to a long and narrow corridor of windowless timber walls dimly illuminated by lanterns.

John eyed the doors on the left as he passed, eventually coming to room four. John put the key into the lock and twisted it with a click. He then pushed the door open and entered, followed by his companions.
They all found themselves standing in a large and cosy looking room. To the right of them was a large window that looked out onto the hamlet outside, it commanded a beautiful view of the distant and dark horizon coloured black against the colours of dusk. The room was spacious and there were five large plush beds covered in thick sheets, pillows and furs. On the floor were some colourful carpets stitched with fantastic and vibrant imagery and against the wall at the back of the room was a large roaring fire. Resting near the fire were some plain wooden chairs and a small table.
John and his friends looked around before they each took a bed for themselves, placing their cloaks, weapons and bags upon them. As Ulva walked round the nearby corner, she was surprised to see there was another door. Opening it, she entered a small adjacent room that contained a tall mirror, a toilet and a large tin basin sitting beneath a small tap. Near the basin were some neatly folded towels,
"Finally I can have a wash", she said,
Whilst John was staring out of the window and looking out at the stars, Ulva sat herself down upon her bed before she removed her gloves and her shawl.
To the sound of Ulva cracking her knuckles and bones as she stretched out, Einar was rummaging through his bag whilst Kit was lying upon her bed tapping the sheets beneath her fingers to the sound of her heartbeat thundering in her ears,
"So what do we do now?", asked Kit,
"Wait for Brenna to return, we can then go downstairs and have something proper to eat", said Einar,
"Great, I'm starving", said John,
Ulva placed her hand upon his belly,
"No wonder, you have lost some weight", she said,
It was true, for John noticed that his belt and shirt were looking a little looser than usual,

"While we are waiting for Brenna, who wants to bathe first?", said Einar,
Kit lifted herself off the bed and stood up,
"Mind if I go first?", she said,
"Of course not", said Einar,
"While you are in there, I can repair that tear in your trousers", smiled Ulva,
"Would you? That would be great", said Kit,
Kit made her way into the bathroom and taking some deep breaths, she walked over and turned on the tap above the basin, releasing hot and steamy gushes of water that caused the basin to ring out gently with a metallic ding. Whilst the bath was running, Kit quickly removed her trousers and pushed the door ajar just slightly before throwing them out for Ulva to sew. She then closed the door and walked over to the mirror hanging upon the wall.
Kit silently gazed at her reflection as she removed her tunic, allowing it to fall and lap at her feet whilst she inspected the many scars and wounds etched across her pale body.
Across her back were four long and deep gashes that stretched from the top of her hip to the bottom of her shoulder. Her arms, legs and stomach were covered in scratch marks, some fresh and some made a long time ago.
Staring into the mirror, Kit brushed her raven black hair to one side, her mind echoing with the sounds of faint and distant memories when the other cultists would mock and bully her.
As voices of disgust and hatred rang in her ears to the blaring pounding of her racing heart, Kit suddenly screamed out,
"Shut up!",
Suddenly Einar burst in through the door,
"Kit, what's wrong?", he asked,
Snapping back to her senses, Kit glanced at Einar in surprise before she looked down at the bath.
Seeing it was now full, she walked over and turned off the tap, her hands shaking as her chest throbbed with pain,
"Nothing, everything's fine", she said,

Einar raised his eyebrow as he eyed Kit suspiciously before he said,
"Okay, but if you ever need to talk or if there is something on your mind, you know where to find me", said Einar,
Kit nodded and dabbed her sweating forehead with the back of her hand,
"Absolutely", she said before grinning sweetly,
"Hm", grunted Einar before he left, closing the bathroom door behind him,
Sighing deeply, Kit slowly stepped into the basin and lowered herself in, grinning from ear to ear as the warm water submerged her cold and shaking body,
"This is nice", said Kit as she ran her fingers through her hair, a faint growl of contentment and pleasure reverberating in her throat as she closed her eyes,
With her mind and heart now relaxed, Kit slid further into the basin, allowing the water to come up to her neck. With the warm water washing over her, Kit slowly began to get drowsy as she was enveloped in a soothing warmth that she hadn't felt in a long time.
After a few minutes of quiet bliss, Kit lifted her left arm and inspected the bandages that spiralled from her shoulder down to her wrist. They were covered in dirt, dry blood and were slightly itchy.
Concentrating, Kit was able to sharpen and lengthen one of her fingernails before she gingerly and carefully began cutting away at the bandages, causing them to fall off and reveal a shocking sight.
Her entire left arm was a gross and sickly pale colour and was covered in deep and weeping wounds that were coloured red, purple and yellow, some of them deep enough to reveal little slithers of exposed bone. Feeling the cold air against her arm made Kit hiss in pain as her wounds throbbed and oozed.
She glanced at the wounds sadly as her mind filled with memories of the time she first transformed, how she would claw at her skin and bite herself in times of anger and grief.

Gritting her teeth, Kit uttered a pained gasp as she thrust her arm into the bath, causing the wounds to flare up with a terrible pain. With her right hand, she began to gently massage her bad arm. Once the wounds had been cleaned, she began washing herself all over with a small cloth.
Once Kit was done, she clambered out of the bath and reached for a towel before she quickly dried herself down. Kit then threw on her tunic and stepped over to the bathroom door and knocked,
"Can I have my clothes back please?", she said,
The door opened slightly and Kit watched as her trousers were thrown through the small gap in front of her.
She put them on before she left and made her way back to her bed,
"Anyone who wants to go next, make sure you refill the bath with fresh water", she said,
"I'll go next", said Ulva,
"By the way, thanks for repairing my clothes", smiled Kit,
"It's no problem, I made a little adjustment so that whenever you feel the need or urge to turn, there's a little pocket flap where your tail can slide through, thus ensuring you don't tear them again", said Ulva,
"How convenient", said Kit,
As Ulva walked into the bathroom, Kit reached into her bag and pulled out a small roll of bandages before ever so gently wrapping them around her arm, grimacing as the painful wounds brushed against the cloth.
As she finished tying the bandages at the top of her shoulder tightly, the door nearby opened and Brenna appeared, carrying a box in his arms,
"Afternoon everyone", he said,
"Ah Brenna, I was wondering when you would return. Did you get everything you needed?", said Einar,
"Yes and something a little extra", said Brenna as he went over to his bed and sat himself down before removing his coat and bag,

Glancing over at Kit, Brenna said,
"Kit, I have something here for you, a little gift to welcome you into our little circle",
Kit's eyes widened with curiosity as she got up and walked over to Brenna,
"A gift? No one has ever given me one before, not even when it was my birthday", she said,
"Well there's a first time for everything", smiled Brenna as Kit sat herself down next to him,
Brenna handed the box over to Kit, who then opened it to reveal a shiny pair of black boots with a silver buckle on the ankle.
With a wide smile etched on her face, Kit said to Brenna, "They're beautiful thank you, are you sure I can't reimburse you for them?",
"Absolutely not, they are a gift and I was happy to get them. You have been through a lot lately and I thought this might cheer you up a little. Besides I won't have you traipsing around barefoot over cold, hard ground", said Brenna,
Brenna couldn't help but grin as Kit suddenly hugged him tightly before she took the boots out of the box and tried them on.
She was surprised to discover that they fitted perfectly, "They're so comfortable, how did you guess my measurements?", asked Kit,
"I didn't, they are designed to stretch and fit. I had them custom made and thankfully the shop was able to make them in a short amount of time", said Brenna,
"What about when I turn, would they still fit?", said Kit,
"Just about", said Brenna,
Delighted with her gift, Kit stood up and began walking about to see how they felt, they were snug and fitted well. Whilst Kit was wandering around the room, Ulva emerged from the bathroom and sat herself down next to John as Einar left to get ready for the night ahead,
"You look nice", said John as he gazed lovingly at Ulva,
"Thanks sweetie", she said,

After some time had passed, the door to the bathroom swung open and Einar emerged. He had removed his chainmail shirt and had changed into a fresh tunic that was coloured a dark cherry red. He looked relaxed and smelt of a sweet and strong fragrance.

Whilst Einar sat himself down and began to tune his lyre, John made his way into the bathroom now that it was his turn to get ready.

After inspecting herself in her little hand mirror, Ulva looked over at Kit and said,

"Are you looking forward to tonight?",

"I…don't know", uttered Kit,

"You don't know?", asked Ulva,

"To be honest I'm a little nervous, I've never been to a gathering before. Whenever the cult would have their parties, I would stay in my room reading books", replied Kit,

"Trust me, you'll have so much fun tonight. We'll make sure of it", said Ulva,

"I hope so", said Kit before she glanced down at her body with a sad gaze,

"Will they care if I go dressed like this? I mean I don't know if I am underdressed or not for such an occasion", said Kit,

"Kit, look at me", said Ulva,

Kit glanced up at Ulva as she beheld her kindly smile,

"You look great and you are beautiful. Besides no one will care about what you are wearing. All they care about is how much fun you have tonight and how many drinks you can chug", said Ulva,

Kit responded with a grin before she blushed slightly,

After John had finished getting ready, Brenna was the last to head into the bathroom. Whilst everyone was waiting for him, they all chatted away to one another and sung a little song together as Einar played his lyre.

After several minutes, Brenna was ready and with that, they all made their way out of the room. John and Ulva were the first to leave, followed by Einar, then Kit and finally Brenna who locked the door behind him.

CHAPTER XXIV:
FOUR HORNS

With their ears filled with the sound of tankards and horns being bashed together, shuffling chairs and boisterous laughter, John, Einar, Kit, Ulva and Brenna all went downstairs and after looking around, they found themselves a large and vacant table at which to sit near the roaring fireplace.
Once everyone had taken a seat and sat down, they all noticed small pieces of parchment that were lying upon the table detailing the specials available for dinner on one side and the desserts and drinks on the other.
As everyone took a piece of parchment and began to read, Kit stared at hers with confusion,
"What's this?", she asked,
"It tells you what you can have for dinner, you make an order and they bring to it you", said Einar,
Kit's eyes widened in surprise,
"You mean I can actually choose what I want to eat? I don't have to eat bone broth and stale bread?", she said,
Einar nodded, which caused Kit to shake with excitement in her seat,
"There's so much to choose from, I don't know where to start!", she gasped,
"Well have a look and when you have made a decision, we'll order for you", said Einar,
"Hard to decide, everything sounds so good", said John,
"Are we sharing a platter or ordering individuals meals?", asked Ulva,
"It's up to you, but this might be our last decent meal for some time, so it's best to fill up now good and proper", said Brenna,

After perusing through the menu, Einar placed it down before he glanced over at Kit. He noticed her eyes were shining as she glanced over the parchment. She was panting heavily as her mouth was salivating.

After a while, the young girl with the snow-white hair and the grey dress that they had seen earlier walked up to the table with a warm smile on her face and a small notebook in her hand,

"Hello there, anything I can get for you this evening?", she said in a sweet voice,

"Yes I'll have the Pinnekjott lamb and a tankard of your finest mead", said Brenna,

"Oh that sounds nice I'll have the same", said Einar,

"And for you?", asked Jetta as she glanced over at John,

"I'll have the marbled rump steak, medium rare with caramelized onions with a side of hot bread and butter, what drinks would you recommend?", he said,

"Well for you I would recommend Valkyrja's Delight, which is alcohol blended with white honeycomb, a juniper berry preserve and double cream. Or perhaps you might enjoy the Frost Giant, a brew concocted from fjelltopp beer, white moonberries, blackberry juice and blue raspberry liqueur from Gallia finished off with a twist of lime", said Jetta,

"Hmm, I think I will go for some hot cocoa", said John,

"Not interested in the Frost Giant?", asked Jetta,

"I don't drink", replied John,

"How come?", asked Kit,

"I have a bad experience with alcohol", said John,

Kit chuckled,

"What you had a bad hangover or something?", she said,

"You could say that", replied John before he sighed, his smile fading into a frown,

"Very well and something light for the ladies?", said Jetta,

"Light?", asked Ulva,

"We have some fresh and crisp glacier grown salads", said Jetta,

"Absolutely not, I'll have the farikal stew to start followed by the prime rib, the rotisserie chicken and fenalar lamb with a side order of garlic and cheese crispbread, reindeer venison sausages and smoked apple sauce. For a drink I will go for that lovely sounding Valkyrja's Delight thank you", said Ulva,
John, Brenna and Einar looked at Ulva with surprise,
"What?", she said,
"That's quite a lot, can you manage it?", asked Einar,
"Of course, I am famished. I wouldn't have ordered it if I couldn't", huffed Ulva,
"Okay and finally for the young lady", said Jetta,
Kit stared at the parchment in her hands and said,
"Um, what's smalahove?",
"It's the head of a sheep, it's quite a delicacy though it might be too much for you, it's usually served as a meal between two to three people", said Jetta,
Putting the parchment down and with a big grin on her face, Kit said,
"I'll have that please",
Jetta jotted down Kit's order,
"Any drinks?", she said,
"That Frost Giant drink sounds nice, I try some of that", said Kit,
"Excellent choices, right I will send these orders to the kitchen, in the meanwhile just sit back and relax whilst we get those drinks for you", said Jetta,
After everyone had thanked Jetta, she walked off with some wooden trays, but not before winking at John as she left,
"I can't believe you just ordered some smalahove", said John,
"Really?", asked Kit,
"It's quite delicious, but when I was young it always used to scare me when it was served during Yuletide. I much prefer that my meal doesn't look at me when I'm eating it", said John,
As Jetta was placing down some tankards of ice water upon the table, Kit said,
"Well I think it sounds quite nice",

"Whatever floats your longship", smiled John as he snatched up one of the tankards before taking a swig,
He then turned to Ulva and stared at her with a loving gaze as she placed a comforting hand upon his knee and stared at him dreamily. John then whispered in her ear, which made her giggle softly and become flushed in the face before they both kissed. Such a sight made Kit a little hot under the collar. She sighed before taking a sip of iced water from the tankard that was nearby.
As everyone waited for their meal to arrive, John said to Brenna,
"Before we leave tomorrow, is there any way we can get in touch with someone regarding Ishellir? I mean the mine is still full of bodies, we should inform someone about what happened",
Brenna took a sip of his tankard before he said,
"Not to worry John, it's all been taken care of. While I was out at the market, I informed the heralds about what happened. Hopefully by morning the authorities will act and begin clearing it out, talking to families, preparing the burials and so on",
"Excellent thank you, they don't deserve to remain down there", said John,
Raising his tankard, Einar said,
"Here's to the fallen of Ishellir and the innocents of Gormwood orphanage, may they be welcomed into Helheim with warmth and love",
As everyone raised their tankards of ice water and took a sip in remembrance, Ulva couldn't help but feel a horrible knot of guilt well up inside of her. She knew she had no control over her actions, but such thoughts did little to comfort her. Such guilt slowly slipped away though as the sight of Jetta returning with delicious looking drinks lifted Ulva's spirit. Brenna and Einar's meads were served in large tankards that were foaming and smelling of honey.

John's cocoa was served in a silver gleaming goblet that smelt of rich chocolate whilst the Frost Giant was an impressive looking drink. It was served in a tall, white and blue marbled ceramic jug, the lip of which was encrusted with sugar. Inside was a sweet smelling and slightly bubbling drink that was shaded a deep purple blue. The Valkyrja's Delight was served in a tall mug and was coloured a beautiful shade of golden crème with layers of deep dark purple.
Jetta placed them down on the table and said,
"Your food will be with you very soon",
As everyone took their drinks from the table, Brenna cleared his throat,
"I would just like to say something before we eat. Even though this journey has been difficult for all of us, I couldn't ask for a better group of people to be doing it with. Let us raise a drink to better times and the hope that this journey shall be successful", he said,
"May we never falter in our journey towards Coldwood!", cried Einar,
"I'll drink to that", laughed John,
"A toast to us all, may we shine brightest when the shadows are at their darkest", said Ulva,
"Skal", said Kit,
Everyone slammed their drinks together before they each took a gulp of their chosen beverages. Kit couldn't help but grin as she felt the refreshing and crisp taste of berries running down her throat, which left a pleasant after-taste. John quite enjoyed the taste of his drink; it was creamy and warmed him up from top to bottom. To Brenna and Einar, the mead was ice cold and was both smooth and sweet. Ulva meanwhile licked her lips as she could taste the delicate flavour of honey mixed in with the sharp taste of juniper accompanied by the taste of the cream.
With the night now drawing in, more and more people were entering the tavern until the place was bustling, from those who had finished work for the day to travellers who were staying for the night and were enjoying the local hospitality.

Eventually after waiting for quite a while, the food arrived, much to everyone's delight.

In front of John, Einar, Brenna, Ulva and Kit was a pleasurable array of hot sizzling meats, warm steaming bread coated with melted butter that ran like liquid gold and delicious looking sides piled upon plates. Even the somewhat gruesome sight of Kit's meal of a whole steamed lamb head with exposed red musculature and gooey eyes slowly sliding out of their sockets did nothing to faze their appetites.

Grabbing their cutlery, John, Kit, Einar, Brenna and Ulva tucked into the sumptuous banquet before them and over the course of a good hour demolished the entire veritable spread of delightful dinners of which they enjoyed immensely.

Ulva was even able to keep true to her word and had consumed the entire plate that she had ordered, leaving not a speck or crumb. It might have been the wolf blood flowing through her veins that had made her appetite more voracious, but then again despite being quite petite in stature, Ulva was never one to shy away from a hearty meal.

But it was fair to say that Kit enjoyed her dinner the most, for as soon as it was presented to the table, she dived right in with a massive smile lighting up her face. Unlike her friends, she did not use cutlery, she did not know how to use them nor did she have any need of them. Instead she simply grabbed the head with both hands and began biting, gnawing, chewing and ripping away large chunks of flesh off the bone before snapping them up without so much as a pause.

As she ate, Kit made soft little chirps and noises whilst she scrunched her nose and happily tore apart her meal.

Though her friends were not concerned about her table manners, Kit did receive some looks and glares off some of the nearby patrons as she loudly scoffed and snarled, though they kept themselves at a distance as Einar pulled back his cloak slightly, revealing the shining sword hanging from his belt whilst giving them a cautionary glance.

Once everyone had finished their dinner and every plate was licked clean, literally in Kit's case, everyone ordered some dessert to polish off their meal. It was safe to say that after they had tucked into some delicious cloudberry cake, hot and doughy smultring with a dusting of cardamom and cinnamon and some fresh and fruity bondepiker, they were delightfully full.

Soon after Jetta took away all the plates and received some coins for her services, John and his friends were startled when the tavern was suddenly filled with the cries and cheers of the patrons sitting nearby, who were clapping and hollering as they chanted in unison,

"Four Horns, Four Horns, Four Horns!", they cried,

After some tables and chairs were pushed aside to make some room, Wyland and Jetta walked into the centre of the tavern carrying a large barrel of frosted beer. Once Wyland cracked open the keg, both him and Jetta stepped away as Yrsa approached it, beaming as the air was filled with the sound of chanting patrons and the knocking of tankards against the tables.

As John and his friends stared in confusion at the sight, Yrsa yelled,

"Good folk of Grontorp, welcome to this week's Four Horns challenge!",

The cheering grew louder as Yrsa said,

"This week sees our very own drinking champion return to the Weary Traveller once more to call upon anyone brave and foolish enough to challenge him to the Four Horns!",

After the patrons had cheered and clapped some more, Yrsa said,

"Please welcome back our champion, the King of Kegs, the man with the iron belly, the dipsomaniac of Krallengard, Bolgr Barrelbreaker!",

John, Einar, Ulva, Kit and Brenna glanced over at a nearby table and saw a tall man stand up.

He was wearing a red shirt, linen trousers that were a dark grey colour and shoes made of leather. Around his waist was a belt upon which was hung a bulging sack of coins and a large drinking horn.

The man's head was shaven and etched into the side of his face and bare arms were many tattoos. His chin was covered in a large dark brown beard and his small blue eyes were framed by a smearing of black powder made from burnt ochre and ash.

To the cheers of the patrons, Bolgr bowed his head before he stared longingly at the barrel sitting in the centre of the inn, "Tonight's first challenger is one of Grontorp's most well-known and respected citizens, it's our very own master shipbuilder Arngrim Arnisson!", yelled Yrsa,

As the air was filled with rapturous yelling, clapping and cheering, John, Einar, Kit, Ulva and Brenna noticed a man sitting near the door stand up. He was slightly shorter than Bolgr and possessed no beard, but he was just as well built and was wearing similar attire, though his tunic was coloured a dark green instead of red. Arngrim's long brown hair was streaked with copper and was braided.

Raising his arms into the air, Arngrim grinned widely as he glanced around at the people chanting his name. Both Arngrim and Bolgr stepped over to the barrel and stood on each side of the keg.

Yrsa meanwhile stood in between them, smiling as the two men shook hands,

"All right, now that we have our champion and the challenger, present the horns!", she cried,

With much curiosity, John and his friends watched as Jetta and Wyland walked over to the barrel, each of them carrying a large drinking horn,

"Because both the champion and the challenger have experienced this challenge before, we shall dispense with the rules and commence at once", said Yrsa,

John glanced over at the tables on the other side of the tavern as he noticed several of the patrons had risen to their feet and were holding their tankards high into the air, yelling and bellowing joyously together.
He then saw Bolgr and Arngrim grab a horn each and hold them out over the barrel,
"Are you ready? Three, two, one, go!", cried Yrsa,
To the loud and rhythmic sound of a drumbeat provided by Wyland, the patrons suddenly began chanting and clapping as the two men standing around the barrel quickly scooped their horns into the ice-cold beer and began to drink, tipping their heads back as they gulped down the beer as quickly as they could,
"Skal! Skal! Skal!", cried the revellers,
John watched as Bolgr and Arngrim quickly finished their horns before thrusting their arms into the barrel to fill them up again. They then proceeded to chug their drinks as fast as they could, the drumbeat getting faster and the chanting quickening as they finished their second drink. It seemed as if the two men were tied for speed, they both had made light work of two horns, but when it came to drinking the third horn, Arngrim suddenly spluttered as he swallowed the beer too fast and he began to choke and cough.
After he had stopped coughing and Jetta had given him some water, Arngrim gasped,
"No more, I yield!",
Hearing this, Yrsa raised her arms and shouted,
"The challenge is over, Bolgr remains the champion of the Four Horns!",
There came the sudden sound of cheering and clapping as Bolgr laughed boisterously, raising his drink into the air before swallowing down its contents in two deep draughts. He then extended his hand to Arngrim and said,
"Bad luck old man, you did good though",

Arngrim took Bolgr's hand and shook it before he staggered back over to his table,
"Who shall be next to challenge Bolgr to the Four Horns, does anyone think they have the fortitude to scale the four peaks and emerge victorious?", said Yrsa,
As everyone murmured to one another, John said quietly to Brenna,
"You wouldn't catch me doing something like that",
"Well you wouldn't, you don't drink", said Brenna,
"It's rather pointless if you ask me, it doesn't require any skill at all nor does it test your mind or body", said John,
"Do we have any people wishing to take on the challenge or shall it be another week of waiting for someone to take Bolgr's crown?", said Yrsa,
Suddenly there came a voice,
"I'll do it",
Everyone in the tavern turned towards the source of the sound and were surprised to see Ulva had stood up.
As the revellers whispered and murmured to one another, John blurted,
"Ulva, what are you doing?!",
"Taking the challenge", said Ulva,
"Are you sure?", asked Kit,
"Oh I am sure, it doesn't look that tough, besides this is meant to be a night of fun, I want a belly full of beer and a heart full of cheer", said Ulva,
As Ulva walked over to the edge of the barrel and stared at a rather bemused Bolgr, Yrsa yelled,
"We have another challenger!",
The tavern was filled with the sound of cheering and tankards slamming down on tables as Ulva glanced down at the frosted beer swilling around in the barrel, it smelt bitter and you could see lumps of dark ice bobbing around the fizzing surface of the keg,
"It's been a while since we had a young maiden take on the challenge, what is your name?", said Yrsa,
"Ulva Forrester of Gormstad", said Ulva,

"Well Ulva welcome to the Four Horns challenge, are you familiar with the rules?",
"No", replied Ulva,
"Well this challenge is a little tradition that goes back a few hundred years. First one to down four horns of frosted beer is declared the champion. If you drop your horn, you are disqualified, if you pause for longer than five seconds between horns, you are disqualified, any questions?", said Yrsa,
"Is there a prize if you become champion?", asked Ulva,
Laughter and chortles of amusement rose from the patrons,
"Yes, the satisfaction of winning and the glory of victory", said Yrsa,
Ulva grinned,
"That's good enough for me", she said,
After Bolgr and Ulva shook hands over the barrel, Bolgr said, "You are quite small, are you sure you have enough room for all that beer?",
"I don't know, but I am sure there's plenty of room in your big head for such a tiny brain", smirked Ulva,
"Oh snap!", yelled Kit,
Bolgr chuckled softly before saying,
"You know you can still back out",
"What and miss the opportunity to see your face once I am finished wiping the floor with you? I think not", said Ulva,
"Okay challengers, ready your horns!", barked Yrsa,
Ulva took the horn from Jetta's tray whilst Bolgr took the horn from Wyland's.
They both smirked at one another as they held their horns out over the barrel,
"Bet you five silvers Ulva drinks Bolgr under the table", said Einar to Brenna,
"Fuck off, I'm not that stupid, of course she's gonna outdrink him", said Brenna,
"Go Ulva!", shouted John,
"Three, two, one, go!", yelled Yrsa,

The air suddenly filled with chanting, cheering, clapping, the thundering of boots and the thumping of tankards against the tables as Ulva and Bolgr quickly scooped up beer into their horns and began to greedily pour it down their throats,
"Skal! Skal! Skal! Skal!", cried the tavern patrons,
Near the fireplace, Einar, Brenna, John and Kit were crying out Ulva's name and shouting words of encouragement as she guzzled down her first horn easily. Quickly wiping the sweet beer dripping from her lips, Ulva quickly refilled her horn and after a few seconds she had swilled down its entire contents. As Bolgr and Ulva started on their third horns, Kit said to John,
"Wow look at her go",
"If you think that's impressive, you should see her during the Midsummer Sigrblot, the barbecue pit always ends up looking like a massacre", laughed John,
Ulva gasped for air as she finished her third horn just a few seconds before Bolgr, who was starting to shake slightly as his belly began to ache from the copious amounts of beer sloshing around in his stomach. With beer running down her chin, Ulva filled up her fourth horn before she tipped her head back and began to drink.
Bolgr was close to finishing his final horn when he had to pause briefly as his vision started to become sluggish, his arms began to ache and he was out of breath.
But just as he composed himself, he noticed that Ulva was beaming at him from the other side of the barrel and she was holding her empty horn upside down, much to his shock and surprise,
"I win", she said,
"We have a new champion!", cried Yrsa,
The tavern erupted into roars of joy as some of the patrons got up and began chanting Ulva's name. Ulva raised her arms in the air, basking in the cheering and the sound of her name ringing out as John swept her off her feet and perched her atop his shoulders so everyone could catch a glimpse of their new champion.

Suddenly there came Bolgr's loud voice,
"Hey!",
Everyone went silent and turned towards Bolgr, Einar glared at him as he brushed his fingers against the pommel of his sword, readying himself in case Bolgr got violent or aggressive.
Bolgr stared at Ulva before he said,
"For seven years I have never known defeat and to bested by such a small woman is surprising",
Bolgr then reached for the horn on his belt before he filled it with beer and held it up,
"I misjudged you, for that I am sorry. Here's to you Ulva Forrester our newest champion. May your tankard never run dry", he said with a smile on his face,
"Skal!", cried the revellers,

CHAPTER XXV: BITTEN

The tavern was filled with the sound of laughter, jovial and boisterous shouting, loud talking and the clinking of drinks as people drunk themselves merry.
At their table, Einar, John, Kit, Ulva and Brenna were laughing as Bolgr finished his story about one challenge he took part in years ago,
"And then he fell head-first into the cider, when we fished him out, he demanded a rematch only to pass out where he stood!", yelled Bolgr,
"What a lightweight!", laughed Einar,
"And that was only after one horn?!", blurted Ulva,
"Aye, poor kid couldn't hold his water, not like us eh champion?", said Bolgr,
"No indeed", said Ulva before she took a gulp of her drink,
Putting her tankard down, Ulva then said,
"Hey listen, I am sorry for calling you dumb earlier. My blood was pumping and I wasn't thinking straight from the adrenaline",
"It's alright, I've been called far worse before. Besides you are right, got more blood than brains in this head", said Bolgr,
Ulva laughed as Bolgr snatched up his drink and quickly gulped down every last drop,
"Forgive me for being nosy, but do you guys live around here? I've been visiting these parts for years and not once have I ever made your acquaintances", said Bolgr,
"We are not from here, we come from Gormstad", said John,
"Ah I remember now, Ulva here said she was from there, are you here for a visit then?", said Bolgr,
"No we are just staying for the night, we are heading north on some important business", said John,
"Might I ask what that is?", asked Bolgr,

John's smile faded before he said,
"It's complicated and secret, I am sorry",
"Don't apologize, I shouldn't be prying into business that doesn't concern me", said Bolgr,
"We are heading towards Coldwood", said Kit,
"Kit!", barked Brenna,
Bolgr spluttered as he nearly choked on his drink.
As Brenna shot Kit an admonishing glare, Bolgr said,
"Coldwood, you mean that big dark forest beyond Bjorndale?",
Brenna sighed,
"Yes, but why we are going there is none of your business", he grumbled,
"Indeed it isn't, don't worry I won't tell a soul. I may be a drunkard, but I ain't no blabbermouth", said Bolgr,
"You know about it?", asked John,
"Oh yes, I hail from Krallengard, a tiny village situated not far from the forest. I have never been there before, but from what I have heard about it, I wouldn't dare go near it",
"What things?", asked Kit,
Bolgr glanced around before he leaned in closer, close enough that you could smell the stench of alcohol on his breath,
"It's haunted, I don't know by what, but there is something dark and unnatural about that place. More than just wolves wander there, the very forest itself seems to be tainted by evil", he said,
John and his friends felt a chill run down their spines as Bolgr stared at them with wide and frightened eyes,
"If you go there, be very careful, people have been known to go missing when they step foot into its forbidden depths", he said softly,
"Thanks for the warning", said Brenna,
"Regardless though, I wish you all the very best on your journey towards Coldwood. I hope you find what you are looking for, whatever that may be", said Bolgr,

"Thanks", said John,
As everyone continued talking amongst themselves, Jetta appeared to collect up any empty drinks from the table. After everyone had ordered some more, Jetta placed the tankards and mugs upon a tray and made her way into the kitchen through an opening behind the counter. Placing the tankards into a nearby sink, Jetta glanced around before she made her way through a nearby door.

After walking through a narrow and dark corridor, Jetta came to a small and rather obscure door that was locked. Plucking a small key from her belt, Jetta unlocked the door and stepped into pitch-black darkness. After closing and locking the door behind her, she illuminated some nearby lamps and found herself standing in a small room that was devoid of any ornamentation apart from a large mirror fixed to the wall, a rickety table and a crooked chair sitting in the corner. Scratched into the floor was a mysterious symbol surrounded by circles of runes.

Standing in front of the mirror, Jetta reached up and removed the ribbons from her hair, allowing her locks to unfurl in a cascading wave. She then rolled up her sleeves and closed her eyes. Breathing deeply as she concentrated, she felt her teeth begin to sharpen and once they had grown to a point, she pulled a glove away from her heavily scarred hand and pierced her skin, allowing blood to run down her arm and onto the floor, dripping profusely upon the symbol beneath her feet.

Once the floor was red with blood, Jetta began to chant a forbidden incantation known only to the Cult of Fenris. As she did, the flames in the nearby lamps began to flicker and dance as if shuddering in fear from Jetta's words. At the completion of the incantation, Jetta watched as the mirror suddenly flashed and beyond its glass surface appeared what looked like fog and rolling storm clouds.

In a gentle yet clear and affirmative voice, Jetta said,
"In the name of Tyr's bane, in the name of the King of Wolves, I call upon Prince Garm of Ulfholl",

The mirror flashed again as there came the low rumbling of thunder, for a moment the mirror was still as the clouds swirled and glowed inside.

After many irritating minutes of silence, suddenly a face emerged in the mirror, a man with piercing yellow eyes and silver hair,

"Who dares summon Garm, master sorcerer and son of Fenrir?", he growled in a menacing and gravelly voice,

"Jetta Snowmane, daughter of the late Jormund of Tarn Gren. With my blood, I have invoked the Rite of Summoning and ask for your audience",

Garm glared at Jetta,

"Why have you summoned me Ulffar of Gren?", he said,

"I have come to inform you that John and Ulva Forrester and their friends are here in Grontorp, in the Weary Traveller Inn", said Jetta,

"I am aware of these people and I am aware of their intention to travel to Coldwood", said Garm,

"Your royal highness, I ask for your advice on the matter of their presence here in the inn. Do I have your permission to kill them and bring Vulthur the Vargslayer to you in the Hall of Wolves?", said Jetta,

"No young Snowmane, they are to remain unharmed and untouched until they reach Coldwood", said Garm,

Jetta snarled at Garm, baring her razor-sharp teeth,

"With all due respect my prince, they murdered my father. The destruction of Tarn Gren was so complete that there were no remains left to bury", she said,

Jetta gasped as the mirror flashed with lightning and thunder boomed as Garm's eyes glowed with anger,

"Have patience, you will have your revenge soon enough, but for now sheath your claws and hide your fangs, your illusion of humanity must be preserved for the time being. Whilst they are here, keep an eye on them and ensure that their journey remains uninterrupted so long as they remain in Grontorp", he said,

"Must I really?", asked Jetta,
"Yes and once they have left the hamlet, I want you to leave the Weary Traveller and come to Ulfholl in preparation for our plans", said Garm,
Jetta sighed and begrudgingly said,
"Very well, they shall be left unharmed, you have my word",
"Good and make sure they are, lest I tear the skin from your hide", growled Garm,
Jetta swallowed past the lump in her throat as she felt her hands begin to tremble,
"So what now your highness?", she said,
"Continue posing as the sweet tavern maid everyone in Grontorp knows and loves and before they leave, give them this", replied Garm,
Garm reached into the folds of his robes and pulled out from one of his pockets what looked like a silver pendant.
Jetta watched in amazement as Garm stretched out his arm through the glass surface of the mirror and held out the pendant,
"Take it my child", said Garm,
Jetta nervously took the pendant and glanced at it with curious eyes,
"What is it?", she said,
"Never mind about that, just give it to either John or one of his friends and when they have left town, make your way to Ulfholl, this I command of you",
Jetta bowed her head,
"Yes my lord", she said,
Garm grinned a fanged smile,
"Excellent, oh and Jetta?", he said,
"Yes your royal highness?", said Jetta,
"I am sorry to hear about your father, you have my condolences", replied Garm,

Jetta felt her heart sink as the mirror flashed and went dark. To the sounds of playing instruments, joyous singing and tumultuous merriment, Jetta quietly and calmly pocketed the pendant and with haste, filled up a bucket and washed away the blood on the floor.
She then pulled down her sleeves, slipped her glove back on, braided her hair and made her way back into the kitchen where she began preparing some drinks,
"Where have you been?!", barked Yrsa,
Startled, Jetta wheeled round and saw the angry form of Yrsa standing in the nearby opening,
"We have people waiting for drinks and we need some meals served!", snapped Yrsa,
"Sorry Yrsa, I had some important business to take care of", said Jetta,
"It can't be as important as serving the customers, now quit standing around and get to your duties", said Yrsa,
"Yes, right away", said Jetta,
As Yrsa stormed back into the foyer, Jetta said quietly and angrily under her breath,
"When the time comes you fat sow, the last thing you will feel will be my teeth against your throat",
After preparing some food and drink, Jetta stepped into the foyer area carrying two full trays. She was slightly taken aback by the sounds that awaited her.
Everyone in the dining area was singing, yelling, swinging their drinks and dancing as a group of travelling skalds had arrived at the inn, all of them singing beautiful and powerful melodies in unison as they played an impressive array of musical instruments.
Jetta glanced over the end of the counter and noticed that Wyland was sleeping. Despite the noise, it barely stirred him. Jetta then walked over to the table where John, Einar, Brenna, Ulva, Kit and Bolgr were sitting, they were all drunk and roaring with laughter as they were telling each other stupid jokes and silly stories.

She could hear Kit talking to Bolgr as she had her arm wrapped around his shoulders,
"You know what...'*hic*'...I think Einar is right...perhaps being a werewolf might not so bad. Just because my father was terrible, it doesn't mean that I am and I shouldn't hate myself for what I am and who I am", she said in a slurred tone of voice,
"Gods I know right? My mother hated me because she said that I reminded her of my father, who she grew to hate after years of loveless marriage. But you know what? I didn't care what she thought and I continued living the way I wanted to, not how she wanted me to live. So I decided to not become a Godi and instead I became a barber and by the gods, I haven't looked back since", said Bolgr,
"Good for you Bolgr", said Brenna,
"Sorry for the wait guys, here are your drinks, enjoy", said Jetta sweetly,
"Thanks!", yelled John despite the fact Jetta was only a few feet away from him,
After Jetta left and everyone had snatched up a drink, they continued to talk and sing loudly, indulging in each other's company as they enjoyed the lively, exuberant and energetic atmosphere of carefree and blithe revelry. At this point, everyone was in such a good mood that every single face was lit up with a bright smile and even John had drunk his fill of delicious cider, even though in any ordinary situation where he had complete control of his inhibitions, he would have outright refused.
As the night wore on, John, Ulva, Einar, Kit, Brenna and Bolgr spent the evening talking, laughing, dancing and singing together all the while becoming incredibly drunk, especially Kit, who at one point nearly unknowingly transformed into a werewolf mid – dance because she was so intoxicated. While most of the taverners were either too drunk or merry to notice, there were a few who witnessed the peculiar sight.

Luckily it was quite easy for Brenna and Einar to explain to the curious, confused and incredibly inebriated patrons why their young friend had grown fluffy wolf ears and a furry black tail whilst howling at the top of her lungs as everyone sung loudly and merrily, they were hallucinating thanks to their drinks. It was an excuse that was easily bought, Bolgr noticed and found it both utterly hilarious and cute.

At one point during the evening, Einar rushed upstairs to collect his lyre, which he played to everyone's delight, even to the musicians, who allowed him to play alongside them during a few songs. As he sang and played his lyre, Einar was attracting quite a lot of attention, especially from the women in the tavern. Of course despite having alcohol flowing through his body, he was never tempted by their flirtations for he knew Maud was back at home awaiting his return, his heart belonged to her and no one else.

As midnight fast approached, the tavern slowly began to empty as the revellers either left to go home or had retreated to their rooms for the night. Kit was the first to go back up to the room because she had drunk so much that the tavern was starting to spin and her heightened senses of sight, sound and smell were warped to the point that the vivid flashing colours, blaring noises and the overpowering scent of alcohol, vomit and smoke was making her feel nauseous. Once the skalds had left shortly afterwards, Einar followed Kit up the stairs to make sure she was okay. Brenna and Bolgr meanwhile stayed downstairs a little while longer and when the last of the revellers had departed, they both stumbled up the stairs after paying their considerable tabs of food and drink.

When they got to the top of the stairs, Bolgr said,

"Well it was nice meeting all of you, good luck on your journey and pay heed to what I said about Coldwood",

"Thank you Bolgr, we will", said Brenna,

As Bolgr made his way to his room, Brenna drunkenly made his way towards room four.

Ulva and John were the last people remaining in the foyer when Wyland, Yrsa and Jetta began clearing up for the evening,
"Are you two going to bed or are you planning on staying down here the rest of the night with the tables and chairs?", asked Wyland in a dour tone of voice,
John hiccupped, which caused Ulva to burst out laughing,
"No, we are going, I just need to grab Ulva and we will be off", he said in a slurred voice,
As Jetta came round and collected up the tankards from the cider drenched tabletops, Ulva grabbed her by the arm and said with a massive grin on her face,
"Don't tell anyone...'*hic*', but I'm gonna ride the hell out of my husband later",
Jetta stared at Ulva with a surprised expression as Ulva stumbled off her chair, causing it to crash against the floor before she began lurching towards the stairs.
Raising her arms into the air, Ulva shouted,
"Like a goddamn horse!",
As John clumsily stood up, he saw Ulva kicking off her shoes before she sighed loudly in relief.
With a stupid looking grin on his face, John walked over to Ulva and picked her up in his arms,
"My stallion has arrived!", yelled Ulva,
Carrying her boots in one hand by the strings, Ulva wrapped her other arm around John's neck. She then giggled to herself before she and John began to sing terribly off key together as they made their way up the stairs, John laughing as he stumbled over the wooden steps beneath his feet.
When they got to the door of their room, John and Ulva began to kiss sloppily,
"Mmmm yummy, you taste good", purred Ulva,
John laughed before he untied the ribbon in his wife's hair, letting her crimson locks fall loose. As Ulva was kissing and nuzzling him aggressively on the cheek, John kicked open the door and staggered in.

Bathed in the warm glow of the crackling hearth, John and Ulva saw that Einar, Kit and Brenna were all fast asleep. Einar was lying on his back, shirtless with his arm lying extended across his face. Brenna was lying flat on his front and was sprawled across the bedsheets. He had made no attempt to undress and was snoring loudly.
Kit meanwhile was tucked tightly into her bed; curled up under the toasty blankets and sleeping soundly. Unlike Brenna, she was barely making a sound and was slumbering peacefully. John walked over to the bed and threw Ulva playfully onto it, where she laughed as she bounced on the sheets.
Putting a finger to his lips, John whispered,
"Shh, everyone's sleeping",
Ulva responded by putting her finger to her lips,
"Shh", she said before chuckling,
John beamed as he dived onto the bed and quickly pulled the sheets over him and Ulva. Giggling under the sheets, John and Ulva embraced and began to kiss passionately before they both began undressing one another, throwing their clothes onto the floor.
Once they were completely naked, John began to pant heavily as Ulva began kissing him gently all over his body whilst he ran his hands down her arms, waist and over her breasts as she laid on top of him,
"Here", said John as he gingerly repositioned himself,
Ulva moaned softly as John gently entered her, pushing his throbbing penis deep inside her quivering body. John then began gently thrusting up and down whilst grasping Ulva's thighs, slowly at first before going faster and harder, all the while ensuring they weren't too loud as to wake the others. John panted as his body glowed with warmth, he gripped the bed tightly, clawing at the mattress beneath him as Ulva nibbled at his neck and ran her hands across his chest.
Ulva moaned as John penetrated deep inside her, slamming against her with subdued ferocity. She gritted her teeth as a growl of pleasure emanated from deep within her throat.

It was a shame that they both had to be as quiet as possible, for if it were in their own home and upon their own bed, they would have been howling and groaning with unrestrained delight and would have even tried some experimentation, but this would have to do for now.

John stared at Ulva as she repositioned herself on top of him before settling into a more comfortable position, putting her legs at his sides and pressing down upon him with her pelvis. John ran his hands up and down Ulva's thighs as she grinded on top of him, Ulva wiping the saliva from her mouth as she became increasingly hot and wet. John winced in both pain and pleasure as Ulva ran her nails down his chest, scratching him enough to make the skin flare and tingle, but not enough to draw blood.

As John was now pounding away at Ulva, she began to shake and her forehead began to sweat as her crotch was now incredibly hot,

"Yes that's it, fuck me", she moaned before she began to play with herself,

John closed his eyes as he pounded Ulva faster, his back arching as he began to climax inside her. As he did, Ulva's mind began to race and her vision began to flash red.

She could suddenly smell blood in the air and could taste it on her tongue as she felt a sudden and primal urge overwhelm her. With her heartbeat pounding against her breast, Ulva let out a loud and long drawn groan of pleasure before she suddenly and instinctively brought her head down upon the base of John's neck and bit hard.

John screamed in pain as he felt Ulva's teeth pierce his neck and a terrible stinging sensation ruptured from his throat and down his shoulder blade. Clutching his bleeding neck, John pushed Ulva off before he rolled onto his side in panic and tumbled onto the floor with a thud. Ulva stared at John in shock as she covered her bloody mouth with her shaking hands, horrified as she watched John cry out in pain as he squirmed on the floor.

Woken by the commotion, Brenna and Einar immediately rose from their beds with Einar even reaching for his sword. Kit was sitting up in her bed with the blankets pulled up to her chin, she was wide eyed and shaking in fright as the noise had startled her,
"What the hell is going on?!", blurted Einar,
Brenna was shocked by the sight of John lying on the floor naked and covered in blood.
Falling to his knees, Brenna quickly grabbed a shirt and pressed it up against John's neck as he sat his friend up against the bed,
"Ulva bit me, that's what's happened", growled John angrily,
"I'm sorry John, I'm so sorry!", squeaked Ulva as tears began to well up in her eyes,
"What do you mean she bit you?!", demanded Einar as he helped Ulva off the floor and onto the edge of the bed before throwing his cloak over her shaking body,
"Well I promised Ulva we would have some intimate fun tonight since it was our first evening of respite since she got bitten", said John,
"Then what happened?", asked Brenna,
"It was great until we came to the end, she suddenly and out of nowhere bit me", said John before he flashed an angry glare at Ulva,
"Why did you do that? You ruined what was to be a wonderful end to an unforgettable night. Worse you could have killed me!", he snapped,
Inspecting the bleeding wound on John's neck, Brenna said, "Come on, we need to get you cleaned up and bandaged",
Brenna helped John up onto his feet before they both hobbled into the nearby bathroom.
With the sound of the door slamming, Ulva wiped the blood from her mouth before she suddenly burst into tears, burying her face in her bloodstained hands.
Einar and Kit sat down beside Ulva and tried to comfort her,
"Why did I do that, why did I hurt him like that?", sobbed Ulva,

Gently rubbing her back, Einar said,
"It's okay Ulva, you didn't mean to intentionally hurt him, I know that and so do you",
"It's not your fault Ulva, it was an accident", said Kit,
Ulva stared up at Einar and Kit and said,
"I know I don't have much control over my actions sometimes, but that doesn't make the situation any better. I must bear some responsibility for the things I have done. I am not completely guilt free, I need to worker harder to control myself",
"If you want to do that, then that's fine, but you need to understand Ulva that the wolfblight will force you to do things against your will and we just need to be more careful in future so no more innocent people are harmed", said Einar,
"Before you bit John, did you feel any urges?", asked Kit,
"Yes, I was in a complete state of euphoria, I...I smelt blood and I suddenly had an urge to bite John. I didn't resist because it felt so good", said Ulva before she buried her face in her hands,
"I just hope he can forgive me", she said,
"He will, I am sure of it, John has every right to be angry, but he needs to realize that what happened was beyond your control", said Einar,
The bathroom door suddenly opened and both Brenna and John emerged. Brenna was holding the bloody shirt in his hand whilst John had a bandage wrapped around his shoulder and neck. He looked bitter and angry; his face was twisted into a cold grimace.
As John sat himself down upon the bed, Ulva placed her hand upon his lap and said,
"I am so sorry sweetie, I don't know what came over me",
John glared coldly at Ulva, such a stare made Ulva's heart sink as her bottom lip trembled whilst tears ran down her face,
"I know that Ulva, but it still happened anyway. You hurt me in a way I thought you never would", said John,

Placing a shaking hand upon John's face, Ulva said,
"I promise you John it won't happen again; I'm going to work harder to keep myself under control, I swear it",
"Why did Ulva bite me?", asked John,
"Sit down, I'll explain", said Brenna,
As everyone sat down, Brenna removed his glasses and wiped them with a cloth before he put them back on,
"Okay Brenna, tell us everything", said Ulva,
"Well to put it simply, despite its horrific and unexpected nature, what Ulva did was perfectly normal behaviour", said Brenna,
"What?!", blurted John,
"Well, normal for a werewolf that is, Ulva did what is known as marking, it is something that werewolves do when they are having sex. Werewolves usually bite their mates during or just after intercourse. It might sound strange, but it is a sign of immense affection. In the throes of intimacy, she showed her love in the most primal and instinctive way a werewolf can", said Brenna,
"So what happened to me was perfectly reasonable and acceptable behaviour?!", barked John,
"For two werewolves yes, but not for two humans, especially if only one of them has lycanthropy. It is rather concerning because Ulva was not a werewolf when it happened. This brings me to my second point", said Brenna before he glanced at Ulva,
"So you know you have promised to try and control your behaviour and actions? I must make you aware that such a promise might be hard to keep, especially as time goes by. It is indeed noble of you to try, but such attempts might ultimately prove fruitless", he said,
"What do you mean?", asked Ulva,

"You biting John was a sign that you are now moving into the more advanced stages of the wolfblight affliction. I must warn you that as you experience more turnings in future, your physical, mental and emotional condition will likely begin to change and deteriorate. What we witnessed might be the beginning of such changes. The fact that you still show relative mental and emotional stability is a good indicator that you are not ready to become a werewolf permanently, but eventually that will change. Time is fortunately on our side", said Brenna,

"So what happens now?", said Einar,

"We prepare ourselves for the eventuality of Ulva becoming less like the girl we know and love and more like a monster", said Brenna before he glanced over at John,

"You are lucky my friend, your wound was deep, but thankfully it's superficial. If Ulva had bitten down harder or had bitten you in a different area of your neck, she could have pierced a vein and killed you", he said,

John glared at Brenna,

"Don't look at me like that, I know this incident was shocking and painful to you, but it was something none of us could have anticipated and it was certainly something that you cannot blame Ulva for, it was an accident, an unfortunate mishap. Try to put it behind you and focus on supporting one another during this difficult time", said Brenna,

John sighed deeply,

"Of course I will support her", he huffed,

"Thank you", said Ulva before she sweetly kissed John on the cheek,

"One more thing before we all return to our beds, I know you guys enjoy a little intimacy from time to time, but from now on, sex is out of the question. John was lucky Ulva had drunk the potion I gave her. If she hadn't then such an emotional act of love making might have triggered a turning and we would now be scraping what's left of John off the walls", said Brenna,

"Damn", grumbled John,

"Don't worry, I'll make it up to you once I'm cured", said Ulva as she began to blush,
"Yeah?", said John,
"Yeah", said Ulva,
"Well now that the situation has been rectified, I think we should all get some sleep and try to forget about what happened", said Einar,
"Indeed, we will need to be well rested for what's ahead", said Brenna,
Standing up, Brenna placed a comforting hand on Ulva's shoulder,
"Dry your eyes my dear, don't worry about what you did and please don't let guilt consume you, you already have enough to worry about as it is", he said,
Brenna glanced over at John, who was staring at the floor with a sullen look on his face,
"And you, try and go easy on Ulva please? She has already apologized and can do no more to make the situation any better", he said,
"I've been going easy on her for years,", muttered John angrily,
Ulva's frown deepened as John's words cut deep into her heart,
"Anyway I'm off to bed", said Einar,
"Goodnight Einar", said Brenna,
"Yes sweet dreams brother", said Ulva,
John said nothing as Einar walked over to his bed and tucked himself in,
"You two going to be alright?", asked Kit to John and Ulva,
"I hope so Kit, I truly hope so", said John softly,
"Good", smiled Kit before she went back to bed,
"Sleep well you two", said Brenna,
John and Ulva watched as Brenna walked over to his bed before he slipped under the sheets and pulled them over his body.

As Ulva got back into bed, she was surprised to see John walking over to the nearby bed and pulling the sheets back, "Where are you going sweetie?", she said,
"I'm going to sleep here tonight, I need to be alone right now", said John,
"Please don't go, I am frightened John. Brenna told me not to feel guilty, but I do and nothing would make me feel better than having the man I love lying next to me whilst I am wrapped in his safe, warm arms", said Ulva,
"I'm just a little shaken Ulva", mumbled John,
"Stay with me...please?", squeaked Ulva,
"Ulva, you say you will try and control yourself, but what's to stop you from cracking open my ribcage in the middle of the night and tearing out my beating heart? What's to say I don't wake up with you chewing on my guts?", growled John,
With tears running down her face, Ulva said,
"Listen to me John, I would never do anything to hurt you if I could help it. When I make the promise that I will try and do everything in my power to protect you from myself, I mean it",
John wiped some tears away from his eye, his breathing trembling as he saw Ulva stare at him with her big, beautiful and tearful eyes.
Feeling his heart breaking, John sighed before he stepped over to the bed and tucked himself in next to Ulva. The second he pulled the sheet over himself, Ulva quickly latched onto his body and curled up next him, whimpering as she wrapped her arms around his chest.
John winced as Ulva pressed against the wound on his neck,
"Sorry", whispered Ulva,
"It's okay", said John softly,
As Ulva rested her head against John, she uttered,
"I love you",
"Love you too", he said,
John winced softly as Ulva applied pressure to his wound, the pain aggravated by the weight of her head against his shoulder.

He was going to ask her to move, but after seeing the gentle and content smile on her face, he decided not to bring up his discomfort and disturb her sleep. Settling deeper into the sheets, John yawned before he closed his eyes and began to drift off to sleep.

Outside the room, Bolgr groaned softly as he stumbled through the corridor and down the stairs into the dark and quiet foyer. To the sound of howling wind, Bolgr walked through the tavern and slowly made his way outside into the bitter night. He wanted some fresh air as he was fatigued and his entire body ached with a dull pain.

As the cold wind enveloped him, Bolgr walked a few yards from the door before he came to a stop and glanced up at the crisp and clear night sky, staring in awe at the veil of beautiful stars that twinkled against the dark twilight. Bolgr stood around for a few minutes before he decided to go back to bed.

But just as Bolgr was about to leave, he heard a metallic crash and the sound of heavy footsteps coming from behind the tavern,

"Hello, is anyone there?", said Bolgr,

Bolgr cautiously walked past the stables and round to the back of the tavern where the sound had originated. He saw in front of him what looked like a large garden enclosed by a wooden fence, at the back of which sat rows of timber chicken hutches. Bolgr stepped forward and noticed that the iron door to one of the hutches had been tore off its hinges and tossed aside. At the foot of the hutch he saw something that made him queasy, a scattering of white feathers lying in a pool of blood strewn with pieces of torn flesh and cracked bones.

Feeling nauseous and disturbed by what he had seen and heard, Bolgr decided it was best that he left and inform Wyland of his discovery in the morning.

As Bolgr was about to leave though, he heard what sounded like growling coming from a nearby storage hut located next to the stables.

Bolgr glanced around and found a spade lying on the floor nearby covered in dirt and frost. After picking up the spade, Bolgr slowly crept towards the hut, his body shaking with fear. As Bolgr got closer to the door, the sound of gnashing teeth and a low growl could be heard alongside the sound of flesh being torn away from bone.

When Bolgr came to the slightly ajar door, he pushed it open slowly revealing an interior that was filled with straw and hay. Bolgr gasped as he saw what looked like a hulking figure shrouded in shadow sitting hunched over in the middle of the hut, it's back facing Bolgr as it devoured something hidden from view.

In shock, Bolgr dropped the spade and tried to flee, but it was too late as the creature suddenly lashed out and grabbed him by the throat with a sharpened claw attached to a large and muscular arm covered in fur. Bolgr let out a screech of terror as he was quickly and violently pulled into the hut, the door slamming shut behind him as the creature snatched him up.

CHAPTER XXVI: WOLFHEARTED SISTERS

Ulva shot up in bed as she heard faint screaming accompanied by the snapping of jaws and the cracking of bone. She didn't know where it was coming from or if it was just her imagination, but she heard it and it unnerved her. Struggling to sleep and with her limbs itching as her skin crawled, Ulva pulled the linen sheets off her naked body. She turned towards John and noticed that he was fast asleep and was snoring, his eyepatch was crooked on his face and his mouth was hanging wide open. As she stared at her sleeping husband, she felt her mouth beginning to water as she smelt the rich and intoxicating scent of blood seeping from the wound on his neck. She inhaled deeply as her heart began to race, shivering with ecstasy as the sweet smell entered her flared nostrils.

Baring her teeth as saliva began to run from the corners of her mouth, Ulva slowly crept towards John, her eyes transfixed on his bandaged neck as her heart pounded in her chest. But just as she was about to tenderly nibble at the bandages to get at the flesh beneath, she suddenly came to her senses and painfully smacked herself across the face, snapping herself out of her moment of madness.

Ulva stared at John in shock as she was surprised by her sudden behaviour. She groaned as she clutched her forehead, gritting her teeth as she could hear a long and terrible growling coming from her throat. She suddenly felt something shift and squirm around within her body. She thumped her chest with a curled fist before she pulled herself out of bed and staggered to her feet, her head now pounding with a sharp and horrible pain.

Though Ulva knew she wasn't going to turn tonight, she came to a horrible realization that the wolf within her was trying to force its way out.

Feeling nauseous, Ulva rummaged around the inside of her bag and pulled out her favourite nightgown, the one coloured a lovely pale pink. Throwing it on, Ulva got out of bed and began to anxiously pace the room, tapping her arm with tapered fingers.

Ulva felt restless and frightened as she didn't know how to calm herself. The entire length of her body was itching and she was stomping about trying to still the raging beast lurking within her. Her anxiety was made worse by the horrible guilt welling up inside of her, she was still upset about attacking John and was angry at herself for even contemplating for one moment that she would feast upon him. Not even humming Lupa's Lullaby seemed to help. She tried quietly dancing, spinning around in the darkness to try and burn off some energy to see if it might help, but that too only made her more fidgety.

Feeling hopeless, Ulva sat herself down in a nearby chair and cradled her head in her hands, muttering to herself as she was shrouded by moonlit darkness, her mind swirling with memories that she wished to forget.

She began to whimper as a soft voice came from the nearby gloom,

"Ulva?",

Ulva glanced up and saw two cerulean coloured eyes shining back at her.

She saw Kit was lying on her side and staring at her with a concerned look,

"It's late, what are you doing up?", she said,

"I can't sleep", said Ulva sadly,

"Hm, you too uh?", replied Kit,

"Yeah", said Ulva,

Kit smiled warmly and said,

"Come, sit and talk, it might get your mind off your worries",

Ulva got up and quietly walked over to Kit, perching herself on the edge of the bed,

"I just feel terrible about what I did to John", she said,

"Still worried eh? You just need to try and forget about it, move on and stop letting it torment you. What's done is done and you shouldn't beat yourself up over it", said Kit,
"You're a fine one to talk about moving on", snapped Ulva,
Seeing Kit's eyes widen in shock, Ulva said,
"Sorry, sorry I said that, I'm just not thinking straight at the moment",
Kit sighed,
"No you're right, I do sound like a hypocrite don't I? I need to listen to my own advice more", she said,
"I appreciate your concern Kit, but I will eventually get over what I did. It will just take some time that's all", said Ulva,
"I understand", said Kit,
Kit watched as Ulva laid herself down beside her and said,
"It will be difficult though",
"I don't doubt that, but we'll be here for you no matter what", said Kit,
"Thanks Kit", said Ulva before she sighed deeply,
"On a different note, why are you awake?", asked Ulva,
Glancing up at the ceiling, Kit said,
"I am just thinking about what Einar told me when we were both sitting together near the northern road. He said that I shouldn't hate myself for who I am, that I shouldn't use my father and his actions as a measure of how to act in this world and how to view it. He told me that I shouldn't be ashamed of being a werewolf and that I should not only be proud of my abilities, but I should use them for the betterment of others",
"That sounds like Einar all right, he has such a golden heart", said Ulva,
"Maybe he's right, maybe I shouldn't see myself as a monster, just as you shouldn't see yourself as one. We are not evil people Ulva, we might have been marked by evil or influenced by it, but evil does not rule our hearts. Perhaps I need to rediscover myself and shed the shackles of my dark and terrible past.

I am the master of my own destiny now and only I can decide on what I should do with my abilities and determine who I am and how I fit into this world", said Kit,
"Does that mean you don't want to cure yourself?", said Ulva as she glanced over at Kit,
"At first I was adamant, but now I don't know, I need more time to think about it", said Kit,
"Well whatever you decide, we will all support you", said Ulva,
"Thanks Ulva, that...means a lot to me", smiled Kit,
It was then that Kit whimpered as her eyes began to well up with tears,
"Kit?", said Ulva,
"Sorry, I'm just not used to having people around me being so friendly and kind to me. You must understand that I have gone most of my life without hearing a friendly word or seeing a friendly face. It will take a long time to get used to this new world and even longer to move on from what happened to me", said Kit as she rubbed her eyes,
"Just like with me biting John", said Ulva,
"Exactly", said Kit,
Ulva laughed softly before she noticed Kit lifting her hand in front of her face. Kit stared at her hand for a moment before she closed her eyes and began to concentrate. Ulva gasped as she watched Kit's hand change into a furry black and white paw. She watched in awe as Kit then extended and flexed her claws, allowing them to shine in the dim moonlight that flooded in through the nearby window. Curiously, Ulva reached up and gently touched Kit's paw, stroking her soft fur before running her fingers across her paw pads.
Kit couldn't help but chuckle at the sight,
"You sometimes forget how soft a werewolf's fur can be", said Ulva,
"Mmhm", muttered Kit,
As Ulva gently rotated her thumb across the underside of Kit's paw, she could hear a soft purr emanate from deep within Kit's throat.

Feeling content and relaxed, Kit said,
"I think I know what might take our mind off our troubles",
"What do you have in mind?", asked Ulva as she felt her heart quicken,
Locking eyes with Ulva, Kit said,
"It's a cool and dry night, care for a walk?",
"I'd like that", said Ulva,
Ulva and Kit got up off the bed, but as Ulva collected up her boots and pulled them on, she noticed that Kit was heading towards the door barefoot,
"It's cold outside you know", said Ulva,
Kit pulled her hood up over her head and shook her hand as it transformed back to normal,
"I want to feel the earth beneath my feet when we go outside. I want to walk like I once did through the gardens of Tarn Gren", she said,
"Okay, but don't complain if you get cold", said Ulva as she fastened up her laces,
Kit rolled her eyes before she pulled the door open and quietly left, Ulva following close by once she had grabbed John's cloak and threw it on to keep herself warm.
Outside it was bitterly cold and the air was filled with the gentle sounds of wind whistling through the grasslands and the flowing of rushing water in the nearby river. As she left the tavern, Kit suddenly stopped in her tracks as she stared up at the night sky. With her mouth hanging open in awe, Kit gazed at the countless stars shining above in a vast multitude of colours.
She could also see milky bands of shimmering stardust amidst the beautiful and pale glow of the moon,
"Are those stars?", she gasped,
"Never seen a star before?", said Ulva,
"Only in the books I have read", said Kit,
Ulva couldn't help but feel sympathy for Kit as she saw her friend's lip beginning to quiver,
"They are so beautiful", said Kit,

Looking up at the night sky, Ulva said,
"My grandfather once told me that stars are the souls of people who have passed on and are making their way towards Asgard and Helheim on a river of light and ice. He said that whenever someone leaves this world, the sky gets a little brighter as a new star is born in the heavens",
"Do you think my mother is up there?", asked Kit,
"Of course, why wouldn't she be?", said Ulva,
Kit frowned and said,
"Because my father said that she was in Niflheim with the other damned souls",
Ulva gently took Kit's hand and said,
"Never believe it for a second",
Suddenly Ulva and Kit glanced up as a bright gleam in the sky caught their attention, a shooting star with a beautiful silver tail,
"Oh look Kit, a soul soars through the heavens, quick make a wish!", gasped Ulva,
"Okay, I wish...", began Kit,
"No, no, you need to say it in your head for if you speak it, then it won't come true", said Ulva,
"Oh okay", said Kit,
Both Ulva and Kit closed their eyes and together they each made a wish as the magnificent comet raced across the sky before fading out of sight towards the star-studded horizon,
"Did you make a wish?", asked Ulva,
"Yeah, I just hope it comes true", said Kit,
"If you keep it a secret, then it just might", said Ulva,
Holding hands, Kit and Ulva made their way down the path and towards the wooden bridge spanning the river that flowed alongside the village.
As they walked over the creaking bridge, Ulva said,
"This was a great idea Kit, ever since we left the Weary Traveller I am feeling a lot better and I am not worrying or even thinking about the wolfblight. My body has stopped shaking, I don't feel any discomfort and even my skin has stopped itching",

"That's good because I worry about you", said Kit,
"Oh you don't have to worry about me", said Ulva,
"But I do, you're my friend and I just want you to be happy and safe", said Kit,
"With you and the guys at my side, I will always feel safe", said Ulva,
Kit blushed slightly before she glanced away,
"By the way, I wanted to thank you", said Kit,
Ulva glanced at Kit in confusion as they both stepped off the bridge and onto a gravelled path that led towards some open fields scattered with large standing stones,
"Thank me, for what?", she said,
"For being so kind to me and for being a good friend. Not just you, but also John, Einar and Brenna, they are good people and though I find the attention a little tiring at times, especially from Einar, I really do appreciate it. You guys have shown me more affection, care and attention in two days than I have ever experienced my whole life", said Kit,
Kit beamed as she felt Ulva put her arm around her shoulders,
"You're welcome and I know that Einar can be a little overbearing, but that is who he is, he just cares about you that's all", said Ulva,
"Really?", asked Kit, her face blushing red beneath her hood as her heart began to flutter,
"Oh yes, Einar has always been a little fussy concerning the well-being of the ones he loves. When I was just a child, there were times when he would give up his food, money and possessions so that I wouldn't go without during dark and lean times. When I was struggling with life without parents, facing my own personal demons and navigating the challenges of adolescence, he would always be there to comfort me, even when he was feeling a little down himself", said Ulva,

Kit's smile faded as she saw Ulva frown,
"There were even moments when I found his affection to be a little too much and I would lash out at him. Looking back on it now, I am ashamed to say that I regret my sudden outbursts and now that he has Maud in his life, sometimes I miss the days when I was the apple of his eye. He's quite the gentlemen and that for me is quite an underappreciated quality that some men I have known in my life could do with learning about", said Ulva,
"If only the cultists I lived with had such manners", said Kit before her and Ulva burst out laughing,
After wandering off the path and into a nearby open field, Kit stopped and inhaled deeply, sighing as she smelt the soothing scents of burning firewood and earthy petrichor. Feeling the grass beneath her feet, Kit stepped forward and lowered her hood so that she could feel the cold wind on her face as she strode further into the field with Ulva walking close behind. Feeling an urge beginning to overwhelm her, Kit turned back towards Ulva and said,
"Run with me",
"What?", said Ulva,
"Run with me Ulva, run with me this beautiful night!", cried Kit as she suddenly took off into the field,
"Kit wait!", cried Ulva,
Ulva suddenly chased after Kit further into the field, passing towering stone columns and the remains of ancient cairns as she raced after her friend, who was now far ahead and sprinting as fast as she could.
After traversing half the length of the field, Ulva suddenly came to a stop as she was panting and her legs were beginning to ache.
Out of breath, Ulva cried out,
"Can you slow down Kit? I can't run as fast as you!",
Ulva coughed a few times before she lifted her gaze, only to find that Kit was nowhere to be seen,
"Kit, where are you?!", yelled Ulva,

There was nothing but silence until suddenly Ulva let out a yelp of shock as something came up from behind her and effortlessly picked her up off the ground. Ulva glanced down and was surprised to notice that she was sitting on Kit's shoulders. Ulva gasped as she noticed that Kit had transformed and was carrying her across the field, her furry arms holding her legs in place as she sprinted across the grassland,

"Didn't want you to be left behind", said Kit,

Ulva laughed as she felt the wind in her face and an exhilarating surge of adrenaline rush through her body. With a wide smile on her face, Ulva held out her arms, imagining that she was flying across the Gormveld. As Kit leapt across grassy bumps and raced over tiny hillocks and slopes of snow, Ulva let out a cry of delight whilst Kit was smiling widely. Kit then rushed towards a nearby standing stone that had fallen onto its side and was tilted like a ramp.

Realizing Kit was rushing towards it, Ulva blurted, "What are you doing?!",

"Hold on!", cried Kit,

Ulva yelled as Kit suddenly sprinted up the stone and catapulted herself high into the air, using her hindlegs and the stone as a springboard.

As Kit got to the height of her jump, she suddenly let out a mighty howl as her body was illuminated by the silver glow of the moon. Ulva wrapped her arms in fright around Kit's neck as they both came back down to earth. Ulva let out a yelp as Kit's paws suddenly struck the ground and as she rushed forward through the field, Ulva was shocked to see a dozen grey wolves appear beside Kit, chuffing and howling as they ran alongside her. As Kit ran, she let out another howl and was surprised when Ulva howled as well. Both Ulva and Kit laughed as they raced into the nearby woodland and barrelled over stones, earth and logs at exhilarating speed, rushing through the trees as the sound of howls echoed around them.

Once Kit had passed through the woodland and returned to the field, the wolf pack running alongside her regrouped and raced away into the night,
"This is amazing!", cried Ulva,
"I could do this all day", replied Kit,
Suddenly as Kit and Ulva were about to do one more circuit of the field before heading back to the tavern, something large rushed up behind Kit and violently lunged at her, sending both Ulva and Kit tumbling to the ground. Ulva painfully struck the ground and heard a terrible and pained howl fill the air accompanied by the sound of gnashing teeth and scything claws. Ulva quickly lifted her head and saw Kit tumbling through the grass as she wrestled and clashed with what looked like another werewolf, except this one was much bigger and covered in dark brown fur that was bloodstained on the front, his eyes glowing a dark shade of yellow.
Ulva stared in horror as Kit snapped at the werewolf and bit him on the arm, causing the beast to cry out in pain. The werewolf retaliated by swiping Kit's legs, causing her to land down hard on her back. The werewolf then lowered its head and tried to bite Kit's throat. Kit snarled as she caught the werewolf by the snout with one of her claws, causing blood to fly. The werewolf staggered backwards as it clutched its bleeding snout. Kit then lunged forward and struck the werewolf hard in the chest, causing them both to tumble into the grass.
Kit then began swiping violently at the werewolf's face and neck, piercing it's flesh with razor sharp claws.
Enraged, the brown furred werewolf swung its massive fist and slammed Kit in the side of the head, causing the she - wolf to yelp in pain as she collapsed and sprawled out onto her back,
"Kit!", shouted Ulva,
Hearing Ulva's cry, the werewolf that attacked Kit suddenly reared its head and glared straight at Ulva before letting out a terrible roar of anger.

The werewolf suddenly sprinted towards Ulva on all fours, its eyes burning with anger and hatred. Ulva suddenly ran as fast as she could as the werewolf chased after her. She let out a squeak as the werewolf knocked her hard to the ground. Ulva rolled onto her back and screamed as the werewolf loomed over her and raised one of its claws high into the air. Ulva shielded her face with her arms and closed her eyes, waiting for the moment the terrible, shining claw would strike.

Just as the werewolf was about to deliver the final blow, Ulva suddenly felt a rushing of wind as something jumped up and slammed the werewolf hard into his ribs, sending him flying towards the ground. Ulva opened her eyes and lifted her head as she saw the brown furred werewolf was now violently clashing with a third werewolf. This one smaller and lither in proportions, its tail whipping the air as it pounded the brown werewolf with small, curled fists and tore into its flesh with a pointed muzzle. The smaller werewolf was covered in snow white fur and had a black nose and claws that were slick with blood, its emerald eyes gleaming with rage.

Whilst the two werewolves were clashing and ripping into each other with fangs and claws, Ulva staggered to her feet and quickly rushed over to Kit to see if she was hurt. She was, Kit had passed out and her mouth was hanging open, her long tongue was sprawled out limp from the corner of her mouth.

When Ulva pressed her ear against Kit's furry chest, she was horrified to discover that Kit's heart had stopped beating, "Gods no!", cried Ulva,

Wasting no time, Ulva started compressing her open palms against Kit's chest to try and get her heart restarted.

As she did, Ulva could hear terrible howls and screams fill the air as the two werewolves nearby were kicking and punching one another, biting and snapping with bloody jaws and slamming each other into the ground, crushing their bones and bruising their flesh,

"Come on Kit, don't you die on me now!", snarled Ulva as her eyes welled up with tears,

Ulva pressed down hard and repeatedly against Kit's chest before she tucked Kit's tongue back into her mouth. After pinching Kit's soft and damp nose, Ulva breathed deep into Kit's throat, causing her chest to rise and fall.

Ulva spluttered and gagged from Kit's bad breath before she began pressing down on Kit's chest again, her hands shaking as her friend was still unresponsive,

"Damn it Kit, come on!", yelled Ulva,

Ulva then began pounding down hard on Kit's chest with curled fists between compressions, hoping the shock would restart her heart,

"Wake up you damn mutt!", roared Ulva,

But just as Ulva was about to stop, Kit suddenly stirred and gasped as her body trembled, her heart shuddering as she came back to life.

Kit clawed at the ground as she spluttered and coughed, groaning as cold air rushed to fill her lungs,

"Kit!", cried Ulva before she wrapped her arms around her friend's furry neck,

"What happened?!", gasped Kit,

"I nearly lost you, you were so close to becoming another star", whimpered Ulva,

"I can't remember what happened, I blacked out", said Kit,

Kit then glanced at Ulva and said,

"Thank you, you saved me, I will never forget it",

"It's okay, come on, let's get out of here", said Ulva,

After Ulva helped Kit get off the ground, Ulva watched as Kit closed her eyes and moaned slightly in discomfort as she changed back into her human shape.

Just as Kit and Ulva were about to leave, there came a roar as the white werewolf had pinned the brown werewolf up against one of the standing stones and was smashing its fists into the werewolf's jaw repeatedly before kneeing him hard in the belly.

The brown werewolf whimpered and whined in pain as it pushed the white werewolf away before fleeing, howling and crying out in pain.

Kit and Ulva gasped in horror as the white werewolf suddenly glared at them with shining green eyes. The werewolf then snarled before it lowered itself onto all fours and dashed away towards Grontorp and out of sight,

"What the hell was that?", asked Kit,

"I don't know, but let's go, I don't want to be out here anymore, I don't feel safe", said Ulva,

Together and as fast as they could, Kit and Ulva made their way back to the Weary Traveller.

As she ran though, Kit couldn't help but ponder over the two lycanthropes she had just encountered,

"*Who were they?*", she wondered,

CHAPTER XXVII: EINAR'S NIGHTMARE

Trapped in the throes of a dark and troubling sleep, Einar tossed and turned in his bed before he suddenly awoke to darkness. As his eyes adjusted to the gloom, he was surprised to realize that he was not in the Weary Traveller and his friends were gone. Instead he found himself in a small room with timber walls dimly illuminated by a nearby candle which caused dark shadows to shift and crawl across the ceiling. With his heart racing with fear and dread, Einar got out of bed and anxiously glanced around before he looked to his left and noticed a door nearby. Cautiously, Einar slowly walked towards it and pulled it open, only to find himself standing in a familiar looking foyer,
"John and Ulva's house, how did I get here?", uttered Einar in a shaky tone of voice,
Einar ran over to the front door and pulled at the lock, only to realize that it was sealed shut. Einar slammed on the door with his fist and tried to pull it open, but it just wouldn't budge.
Suddenly there came a piercing bloodcurdling scream from deeper inside the house followed by the sound of a terrified voice,
"Einar!", cried Maud,
"Maud!", yelled Einar,
Einar stormed down the corridor towards the cries of his wife. At the end of the corridor was a wooden door, which suddenly burst open, revealing a bloody and wounded Maud who staggered out.
Her dress was torn and her arms and face were covered in gruesome claw marks, her eyes wide and teary,
"Einar, help me!", wailed Maud,
"I'm coming my love!", shouted Einar,

Suddenly Maud screamed as a clawed arm grabbed her by the ankle and snatched her up with incredible speed, causing her to fall with a painful thud.
Maud screamed as she was dragged through the door before it slammed shut behind her,
"No!", roared Einar,
Einar tried to open the door, but it was locked. To the sound of Maud's petrified moans and terrified screams, Einar slammed his body against the door, trying to break it open. After several attempts, he stepped back and kicked it open, shattering the lock and nearly sending the door flying off its hinges. Stepping into the room beyond the threshold, Einar was horrified to see the terrible sight of blood splattered and smeared across the floor alongside bloody footprints. He saw the blood trail off towards a corridor and could hear Maud's distant cries and screams accompanied by the sound of tearing and snarling. Einar stepped over to the entrance of the corridor, just in time to see Maud lying on her side at the other end, grabbing onto the wall with her fingernails. She saw Einar and called out to him,
"Help me!", she screamed,
Maud then suddenly disappeared around the corner followed by the sound of a door slamming violently. Einar ran down the dark corridor and soon found himself in front of another door. As he approached, he heard what sounded like a scuffle and the sound of something being dragged. He then heard screams and the sound of gargling accompanied by the snapping of bone. Fearing the worst, Einar kicked the door open and saw a sight that horrified him, causing his legs to become weak and the blood to drain from his face. He saw Maud lying on the floor in a pool of her blood. She was motionless, her eyes frozen in a blank and lifeless stare as her mouth hung open uttering a soundless scream. Kneeling on top of her was a hunched over figure that was burying its face into Maud's chest, which had been torn open.

As the figure wrenched out a string of dripping flesh from Maud's shattered ribcage, the figure snapped it up, snarling and snorting as bile ran down its chin,
"Maud no!", cried Einar,
The figure suddenly lifted its head and stared at Einar with piercing eyes, who was horrified to learn that the figure was his sister Ulva.
Seeing Einar looking at her with his eyes wide and his mouth agape, Ulva grinned a bloody smile before she wiped the blood and saliva from her mouth and said,
"My dear brother, you have caught me at a bad time. You see I was hungry...so very hungry and I needed to feed",
Einar staggered back as Ulva suddenly stepped off Maud's twitching body,
"And she was the only thing around here with a pulse", she hissed,
Einar shook his head in disbelief as Ulva began walking towards him,
"What have you done?", he gasped,
Einar watched as Ulva's smile widened, her lips peeling back to reveal bloody teeth between crimson and grisly gums,
"Looking at you now, I wonder how you would taste dear brother", she said,
Einar stared at his sister with wide and horrified eyes as Ulva cocked her head to one side and said,
"I wonder what it would be like to feel your blood wash against my teeth, to feel your bones grinding against my fangs, to pop my claws and drag them deep across your beating heart before I taste it",
Einar raced for the door behind him as Ulva growled,
"Let's find out",
Einar grabbed the lock on the door and pulled hard with all his might, his heart sinking as he realized it was sealed shut and wouldn't budge an inch. He wheeled round as he could hear Ulva suddenly let out a pained moan as she began to turn.

Einar began slamming on the door, crying out for help as he could hear Ulva's bones begin to crack as she cried out in pain.
He watched as Ulva reached up and began pulling at her face, "This face is much too tight", she groaned,
"Somebody help me!", yelled Einar as he pounded his fists against the door,
Suddenly the door swung open, sending Einar stumbling backwards into Ulva's arms,
"Come to me Einar", hissed Ulva before she opened her mouth, causing blood to drip onto Einar's terrified face,
Einar quickly pushed his sister away and raced towards the door but was stopped by a shadowed figure that appeared in the doorway. The figure stepped forward, revealing his face, it was John. His skin was grey in colour, blotched and covered in deep, seeping wounds whilst his one visible eye was bloodshot and watery. With an angry scowl on his face, John silently lumbered towards Einar before he grabbed and held him in a tight embrace, forcing him to watch Ulva turn before his very eyes.
With Ulva crying out in pain as she peeled and tore the skin from her flesh in an act of gruesome self - mutilation, Einar tried to look away, but John forcefully grabbed him by the back of the neck to keep his head still,
"Look at her Einar", he growled,
Einar then closed his eyes before John wrenched Einar's head back and bellowed at him,
"Look at her, you will watch your sister turn just as I did, look at her!",
Unable to move his head or his body, Einar could only cry out in horror and watch as he saw Ulva let out terrible screams as she peeled the skin away from her face before she stretched it out as it began to change into a wolfish snout. Ulva then began tearing at her dress as she transformed.
With the smell of blood rising on the air and the sound of cracking bones and snapping sinews filling his ears, Einar watched as Ulva's body began to contort.

Unable to watch any further as he felt sick, Einar quickly and forcefully stamped on John's foot, causing him to cry out in pain. Feeling John's grip loosen for just a moment, Einar pushed John to the floor and sped through the door and down the corridor, gritting his teeth as he could hear Ulva screaming out in anger and pain. Realizing the front door was locked tight, Einar knew he had to hide somewhere. Einar raced into the foyer, whimpering as his heart pounded against his chest.

As Einar could suddenly hear the slow and rhythmic stomping of heavy paws against creaking floorboards behind him, he ran over to the table and picked up a knife before he fled into a nearby room, which was small and furnished with two cupboards, a bed and several chests.

Without thinking clearly, Einar quickly dived under the bed and curled himself up in the corner as he could hear Ulva step into the foyer to the sounds of heavy breathing, low guttural growls and snarls uttering from her lips.

Einar could then hear Ulva talking in a horrible voice that sounded gravelly and coarse, but also sounded like Ulva when she was an ordinary young woman, her lovely voice desecrated by the hissing, rasping and growling vocals of a wolf,

"Come on out Einar", she growled,

Stepping forward as she glanced around the room, Ulva said, "Don't you want to see how lovely I look? It took a lot of effort to get all dressed up nice and pretty for you",

Einar tried to soften his breathing as Ulva began making her way slowly through the foyer,

"By the gleam of my teeth and the glint of my eye, I smell someone who's going to die", she growled,

Einar could hear Ulva's footsteps thud against the floor as she got closer to the room in which he was hiding in.

With his entire body trembling, Einar gasped softly as he could hear a door burst open as Ulva violently lashed out with a powerful kick,

"Hide all you want Einar, I will find you", snarled Ulva,

Einar gasped again as he heard the startling sound of a door being broken apart as Ulva punched her fist through its frame,
"Come out my dear brother, come out wherever you are", sang Ulva,
Einar covered his mouth with shaking hands as he heard Ulva's sharp claws scraping against the wall as she stomped closer towards the bedroom. With his heart racing and with tears running down his face, Einar watched as he saw the looming and crooked shadow of a werewolf appear on the wall opposite the bed. As he stared out from his hiding place, Einar could hear the sounds of dripping, the swishing of a large and bushy tail and the creaking and moaning of floorboards beneath heavy and clawed feet.
As Ulva slowly entered, she began to talk in her terrible wolven voice as she stepped through the threshold,
"There was once a girl trapped inside a wolfskin,
Because she let the vicious wolf in,
And in her search of a good meal,
She conducted with bloodthirsty zeal,
The slaughter of her family and kin,
All because she let the wolf in",
Einar held his breath as he saw a pair of red and white paws appear under the bed, tapping against the floor as Ulva gazed around the room searching for her brother.
He squeaked as Ulva grabbed one of the nearby chests and tore off its lid, slamming it angrily against the wall where it splintered into dozens of broken pieces,
"You can't hide from me Einar, I can smell your fear, the sweet scent of your curdling blood", snarled Ulva,
Einar gasped as he heard Ulva rip the lid off another chest and throw it against a nearby window, causing it to shatter loudly and spray broken glass against the floor.
With lightning flashing through the broken window and the sound of tapestries fluttering in his ears, Einar heard Ulva pull the lid off the third and final chest.

Realizing the chest was empty, Ulva angrily tossed the lid to one side before she sniffed the air. Catching Einar's scent, Ulva turned round and glanced down at the nearby bed. A sinister smile appeared on Ulva's face before she said, "She snarls as she takes a bloody bite,
And feeds and feasts throughout the night,
She gorges herself until she is flush,
And like a crimson rose,
Her coat is ripe and lush,
Coloured a beautiful and crimson red,
With the blood of her brother,
Who's hiding beneath the bed",
Einar screamed as Ulva suddenly snatched up the bed in her claws and lifted it up, revealing Einar cowering in the corner. With the knife in his hand, Einar quickly got to his feet and stabbed Ulva in the leg, nearly stumbling as he rushed out of the room. Ulva screamed in pain as blood ran down her calf before she dropped the bed, causing it to break and shatter upon impact with the floorboards.

As Einar ran through the foyer and towards the front door, the entire house trembled with the angry and ear-splitting howl of anguish from Ulva, Einar screaming in terror as the lamps hanging on the walls shattered from the noise and darkened the room. Einar reached for the lock of the front door and wrenched it open, turning back to see Ulva stagger out of the bedroom, her blue eyes and white fangs glowing in the dark. Snarling and growling, Ulva angrily glared at Einar as he rushed through the front door and slammed it shut behind him before locking it tight.

Einar looked round and was disheartened to find himself standing in front of a long corridor illuminated brightly by a red light.

It wasn't what he was expecting, he was expecting to either be outside in the street or back in the Weary Traveller, but he had no choice but to follow it and see where it led to, "Einar!!!", screeched Ulva,

Einar yelled as Ulva smashed into the door behind him before she began tearing at it with claws and teeth.
Seeing his sister's bloody snout emerge through a freshly made tear in the door, Einar quickly ran down the corridor, the angry howls and cries of his sister echoing around him. Einar turned a corner and found himself in another corridor. As he ran, he heard the door shatter followed by the sound of quickening and thunderous footsteps against the floor. With his heart thundering in his chest, Einar ran until he was greeted by a dead end. Panicking, Einar patted the wall, trying in desperation to find some sort of lock or switch that might release a passageway in which he could escape. Realizing that he was trapped, Einar spun round and backed up against the wall, holding out the bloody knife in his hand as he saw Ulva's shadow emerge from around the corner.
As Ulva got closer, Einar heard her voice thundering in his ears,
"I shall chew on your flesh and swallow your bones,
To the delightful sound of your dying moans,
Now that you are trapped, I shall take your life,
Just like I took your darling wife",
Einar gasped as Ulva appeared at the end of the corridor, her face lit up by a terrible grin.
Einar screamed as Ulva suddenly rushed towards him on all fours and after a few seconds of slamming his fists against the wall in panic, he let out a cry of terror as Ulva lunged at him with flashing eyes, teeth and claws before everything went black and cold.
Einar awoke screaming with his heart pounding and his pale body covered in sweat. Startled and panicking, Einar threw himself out of bed and tumbled to the floor.
The noise woke the others, who shot out of bed concerned and alarmed,
"Einar, what's wrong?", said Ulva,

With his mind still spinning with terrifying images, Einar saw Ulva staring at him and let out a cry of terror before he reached for his sword and pointed it towards his sister, much to everyone's shock and horror,
"Stay away from me!", yelled Einar,
"Einar put the sword down!", snapped Brenna,
"It's okay Einar, it's us", said Kit,
Einar glanced around and as he came to his senses, he realized that he was back in the Weary Traveller. Horrified, he looked down and saw the sword in his hand. When he glanced over at his friends staring back at him looking frightened and worried, Einar realized what he had done. He dropped his blade and fell to his knees before cradling his head in his hands.
He then wept as Ulva knelt beside him and comforted her brother in a tender embrace,
"I am so sorry Ulva", he moaned,
"It's okay Einar, you just had a nightmare that's all. It's all over now", said Ulva,
Einar shook his head and said with a trembling voice,
"No, until you are cured, this nightmare will not end",
"She will, I promise", said Brenna,
"Gods I hope you are right", said Einar,
It took a while, but eventually Einar calmed down and after a cold drink of water, he returned to his bed after some consoling and comforting words from his family and friends and soon fell asleep once more.

CHAPTER XXVIII: LEAVING GRONTORP

Thankfully Einar did not have any more nightmares over the course of the night and soon enough it was a cold, bright and sunny morning over Grontorp. After waking, getting washed and dressed before making their way downstairs, John, Einar, Ulva, Brenna and Kit sat themselves down to enjoy some breakfast, which consisted of tea, milk, some pancakes and buttered toast. They were the only patrons in the tavern that morning and despite the appearance of a delightful spread and the promise of a beautiful early spring morning, everyone was in quite a sombre mood. Einar, Ulva and Kit were exhausted and aching, their bodies weary and their heads throbbing with a dull pain. Brenna was quite despondent whilst John was preoccupied thinking about the previous night. No one looked up from their plates as Jetta came over to the table and placed down a small pot of cream to put onto their pancakes.
She glanced round at everyone and said,
"Are you guys okay?",
John glanced up at Jetta,
"We're okay", he said with a warm smile,
"Good", said Jetta,
Reaching into her pocket, she pulled out a silver pendant and placed it upon the table in front of John,
"What is this?", he asked,
"A small token of appreciation from all the staff here at the Weary Traveller for being such lovely guests", said Jetta,
John picked up the pendant and said,
"Thank you, that's very sweet of you",
"It's no problem and please let me know if you need anything before you leave", said Jetta before she walked away,

John tied the pendant around his neck and stared at it as it shone and shimmered in the sunlight that filtered in through the windows,
"Fine craftsmanship", he said,
After John had sipped his tea, he glanced over at Einar and said,
"How are you feeling brother?",
"Tired, I had a terrible nightmare last night", said Einar sadly,
"Do you want to talk about it?", asked John,
"What would that achieve? No, I would rather forget about it", said Einar before he shoved a large piece of pancake into his mouth,
"And you Kit?", said John,
"Ulva and I went for a walk last night to clear our heads. I regret going out, all that cold air and running about, it's drained me", said Kit,
"Well hopefully when we get back on the road, we'll feel a little better", said John,
"I hope so, I can't wait for this all to be over", said Ulva,
Ulva reached into a pouch on her belt and pulled out the bottle that Brenna had given her,
"So Brenna, when can I drink this again?", asked Ulva,
"Preferably when we arrive at the town of Bjorndale just beyond the Krallenthroll Forest. Should we not get there before sundown, then you can drink it sometime before then. Once the bottle is empty, we will have no choice but to camp in the wilderness away from innocent civilians", said Brenna,
"Fine", said Ulva sadly before she put the bottle away,
After eating and drinking their fill, everyone got up and collected their belongings and bags as Brenna said,
"Wait here, I'm going to pay for the food and thank Wyland, Jetta and Yrsa for their generous hospitality",
Brenna walked over to the counter whilst Kit, John, Ulva and Einar stood in the middle of the inn, shuffling their feet and glancing around silently as they waited for Brenna.
It wasn't long before he returned,
"Right, let's go", he said,

With haste, John, Einar, Ulva, Kit and Brenna left the Weary Traveller and made their way down the path and onto the northern road.

Before they left Grontorp, they noticed a dozen guards going from door to door talking to any townsfolk they happened to come across,

"Why are there so many guards about?", asked Kit,

"I don't know, but we're not hanging around to find out", said Brenna,

"So what is our next destination?", asked Ulva,

"Bjorndale beyond the Krallenthroll Forest", said Brenna,

"The Krallenthroll Forest?", asked Kit,

"It is a vast and dangerous forest that we need to pass through in order to get to Coldwood", said Brenna,

"How long will it take us to get there?", said John,

"We should be there by late morning", said Einar,

"So does anyone know much about the forest?", said Ulva,

"Well the forest is home to a group of people known as the Hjortur, though what they call themselves is a mystery to me. The Hjortur are a mysterious people who reputedly come from a distant island known as Britain. They came to Norway after they had fled their homeland many centuries ago when the men of ancient Rome invaded and attacked them. They settled on the edge of the Gormveld and created the Krallenthroll Forest. The forest itself was created as the result of an ancient custom that the clans of the Hjortur follow. When one of their own dies, they bury the body in the ground and plant a seed within the remains. As the body decomposes, a tree emerges from the body and grows, using the buried corpse as a source of nutrients. The forest is the result of burying thousands of their dead over the course of many centuries, in short, the forest is literally a naturally grown graveyard of monumental size", said Einar,

"Impressive", said John,

"I would say eerie", said Kit,

"The trees are sacred to the Hjortur and as such are fiercely protected. To damage, harm or destroy one of the trees is to commit the greatest insult in the eyes of the Hjortur. The trees are quite remarkable in that they never lose their leaves, even in the harshest of winters. I visited the forest once before Ulva was born, but I never saw any of the Hjortur. We should be cautious going through, people have been known to disappear when they enter", said Einar,

"Anything else we should know about?", asked John,

"Yes, when we leave the forest, we must stay away from the tower of Vargoth that sits on the other side of the Krallenthroll", said Einar,

"Who's Vargoth?", said Kit,

"A dangerous necromancer who is said to live near the outskirts of the Krallenthroll. He is feared by many and few dare to venture near his tower. I don't know much about him other than it is said that he tinkers and toys with the dead and conducts horrible experiments on all living things", said Einar,

"He's sounds horrible, anything else we should be wary of?", asked Ulva,

"Yes, we should beware the May Queen who rules over the Krallenthroll. Lucilla is an iron fisted tyrant who does not care much for strangers walking through her forest. She only lets them through because she has been commanded to do so by the ultimate authority of King Snaebjorn. He knows that the forest is an important route for travellers and though he respects the wishes of the May Queen, he will not allow her to close off the forest to outsiders", said Brenna,

"When we go inside the forest, we should be respectful of the forest's sanctity. We can walk through the forest so long as we stay on the marked path and ensure that we don't destroy or damage any of the trees. Also we must not walk through the stone circles located deep within the forest. We can walk around them, but we cannot touch them nor walk through them, for they are sacred to the Hjortur heathens", said Einar,

"Tyrannical rulers, manipulators of the undead and forbidden stones, this forest seems to be full of dangers. Can't we just go round it instead and avoid all the trouble?", said Kit,
"Out of the question, the forest is much wider than it is longer. It takes three days on foot to go around it from the west and a day to walk around it from the east", said Brenna,
"Uh, the east doesn't seem too bad", said Kit,
"From the east you would have to pass through the vast Hjemsoktopp Mountains, a place full of trolls, witches, ghosts and worse, winged spiders the size of your head and flesh-eating fungi. No it's better that we go through the forest as quickly as possible. With any luck we will be within Bjorndale by the time Ulva transforms again", said Brenna,
"I wish I could drink some more of the Vokvir and have another night of peace", said Ulva sadly,
"I know my dear, but we only have enough for one more day and we should keep it for later just in case we run into any unexpected problems or delays", said Brenna,
Ulva frowned at Brenna's words but perked up a little when John took her by the hand and gave her a peck on the cheek. As John, Kit, Brenna, Ulva and Einar continued making their way up the northern road, they could see lush fields and farmland, flowing rivers and snow-capped hills.
Eventually they could spot in the distance a vast forest that sat beside a ridge of mountains crowned by towering summits, it was the dreaded Krallenthroll Forest.
When they arrived at its foreboding entrance, John, Kit, Ulva, Brenna and Einar noticed that the road split into three paths, one going east, one going west and one going straight on into a dark sea of trees.
Near the entrance stood small totems and pillars of stone etched with runes, hanging from which were long pieces of string decorated with the bones of animals that swung gently in the breeze.
To the sound of whistling wind, Brenna stepped forward cautiously and said,
"Are you all ready to go in?",

"I guess so, what other choice do we have?", said John,
"I have a bad feeling about this", said Kit,
"We should be fine, remember that we are armed, well rested and ready to face anything that dares to cross our path inside", said Einar,
"That's the spirit Einar, if we keep to the path marked with ancient stones, we should be out in no time", said Brenna,
With his heart beginning to race, Brenna was first to enter the forest, followed closely by John and Ulva, then Einar and Kit. As the sun disappeared behind them and they were enveloped in cold shadow, everyone felt uneasy, apprehensive and fearful, for if what Einar and Brenna said was true, they were walking straight into a very dark and dangerous part of Norway.

The Wolfblight Saga will continue with '*Coldwood*'...

ABOUT THE AUTHOR

Simon Steele is an amateur historian, writer and archaeologist, possessing a BA in Archaeology and Heritage Studies from the University of Worcester. Born in South Wales, Simon has always possessed a strong passion for creative writing, his first publication being a short horror piece for a collection of stories by Welsh students in 2003 at the age of eleven. Coldwood is the culmination of Simon's passion for writing stories and when he is not writing for personal pleasure, Simon spends his free time reading books of history, horror and fantasy, hanging out with friends and family, listening to music and indulging his casual interest in all things spooky, gothic and supernatural.

Printed in Great Britain
by Amazon